Blue Stars

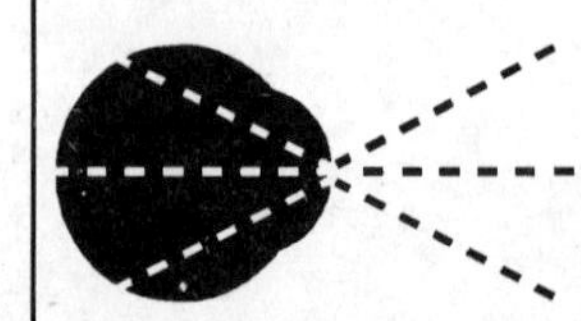

This Large Print Book carries the
Seal of Approval of N.A.V.H.

Blue Stars

Emily Gray Tedrowe

THORNDIKE PRESS
A part of Gale, Cengage Learning

GALE
CENGAGE Learning®

Farmington Hills, Mich • San Francisco • New York • Waterville, Maine
Meriden, Conn • Mason, Ohio • Chicago

Thorndike Press, a part of Gale, Cengage Learning.

Thorndike Press® Large Print Women's Fiction.
The text of this Large Print edition is unabridged.
Other aspects of the book may vary from the original edition.
Set in 16 pt. Plantin.

LIBRARY OF CONGRESS CATALOGING-IN-PUBLICATION DATA

Tedrowe, Emily Gray.
Blue stars / by Emily Gray Tedrowe. — Large print edition.
pages cm. — (Thorndike Press large print women's fiction)
ISBN 978-1-4104-7884-9 (hardcover) — ISBN 1-4104-7884-X (hardcover)
1. Female friendship—Fiction. 2. Iraq War, 2003–2011—Veterans—Fiction.
3. Large type books. I. Title.
PS3620.E4354B58 2015b
813'.6—dc23 2015001860

Published in 2015 by arrangement with St. Martin's Press, LLC

Printed in the United States of America
1 2 3 4 5 6 7 19 18 17 16 15

To my brother

To an army wife, in Sardis:

Some say a cavalry corps,
some infantry, some, again,
will maintain that the swift oars

of our fleet are the finest
sight on dark earth; but I say
that whatever one loves, is.

— SAPPHO, "TO AN ARMY WIFE, IN SARDIS,"
TRANSLATED BY MARY BARNARD

Part One: Home

1

Madison, Wisconsin
January 2005

Ellen Silverman adjusted the cookbook stand so she could see the page in between bursts of chopping vegetables. Beneath the spattered plastic shield was a new collection of essays about Edith Wharton she was to review. (It had been years since she'd needed to refer to a cookbook.) Each time she scooped a handful of peelings and carried them to the garbage can Maisie, their twelve-year-old golden retriever, lifted her head to assess her chances, dropping it back to her paws when Ellen returned to the counter. Black bean chili sputtered on the stove, a chocolate torte from the bakery was in the fridge, and after the salad was finished all she had to do was set the dining room table. Her daughter Jane's nineteenth birthday wasn't until the end of next week, but since her son Wes would drive back to school tomorrow, they were celebrating tonight. It was good luck that Michael was also free. His motley jobs — snowplow driver, parking lot security, landscape worker — made for an unpredictable schedule.

The holidays were over, which was a relief. She would have time to read, to work. But this winter was a hard one, with two bad blizzards already. Even now there was a foot of new snow on the ground and more to come tonight. And the war in Iraq, brutal and pointless . . .

"Wharton's famous *tableaux vivants* scene, in which Lily's controlled stage fright rehearses the more intense fears to come, a cycle of terror revolving from loss of social status through loss of life —"

"Stage fright," murmured Ellen, wiping the paring knife on her apron. "Stage fright? She's happy as a clam, with everyone staring at her!" Maisie opened her eyes. Ellen leaned closer to the book, scanning the page. Hard to believe that a scholar (who was it, oh yes, the one from Iowa) could so mischaracterize one of *The House of Mirth*'s central scenes, even in a throwaway line unrelated to the essay's larger point. Ellen lifted the lid on the chili. She opened and closed the refrigerator door. Then she laid a dish towel over the salad bowl and went up the stairs to her study.

For the first time in longer than Ellen cared to remember, after four books, countless articles, and numerous presentations focused on Edith Jones Wharton, there was no project of her own under way or on the horizon. She'd come to a stopping place. She needed to look around. Hence, this minor book review, a bit of busywork taken on while Ellen adjusted to the discomfort of her freedom.

Maybe I should find something else, she thought, standing in the middle of her room, *someone other than Edith, to write about.* Unimaginable. She might as well become another person.

Ellen took down her reading copy, the compact off-white Penguin one (same as she'd owned as a girl) and found the right page even before she was seated in her armchair. Still in her apron, she read just enough to reassure herself that Lily was anything *but* nervous when she took her place in the gaudy party scene. Still, it was a potentially interesting notion — the idea that social fear and life-or-death fear were entwined, and often confused, within the novel's various performances. Ellen made a note on a pad on the side table before flipping back a few pages, to enjoy Lily's whirlwind preparations for the extravagant *tableaux.*

Some time later, a rhythmic scraping drew her attention out of the book. Outside, a familiar figure was shoveling off the side stairs. Ellen watched her ward — the young man who used to be her ward — fling snow left and right over the metal railing, working his way down the buried stairs she hadn't used in weeks. "Idiot," she whispered, heart full. He knew she used the front door when it snowed this much, but he was shoveling for Maisie, who reliably trotted to this entrance morning and night, baffled each time that Ellen tugged her away to the front. Ellen rose to go but stayed to watch as a slighter figure crept up on Michael from behind. Her daughter Jane, long tangled hair spilling out from under a felt hat, scooped snow off the bushes and packed it hard. Just as she pulled back to throw, Michael turned to whip a shovelful right at her face. He'd faked not hearing her approach. Janey's scream reached the rafters. She went to tackle Mike but he blocked her. Ellen watched for one more moment while he held her still, wiping snow from her face. Their laughter grew louder when she went downstairs and into the kitchen.

Now they'd let Maisie out, and she charged up and down the half-cleared stairs, deliriously. Jane grabbed the dog to give her a kiss and Michael wrestled her for a chance to pet Maisie. Ellen rushed over to the open door.

"You forgot to shut the door!" she shouted. Cold air along the kitchen floor. She blew kisses through the glass and mimed *come in, it's freezing!* They waved back and then ignored her. Jane stuck a handful of snow down Michael's collar; he lightly toppled her into a giant drift pile and then picked up the shovel.

Ellen pulled the door open a crack. "Don't worry about that, just come in and get warm!"

"I was warm until your bratty daughter showed up."

Jane pushed past him and flicked her snow-covered mittens his way. "Whiner."

"Baby."

"Suck-up."

"Jane, your boots!" Ellen dragged her in to a towel on the floor and backed away from the spray of cold snow.

Michael stuck his lip out and pretended to shiver. Jane pounded the glass door and shouted, "Break's over — get back to work!

Earn your keep!"

"Jane!"

"What?" Laughing, her daughter toed off her snow boots and shrugged out of her soaking coat with Ellen's help.

"Don't say that to him."

"Mom, relax."

"Why would you say that?" Michael's broad back, the muted scrape of his shovel.

"Mom! He knows I'm kidding. God, if there were any iota of truth to it, do you think I'd say it, even joking?" Jane twisted her hair into a rough knot and strode away, through the kitchen. Ellen held her dripping coat. Once again she wondered about the fault lines underneath the four of them. Michael was part of their family now, and had been for nearly five years — but even so . . . Did he feel, somehow, that he *had* to shovel the walk? Did a joke like Jane's make him feel more welcome, or less? Did her own reaction make things worse, or worse in which ways? *Text and subtext.* Ellen hung up the coat and eyed Jane's damp sock prints as she went over to stir the chili. As usual, birthday or not, she and her daughter were off on the wrong foot.

It was hard to say exactly when Michael Cacciarelli became one of them. Was it the day he and Ellen had the notary sign the forms for Wisconsin petition for guardianship? Was it before that, when he was crashing on the basement couch? The day she gave him a set of keys? When he began to leave grocery money, a wordless ten or twenty, magneted to the fridge? The night he allowed Ellen to take him to the ER for the cut above his eye, the one his aunt's boyfriend gave him, the one that made him tell her everything?

Ellen's son Wesley met Mike during the summer before his senior year in high school; he was seventeen, Mike sixteen. A friend of Ellen's had gotten Wes a job with the city. It was a kind of youth program not really designed for bookish middle-class kids from the university neighborhood, but Ellen decided for reasons she couldn't really remember now (fear she wasn't exposing her son to more manly pursuits or the use of power tools at least) to sign him up. Wes gamely braved it all: the 5:00 a.m. honk of his crew outside; packing both a breakfast and lunch; and weathering what Ellen is sure must have been a fair amount of hassle from the rougher guys much more used to the work than slender, straight A's Wesley. They laughed about it now, with Wes in his first year of U.Chicago's graduate program for philosophy. But what had she been thinking?

"He's a good guy, Mom." That's all Wes could tell her, once he started hanging out with this new Mike she began to hear so much about that summer: *Mike says, Mike once went to, Mike and I are going to . . .*

But Ellen didn't like it, Wes bolting dinner and hurrying to the beat-up two-seater idling at the curb. Where did they go? *Just drive around, get pizza.* Where does he live? *Like on Hammersley or something, over in the Southwest side.* And his parents? *I don't* know, *Mom.*

"So you're worried about . . ." Her best friend Serena prompted. "Drinking, drugs?"

"No. I mean, maybe — but that's more a Janey worry. It's just . . . well, he's never had a friend from a different school before!" Most of his Whitman friends were doing summer internships at the Capitol. "What was I thinking?"

"That you'd like him to make friends from different schools?" Serena had smiled gently, too kind to point out what they both understood: by "different school" Ellen meant "shitty neighborhood." So yes, a great part of her confusion about this Mike Cacciarelli came from the fact that he lived in the Southwest, a gritty part of town featured regularly in the *Journal*'s articles on crime and racial tension. Ellen wasn't sure what to do, if anything. Not for the first time, she wished she wasn't alone in figuring it all out.

Her husband, Don, had died when the children were young. Why hadn't she remarried? It was a question asked, in varying forms and tones, by friends and family occasionally over the years, or by one man or another who clearly thought he had earned the right. Even the kids, once they were old enough, would ask. Ellen's answer — bright for friends and family, loving to her kids, stringent toward the man — was essentially the same. She had enough, in this life. Two lovely and complicated children, absorbing work, a creaky old house . . .

As for love and sex? (Because that was what most people meant, after all.) Well, she had that too, not that it was anyone's business. For years she had been "dating" Paul West of the UW's Whitewater campus — a well-regarded Woolf scholar and a good friend to her children. They had meals together, they had sex, they often accompanied each other to weddings and department functions. But marriage . . . no. Neither of them — as far as Ellen knew — had seriously considered it.

“Invite Mike for dinner,” she finally told Wes. “He sounds great, and I want to meet him.”

“Okay, sure. But Mom?” Wesley, thinking. “It doesn’t have to be, like, a big fancy thing because I don’t know if . . .” He trailed off and Ellen read his mind: *If it would make Mike feel uncomfortable, the way we are in our big house and everything.* Oh, her sensitive beautiful boy, almost a man.

“No, we’ll just grill burgers or something. Chips and soda.”

The afternoon Mike first came over was utterly unexceptionable, although likely all of them wished they could remember the particulars more. Because soon after, it all began to change — their longtime unit of three altered its shape and became four. And Ellen, as it turned out, was changed most of all.

No one sat at the head of the dining room table. Ellen didn’t like to, didn’t like the feeling of separation from the kids. Occasionally she put Wes or Jane there, though mostly they ate in the kitchen. She had tried with Mike too, but he always refused, picking up his silverware and plate and moving around to the side. It never felt right to any of them. So there they were at Jane’s birthday dinner: two and two, facing each other across candles and serving dishes and the ironed tablecloth. Ellen and Wes on one side; Mike and Jane on the other.

But on that night Ellen thought she might have liked to be at the head, with an outsider's perspective on this happy sight: three young adults, talking over each other and dishing up the food. After the last-minute rush to get it all out here, she would be content to simply sit for a moment and watch them. Wesley wore the gray shirt she'd given him for Christmas, and a new pair of glasses. A few nights ago he had appeared in the doorway of her study, on his way out to a movie. *If you get a chance,* he'd begun, overly casual. Would she mind taking a look at a file he'd just e-mailed her? Nothing major, just a draft of a paper he would give at a conference this spring, his first. If she had any comments, great, or just . . . maybe she'd want to see it. *I do,* Ellen cried, delighted. *I'll print it right now.* Wes had failed to hide his proud smile, saying *no big deal, no big deal* and then hurrying away downstairs.

"Mom?" Jane was tilting the wine bottle her way.

"Just a little. That's enough, that's plenty." Ellen said nothing as Jane refilled her own glass with a generous amount of red wine. It was, of course, Jane's nineteenth birthday — and Ellen had never needed some arbitrary law dictating when it was appropriate for her children to drink, especially in her home. Still, it was just like Jane to go ahead like this, without checking.

The wine had brought a pretty flush to her daughter's cheeks. Her wide, open face never hid any trace of what she was feeling, and right now she was describing an internal argument in her animal rights group. Ellen studied her, curvy and passionate and messy, in a raggedy oversize sweater and half-braided hair. She willed herself not to come near any topic related to her younger child's life-in-flux. In a way, it was a relief, Jane's semester off college — for now — after the battles over her UW grades and dropped courses and eventual academic probation. Now she was living in a co-op house near campus and working as a receptionist at a veterinarian's office.

"I got her on my team," is how Mike put it, when he wanted to wind Ellen up. "Dropouts represent!"

"Dropping out?" she had retorted. "When were you *in*?" And instantly regretted it. Failing to get him to enroll was still painful.

But Mike had only grinned. "Boom! Ellen

for the win!"

"So now they're threatening to back out, you know, like to leak the whole plan to the bloggers. I heard this one douche might even tell some guy he knows who *works* at Petco!"

Ellen tuned in late to Jane's story. "What plan?"

"Mom. What I just said."

"I mean, it is pretty harsh," Wes said. "You guys pretend to be on their side, but then you turn around and smear their whole business. How's that going to make them want to work with you again?"

"Fuck them," Jane said. "They buy from this puppy mill, we just know it. We do. So we infiltrate, and expose."

"Just like Buffy!" Mike said.

"I guess I should have bail money at the ready," Ellen said. "You and I are going to be on a first-name basis with the cops soon."

"Well, if you don't want me to call you, I won't," Jane flashed. "You're the one who teaches *Civil Disobedience.*"

"Of course I want you to call me," Ellen said. "It's just that seeing those bruises . . ."

"She did it to herself," Wes pointed out. This was last summer, when Jane and six others were arrested for chaining themselves to dog cages outside the Capitol. An *Isthmus* photo from the incident, two officers lifting a cross-legged Jane up from the grass — dog collar around her neck — was pinned to the bulletin board in her room upstairs. Passing through sometimes to open or close the shades, Ellen would stop to look at it. She knew that expression her daughter wore: determined, angry, *you'll break before I do.* She had known it since Jane was a toddler.

"Anyway, the chili is great, Mom. It's from one of my cookbooks, right?"

"Now why'd you have to go and remind us," Mike said, his spoon clattering down to his plate. "Food for freaks."

"Fly your freak food flag," Wes said. "Whoa. Try that one ten times fast."

"Freak flood fag. Fleak food flag. Freak frood —"

"Ignore them," Ellen said. "I don't think you miss the meat at all!" She did miss real stock, however; shiitake dashi left a sour aftertaste.

Snow continued to fall heavily; they could hear the groan of snowplows down the block. Classes began tomorrow. Ellen hoped the secretary would have her syllabi copied and ready. With no book project under way, just think how much time would be freed up to actually pay attention to her students.

"Save room for cake," she said. Clink of flatware on plates.

"So, actually . . ." Mike began, and they all looked up. "Okay, so the thing is —" Maisie's whine and scuffle. "I'll get her."

"It's fine. She just went a few minutes —"

But Mike had already jumped up, was off to the kitchen.

Ellen looked to Jane, who shrugged. Next to her, Wes broke his corn bread into small and smaller pieces.

"She didn't have to go after all," Mike said, with an invisible halo of cold as he sat back down. "Just checking out the snow."

"What were you saying?"

"About . . . ? Oh. Yeah. So I joined the Marines. Last week." Mike ate a big mouthful of chili, chewed and swallowed it. "Sounds all weird and heavy, when I say it like that. Like a commercial or something." He made his voice low and mock-stentorian. *"Joined . . . the . . . Marines."*

Ellen and Jane stared at him; Wes looked at his lap.

"Don't wig out," Mike said, nervously. "You're not going to wig out, are you?"

"This is a joke," Jane said. "Right?"

Ellen's thoughts ran thick and slow. *Not the Marines as in,* The Marines, *obviously. Because there's a war. Two wars. I should take the ice cream out, let it warm a little. Although, did soy ice cream actually need defrosting?*

"— Go to Camp Lejeune for infantry, that's after basic at Parris Island —"

" 'Basic'?" Jane spat. "Did you just say 'infantry' and 'basic,' like you know all the fucking lingo now? What are you talking about?"

"I'm talking about it's a good option for me, with regular pay raises and . . . the recruiter says that the benefits are ridiculous, you get, like, free health care for the rest of your life, plus they'll pay for college, and —"

"WE can pay for you to go to college! God, she's only tried a million times!"

"Jane."

"And what recruiter? Those guys get *paid* to sucker you into signing your life away. Literally! I mean, how fucking dumb are you, Mike. You think he gives a shit about you? What, did he tell you how *strong* you are, what a big *man* you are, how you'll rock all those push-ups and —"

"Actually, I think he does give a shit. He came up on the Southwest side too, and now he's got like a family and owns his own place and . . . I already rock push-ups." Mike risked a sweet smile.

"Mom," Jane begged, her eyes wild. "Say something to him!"

But Ellen couldn't. She could barely look at Mike. Too much was happening, all at once. And Jane's outburst, as usual, had pushed aside any room for her own feelings.

"You knew about this," Ellen said quietly. To Wesley, at her side. "Didn't you?"

He blew his breath upward, toward his floppy bangs. "I don't think it's a good idea, but . . . it's his decision."

"Thanks, man."

"I don't believe you," Jane said. "You were in on this? You let him? Oh, I guess you probably think bombing Iraqi civilians is okay now, and obviously torturing prisoners held illegally at Guantánamo is fine, and — yeah, and Mike'll get his face blown off on a desert road, that's cool, just as long as we get the oil, right?"

Ellen stood up and walked out of the room, shaking. In the kitchen she took out four spoons and then held them, for a long moment, unseeing. She opened the freezer but didn't recognize the soy ice cream at first. When she tried to read the label the words were meaningless. They were probably in there whisper-arguing about who should come in to see if she was okay. Wes, they would send Wes.

And here he was, just as she closed the freezer. "I know it's crazy . . . Look, we don't have to talk about it anymore," he said, with a worried smile. "Not right now anyway. Jane says she's not hungry, but at least she's not, you know, still going on about it. Do you —"

"Start the coffee if you want," Ellen said, walking quickly past him. "I'm going upstairs. I need to work because I — I forgot to do something earlier, and I think I should —"

"Mom, it'll be okay."

"Soy Dream," she called back, a half-angry sob, from the stairway. "Ask your sister what to do with it!"

Ellen managed to get into her study, and pull the door shut. She moved around aimlessly for a few minutes, once in a while picking up a book or a folder, and putting it back down. Then she found herself in her reading chair, with the lamp off.

She had failed. They all had. Pretending they were a family, pretending everyone was equal. That Mike's background, full of abuse and truancy, had dissolved for good because of twenty months when she had acted as his official guardian.

Guardian. The word raced through her like nausea.

He'd said it, without saying it: *Came up on the Southwest side. A good option for me.* As if he knew that this home full of books could never be where he belonged. That Wes and Jane, grad student and vegan activist, were on a different path, one that was closed to him no matter how nice this professor lady had been.

Goddamn him. Did he think so little of her, of her love for him?

A memory: driving out at midnight to a bar to get him, after Wesley had woken her. *I think Mike's in trouble.* And he was — handcuffed and shoved up against a squad car. *Shit,* he said, when he saw her. *Go home. Please.* But she'd stayed, and her anger at him quickly dissipated when she saw how rough the police officer was, how he taunted Mike, how he hit him. Ellen surprised everyone, herself included, when she got up close and demanded he stop and when he didn't, she held up her cell phone and shouted that it was all on video (not true), that she had his badge number (not exactly). It worked, sort of, in the sense that Mike got put in a car and taken to the station while another weary cop escorted Ellen away and lectured her on obstruction. By dawn, Mike was released into her custody with a summons. On their way home they stopped at a diner and ate breakfast in silence. Mike paid the check.

Surely it wasn't too late. Whatever he'd signed could be unsigned, torn up. She would talk him out of it. Ellen looked down at her hands, and the four spoons they were clutching. She hadn't foreseen this but now she would manage things. As usual, the sight of her bookshelves ringing the room brought calm; her thoughts settled into orderly rows as she ran her gaze over them. Built-ins of cherrywood, they were probably the most expensive thing she had ever purchased on her own. She'd had them put in about two years after Don had died, designed to her exact specifications using a contractor Serena recommended. One or two less bookish friends had admired them but asked if the renovation wouldn't tug down the home's resale value. How many people, after all, needed shelving of this magnitude? Missing the entire point. Ellen had built herself a home in this room.

Somewhere in all these books, in all these words, she would find a way to get Mike out of going to war.

She should go downstairs. She should be with Jane, at least, for her birthday. Spoons still in hand, Ellen picked up *The House of Mirth* and switched on the lamp.

■ ■ ■ ■

Ellen woke cold and cramped, curled up in her chair. She wrapped a mohair afghan around herself and went out onto the landing, where she stood for a moment, disoriented. The house was quiet. She wanted to go to bed, but hunger drew her downstairs. In the kitchen, she made toast and tea, and was about to bring it back up when she saw flickering light in the strip of space under the basement door.

Mike, on the couch in front of the TV, looked up guiltily with his fork in about half of Jane's birthday cake.

"Don't be mad. I know you are, and I get it, but . . ."

"Move over." She set down the tray and poured tea into two mugs. "Just don't blame me. No butter or eggs, what can you expect?"

"It's not bad. The texture's a little weird. Like, gummy."

He put the TV sound back on. "We can change this," he said, picking up the remote. She shook her head, mouth full of toast.

"Whatever you have on is fine."

He flipped through the channels, pausing briefly to assess. Cable news; shots of Iraqis holding up ink-stained forefingers.

"No."

Mike glanced sideways at her. In the end, they settled on a *Law & Order* rerun, one of hundreds they'd seen together. It was an episode from the mid-1990s, with coiffed hair and cell phones the size of a man's shoe. Briscoe and Curtis wandered around a stable.

"This is the one about the horse?" Ellen said.

"Mr. Wicketts." Mike made a sad face.

She ate some cake, he dozed off. After a while, she shut off the TV and shook him gently.

"Bed stuff is in the laundry room." Of course he knew that. He hadn't stayed over much in recent months, but for a long time this basement had been his room, the pullout couch his bed.

Mike didn't open his eyes. "You okay with that?"

She ached, she ached. Ellen punched him in the shoulder, and went up to bed.

2

Bronx, New York
January 2005

Lacey Reed Diaz unzipped her Yankees sweatshirt and laughed. "So I just strip, right here? Three o'clock in the freaking afternoon. Totally sober."

"That's your own fault." Martine drank straight from the champagne bottle. "Let's see it, girl."

Lacey took a deep breath, dropped the sweatshirt on the floor, and shimmied out of her jeans. "I get called a lot of things but you know —" T-shirt over her head, she tossed it aside, with a flourish. "Prude ain't one of 'em!" She shut her eyes and struck a pose to the cheers of her friends, the snap of the shutter.

It was called "a boudoir photo shoot." Somehow the classy French word made it sound more trashy. The upshot was $250 split three ways bought ninety minutes of studio time with one photographer, one "set assistant," one bottle of cheap champagne, and a handful of six-by-eights plus the hi-res digital files. It had been Mart's idea, of course. The week their husbands got the official orders — they had all known another deployment was coming — she booked it, using an online coupon to reserve this second-floor studio on Baychester. Lacey said what the hell, and then they somehow roped in devout, petite Felicia.

Lacey perched on the edge of the frilly cushioned chair, knees together, back arched. It was easier to watch herself in the tilted oval mirror than to look into the blank black eye of the camera. It wasn't fun to have these hot umbrella lights shining down on every bulge and wrinkle, but they could do a little retouching, right? Actually, when she sucked in her middle, she looked pretty good. For getting toward forty, anyway. Lacey had always been one of the tallest girls around — and the toughest. Even now, in this froufrou setting, her bare arms and legs showed their strength. Great tits, good hair, nice eyes. She didn't love her ass, or how it had spread over the years, but that's why she was on the chair. The other girls had splurged on new lingerie, but Lacey posed in her own: white cotton panties and matching bra. She wanted Eddie to think about the real her while he was gone, not some fantasy.

"I'm out!" Lacey hopped off the stage with relief. "Who's next?"

"I gotta get this over with," Felicia said, sighing. "Before I come to my senses." They helped her up the platform in her three-inch heels. She let her silky robe slip off her creamy black shoulders and aimed a fierce pout right through the camera. She knew what to do. "Vanessa Williams? Eat . . . your . . . heart out!" Lacey and Martine whistled and clapped while little Felicia, in nothing but a camisole and a red lace thong, worked it with pose after pose.

The three knew each other from the well-organized branches of a Family Readiness Group that served the army families who lived north of the city. Lacey and Edgardo lived in Mount Vernon, with Lacey's twelve-year-old son, Otis, in a two-bedroom condo just off Gramatan. It was a long commute to Fort Hamilton in Brooklyn, where Eddie was based, but he insisted on being near his mom, who still lived in the City Island house where he grew up. Unlike the others — Martine and Felicia were well into double digits with their husbands — Eddie and Lacey had been married for less than five years, or one deployment (Iraq, Sixth Battalion, Twenty-seventh Field Artillery). In fact, they had been apart more than they'd lived together.

That first deployment had gone by in a blur — it always does, Martine told her — but now Lacey knew what to expect. Although that, she thought, watching Felicia show off her ample curves, wasn't necessarily a good thing.

"Me, me, me," Martine said and killed what champagne was left in the bottle. Felicia conceded the stage and Mart took off her shirt. "Check this out, you guys." She motioned the photographer to come closer, and turned around. Then she tugged down her tight jeans to reveal the top of a multipart tattoo, rippling U.S. flag, dog tags, eagle. And some cursive lettering.

"What's that say?" Felicia asked.

Lacey leaned forward. " 'Proud Army Wife' . . . nice . . . what are you laughing about, Mart?"

Martine stepped out of her jeans and there, on her bare ass cheek, was a cartoon Iraqi insurgent caught in the crosshairs, and a big red-white-and-blue smooch across his face.

" 'Kiss My USA Ass,' " Felicia read out. "Lord, lord. Tell me that's not on your body forever."

"Why? Doesn't every girl want a little rag-head art on her behind?"

"Martine."

"No, no, of course not. It's that kind they airbrush on; it'll be off in a few days. Thing is, I want it to be a surprise for him — for when he's over there. Right?"

"Yeah, so what's the problem?"

"Keeping him out of my pants until I can scrub this thing off!" They all cracked up.

After the shoot, they waited while the studio assistant processed their forms. Lacey was dressed but barefoot, and Martine and Felicia wore various combinations of underwear and clothes. Outside, the winter sun had disappeared.

"I got to go pick up my kid," Lacey said. But she didn't move.

"Crap," Martine said. "I forgot to take the chicken out to defrost. Oh well, pizza night. They'll be — hey, what's going on? You okay?"

Felicia had her forehead on the heels of both hands. Tears slid down her wet cheeks. "I hate it. I hate it. I want to be strong, but God knows, each time I just hate it."

They rubbed her back. They told her, It's okay. It's going to be okay.

"We're pushing our luck." She sobbed.

"Third time out, second to Iraq? Deployment's fifteen months now? How much longer before . . ."

"You can't think that way," Martine said.

"But it's the numbers," Felicia said. "The odds. Probability. It gets harder and harder to ignore!"

Now even Martine grew serious, quiet. Lacey stood up and went behind the studio desk to the minifridge, where she took out another bottle of champagne.

The assistant was dubious. "Actually, your package only comes with —"

"Please. This stuff goes for five dollars a bottle." She gestured toward Felicia's cup. "Come on. It's medicinal."

"She's the boss."

Once they each had a refill, Lacey got down to business. She took out both her phone and her overstuffed day planner. "Here's what we're going to do. Get your calendars, come on." Felicia and Martine, sad and in lingerie, hadn't moved. Lacey went and got their purses and dropped them in their laps. "You remember what that crazy girl did last time? From our group?"

"Which one?" Martine said, and Felicia had to laugh. There was a mostly unspoken divide in their military wives support group between the more mature and settled women like themselves and what they called the "girls" — nineteen- or twenty-year-olds who had married too young, got pregnant before they should, and generally went haywire in one way or another after their PVTs shipped out. They bailed out of college courses, partied too much, mismanaged the budget, or Skyped soldiers nonstop with daily complaints. Lacey thought of it as her job to teach them how to behave, how to earn the trust and respect a military family deserved. She may have been new to the army herself, but it had given her life more purpose and meaning than she'd ever known — except for raising her son.

"You know which one. Went with her girlfriends to Ladies Night at that topless place on North Avenue? Brought in by the cops for — well, I don't know what exactly. Being a drunk fool."

"Lewd acts in public," Felicia put in glumly. "Wandering around the parking lot with her boobies out."

"It got online too."

"Most of them can't handle the pressure of being on their own for a year," Lacey said.

"Quickie benefit marriages." Martine scowled.

"Maybe so. Either way, they're in it same

as we are. So it's up to us, unless we want these girls causing drama and embarrassing us all."

"She's right," Felicia said. She shrugged out of her silk robe and pulled on a sweater. "I'll head up Bible study again, unless you know of someone else."

"No, that's perfect." Lacey flipped around in her daybook. "And I was thinking, Felicia . . . do you feel like doing something about Facebook, social media — what's appropriate, what's not? Either a onetime workshop or a short class?"

"Yes, *please,*" Martine begged. "They post dates and locations of missions. All the wrong info, of course, but still. 'Godspeed two/three! Send good thoughts, they're heading out tonight in Anbar!' Makes me want to throttle someone."

"I don't know . . ." Felicia said. "I'm not on Facebook much. Now that my teenagers are all over it." She thought a minute. "But my team did a security presentation at work last month. I could adapt that for us, probably." She tapped quickly on her phone's screen.

"I'll run the kiddie co-op again," Martine said. "I had a toddler in diapers during last deployment, got another for this one. Kill me now."

"And the parenting support groups," Lacey said, consulting her list. "Break it down by ages again? Think we can get a few speakers this time?"

"Sign me up for the smart-mouth teen group. I'll bring the wine."

The studio assistant handed out copies of their receipts and then pointedly began to straighten up her desk and switch off lamps.

The women put on their coats, exchanged hugs, laughed at the prospect of getting their portraits in the mail. They went out to the street and hugged again in the windy dark, under a streetlight. Martine and Felicia went arm in arm to their cars around the corner. Lacey watched them go.

Rush hour traffic didn't get really bad until she crossed Nereid Avenue. Lines of red headlights waited to crowd onto the Bronx River, crossed with white headlights backed up getting off the Cross Bronx. Plus you had Metro-North, people picking up commuters at Nereid or the Wakefield stop. In her overheated Pontiac Lacey used the time to mess with her bangs, arranging and rearranging them in the visor mirror. She kept the radio on scan, singing along to almost every scrap of song before it disappeared. Redid her lip color. Got honked at for lagging. Honked at some guy who tried to cut in.

She was buoyant, hardly feeling the effects of yesterday's double shift at the gym. (All those New Year's resolutions meant a swarm of new clients and full classes.) So many plans, so many ideas. That extra cash could go to that mil-kids spring break camp Otis had wanted to go to last year, the one in New Jersey. They should start writing letters for Eddie now, considering how much Otis dragged his feet on that. Tonight he could help her get out that whiteboard from his closet — she would set it up in the kitchen for lists, notes, group phone numbers. And how about a family social one night closer to deployment? Probably Nathan's on North Avenue would give them a good deal, let them take over the back room. The kids could play in the arcade.

When that Destiny's Child "Soldier" song came on, Lacey turned off scan and spun up the volume. She pretended she was street, singing along. She pretended that she was twenty years younger, and a whole lot dumber. Like those girls, the ones they had snarked about in the studio.

Thugs and gangs and street life. "Soldiers." Lacey made a slow right onto Fifth Street. Her face grew hot and she snapped off the radio. What was she doing? Eddie wasn't in the car, but it suddenly felt like he was, and what would he think if he saw her bopping along to this stupid song that was the antithesis of everything his disciplined career stood for.

It wasn't just the army. Ever since Eddie got the promotion at his civilian job — he was now regional safety manager at Hess — it was like he'd climbed up to a level where he had a better view, where he could find more problems with Lacey. He didn't even have to say anything, she could just tell — feel his eyes on her when she went for that weeknight third beer, turn the music down when he came in a room, frown at the take-out containers. She knew what Martine would say: *They always end up wanting their mom, no matter what they tell you in the beginning.*

She should have seen it from the start, their fundamental incompatibility. After all, she picked him off a list *because* he was in the army. So who's the dummy here?

Before she'd started getting her own clients, before she'd moved heaven and earth to get the coveted part-time schedule she had now, Lacey had been full-time at Rudy's Gym in Pelham. Four days a week she got there at 4:30 a.m. to unlock the doors, turn on the lights and heater, start up the computer system for the front-desk girls who never rolled in before they opened at 5:00 a.m. When she couldn't get a sitter, Otis would sleep on a sit-up mat back in the office. Then she'd partner with Gwen to work out the onslaught of commuters who had exactly fifty-five minutes each for cardio, machines, stretching, body-weight exercises, and a shower. Slowdown after that, a couple of walk-ins maybe, people cashing in those endless damn coupons for a free session, then it would pick up again at lunch, a group class for the stroller mommies and some lunch-hour locals. Early afternoons were for one or two regulars and the inevitable freak — you could tell right off the bat, the ones who stood too close and requested a lot of "adjustments" — before clocking out and racing to get Otis after school.

Aside from that? She went out, alone, to bars. Met men who could barely hold up their end of a conversation when sober, and slept with too many of them. Lacey was trying, in her way. She wanted Otis to have a dad someday, a good one, and there was a long way to go in that department. She and Otis would have to overcompensate for his genetic legacy, thanks to the Asshole. But the pickings were slim in all seasons at

Mazzy's, at the Bayou, no matter how many Jack and Cokes she let men buy her.

Then she said yes, once or twice, to clients who asked her out. On paper, they were better — these men were usually divorced locals with thinning hair and tight shoulder muscles. Decent jobs. But they either bored Lacey or were taken aback by her loud laugh, her messy life.

By the time Gwen and the desk girls called her over to the front counter one slow afternoon, Lacey was done. One of Otis's preschool teachers used to have a singsongy mantra: *You get what you get, and you don't get upset.* Annoying as hell, but . . . something to think about. She had a job — best she could expect after squeaking through Iona — she had this beautiful chubby smart-mouthed kid, she had some crazy fun girlfriends and maybe that was it for her, you know? Despite the nagging feeling that she was meant for more.

But the desk girls had too much time on their hands, and had mocked up a whole page for Lacey on Match.com. She couldn't be too pissed: "Smoking physique of a girl who still holds the state record for most steals in a play-off game."

"Oh the glory," Lacey muttered, scrolling up and down the page. "What do you think the ratio of skeevy to normal is here?" But she was touched, and that night fell down the online dating rabbit hole, which called for multiple vodkas with orange juice. As expected, there were too many "winks" and "waves" from desperate losers, long unhinged messages from the nut jobs, and just a staggering number of people out there in greater New York who wanted sex and love.

She was one of them, after all. So Lacey scrolled and clicked and deleted and narrowed it down until the same guy kept popping up, kept catching her eye. It wasn't so much his photo, although she liked his serious face and even that mustache — bold choice! Nor did it bother her that he didn't have kids, and had never been married. What drew her attention was his army job, and the way he wrote about it: "As a major in the Army Reserves, my MOS is infantry. That means I command men and women on missions that could put their lives in danger. They depend on me, and I've got their back. It's an honor to lead them. Nothing or nobody could take away what that means to me." There was a photo of him in uniform, kneeling down and handing out soccer balls to a group of kids in sandals, somewhere in Iraq she guessed. "My goal in life is to find a woman who can be my partner, someone I can depend on. Someone who understands what it takes to be part of something bigger." For hobbies, he'd put, "sometimes."

That was Eddie, six years ago.

Lacey, in a moment of vodka-fueled inspiration, wrote this army guy a note — *she could be part of something bigger, after all!* He wrote back. What started as a dare to herself — playing up her responsible-mom side, using the words *aspiration* and *dedicated,* cramming on politics — became exciting in and of itself, became a habit. Changed her. So that by the time they met, Lacey had already begun the long process of shifting toward someone she thought he'd like her to be. Which mostly fell in line with who she wanted to be too.

So what if this was the best thing she'd get out of it all, this marriage? I mean, who wouldn't take it, the last-ditch chance to pull yourself together, to go from being the last girl at last call to someone who knew her Sunnis from Shiites and why they were all screwed? Who could explain it to her ten-year-old, using age-appropriate terms, while cooking a hot meal for the man who brought home a steady paycheck and the respect of their neighborhood, not to mention of the whole nation? Lacey saw it as her ticket out, maybe the last one she'd be offered. She knew when to cut her losses. Those sloppy mistakes she'd made, the bad decisions, the wince-inducing scenes she'd caused . . . they could be erased in this trade. As it turned out she liked being the one to organize other wives, to set up potlucks and babysitting co-ops and prayer groups. They needed her. She was good at it.

Plus, what did she think she was entitled to, true *love*?

She pulled over, agitated. Her hands were cold; she shoved them under her thighs. What made her think she could play this role, upstanding do-gooder army wife? She wasn't real, not like Martine and Felicia. She was faking it and someday they'd find out. Also, what if those photos embarrassed Eddie, made him see her as some kind of flighty slut? Lacey rocked a little, back and forth. She should get going.

Or . . .

Belluzzi's Lounge, right up the block. She'd even parked in a fifteen-minute flashers zone. Gathering scarf, keys, purse, and phone, Lacey told herself, *just one.*

Standing at the bar she texted Sue: *Running late, okay if Otis eats with you guys?* Reply: *He already did.* Lacey squelched the guilt, because she could, because the bartender had just set up her double Macallan, straight, because she knew she could handle this. Lacey could handle all of it: these happy-hour winos eyeing the tall blonde, drinking alone; that dip in Otis's grades (she'd confiscate his DS until they came up); the mess in the house (she'd clean at night! instead of TV!). Most of all, she could handle Eddie, and the deployment. She'd prove herself this time.

Meanwhile, this guy who'd sidled up next to her clearly thought they were in the same camp. "So I was telling my friend over there that you've got to be the only —"

Lacey put a twenty on the bar and finished her drink. "Another time, all right?"

"C'mon, you're not leaving yet!"

The fiery glow of the drink and her newfound calm kept Lacey from all the cutting remarks she could have chosen. Nothing could touch her. She shouldered her bag and gave him a dazzling smile. "Don't move. I'll be right back."

"Seriously?"

"Save my seat," she called back, pushing out the door onto the windy dark street. There was so much to do.

3

"I'm going to stay out of it." Ellen could barely hear her own voice over the lunch hour din at Memorial Union, the U's dining center. Red and pink paper Valentine's Day decorations were taped to the walls; a flyer on their table urged everyone to attend Sex Week's different events. *Learn about the REAL "Student Body."* She tried a bit of humor. "I ain't got no quarrel with them Vietcong."

"What?" Serena frowned at her chef's salad, using a knife and fork to transfer pieces of ham off her plate onto a napkin.

"Isn't that how he put it, Muhammad Ali?"

"He was about to be drafted," Serena said. "There's a difference." She blew on her coffee before taking a first sip. Ellen wasn't sure what difference she meant, and didn't ask. She thought about how similar she and her long-time friend must look to the others, mostly students, crowded at tables in the Rathskeller's big drafty dining room. They had a standing date for lunch on Wednesdays, after Ellen's morning lecture and before Serena's afternoon seminar. Serena was a George Grosz specialist in the art history department. Years ago she and Ellen had served on a committee on student retention in the liberal arts; the two of them had bonded over the pointless academic bureaucracy and the chair's disgusting habit of slipping off his smelly shoes during the long meetings. Serena wore her silvered hair short, in a bob — not quite as short as Ellen's crop — and liked severe, modern jewelry and eyeglasses, which she had picked up on sabbatical in Berlin. That said, today she and Ellen were both wearing good leather boots and warm, understated pieces in cashmere and herringbone. Each woman had a stack of files and books on the table next to her tray and, hanging off the back of a chair, a handsome briefcase that she had bought herself in order to celebrate a personal academic achievement.

"I just can't get involved."

"You are involved. He's already over there, isn't he? I mean, he will be soon."

Ellen stared. "He's just in training," she said. "It's exercises, classes."

"It's boot camp. And then Iraq. Don't pretend — it'll make it harder for you."

Ellen shook her head. "The next step isn't to go overseas anywhere. They get stationed to a base, and his would be in North Carolina, Mike says. The point is, I'm not going to get all wrapped up in what might happen, or get fixated on the worst-case scenario when for all we know he could get a job driving a truck around North Carolina . . . or Europe . . . and end up with a shaved head and a savings account and some new identity after having spent a year or two playing soldier." She let out a long breath and bit into her turkey and avocado sandwich, trying to steady herself. *A year or two playing soldier.* How stupid that sounded, how willfully misinformed. Of course it would be more than that. But this was why she couldn't get into it, what Mike had done, even with someone as close as Serena. There was so much she didn't understand, and Ellen had the stubborn sense that if she kept herself from knowing too much, then there could exist all other sorts of possibilities for what would happen next. Not *all* Marines were going to Iraq, surely. And by the time he finished boot camp — Mike's letters from Parris Island were brief, misspelled, and mostly about food he missed — well, it could be that the entire situation would have changed for the better.

This last thought was so tempting that Ellen made a mistake. "It's becoming more stable," she said. "With Saddam Hussein captured, and the Shiites winning the election . . . most likely they'll draw down forces until it's nothing more than policing. A peacekeeping mission."

"More stable?" Serena stopped, her fork in midair. "This helicopter that was shot down — that happened *because* of tensions rising around the election! Things are more volatile, if anything. Ellen, thirty-something Marines died on that one day alone —"

"We don't know it was shot down!" Ellen noticed glances from other tables and modulated her voice. "They think it was just sand in the rotors. Or the motors. I heard it on NPR."

"All the more reason to agitate against this war in any way we can. Cheney keeps sending them there in droves, unprepared, unequipped — it's Vietnam but worse. Urban fighting, a civil war that's going to stretch out for decades. Absolutely no reason for Americans to die there."

"I know, of course." Ellen pushed her tray an inch away. They had spoken like this before. She knew how active Serena was in the university antiwar effort; both Serena and her partner, Jill, were on all the faculty-student committees that organized vigils and protests. They wrote defiant letters to the administration whenever the president made moves to quell large gatherings at Memorial Union, or in the quads. Ellen signed every one of these petitions when they were e-mailed to her. She felt like reminding Serena of that now.

"You can use this." Serena leaned forward, over her plate. "Incorporate it into your work. Make connections across the . . . didn't Wharton write about World War I? She did, didn't she? She had the perfect vantage point on the ramp-up to war as an American in England —"

"Paris," Ellen corrected.

"Well, it's ideal!" Serena exclaimed. "For an essay, an article. You've never written about this aspect before, and you yourself said you're looking for a new project —"

"I don't really think —"

"A comparison between then and now. How nothing's changed. The horror of war, the useless waste of an entire generation of young men —"

"Serena," Ellen said, more sharply than she'd intended. "Wharton was avidly *pro-*

war. She was furious at how long America stuck to neutrality. Her texts around that time are full of borrowed French nationalism, she practically beats the drum for engagement —" Ellen snapped the plastic lid onto her soup container.

"Oh." Serena's disappointment shaded into further strategizing. "I suppose you might work that in somehow . . ."

"Do you actually . . ."

"What?"

Ellen shook her head, ashamed. Had she really been about to ask if Serena herself knew anyone in the war? As if that would or should temper her friend's own ideas about the matter, as if it gave Ellen some moral high ground to have Michael away at Parris Island. Her hands went cold and suddenly she wanted him away from there so badly she thought she might cry.

Serena reached out and touched Ellen's arm. "Let's talk about something else. Tell me about Jane. What is the latest?"

Ellen straightened her back. It was a peace offering. Only with Serena was she comfortable enough to complain — in a loving way — about Jane. Serena herself had no children, but her partner Jill's daughter, now grown and living in New York, had also been a wild one, and so she could understand.

"To tell you the truth, I don't know. I'm not happy about this place she's in, that's for sure."

"The Friends co-op? On Johnson? They're not bad kids. I have a couple in my senior seminar."

"It's not Friends, it's a new place. An apartment on Denham Street. She moved there a few weeks ago with . . . well, how many people I don't know. Nor who they are. Whenever I ask for details she says, 'They're just, like, normal people, *Mom.*' "

At this, Serena matched Ellen's expression. "Have you been over there?"

"No, because she says it's not clean enough for me to visit. Having been over at the co-op when she called it 'clean,' I can only imagine."

"Be grateful." Serena laughed. "Shudder."

"But I've driven past it. A run-down house, bikes everywhere out front, a ripped-up couch on the porch. None of the neighbors, no one on the block, looks connected to the university. It bothers me, of course. Wes says I shouldn't pick this battle. He's right. We're not on great terms and I get the feeling that one more blowup between us . . ."

"Oh, they always come back," Serena said. "Nothing's irrevocable. It's a phase. Like the terrible twos."

"The terrible teens," Ellen agreed.

What she didn't say was that she feared this latest from Jane had to do with Michael, with his leaving for boot camp. Jane had come by the house last week with several boxes of her stuff she wanted to store in her old room. Ellen had done exactly what she told herself not to do, even as she was doing it: follow her daughter from room to room, asking ineffectual questions.

"So they're not the animal rights group?"

"They're not *not* into animal rights, if that's what you mean. They just have broader interests. It's not like we all have to fit into some little box."

"What I meant was, how do you know them?"

"Friends. Friends of friends."

"Do they work at the vet with you? Are any of them enrolled?"

"No. I mean, yeah. This one girl is in the poli-sci program. I think."

"Jane."

"What?" Ellen couldn't believe the way her daughter jerked away from her touch. She looked pale and tired, and her face was puffy.

"Can't we sit down for a while? I'll make some tea."

"I have to get going."

"Let me give you something to eat. Or to take with you. There's soup, or —"

Jane had stopped stock-still while tearing through the upstairs hallway, and Ellen almost ran into her. She crouched down and pulled open the flaps of a large brown box. "Is this . . . this is Michael's stuff?" She took out objects slowly, one at a time: a handful of CDs, a polo shirt, one enormous Nike sneaker.

"It didn't fit in the basement closet so I thought I'd put it in Wes's room."

"Why not mine?"

Ellen watched Jane, sitting on her heels, take out Michael's belongings and study each one. "If you wouldn't mind. It doesn't matter to me." DVDs: *Harold & Kumar, Mission Impossible 2,* and . . .

"The Notebook?" The cover showed a couple passionately locked in a kiss, in the rain.

"I gave it to him," Jane said. "Inside joke."

Inside Ellen a ticking alarm went off; she wished she could see Jane's face more clearly. She and Michael weren't . . . They hadn't ever . . . Had they? Off and on throughout the years she had wondered if there was more to their relationship than quarreling and ignoring. Certainly it had been a concern when she allowed Mike to sleep in their basement, when she gave him a set of keys. Jane had been fifteen then. Ellen had kept a sharp eye on all their interactions, with the intention of throwing him out at the first sign of misbehavior. Satisfied that Michael wasn't showing any signs of interest — and by Jane's eye-rolls and "meathead" comments — she mostly gave up worrying. But now . . .

Jane flipped through a stack of photographs she had taken out of an envelope. Ellen held herself back from telling her to stop going through his things. Instead, she sank onto the hallway carpet next to Jane.

"So basically," Jane muttered to herself, "I'm bringing boxes of stuff to keep here and *he's* left boxes of stuff here. Perfect."

Ellen stroked Jane's head, tucked a dreadlock behind her ear. "It's hard," she said quietly. "And confusing. Why does he want to do this? I'm incredibly angry at him but I —"

"You are?" Jane shot her a look. "Did you tell him that? Before he went?"

"Well, not in so many words."

"I knew it." Now she was slamming Michael's things back in the box. "I knew you hadn't even said *anything.* Right? Because Big Mike can do no wrong. Even when he couldn't be wronger."

Startled by Jane's sudden fury, Ellen couldn't respond. And then in a flash Jane was up and off, leaving her mother to wonder what she had done this time.

In the restaurant now, Serena was reviewing the notes for her seminar. Ellen took both of their trays to the cleanup area and emptied them. She said hello to several students, colleagues. Slowly walking back to Serena at their table, Ellen felt the space around her expand; she had a mental image of the tall-ceilinged beer hall, the rest of the Union building, the spreading ice-covered Terrace with its gray stone steps leading down to placid Lake Mendota.

How could the fate of Iraq matter here? How was it possible that decisions and reversals in that desert country half a world away, a suffering place, steeped in wholly other languages and customs, whose history stretched back through the rise and fall of empires, could touch Mike's life? That a boy from the frozen upper Midwest should play any part in Iraq's woeful current mess was absurd to the point of existentialism. What did Mike's life mean, what did anyone's, if it could be hurled around the planet like a marble in a sandstorm?

For a moment, she had to hold on to the

back of a chair. Then she found her stride again.

Serena had gathered up her things, put her coat on. She held a thin paperback in her hands.

"I took this off my shelf on the way out to meet you. You know it, I'm sure, but it just seemed necessary for what you're going through."

How do you know what I'm going through? Ellen heard herself think. She told herself to shut up.

"What is it?"

Serena handed her the book. "Simone Weil. 'The *Iliad,* or the Poem of Force.' "

"Ah."

"I'm sorry about the markings inside. I must have years of margin scribbles in there. What she begins as literary criticism turns into a pacifist polemic of such —"

"Yes, I've read it, but years ago." Ellen put the well-worn book in her briefcase. "Thank you."

Serena stood and pulled her in for a tight hug. Her friend's embrace was familiar, her sharp scent of tobacco and French perfume. "You don't have to stand by while this happens," she heard Serena whisper urgently. "There's time still. I can help you get him out of it before —"

Ellen pulled away. "I have to run." She covered over apologies and protests with *have a good class* and *lunch was lovely* and *I'll talk to you soon.* And then she fled.

That evening at home, Ellen graded essays and wrote a recommendation for a former student. She made her nightly phone call to her mother in the nursing home downtown, and ordered a belated wedding gift online for one of her nieces. She ate a little chicken salad while reading *The New Yorker,* then watched a *Seinfeld* rerun with Maisie's head on her lap.

All the while she fumed. At Serena, for acting like a thoughtless prig. At Jane, for selfishness. At herself, for feeble efforts and unkind thoughts. At Michael, for enlisting.

Finally, around eleven, she took a small glass of bourbon on the rocks up to bed and read a new novel until she could fall asleep.

A few hours later she was lying awake, listening to the wet swish of an occasional car going up Willow, or Maisie's toenails clicking along the floor downstairs. No one in Ellen's family had ever served in any branch of the military, as far as she knew — she counted back generations to be sure, and then went sideways along her own cousins, their children. No friends, none of their children. Her husband, Don, had been slightly too young for Vietnam; Paul West was just slightly too old. During the Gulf War in 1990, she remembered photos in the *Wisconsin State Journal* of tree trunks tied with yellow ribbons, but she had never seen any in her own neighborhood. There was ROTC on campus, it was true. Cadets occasionally wore the camouflage uniforms to class, during their training periods. But Ellen realized she had only ever considered the program a good way for lower-income students to pay for college. She hadn't thought about what happened afterward, when the students accepted commissions for active or reserve duty.

How foolish it seemed now, in the middle of the night, her blithe life-long assumption that war would never reach her personally. That it was the business of other people; that what happened on the news was only theoretical. It might have continued that way, she thought, had it not been for Michael.

Ellen flung off the covers. In the dark bathroom she drank a full glass of water and then pressed wet fingers against her hot cheeks.

At her study desk she opened her laptop and found the Web site she had only glanced at once, weeks ago, to get the address: Marine Corps Recruit Depot. This time she settled in, clicking through each page and each series of photographs: young men in green T-shirts and camouflage pants, lined in formation, crawling under an obstacle course, clinging upside down to a beam. Maisie trotted upstairs and covered Ellen's bare feet under the desk. Ellen read about Honor and Courage and Commitment. She read about no sending of care packages (she hadn't been) and the necessity of writing upbeat, encouraging letters (hers had been, mostly). Military history and customs. Swim/water survival qualification. Rifle range. The Crucible.

None of it really scared her, though. It was too easy to deconstruct the jingoism. *This is how they get them,* she thought. The ones, like Michael, who don't have the luxury of higher education, the skills to see through this rhetoric. Only one part of the Web site gave Ellen pause: graduation. *The day a Marine graduates from Basic Training is one of the most important in his or her life. A Formal Ceremony establishing your Marine as one of "The Few, The Proud" is held Friday morning on the Depot's Parade Deck . . .*

"But he never said anything!" But then of course he wouldn't. Mike had never asked her to do anything, because he already felt beholden enough. Even when she and the kids came to a few of his football games that last year he was in school, she could tell it made him uncomfortable. Did he want her to come? Did he not? Was he waiting to see what she would do? Ellen zipped past pictures of parents hugging stern men in dress uniforms to find the dates. Two weeks from now. She sat back, closed the computer.

Long past the point of sleeping again, Ellen wrapped herself in a blanket in her reading chair. She dug in her briefcase for the Simone Weil, willing to take Serena's test, willing to dare herself into facing it. *If not now, at 4:00 a.m., then when?*

The act of reading literature didn't fail her, as it hadn't ever, in life. Drawn in by Weil's fierce intelligence and bold insight, Ellen understood how Homer's ancient war poem must have given impetus and urgency to the French intellectual's essay, published just as world war approached again. Weil announced that *The Iliad*'s true subject is force, and the way force, throughout the poem, turns men into things. Human beings become torn flesh, corpses, garbage: "Dearer to the vultures than to their wives." Logical and inexorable, Weil wrote of the blind qualities of force — first the Greeks advance, and then the Trojans, and back and forth until specific meaning slips away from the conflict. Whoever tries to wield force will inevitably be brought down by it. This is the very nature of war, its "geometrical rigor."

Ellen read the following lines, then made herself reread them.

"For other men death appears as a limit set in the future; for the soldier death is the future, the future his profession assigns him. Yet the idea of man's having death for a future is abhorrent to nature. Once the experience of war makes visible the possibility of death that lies locked up in each moment, our thoughts cannot travel from one day to the next without meeting death's face. The mind is then strung up to a pitch it can stand for only a short time; but each new dawn reintroduces the same necessity; and days piled on days make years. On each one of these days the soul suffers violence."

No sun yet, but a thin gray light began to contrast the black shapes of trees and the houses across the street. Ellen stood stiffly and turned off the reading lamp. She put Serena's book away; she wouldn't need it again.

"Hungry, Mais?" The dog raised her head.

"Yeah, me too. Just give me one more minute up here, okay?"

Back at her computer, Ellen bought a round-trip air ticket to Savannah/Hilton Head International. Professor Silverman had never missed a graduation ceremony in her life, and she wasn't about to start now.

4

Fort Hamilton's farewell party was being held in a local church basement. Banners were hung from rafters: ALWAYS IN OUR HEARTS, ALWAYS IN OUR PRAYERS and SERVICE IN THE NATION'S HONOR. Everywhere were black-and-gold army stars, Reserve insignia, and posters of men and women in uniform.

"For once we get our own digs," Eddie said. "I lose my appetite when I have to stare too long at the jarhead paraphernalia." Fort Hamilton served army, Marine, and navy units, so the intraunit slagging was frequent.

"Screw the jarheads," Otis said, testing the waters. Lacey watched to see if he would get reprimanded, but on this day her uniformed husband grinned and made a *you-got-it* noise.

"But the navy's okay, right?" Otis went on. "Jon Weible's dad is in it. So is Ross's, and —”

“The navy is just fine,” Eddie said. “Don’t let anyone tell you different: they do an absolutely fantastic job” — the other two waited for the punch line — “of getting us real soldiers to where we do the fighting.”

Otis whooped, and Lacey didn’t shush him. The three of them were united in high spirits this afternoon. Eddie was packed and ready; he would ship out day after tomorrow. He looked so fine, she thought, in the dress blues they had carefully pressed and laid out for him. Lacey had never thought she’d be so familiar with an iron, but she now owned four different kinds of spray starch. She caught Eddie patting down the sides of his mustache, a nervous habit — he’d spent forty minutes this morning trimming it in the bathroom.

Early on, she used to tease him about it: how’d he get away with a mustache, given those tight-ass commanders? Until one day he actually showed her a PDF of the Uniform/Appearance reqs, scrolling down until he found the right page. “See? That’s me.” Sure enough, there was a meticulous line drawing of authorized mustache length, shape, and fullness — Eddie’s matched it so perfectly, it could have been a picture of him.

Mustaches are permitted; if worn, males will keep mustaches neatly trimmed, tapered, and tidy. Mustaches will not present a chopped off or bushy appearance, and no portion of the mustache will cover the upper lip line or extend sideways beyond a vertical line drawn upward from the corners of the mouth (see figure 1-1). Handlebar mustaches, goatees, and beards are not authorized. If appropriate medical authority prescribes beard growth, the length required for medical treatment must be specified. Soldiers will keep the growth trimmed to the level specified by appropriate medical authority, but they are not authorized to shape the growth into goatees, or "Fu Manchu" or handlebar mustaches.

Lacey had laughed until she couldn't breathe. "No 'Fu Manchu'? No handlebars? Oh my God, I wish they had a drawing of *that.*"

Eddie tried to close the document, but she blocked him, sitting on his lap at the computer. Back when he let her do stuff like that. "Yeah, well, that's the army," he muttered. "You should see the section on tattoos."

"What does this mean about beards getting the okay from medical authority? If you're in sick bay, they cut you a little slack?"

"Nah, that's if you get your face torn up by shrapnel they don't make you keep shaving right over that." Lacey had felt chilled, lightly reprimanded. A glimpse of what she was getting into.

Now in the church hall Otis saw two of his buddies and ran off to join them by the punch table. Eddie was standing as straight and tall as he could, shoulders back. As usual at one of these events, Lacey had worn her flat boots; she had an inch (or two) on her husband, which, she'd learned, was not to be joked about.

Kids were gathered around a man twisting balloons into animal shapes; the older ones around a couple of coin-op video games. There was a DJ playing easy Motown hits, and three long tables were set up with food and drink. Soldiers wandered around in greens and blues, covers on; occasionally it was the husband in civilian clothes.

"Should we hit that first?" Lacey meant the table where his commanding officers sat. "Get it out of the way?"

"Nah, I'll take care of it. You go on, get some food."

"Really? I don't mind." She was relieved to see that the CO wives were in jeans too, like the nice dark pair she'd settled on. Although her Forever 21 blazer was wrong, too uptight, probably too *tight.* Those women, so sleek and confident, wore thin cardigans and not much jewelry. Lacey tried to look unobtrusive as she slid out her dangly chandelier earrings and tucked them in her purse.

"Where've you guys been?" It was Martine, in a short black dress. "Otis found our table — we're over there. Get me more of the potato salad, all right? And some rolls?"

Later, a chaplain led a prayer, but his microphone cut in and out, interspersing his words with feedback squeal and thumps and finally a long silence. People lifted their heads to check on the status, was he done? He was. Then a performance of "Battle Hymn of the Republic" by a youth chorus. Finally, the chair of the FRG program — a woman named Anne Mackay — said a few words. Lacey made a sour look back at Martine, who couldn't stand these perfect types, but in truth she watched with envy and admiration. Anne Mackay was a child psychotherapist with soft brown hair and a funny, self-deprecating manner; her husband was a captain. They had been to the

Mackays' home near the base once. Lacey's eyes had roved the spacious rooms: all the books, all the strange art — real paintings, not posters. She wanted to scoff at Anne like Martine did, but she couldn't deny that the woman was good at this. She made a face at the malfunctioning mike, and stepped away from it, raising her voice naturally to carry throughout the hall. She talked about how hard it was the first time her husband was deployed, how it was her friends in the FRG who saved her. There was the night two girlfriends stayed over until 1:00 a.m. to help her glue two hundred sugar cubes onto a plastic bowl for her kid's history project (igloos). The morning everything had gone wrong and she dropped her car keys into a nasty pool of watery mud, and just lost it, how she had called a milwife friend who let her vent and cry until it was time to roll up her sleeves and fish around in the sewer water, alone.

"Now I'm sure some of you have seen *that* TV show," she said, to laughter. "And whether it represents what our lives are like, I think I'll just . . . reserve my comments on that. Find me over a glass of wine later, and we'll talk.

"But I will say that the show with that title has made me think. Am I just an 'army wife'? Are you? What does that really mean in today's world? I have a job, a life, kids . . . this isn't my whole world, you know?" Women nodded, clapped.

"And yet, I *am* an army wife. I'm proud of it. And I know you are too. So let's be there for each other — army husbands too, I'm not forgetting you guys! — during this next year. God bless our troops, and God bless America." Amid the cheers and applause, Lacey was surprised by tears, which she quickly blotted away with her napkin.

"What'd you get?" she said to Otis, who was unwrapping a gift that had been passed out to all the kids at their table, and throughout the hall.

He held it up. "Laaaaame."

It was a book called *Daddy, Come Home! Helping Kids with Deployment.* The cover featured a cartoon of a saluting dad in uniform with two kids looking up at him, smiling mom observing it all.

Martine leaned over to Lacey and read in a whisper from the introduction, " 'Deployment can be hardest on parents left at home who are not only contending with their own anger, sadness and fear, but must deal with misbehavior issues stemming from their children's anger, sadness and fear.' Super. Really psyches you up, huh?"

Her husband Greg raised a hand, a toddler on his lap. "Uh, did someone just say that deployment is hardest on the folks at *home*?" A couple of guys laughed. Martine tossed a balled-up napkin at him. Eddie was looking elsewhere, scanning the room.

Otis pulled the book away from his mom. He and another boy took turns reading aloud in a high, whining voice: "Daddy, I *miss* you!" "Let's draw a picture together of the United States flag. Isn't that a special symbol?" "Punching a pillow is a good idea to get your anger out. Punch, punch!" "But Daddy, I *miss* you!"

"That's enough," Lacey said, taking Otis's book away. "Knock it off. Go see if they put out the ice cream."

Another woman, a friend of Martine's, said, "You guys'll think I'm crazy, but I'm actually having one of those Deployment Dolls made for Tara. You seen those? Hug-a-Hero dolls?"

"What are they?"

"I can give you the Web site. You send in a photo of your soldier in uniform, and she prints the image on fabric and makes a stuffed doll out of it. It's about a foot tall."

Lacey said nothing. The woman blushed. "Believe me, I thought it was creepy at first too. But my girlfriend is at Fort Hood, and she said it really helped her daughter with the stress of it all. She sleeps with it every night."

"What's the Web site?" Martine asked. "They're not just for girls, are they?"

A doll wasn't going to help Otis, though. Lacey watched him goof around with the other boys. A chubby kid with glasses, Otis resembled her more than his father, thank God. He had Lacey's sandy-colored hair and dark blue eyes. The last time Eddie was away it hadn't seemed to bother Otis that much — or maybe she hadn't been able to tell. But now that he was older . . . how hard would it be for him? Lacey knew that it was "cool," among his friends, to have a soldier dad — most of his buddies did. And she wanted him to have access to every scrap of cool he could afford. Middle school wasn't easy for a sweet, slower guy like Otis.

"Excuse me, is one of you Lacey Diaz?"

Anne Mackay stood at their table with a clipboard, tucking a piece of hair behind an ear.

"Oh man, am I in trouble already?" She stood up, yanking her blazer down. "I'm Lacey."

"Of course! So sorry, I know we've met before." They shook hands. "Do you have a second? I don't want to interrupt your lunch." Anne led her away from the table a few feet.

"Thanks for the books, by the way." Lacey held up *Daddy, Come Home!* "I'm assuming they're from you."

Anne made a face. "You know, a friend of mine donated them so we felt they had to be given out, but . . . honestly, I know it's not right for your boy's age. He's what, eleven or twelve?"

"Twelve." Lacey was impressed.

"Well, we've got something better planned for later. Tell him not to worry. But listen, I've been hearing such great things about your FRG volunteer work —"

"Oh . . ."

"And I'm hoping to ask you for a favor. I'm starting a series of weekly counseling groups for wives, and I was wondering if you'd run one for me up in Yonkers. As an informal leader, of course. I'll handle the base groups with more serious issues around depression, anxiety, substance abuse . . . but yours would basically be a group of women who come together in a safe space to talk about their feelings during deployment. Managing stress, nightmares, how to deal with the news — that kind of thing."

"But you're a therapist, and I've never done anything like that." *Never even needed therapy,* Lacey thought.

"That's perfectly fine. Like I said, you'd be an informal discussion leader, just kind of helping the women feel welcomed, and encouraging people to talk — or to take turns listening, as the case may be. I have a feeling, especially with your volunteer expertise, that you'll be great. And you might also get a lot out of it."

Lacey hadn't really thought of herself as being a volunteer "expert," but she liked the sound of it. For a moment she imagined herself holding a clipboard and wearing ballet flats like Anne's, holding out a box of tissues and murmuring, "Tell me about your mother."

"I guess . . . Sure, okay. I'll have to figure out my work schedule, and —"

"Oh, fabulous," Anne said. "This year we really need some of the older wives to step up — I mean," she said, waving her hand across her face. "Scratch that. Not *older,* but . . ."

"Wiser. I'll set a good example, with all my wisdom."

Anne held out her pen. "If you can put down your e-mail, I'll be in touch and we'll work out all the details."

When she returned to their table Martine mouthed, "What was that all about?"

"I think I just became a shrink." But Lacey's eyes were on Eddie, talking with some of the younger men in berets who had come over to say hello, nervous around their major. Eddie put them at ease; he stood up when they approached, and spoke quietly, making them laugh. No one could have a better company leader. He'd take care of them; they'd have his back.

Lacey twisted her hair up into a knot; a powerful surge of pride hit her hard. Two days, only two days until he left. She stood abruptly and began to stack up the table's empty cups, paper plates. The DJ was spinning Bob Seger and she wanted a drink bad, deep down, a cold pull. You think they'd have some beer at least.

"Where you going?" Martine said. "Leave that stuff, don't worry about it."

"I'm good." Lacey dumped the trash and went over to Otis, who was crowded next to the couple of arcade games. "You doing okay?" He nodded without looking at her. She gave him a five-dollar bill, said she would be right back. The church hallway was quiet, empty. Lacey wandered up and down past darkened offices and child care rooms until she found what she was looking for. Then she hurried back to the main room.

"C'mere," she whispered to Eddie. "I need you for something." He frowned but allowed himself to be tugged away from their group. She led him quickly down the hall; there probably wasn't much time.

"Where we going?"

"Just . . . in here, right in here." She pulled him into the small supply room and shut the door behind them before he could protest. Lacey kissed Eddie, pressing her body against his. Startled, for a few seconds he kissed her back, before breaking away.

"Lace. What are you doing? What is this?"

"What am I doing?" She put her face in the crook of his neck, ran both hands up the inside of his thighs. "You tell me."

"This is nuts. Come on . . ." A sharpness of bleach burned her eyes. She kissed him again, rubbing his crotch through the pressed blue fabric until she felt him get hard. "We gotta get back out there," Eddie mumbled against her mouth, but his hand went dutifully up her shirt and into her bra. "This is a church," he pointed out, thumbing her nipple. Lacey moaned. She unbuckled his belt, pushing the dress coat up and out of the way. Medals clinked.

"No. Let's wait. Tonight, okay?" Lacey hated that chuckling sound in his voice.

"Let me go down on you," she begged,

opening his pants. "I'll do it quick, you know I can —"

"Not here! This is —"

When her mouth reached his skin he shut up for a moment. The quiet in the janitor's closet was broken only by Eddie's sharp intake of breath. Then he pushed her aside and Lacey rocked backward off her heels where she'd been squatting. Eddie had pushed her aside hard. He turned away to zip up. "Jesus, Lacey. What's wrong with you?" Sprawled on the cold concrete, she gaped up at him, her husband.

He tried to help her stand but she scrambled to her feet, pissed. They faced each other in the smelly dark. "It's my boss out there! And Otis, and —"

"I know! Forget it!" She shut her eyes. "Go back. I'll be there in a sec."

"But why would you —"

"Go!" She kicked a wheeled mop bucket and sent it crashing. He left. Lacey stalked around the small space, hands over her ears. What would Anne Mackay think now? *I always fuck it up.* Eddie's face . . . Bewildered. Kind of angry. And — yes — disgusted, a little. If she didn't have to go back out there, Lacey would have smacked herself in the face, again and again. Instead she let humiliation jet through her, and left the closet with it still flooding her insides.

5

Ellen had always thought of herself as someone well acquainted with death, with the whole spectrum of that experience: knowledge, shock, action, anger, sadness, calm. Maybe it was a point of pride, but she considered that what she'd been through with her husband Don's sudden death gave her some kind of qualification in these matters. Stamped her passport.

When Don died, Ellen was stuck in a day-long department planning meeting. It was September 1988, temperatures in the nineties, and in the un-air-conditioned English building she and several other younger faculty members trudged through pages on pages of course scheduling. Occasionally they chatted about the Olympics, taking place in Seoul, and who had won which medals. The night before, Ellen and Don had watched the recap of track-and-field events; a young American sprinter nicknamed Flo-Jo was tearing up world records. Ellen was mostly struck by her outlandish outfits: one-armed sparkly leotards, crazily long fingernails. But Don, excited by her speed, got caught up in the two-hundred-meter race and started shouting at the TV: *Go! Go! Go!* That brought seven-year-old Wes out of his room, startled awake and a little teary. Ellen wanted to put him right back to bed but Don took the boy onto his lap so he could see a replay of the flamboyant sprinter breaking another world record, second in a week.

When they broke for lunch, Ellen's answering machine was blinking: several hang-ups and a wrong number. It had to have been a wrong number, because the male caller said only, "County police," waited a long moment — clicking and voice noise in the background — and then hung up. Ellen didn't worry. The department phones were always doing weird things. Forty minutes later when the secretary opened the conference room without knocking, a policeman standing behind her, Ellen still didn't understand that it might have anything to do with her. Or Don.

He had collapsed on Langdon Street, a block away from the state building where he worked. His assistant later told Ellen he had stepped out to buy a cup of coffee. Bystanders gathered; an ambulance arrived. He was taken to Meriter, but by the time Ellen arrived via a swift police escort, soundless lights flashing, he was already dead. Gone at age thirty-five from a cerebral aneurysm.

Because it was an asymptomatic onset, with no discernible cause, Ellen was left — in those chaotic days and weeks afterward — with bizarre speculations, heart-pounding guesses. Were the meals she cooked too fatty, not fatty enough? Was it because of a childhood spent riding bikes without a helmet, climbing trees and occasionally falling out of them? Could it be related to Flo-Jo, the way he jumped up and screamed when she burst across the finish line? She didn't want to obsess in this manner, she wanted to do as she could tell everyone wanted her to do: come to accept what couldn't be understood, with grace and forbearance. So she let it go, the *why.* And plunged into the *what now.*

Her mother moved in, for a while. Her classes were reassigned. Her children, too young to really understand, asked over and over where Daddy was, and she learned how to answer. The first *this,* the first *that.* She allowed herself certain moments of wild theatrical weeping, a couple all-nighters of regret and existential doubt, a journal she never wanted to read again. Little by little Ellen taught herself to get through it, this life after Don had died.

Over time Ellen's own narrative of her life had incorporated Don's early death as a formative event. An essential, isolated incident that determined a good deal of her personality and the way the family functioned; a background sadness that came to seem inevitable but had been overcome. So why now, at age fifty-five, in the Parris Island parade stands facing a Marine Corps marching band — dozens of blue pant legs with one red stripe, stepping in unison — did she begin to revise the assumptions she had made, about life and death and her experience with both?

"Ladies and gentlemen," said the buoyant female voice on the loudspeakers. "Please rise as the nation's flag passes directly in front of you."

Ellen shaded her eyes and tried to differentiate among the hundreds of new Marines in their identical tan shirts and dark green hats. "Covers," they were called. Last night at the Family Day ice cream social with Mike she had met some of his fellow recruit friends. "This is Ellen Silverman," Mike said each time. "Great to meet you, Mrs. Silverman," these strong, tanned boys said while shaking her hand. "Great to meet you, ma'am." And then they would proudly introduce Mike to members of their family.

Now she couldn't tell which one he was — and that was the point, wasn't it? That they be interchangeable. Disgusted, she glanced around the audience. Surely she wasn't the only one here who harbored doubts, who refused to be impressed by these shows of military pomp? But as with all things President Bush, there was no room here for uncertainty or dissent or debate or intellectual consideration. Just rigid formats, blind acquiescence, and knee-jerk obedience to the red-white-and-blue.

Ellen wished she had brought water; the parade grounds were muggy, with no shade anywhere. She wore a black-and-white-striped sleeveless silk top, and black linen pants. A folded jacket lay in her lap, getting wrinkled. Most people in the stands wore specially ordered Recruit Graduation T-shirts, coded in colors based on battalion and company.

The Marines marched around and around, grouping on one side of the depot and then the other. Ellen thought they looked like rows of uniformed Fascists from a grainy 1930s film; she enjoyed this bitter comparison in the privacy of her own mind. Finally they came to order just in front of the stands. Legs apart, hands behind backs. Now the announcer was a male voice: "Today we graduate three battalions from the United States' most respected branch of the service. Let me tell you a little bit about what these men have gone through in the past twelve weeks, and why we are proud, today, to call them Marines." Then a list of various training activities, weapons instruction, learning the history of Marines . . . Ellen stopped listening. Instead she thought about the letter to Michael in her purse, the one she had labored over night and day for the past two weeks.

It was a document that mixed all sorts of rhetorical styles; not her best work, but it had been attacked with research and revision in the manner of her best scholarly articles. First, she acknowledged his right to make his own decisions, and that she trusted his good sense and judgment. Then she wrote, not truthfully, that the goal of the letter wasn't to make him quit, per se, but to enable him to fully understand what he was getting himself into. To consider additional perspectives. Various parts of the letter then talked about the misbegotten origins of the Iraq War, the Bush administration's callous disregard for what the UN weapons inspectors found, i.e., nothing. She reminded him of "Mission Accomplished" idiocy and the death tolls of U.S. service members so far. She threw in Blackwater and Halliburton and Cheney. She quoted from Iraq Veterans Against the War. *I know it's the socially acceptable custom to say "support the troops,"* Ellen had typed. *Or for soldiers to say "I'm just doing my job." But individual Marines don't get to stand outside what's being perpetrated in Iraq, even if they didn't make the decision to go there. You don't get to wash your hands of the larger reasoning.* Switching tactics toward the end of the letter, Ellen went for the jugular. What it would do to her if he got killed. What it would do to Wes, to Jane. She laid out the basics of a carefully designed plan (put together with the help of a lawyer to whom she'd paid three hundred dollars) for getting him out of his contract. She promised job help and that they would never mention this letter again. She tried to think through every angle of his pride, which Ellen was sure would be the only obstacle. They couldn't have gotten him yet, not with push-ups and being yelled at and marching in parades. After today, she'd found out, Mike had ten days of leave before reporting to Camp Lejeune. She'd give him the letter soon and then there would be plenty of time, in that ten days, to work out the details.

The announcer droned on. "Nobody's said one word about Iraq," she whispered to herself. Noting it, as if for the record.

"And now, ladies and gentlemen, I have the honor of introducing you to the newest members of the Marines." With that, all the khaki-green-clad men turned around, someone yelled a guttural *Oo-rah,* and then they broke ranks. Now the Marines were hugging each other. The audience didn't seem to know what to do — they were all so far off from what was happening on the parade deck. Desultory clapping broke out, but it was unclear if the happy new Marines noticed. Ellen sat still.

The sun was in her eyes. People were climbing down from the stands, streaming toward their sons and husbands and boyfriends. Ellen stayed put. *Let him come over to me,* she thought. She was so tired, parched.

"This is bullshit," she said aloud. A family passing by glanced at her, curious.

But then, quick-crossing the shimmering concrete, a man came toward her. Michael.

Had he ever been dressed this neatly, knife-crease pants and gleaming shoes? It was easier to look at his clothes than in his face. He hugged her and didn't let go for a long moment. Oh, Mike. There was a newness in his stance, in his body itself — always a big guy, now he had a bearing to match his size. And muscles.

"She's crying!" Mike pulled back, pretended to gesture at onlookers. "A-ha! We get 'em all, in the end."

"I am not," Ellen said, dragging the sleeve of her jacket across her face.

"Funniest thing," Mike said. "Our one toughest DI, Sergeant Gunnery Dean, he got all up in our faces 0600 this morning and was like, 'I don't care how emotional you feel, with your mommy and daddy watching you graduate, if I see any one of you out there in uniform crying like a girl . . .' " Mike chuckled. "Only that's not exactly how he said it."

"Well, don't spare us on my behalf."

Mike just grinned. "No profanity around women, ma'am."

"Could I get some water?" Ellen asked. The two of them made their way across the sun-baked depot toward one of the low buildings on the side. There was a sign over the entrance:

THROUGH THESE PORTALS PASS
PROSPECTS
FOR AMERICA'S FINEST FIGHTING FORCE

People were gathered underneath, taking turns taking photos of Marines and families. Someone, a friend, shouted for Mike to join in a photo. A small group arranged themselves under the sign, facing outward. Ellen hung back, watching. Mike stood ramrod straight, his arms flat against his sides, shoulders back. His feet, heels together, were angled out in what Ellen recognized as ballet's first position.

So like a college graduation. UW even had a doorway like this, a mythic arch only graduates could pass through, where every spring parents took photos of their cap-and-gowned children. *Oh why couldn't this be his college graduation?* It was unnerving how easily Mike broke away from his attention pose, after the photo was taken, and how easily he had snapped into it.

Ellen began to think as she waved to him, *Yes, I'm coming,* that her mission was going to be more difficult than expected.

Back at the hotel for an afternoon rest before dinner. The shades were drawn; lines of dark yellow sunlight edged the window, escaping into the room where Ellen lay in bed. Dust motes spun in the air. Muffled noises came from the carpeted hallway — trolleys and key cards. She was thinking about Virginia Woolf. Woolf's agony when England began ramping up for war again, in the late 1930s. Hadn't she during that time written a stinging essay against nationalism, against patriotism? Ellen almost wished Paul West were here to ask. It was conventional wisdom that Woolf's last depression, the one that brought her to put stones in her pockets and walk into the Ouse River was brought on in part by anger and despair as a helpless pacifist. But what Ellen wanted to know was Woolf's inner state, her personal experience. She couldn't remember who, if any, of the men in Woolf's life — not Leonard, she thought — were in the Great War. If any cousins or relatives had been injured or killed. How had she known about soldiers and war? Had she come to hate the fighting only because of news and talk and that singular blend of imagination and uncompromising intelligence? Or maybe it was intense fear itself, when the bombs fell on her home in London, that had made her want to give up.

Carefully slipping from bed, she put on her blue flowered kimono. On the hotel dresser next to the coffee machine were some papers from Parris Island, among them a large manila envelope. Mike had taken her on a short tour after the ceremony; what he wanted most was to show Ellen the barracks where the recruits had all slept during training. As she expected, it was a long, plain room with dozens of metal bunk beds lined up on either side. Mike pointed out how tightly his thin green wool blanket was tucked around his bed — *not like this shlub,* he said fondly, pointing to a friend's bed nearby, which to Ellen looked identical — how everyone hung his small brown towel on the rungs of the bed, draped down neatly like a hand towel in a guest bathroom. He showed her his locker, back to back with another locker at the foot of his bed. He opened it to show what was inside, arranged in battered wood drawers — folded cammies, notepad, toiletries — and while he was bent over Ellen saw how close the hair had been shaved on the back of his head, how finely it shaded into the skin of his temple, and behind his ear. She ran a finger across it and Mike made a face.

"Classic high and tight. Six bucks, razor number one point five." Mike ran his hand where Ellen had touched. "Wes is gonna be relentless."

"What's this?" Ellen picked up a corner of the large envelope that lay on top of the other items in the locker.

"No, yeah, that's just something they make us do, our dress-blues photo. And a platoon one. We had to fill out forms on the spot so I ordered one . . . kind of by mistake. Also the yearbook, but I think they mail that to you later."

"There's a yearbook?" Ellen slid out a cardboard folder from the envelope and opened it carefully. Mike, unsmiling, in a white hat with gold insignia, buttoned blue jacket, against a lighter blue backdrop and an unfocused American flag.

"Handsome," she said. Mike, embarrassed, took the photo out of her hands and put it back in the envelope.

"I didn't know it would be so big," he muttered.

"May I keep it?" Ellen asked. "Unless you had other plans."

Mike looked at her. "No other plans."

In the hotel bathroom, Ellen ran hot water in the shower until the mirror fogged. She rummaged among her cosmetics, then squinted at the small complimentary bottles of shampoo, conditioner, body lotion. Then under the spray of water, a rush of realization. That photo . . . she knew that photo.

She knew its elements, its setting, its shape and form. It was the portrait newscasters ran, in a corner of the screen, when reporting the recent death tolls. Every man in that photo: young, tanned, hard faced under the white cap. *Through these portals pass prospects for America's finest fighting force . . .*

Ellen began to cry. And its size . . . there had been a framed one of Don at his memorial service, that same eight-by-eleven print. She couldn't remember who had set it up, maybe Don's brother. But she knew without a doubt it was the same dimensions, propped on a table near his casket, a life-size image of his laughing face, what she'd had to stare at all service from the front pew of the church.

Angry and afraid, she cried and washed her hair. She cried and washed her body.

"Screaming at the top of your lungs, you go, 'Sir! Recruit Kirkson requests permission to speak to Senior Drill Instructor Staff Sergeant Michaels!' And he'll be like, 'What the hell do you want, Kirkson?' 'Sir! This recruit requests permission to make a head call!' "

"That means, go to the bathroom," Mike's friend Tom said, interrupting his own story.

"Duh," Tom's little sister said. "We've all

seen *Full Metal Jacket.*"

"Why do you have to say 'this recruit'?" Tom's tall, friendly mother asked. "That I don't get. You can't say your own name?"

"You can't even say 'me' or 'my' or any of those, what are they called . . ."

"Personal pronouns," Ellen mumbled. *Stop it,* she told herself.

Tom blew out his breath. "Oh man, and if you do . . . Remember Gerhardt that day?" He and Mike cracked up.

"What happened?" the teenage sister demanded. "Did you have to haze him? Was there a blanket party?" To her mom, she explained, "That's when they pin the guy down and beat him with —"

"Jeannie."

Tom and Mike just laughed. Whatever they had done or seen done in training they wouldn't be describing here, at the dinner table with their families in a bunting-swathed room called Chesty Puller Hall. Ellen couldn't help but be happy, hearing Mike joke around with skinny, amiable Tom — it was clear they were good friends. She'd never met one of Mike's friends before, but she knew this relaxed goofy manner: it was how he was with Wes. But still, she didn't like the way his experience, their secrets together, separated him from her. Already today she'd been referred to as a "civilian" one too many times.

"Want to go find Crum? See if his girl showed?" Tom asked. Mike looked at Ellen; she nodded. The boys crossed the room together. Tom said something that made Mike rock his head back, clap sharply.

Tom's mother scooted her chair next to Ellen's. She too had been watching them go. "Never thought I'd be here doing this," she said. "Last time he wore a uniform it was Cub Scouts."

Ellen smiled.

"All right, now don't judge me but . . ." The woman opened her purse to show Ellen — inside, a flask-size bottle of Maker's Mark. "I was thinking of making my tea into a hot toddy. Will you join us?"

"With pleasure. But will we end up in the brig?"

"They've got bigger problems than two moms who could really use a drink. I'm Grace, by the way."

"Ellen." She pushed her cup closer, thankful for the generous slug of whiskey Grace neatly tipped into it. It was nice to be with a family. The two women clinked mugs, and Ellen felt her shoulders loosen for the first time since touching down in Georgia. She also let Grace's "two moms" pass without comment, an omission she couldn't remember making before.

With that, the two women began to talk, and after mutually testing the waters, started a real conversation about their doubts and fears. Grace, a dance teacher in Connecticut, admitted in a whisper that she was a registered member of the Green Party. Ellen described a few of Serena's more controversial actions, one involving an effigy of Donald Rumsfeld. She even acknowledged being there. Another round from the purse flask, and they were talking about how dumb the broad-brimmed drill instructor hats were, how much they hated "oo-rah," and how annoyingly proud the guys were of having cleaned toilets and made beds.

"Okay, here's a joke," Grace said, leaning in toward Ellen and her husband. "An Army Ranger is stationed in Louisiana, and really wants a pair of these fancy alligator shoes he sees everywhere. But in all the stores, they're priced way out of his range — five, six hundred dollars. So in frustration he says to one of the shopkeepers, 'Maybe I'll just go over to the swamp and kill one of those suckers myself, make my own damn shoes.' Shopkeeper says, 'Be my guest — maybe you'll run into these two Marines who were in here today saying the same thing.'

"So the Ranger gets down to the river, swamp, whatever . . . he's standing onshore and sure enough, he does see two Marines there, up to their thighs in swamp water."

"How does he know they're Marines?" Tom's father asked.

"Because it's a joke, and he just does." Grace pushed her hair back and made a face. "Anyway, as he's watching, a giant gator comes slowly swimming toward the Marines. One of them grabs it by the throat, strangles it to death with one hand, and easily tosses it out of the water and up onshore. They flip it on its back. Lying next to it, the Army Ranger realizes, are several other of the huge creatures.

" 'Goddamn it all to hell,' one of the Marines says. 'This fucker ain't wearing any shoes either!' "

Tom's father's laugh rose above the rest of the table's in a short, sharp blast. Ellen thought about how sourly Jane would have reacted to this joke, and how nice it was — *bad, bad* — not to have to deal with that awkwardness.

The boys came back, bearing slices of cake. Everyone ate dessert as a screen was unrolled and a slide show began. Ellen rolled her eyes at Grace, who giggled. Mike and Tom dragged their chairs into the middle of the hall, with other Marines, so they could hoot together at the various images of themselves in training, covered in mud, doing pull-ups, sweating out a run.

"I've been wincing every time I hear another parent say the phrase 'my Marine,' " Grace whispered, shaking her head. "But I confess it's starting to seem like it'll be in the realm of possibility."

"Don't do it, Grace! It's a slippery slope to that T-shirt . . . You know the one." Earlier, they had ogled a woman passing by in a spangled shirt that spelled out, in glittery red-white-and-blue: *MY MARINE SON IS MY HERO . . . AND YOURS!*

Mike's profile was lit by the projector's beam. Whatever happens, Ellen thought, quickly ignoring what she meant by *that,* it was good to see him this way, accepted, successful, with friends. Maybe it would be all right. Even though the pendulum had swung too far to the other side, at least she wasn't worried about him huffing paint and doing 360s in the Goodman pool parking lot.

"Is it possible to imagine some good coming from this?" she asked Grace, eyes on Michael bathed in the film's blue light. "That at the very least they may have learned how to take care of themselves?"

"And each other," Grace pointed out. "When they're over there, that's going to be the thing that gets them through it."

A shiver went off deep inside Ellen, a gathering rush. *Over there.* "What do you mean?"

"In . . . well, in Iraq."

"But how do you — I mean, it's not for sure they *will* go there. Is it? Or did you just mean, in case they do."

Grace was worried. She glanced at Tom's father. "I thought — well, didn't Michael tell you?"

"Tell me what?"

"Maybe I shouldn't have said anything. I'm sorry, I wish I hadn't raised it —"

"Tell me what."

"Tom told us on the phone a few weeks ago . . . that both platoons heard unofficially but essentially, they'd be going. First to Lejeune for infantry, and then deploy to Iraq right after that. This summer. June, most likely."

"That doesn't mean it's final," Tom's father said. For Ellen's benefit.

"Tom seemed to think it was," Grace said quietly. "The officers have been talking about it to them all throughout the end of training."

Ellen pushed back from the table a few

inches. If anyone spoke to her she might scream. In a whirl of thoughts, she isolated a surprising anger toward Grace, in all respects a perfect stranger: *What do you mean by sharing this meal and pretending to be on my side?* Also, *How can you do it — chat and joke and have known it all the while?* She had been duped.

Table conversation all but stopped. Mike and Tom came back to say good night. They were off to get rip-roaring drunk with the other graduates. Or so it was implied. Ellen accepted his kiss on her cheek and automatically told him to be careful. Tomorrow they would meet for breakfast before her flight; he had plans to drive up to New York City with Tom to spend the weekend and would fly to Madison from there. Grace and her family got ready to leave and said good night. Ellen brightly fended off the other woman's awkward concern, her apology.

For maybe she knew more than she would admit about how to behave in this new world. Throughout the hall caterers bunched up paper tablecloths, broke down folding chairs. Ellen put on her coat, took up her purse with its letter inside. She walked calmly to the parking lot. How strange to realize that manners and politeness and social convention held sway even now. One didn't scream with fury at the Chesty Puller dinner party for one's newly minted warrior. One didn't make a scene.

Because that's all it would amount to, Ellen thought dully as she drove back to the hotel. Her careful plan, her passionate arguments, her letter. It wouldn't do any good. It was too late. Mike might hear her out but ultimately it wouldn't matter. A time when Ellen might have been able to change his mind had passed, if one had ever existed. He was in it now, and she was too much of a coward to make a scene.

6

Eddie had been gone five weeks. His division went from Germany to Kuwait to Baghdad. He'd called and e-mailed when they were still in the Green Zone, but now he was out in Sadr City and she hadn't heard from him in over a week. Lacey wasn't worried; right now the Mahdi army, controlled by Moqtada al-Sadr, was mostly calm. If Mookie stayed quiet, the army could make progress on stabilizing the slum, which she knew was one of the worst in Baghdad. No plumbing, no electricity, sewage running raw through the streets.

At the computer in her kitchen, Lacey clicked past a photo of young boys jumping up and down in their blue rubber sandals. They were waiting for the food trucks to arrive. She focused on the next series of pictures — Second Brigade, First Army guys out there with new Iraqi soldiers. These were taken before Eddie's unit arrived, but they showed what would be his main mission: training Iraqi soldiers to find explosives, quell insurgent fire, and provide on-the-ground support for any coalition movements.

"What a nightmare," Lacey muttered, thinking about Eddie's anal-retentive nature in contrast to the haphazard Iraqi discipline and organization. One photo showed an Iraqi man getting a retinal scan. He was applying to be a neighborhood guard. But so many of these guys had untrustworthy backgrounds — connections to insurgents, hostile to Americans — it was a risk just letting them do the grunt work. They were broke, desperate. They'd say anything to get a job. And then turn tail, inform to the Mahdi army, if that would get them more money. Lacey glared at the man holding open his eye for the camera. She checked a couple other threads, but not much was going on. Weekends tended to be slower on the boards.

"Otis!" she yelled in the direction of the bathroom, shower still running. "Let's go already!" Was he masturbating in there? But that would take two minutes, not twenty — wouldn't it? Lacey wished someone could have a talk with him about all that guy stuff, with pointers for when and where. She was fine with male hormones in theory, she just didn't want to think about them in her bathroom.

Before she shut down the Internet, Lacey swung through the chat rooms at www.marriedtothemilitary.com, an anonymous online forum for military wives, girlfriends, and anyone else who had the army in their business. Most of the questions were about care package protocol (no sweets, no glitter, hide the porn) or on-base questions about housing and paychecks. There was one thread, though, that Lacey couldn't stop thinking about. It had started several days ago when a poster who called herself "InfidelGirl" confessed that she was thinking about cheating on her Marine boyfriend. The board had erupted with outrage and scorn, blasting InfidelGirl as a homewrecker, a bitch, a slut, and a thousand more epithets that had brought the board moderators in several times to remind everyone to keep it civil. *I haven't done it yet,* InfidelGirl wrote. *And maybe I won't. I'm just lonely, and at least I'm honest enough to say it. He'll never know, anyway.*

She just wants attention, Lacey told herself. No update from InfidelGirl. Probably it's all fake. Some people have nothing better to do, right? Lacey shut the computer, feeling vaguely dirty.

Finally Otis was out and dressed. Lacey noticed he was wearing a short-sleeve shirt over a long-sleeve one. Was that a thing now? But with his short-sleeve tighter and the long sleeve one baggy, the look came out bunchy and weird. She gave his head a kiss and made a mental note to check Marshalls for shirts with the right proportions.

Her car stalled twice before they could pull up the ramp leading out of the apartment's garage. Lacey's face grew hot as she motioned people behind her to go around. She jammed the clutch, pumped the gas, and cursed a lot.

"Is it the battery again?" Next to her Otis was flipping through a Legos catalog. He didn't sound all that concerned.

"I think it's the hoses or something," Lacey said. "Better be." Last time, though, the mechanic had murmured something ominous about the carburetor before she shut him up. She did *not* have an extra seven hundred bucks lying around. Finally they were out, on a cloudy warm spring day, windows down and Z100 on the radio. Mother and son both sang along to "Hollaback Girl" with Gwen Stefani. Otis had a little thing for Gwen Stefani, and Lacey couldn't deny she was cute. And extremely athletic: what was up with all those push-ups during her shows? They took the Hutch South through Pelham, crossed the New England Thruway, and went around a series of clover turns as they entered Pelham Bay Park, a confusing mix of parkland and public beach. Lacey missed the first turnoff so they went around again, finally pulling onto the dinky little two-lane that led over a bridge into City Island.

"The Seaport of the Bronx," Otis intoned. The sign made them crack up every time.

"We're late." Lacey sighed. She hated to give Lolo anything else on her. It was still weird to her that Eddie had grown up here, on this seedy spit of land in the Eastchester Bay. While she had spent her teenage years strolling every mall in Yonkers, he'd worked in the fading boatyards in the putt-putt, driving weekenders out and back from their docked fourteen-footers. You'd think he would have joined the navy. And it was white, white, *white* here — Irish, Italian, a little Greek. Eddie claimed he hadn't been the only Puerto Rican kid at P.S. 175, but as far as Lacey could tell, his mother Lolo cornered the market on color.

When they pulled to a stop in front of her two-story A-frame on Carroll Street — you could always find parking out here — Otis said, "Yeah. She's sitting in the window. You're screwed."

"Look, no more with the screwing, all right?" Otis snickered. "You know what I mean."

He jogged up the steps and the front door opened instantly. "Hi, Lolo!" "Hi, baby. *Finally.*" Lacey got the grocery bags from the trunk. Lolo hadn't e-mailed her list until yesterday at 6:00 p.m., which meant then she and Otis had been out at Wesselman's and the discount grocery place until ten. She shouldered open the door and carried bags right into the kitchen. "Hi, Mom."

Lolo came in the doorway, one arm tightly wrapped around Otis; they were about the same height. Petite, fully made up, hair done . . . it was clear that the visit wasn't a casual one for her mother-in-law. Lacey put away the milk and eggs, lugged the cat litter under the bathroom sink. She felt scrubby and huge, as usual, whenever she was out here. "They didn't have Genoa salami. This is the same thing, right?"

Lolo barely glanced at the package she held up. "It is what it is. Let me get my checkbook."

"Forget it, Ma." Otis grinned. They went through this each time.

"I'm not a charity case. Now tell me the total."

Lacey put the soda liters on the lower shelf of the pantry. "Zero dollars, and zero cents. Today's bargain only."

"Well . . ." Lolo shook her head at the ceiling, *what can I do,* deeply disappointed yet again.

"Otis? You waiting for an invitation?" Lacey pointed to full grocery bags on the floor.

"No, no, he has to come tell me every single thing about school. Get a glass of milk first, sugar."

Otis shrugged happily. "I have to go tell her every single thing about school."

As he reached into the fridge, Lacey gave him a noogie. Actually, she was glad for a moment's quiet in the kitchen. And for the ferocious love Lolo had always shown Otis, another man's son, even if it was on the bossy side. It had been five years, but Lacey still felt like Lolo was judging her, waiting for her to mess up. She'd confided this to Martine once, who had snorted and said, "Uh, *yeah* she is. You married her only son, what do you expect? She was hoping for J.Lo, she got you." Lacey didn't think it was the PR stuff standing in the way, though — Eddie'd had a white dad. In fact she and

Lolo had more common ground than they admitted. Lolo had raised Eddie on her own, after his father split. She'd put in long hours as a secretary in a career that went from medical offices to local colleges to working for the Bronx borough president. But for whatever reason — *the obvious ones,* Lacey could hear Martine say — they couldn't get along.

In the living room, a plate of almond sugar cookies, *mantecaditos,* was set on the table. Tego, the cat, jumped into Lacey's lap, but she shoved him off with a forearm. She went over to the front windows, which gave out practically right to the street, and looked at the houses on the other side: modest, neatly kept up, several American flags. Attached to Lolo's window with a plastic suction cup was her red-and-white service banner, same exact one Lacey had. She lifted it to peek at the blue star on its front; several others of the same flag were hanging in windows on this street alone.

"Sit down and relax, Lacey. What are you doing over there?"

"Nothing." This place always made her feel antsy. "I printed you out a couple of e-mails. We should get a call from him any day, but you know when they first arrive it's all so —"

Lolo was motioning, *give me, give me.* She took the folded papers and put on her glasses to study them. Otis flopped sideways on the couch whispering *pleaseplease-pleaseMom* — he'd been begging to stop at Seafood City on the way out for hot dogs and video games. She made a *just chill* face.

"What does he mean about 'not happy but I'll get over it'?" Lolo pointed to a page.

"Some drama with one of the other unit COs. They had a mix-up about supplies, and Eddie didn't get what he wanted."

"So why didn't he?"

"I don't know, Mom. It doesn't always go his way over there."

"Pff." Then she told the story of the time in high school when Eddie and a friend got rear-ended in a "borrowed" car out by the Co-op City complex. The friend ditched, but Eddie owned up to everything. He had to do chores nights and weekends for a month until Lolo let him off the hook. And he never ratted out his buddy. Otis was rapt — he liked the part about Eddie in trouble — but Lacey had heard it before. She knew, she knew, Eddie could do no wrong, even when he *was* doing wrong.

Lacey let her gaze travel around the small room, worn flowered furniture, Lolo's cane leaning against her chair, no TV, framed photos everywhere, mostly of Eddie, one of Otis. There was one from her own wedding on a side table: Lacey angled to the side, bangs falling into her face, idiotic smile; Eddie, straight-on, jacket off, calm. But the biggest one, the best — they would all agree — was Eddie in ACU battle dress, digital cammies and black beret. Last year, Lolo had paid for him to go to a studio in town here, since he'd never had an official portrait done after ROTC. Lacey remembered him bitching about it, but now she was glad Lolo had won. Framed and huge and placed on a shelf all alone, it showed the real Eddie: confident, determined, unsmiling.

There was so little to talk about here. Eddie had made her promise not to bring up any news, no matter what. After a few more minutes of chatting, Lacey couldn't contain herself. "Okay, Mom, you got a list for me?"

"Why are you in a hurry?"

"It's a school night. Otis has homework. What do you need me to fix?"

"Well, I don't keep a *list,* like for a handyman."

"All right. Then we need to —"

"But the TV upstairs. I can't figure out what's happened." The three of them trooped upstairs. Lacey let Otis take care of the TV remote situation — Lolo had pressed an input button and couldn't get out of a black screen that said "Video 2" — while she popped into the bathroom to check the medicine cabinet.

"Mom, you're low on Prandin." She shook the pharmacy bottle of diabetes pills. "You have to take these three times a day, before each meal."

"I have another in the kitchen," Lolo called. "This one's just if I forget. So I don't have to go back down the stairs."

"Right, well, the idea is not to forget," Lacey said to herself. She checked the bedroom — fine, tidy — and picked up the laundry basket. Above Lolo's protestations, she started a load and then attended to other things on the list. Lolo had, in fact, made a list. However, Lacey point-blank refused the last item.

"Lolo, I am *not* clipping any cat's toenails. Disgusting."

"But it only takes a minute! He won't hold still for me. You should see what the claws are doing to my bedspread! Here, Tego. Come here, Tego!"

"Uh-uh. Negative. Let's go, O."

In spite of her theatrical disappointment — you only just got here! — they gathered coats and hugged Lolo and said good-bye. Lacey could almost feel herself lighten, out on the street, unlocking the car.

"You call me," Lolo ordered from the doorway. "Any minute that you hear from him."

"Of course we will, Mom. Love you. See you next week." Pulling away, Lacey glimpsed her mother-in-law in the window, curtain aside, watching them above her service flag.

"Mom. *Pleasepleaseplease.* I am so hungry. I'm starving."

She glanced at him. He was a good kid. "All right, I'll make you a deal. We can stop for dinner, but I'm not going to that seafood place, it gives me a headache." And it was insanely expensive; eighteen dollars for a paper plate of fried clams. "Bring your backpack."

They went to the Snug, a recently renovated pub next door to the diner. The Yankees were on three TV screens, and only two or three people were sitting at the bar. Lacey led Otis to a table along the side of the room and went up to the bar for menus.

"I got you," the bartender said, waving her back to the table. He came over with menus, place settings, and two glasses of water.

"What's the score?"

"Detroit's up by two. Something to drink?"

"He'll have milk and —"

"Sprite, please, Mom?"

"One Sprite and I'll have . . . what the hell is 'City Island Beer'?" she said, squinting at the tap.

One of the barflies called back over his shoulder, "It's six-dollar Michelob with a fancy label." Cackles.

"I'll take a Miller Lite." Meanwhile, Lacey was unpacking Otis's backpack and handing him his math workbook and reading folder. "No watching the game until I've checked these."

"Mom, Jeter's up!"

"Look, I'm working too." Lacey pointed to her thick, stuffed binder: a combination agenda, scheduler, and file folder. She turned to the section labeled "FRG Group." Each woman had filled out a sheet with some basic information as well as a space for what Lacey had called "Concerns and Life Stresses." Anne had suggested that she have each person describe what her main problems were, and then take notes based on that. But Lacey had wanted the women to put it in their own words. Which, thank God, because the first meeting had not gone as expected.

There had been six of them in a dingy room in the Yonkers Community Center. Two black women who were longtime friends and had husbands in the National Guard; one bitchy girl with a newlywed in the Marines; one freaked-out mom of an army PFC; and one woman who didn't say a word the entire hour. Nervous, Lacey had been too energetic. She aimed for Anne's funny enthusiasm but landed on loud and manic.

In any case, no one had listened much to her. They immediately took over the discussion with intense questions and arguments about TriCare, the DoD's health care plan. Which plan, Prime or Standard? Why those hellish new deductibles in Standard? And how come they were so slow to reimburse? One woman said her kid's broken wrist from last winter was still on her credit card. Lacey listened, agreed — and tried to change the subject. Weren't they supposed to be doing feelings?

The women ran right over her overtures. Next up was pay grade, of course, that endless source of gripes and confusion. Right away, Lacey got tense. As the wife of a reserve NCO, Anne had told her, she was supposed to be mentoring these women on good personal finance practices. But the truth was, she was already scrambling; Eddie's active duty pay was less than three-quarters of what he made at Hess. Last time, they toughed it out for a year, but now deployment meant fifteen months. So they were making up the difference out of savings. Problem was, they'd used a chunk of savings last year to help Lolo after her surgery . . . and now with Lacey having to reduce her private-client hours to spend more time with Otis, it could get ugly. She didn't like to think about it, to be honest. But most of the women were in similar situations, and they volleyed questions at Lacey about basic pay, allowance for housing, loss of BAS food money, hazardous duty pay, family separation pay . . .

Then it was over, Lacey feeling dazed and disappointed.

"You're from Great Neck, aren't you?" The bartender had just put down Otis's cheeseburger and was staring down at Lacey. "Did you go to North?"

She glanced up at him and away. "Maybe. Can we get some ketchup?"

"Thought so." To her surprise and relief, he merely brought a ketchup bottle from another table, and went back behind the bar.

"Mom. I can't do this one."

The sum of the interior angles of a quadrilateral is equal to 360 degrees. How many degrees are in the fourth angle of a quadrilateral whose other three angles are 80 and 110 and 95?

Lacey's heart pounded. She ate some of Otis's fries and read the problem for the third time without understanding it. Who was this guy? How did he know her from high school? Worst thought: What if he'd been one of the Asshole's friends? What if he mentioned him to Lacey, asked about him, saw the resemblance in Otis, said the Asshole's name out loud?

"Is this what it looks like?" Otis had sketched a crazy, tilted four-sided shape on his paper place mat.

"Okay, but drawing it might actually be more confusing. Try this." She wrote out an equation next to it subtracting 80 and 110 and 95 from 360.

She snuck looks at the bartender. Fortyish white guy with salt-and-pepper hair, a little potbelly, decent face. He watched the Yankee game for a minute, and then turned back to rinsing glasses. When he caught her looking, he pointed to her empty beer glass without expression. She nodded.

"So how do you know Great Neck?" she

asked when he brought her a fresh one.

"I graduated '89 at North," he said. "Just a few years ahead of you. Your brother Bob — right? — was in my class."

"He lives in San Diego now."

"Nice. Good for him."

"Is this right, Mom?" She tilted her head to check Otis's equation.

"Yes. Now copy it real neat into the workbook." *What's the problem, just be normal.* "Lacey Diaz," she said. "And this is Otis."

The bartender wiped his hand on his towel and held it out to both of them. "Jim Leahy. You don't live on the island, do you?"

"Which one?" They each laughed. "No, we're in Mount Vernon. You live here?"

"Pelham. I'm managing a place out there, and then I fill in here most weekends."

"You got a family?"

"I got three pretty girls, but no. Divorced."

After a bit of silence, Jim rapped on their table and went back to the bar. Lacey took a big swallow of the beer. So, that was it. She wouldn't have to account for all the shit that happened back then, maybe she'd been able to skate right past those screaming fights with her parents, the bad places she'd been stuck in, the way the Asshole had messed her up. *This is who I am,* she told herself. *Not that girl, not anymore.*

The beer filled her with warmth from deep inside. The Yankees went up by a run on an A-Rod homer. Otis whipped through the rest of his homework with no whining; Jim brought him over a small dish of ice cream, on the house. Lacey read here and there amid the group members' Concerns and Life Stresses; she couldn't remember who was who, couldn't put faces with the names. She didn't focus on the content of the comments so much as on the handwriting. One woman had pushed down so hard on the ballpoint she nearly went through the page. Another had schoolgirl script. One added smiley faces. Another used feathery, incoherent lettering.

When she paid the check, nearly half of it had been comped. She tried to thank Jim, but he shook it off brusquely. She left a big tip and said, "I'm just glad you didn't make me relive high school."

"Next time," Jim said, meeting her eyes once.

7

Dear Mike,

There was one day when I got my first sense of the way you'd had to live, before you came to be with us. This was in fall of 2002, after the summer you and Wes worked for the park district. I'd noticed, of course, that you were crashing in the basement pretty regularly, after you and Wes hung out — or even after you'd be out with other friends. I knew you were careful to keep out of our way as much as possible. (Remember how you set an alarm and left before eight sometimes, even on Sunday mornings?) But that engine in your Ford Probe never failed to wake me up. I wonder now where you went then. I should have made it more clear that we wanted you to stick around, to have some pancakes at least.

Anyway, one day that fall, your senior year, I went down to the basement with a basket full of Wes's and Janey's laundry. Why I was still doing my sixteen- and fifteen-year-olds' laundry is a good question. That day, for the first time, I decided to throw some of your things in the wash too. At first I hesitated, though — would you be offended? Would you think I was too forward, or meddling? Also, I have to admit, I wondered whether it would set a bad precedent. Would you expect me to keep it up?

I opened the closet door where you used to stash your stuff before we brought that dresser downstairs. What was I expecting? Probably a pile of dirty clothes on the floor or stuffed in a backpack. I liked the idea of you finding fresh clothes all folded up, the next time you came over. Instead I saw . . . well, I saw your setup.

On the floor of that storage closet were small bundles of tightly rolled and folded clothes. Arranged in seven piles, each had a T-shirt, a pair of boxers, socks bundled together, and maybe a sweatshirt stacked underneath. You had one pair of jeans, inside out, neatly rolled and lined up to the side. There was a pair of your sneakers. There was your football jacket. All of them rolled or tightly wrapped so as to take up as little space as possible.

And then there were the notes. Forgive me. I read them. I turned on the overhead light: *Mondays, 9/16 (wash 9/24), 9/23 (wash 9/24 — shrunk! no dryer!), 9/30,* etc. You were keeping track of when you wore certain shirts — the Pac-Woman one, the flannel button-up, the rock concert one — because you owned so few. You notated which were clean, when you needed to wash your socks . . . you must have done it late at night. There was a plastic bag on the floor too, full of powdered detergent that you must have swiped from somewhere else (the school gym? a friend's house?). You were so determined not to impose on us any more than you already had that you weren't even using my detergent. You were carefully parsing out your clean clothes, making sure not to be seen in a shirt two days in a row, making sure to only run one load per week. And with these little notes that kind of broke my heart that afternoon.

Have you ever had the experience of flowing straight into someone else's mind and heart? I sat on the floor in front of that closet and felt myself dissolve. For a few short moments I knew what it was like to be *you,* bouncing from house to house, hoarding and organizing your few, scattered possessions — essentially homeless. Proud and secretly afraid. Thick-skinned and confused, angry and grateful. Seventeen years old.

Although I'm embarrassed to write this, up until then, I thought you were my good deed. You know I worried you'd corrupt Wes, we've joked about that. I also liked to think of myself as a "cool mom" — *sure, no problem, enjoy my pullout couch.* I liked the way it made me look — the way *you* made me look: to Wes and Jane, to my friends, to myself. But I'm ashamed to admit I didn't spend much time really feeling what life was like for you. When I did, thanks to a nosy laundry idea . . . well, it jolted me out of complacency. I didn't run to get the guardian forms (you know that took a while for both of us to get our heads around), nor did I scoop up your clothes and find a better place for them than the floor of that old storage closet. After some time I quietly closed the door, leaving your system intact. Probably you didn't notice any change in my attitude toward you. But you became more of a person to me that day.

This photocopy is a very short story called "The Huntsman" by Anton Chekhov. It's barely four pages, don't roll your eyes like that. On the one hand, nothing "happens" in this story, right? A hunter meets a peasant woman in the woods, they speak, he walks on. But then again . . . do you see the moment where his attitude shifts, regarding her? What makes him ask her "how do you live?" Why does he want to know?

Surprisingly, you didn't have to do much differently when mailing a letter to Iraq than when you mailed one to your mother in her retirement home one county away. At first, Ellen hadn't believed the post office worker who shrugged off her inquiries about special stationery, stamps: *Just put the FPO address on it,* she was told, *and a regular old thirty-seven-center.* But a few minutes of searching online confirmed that. So she typed on her computer, printed off on copy paper, and folded the pages inside a plain white number ten envelope. It was strange to see those letters to PFC Michael Cacciarelli in a stack of Ellen's other correspondence on the hall table, waiting to go out. Same postage, same appearance. Like we might be tricked, Ellen thought, into forgetting how far away these soldiers are.

Mike had been gone just over a month. "Over there." Any week now would tip the scales — this would be the longest she, or any of them, had gone without seeing him. All they knew was that he was in Anbar Province; although that, Wes said, meant nothing. "It's a catchall term for the western area, full of Sunni militia. Where they send almost all the Marines. It'd be like saying you live in the Midwest, Mom. Almost impossible to guess which city."

Ellen understood this and didn't. She knew that Wes and Jane were in more contact with him, had talked to him more before deployment, were more clued in. She didn't ask and they didn't tell, an old pattern left over from the days when Mike's whereabouts would have upset her, so were deliberately withheld. Actually, Ellen thought, back then her kids underestimated her quite a bit. Maybe they imagined that Mike's drinking and fighting and general troublemaker lifestyle were too much for their ivory-tower mom to handle. Or that she'd never spent time around drugs herself (she came of age in the *1960s,* for Pete's sake). Or that Janey's own phases of secrecy and excess hadn't schooled Ellen in both steely resolve and a Zen-like not-clinging-to-expectations. In a way, she encouraged that "don't tell Mom" three-against-one setup when Mike was living with them. She loved their growing closeness; she wanted Mike to have allies his own age. And she had enough trust in the surprising force of their own relationship — hers and Mike's — that she could allow the division between them.

Also, the guilt. She and Mike had an unspoken agreement about their closeness. Neither of them alluded to so many conversations — those late-night talks while watching TV, the things they told each other driving around Madison — when the others were around. One morning at breakfast, Jane had gone from bleary to animated over her mug of tea, reading an article out loud, the idiotic story of a criminal who "butt-dialed" 911 while robbing a liquor store. Ellen watched in amazement — and quickly followed suit — as Mike listened carefully, even asking a few laughing questions, as if the whole thing were new to him. When in fact the night before she and he had caught a segment about it on the late-night news, which even included audio of the recorded call. But he pretended, and so she did.

Maybe Mike was embarrassed, later, about how much time they'd spent together. Or maybe he didn't want Wes and Jane to feel weird about it, to get territorial. So why did Ellen go along? Why did she always feel she was keeping something from Wes and Jane? Part of it was not wanting the inevitable taint of sex to cloud the air. She knew how it looked — a lonely older woman, a young attentive man. As a longtime teacher, Ellen had had her fair share of classroom crushes. She wasn't unfamiliar with the ego boost and inward thrill that an attractive, interested student could provide. But it wasn't that. Or, it was more than that.

Over the weeks he'd been gone, her letters to Mike had taken on an importance that was hard to shake. Ellen worked on them constantly, essays she composed and revised over the course of a feverish three or four or five days. She discarded the hysterical style of that first letter, in which she'd foolishly tried to convince him to go AWOL. (Why had she thought that would work on him?) What she was going for now: a lifeline made of literature, a rescue built of the only power Ellen believed in. The study's once-organized bookshelves became messy and caved in, so many volumes pulled out, scanned, discarded. How to find the right text for a boy (a man, a man, she knew she was meant to think of him that way) who'd barely squeaked through a mediocre high school? How to find the words (others' and her own) that would keep him tied to humanity, to himself? That would save his soul — for her aim in these letters was nothing less.

One night when he was on leave from base, about a week before he was flown to Al Asad, Mike came to dinner. It was just the two of them; Ellen made meat loaf with extra ketchup and bacon slices on top. Maybe he was nervous and couldn't wait, or maybe he wanted to get it over with, but before they'd even finished eating, Mike took out a folder he'd brought.

"You're not going to like this," he said. "But procrastinating will just make it worse, so . . ."

The same phrases she'd used to get him to tackle overdue homework assignments!

Mike said, "So this is, like, my will."

Ellen wiped her hands on her rough linen napkin and took the sealed envelope. "I'll keep it in the file cabinet in my study, with the other papers." Their guardianship forms; her own will; all the kids' medical and identification files.

"A few other papers: copy of the deed to my car. I sold it last week, but just in case the guy turns out to be a douche. This one's my credit card info, my bank account numbers."

She accepted the pieces of paper one at a time as he handed them to her. In the kitchen above their round wood table, an overhead lamp draped them both in soft light; NPR murmured from an upstairs radio, where she'd forgotten to turn it off. This big, dear young man was here, was so physically *here,* in existence, in his faded black White Sox T-shirt and cheap deodorant fumes, that it seemed impossibly wrong to be planning for a theoretical time when he might not be.

Ellen pulled a brochure out of the stack of papers he was sorting through. *Letters to Your Service Member.* She skimmed the advice that came in boxes next to photographs of beaming parents, arms slung around uniformed young men and women. *Receiving a letter from home is the best part of a soldier's day. Take care that your words ENCOURAGE and UPLIFT him or her. Leave out all complaints and worries. Remind your soldier that YOU ARE PROUD of him or her, and that YOU BELIEVE IN THE GOOD WORK he or she is doing. Below is a sample letter you may wish to . . .*

"This is embarrassing. I'm actually embarrassed on the military's behalf."

Mike peered over the page. "Whatever, they just give us all this crap."

"Do they actually think parents will copy a preset letter written by some functionary? To mail to their child? I thought propaganda was meant for the enemies."

"Toss it. Now, this is —"

"And this capitalization . . . What are we, morons? I know you don't expect me to write how I BELIEVE IN THE GOOD WORK you're doing."

Mike sighed and tried to tug the brochure away from her. "Letters are overrated anyway. That's like, a holdover from World War II. 'Dear Mother, Though the bombs are falling, I can picture our farm . . .' " He snickered.

Ellen yanked it back. "Don't joke about that. Don't say letters aren't important! Of course I'm going to write you — we all are. And you'd better write *back,*" she said, wishing she hadn't brought it up. A fearful memory of Mike dragging his feet about even the most undemanding compositions . . .

"Right. Pages and pages about Maisie and Edith Wharton. And am I staying out of trouble."

"What — what would you like me to write about?" A sudden shyness fell between them.

He swirled the last inch of beer around in his beer bottle. "Whatever. Just — you do your thing. I'll write back, obviously." He glanced up at Ellen.

"I want to write something you'll look forward to. Not some pro forma thing about the weather."

"Tell me, like . . ." He shook his head.

"What?"

"Stories about you guys. About us."

Ellen held back her excitement, a dozen questions: *Old stories? New ones? Those you know, or . . . ?* He was staring hard at the papers in front of him. She wouldn't push it, but an idea bloomed. What she could do, with writing, for him.

"What's this?" She unwrapped a piece of red felt cloth, rolled into a tube. It was a banner about a foot long, attached to a wooden dowel with a gold tasseled cord. On its front, a white velvet rectangle with a blue star in its center. Included in the packet was a suction cup hook and a piece of paper: *Rules for Proper Display of Service Flag.* "I see I'm supposed to hang this in the front window." Ellen tried to picture herself doing that. And if anyone noticed it — the postman, the cleaning woman — would they even know what it meant? *Outdated and maudlin,* she thought, repulsed.

"I don't know what all this crap is, I'm just supposed to give it to you. Junk it for all I care. What else? Oh, right. They want us to hand over copies of birth certificates and Social Security cards, so . . ."

"I do have these, upstairs. But it's good to keep all of this together." She unfolded the birth certificate copy and they both stared at it in silence. *Proof of Live Birth. Michael Cacciarelli,* infant: male. Date: November 23, 1975. *Mother: Renee Milio. Father: unspecified.*

"Not a lot of relevant info there," Mike said. He bounced a knee up and down, finished the beer.

"Would you like to . . . give at least some of this to your aunt? Or I can make copies of all of it for her, and —"

Mike shook his head. He snapped back into action, flipping through pages in his folder. "She's not even in Janesville now, I don't think. Anyways . . . look, do you want to do this or not?"

Not. "All right. Yes, go on."

"Well, I guess the next one is . . . yeah. Here, you just have to sign a few places."

Consent for notification, Killed in Action. Ellen breathed out. "Where do I . . . okay, I see." She initialed several places to confirm her name and address. *Don't you dare be funny,* she told him in her head. The red service flag lay curled on the table between them, drawing her uneasy attention like a live thing.

"One more. Last one." Mike pushed a form toward her and went back to eating meat loaf. It was a life insurance policy he'd taken out, with Ellen named sole beneficiary.

"Michael, no." There was also a federal payment in case of death or injury attached to the forms. Someone had helpfully attached tiny yellow Post-its at all the "signature" spaces.

"Why not? Someone should get something if I buy the farm —"

"Don't —"

"— And we get a death gratuity too, so make sure none of this gets wasted on funeral exp—"

"Stop it."

"Plus, you know, it's probably like the only way I could ever pay you back for all the —"

"Fuck you." The shock of what Ellen had just said propelled her out of her chair. "I'm

sorry, I didn't mean it, I didn't mean you — but — *fuck* this, honestly, *fuck* all of this —" Hands over her mouth, she went in useless circles around the kitchen. Mike hovered nearby, saying something, he was trying to pat her back, but she was fighting hard for control as wave after wave of horror passed through her. After it had, she rested against the counter and studied Mike: worried, out of his element.

"Do you . . ." She sniffed hard, wiped her face with a tea towel. "Do you have food in your mouth?"

He tried an experimental chew, and then swallowed, giving the thumbs-up. "Caught me off guard with all those F-bombs. I thought I was going to have to —"

"Actually hug me?"

"Whatever. What*ever,* Ellen." He pulled her into a big hug and they rocked there for a long time, by the stove.

One of the only breaks from composing Michael's letters that Ellen allowed herself was a movie date with Jane. Of course Jane was late. From the movie theater lobby, Ellen tried her cell, but it didn't even ring — "call failed" — which made her suspect Jane had stopped paying the bill again. It was a Thursday night at seven, and the Marcus cinemaplex was crowded; Ellen went around the concessions stand to double-check, but no Jane. Frustrated but not surprised, Ellen got into the long line for tickets. Even if she was stood up by her daughter, she was going to try to find a movie to enjoy. Not *War of the Worlds,* although apparently that's what most people were here to see. Maybe she would try that remake of *Bewitched.*

But then Ellen heard Jane calling for her. Outside the rows of ticket buyers, Jane waved both hands, *here I am.* Ellen pointed up at the board of titles and showtimes: What do you want to see? Jane shrugged: You decide. Her daughter would scoff at *Bewitched,* she felt sure, so Ellen made a split-second decision at the cashier and came away with two tickets.

"Batman Begins?" She gave Jane a one-armed hug.

"I've seen it, but sure, whatever."

Ellen stifled her response to this and instead they went to get popcorn and drinks. Jane claimed she wasn't hungry; Ellen ignored her and paid for one of the specials that got you a giant bucket plus two sodas. She was going to have a good time, despite Jane's attitude.

It was difficult to find seats in the dark, with strident commercials blaring. Ellen stumbled over someone and spilled a little popcorn; Jane reached her hand back to guide her mother. When Ellen did sink in relief into a seat Jane was staring up at the screen in disgust.

"What?"

Jane merely held out both of her open hands. *This, this!*

"Finding your own power and using it for good. Being part of a team. Protecting America, one day at a time."

On the screen, images of men rappelling out of a helicopter, racing up a dirt hill, grinning under their face paint and helmets. Some sort of country-power-pop anthem built to a climax while the narrator intoned: "Always ready. Always there. The National Guard."

Jane leaped to her feet, her bag and coat sliding to the floor. She shouted, "Boo! Booooooo!"

Next to her, Ellen could practically feel her young daughter vibrating with intensity. The audience laughed, a few people clapped. One called, *You tell 'em girl.* Jane slowly sat down. Ellen took her hand and Jane let her hold it. She was filled with pride. When was the last time she herself had taken such a stand?

At the same time, Ellen worried. What did

it mean to shake with that kind of righteous fury, to find so much of the world unbearable? Would it have been different if she'd grown up with a father in her life? Jane suddenly appeared porous, undefended. Far too vulnerable.

Batman Begins began. Jane slouched down in her seat and took a giant handful of popcorn. Ellen let the last few days fade away, the fevered intensity of her letters to Michael, and allowed herself to be drawn into the origin story of a comic book superhero she didn't care about one way or the other. Luckily, there was no need to know much: Bruce Wayne, Gotham City, Alfred the butler, the vault with the rubber suit. She liked the long sequence set in Asia where, as part of his training, Bruce is drugged and has to fight wave after woozy wave of black-suited ninja warriors.

After a while, Jane scrunched closer and put her head on Ellen's shoulder. Ellen kissed the top of her head with its tangled, dirty hair. They watched Batman acquire some new weapons. Ellen wished time would stop.

"Mom?" Jane had her mouth very close to Ellen's ear; she could feel her warm breath around the words. "I think I'm pregnant."

8

"No way, lady. You're not going anywhere yet." Lacey leaned her forearm against the thrashing toddler's stomach while she wiped poop off the girl's legs and bottom. She wasn't sure what this one's name was, but she could tell what she'd had for breakfast. "Good lord. Hey, need more wipes in here!"

One of the other moms dashed in with some. "If you're done, we may have another for you."

"How'd I get on this detail?" Lacey asked. It had been a long time since she had changed a diaper and she wanted some verification she got this "pull-up" kind the right way, but the other mom had already fled the designated changing room. Lacey sat back on her heels and helped the fussy toddler to her feet. As soon as she was upright, the girl shot back out to the living room, where there were toys, snacks, and "Yo Gabba Gabba."

Lacey bagged the dirty diaper, scooped the towel into the laundry bag, and washed her hands. "Next?" Felicia carried in a sleepy baby and laid him gently on the bed.

"I was just about to put him down, but I hate for him to sleep in a full diaper," she whispered. "The last thing she needs is for him to get a bad rash."

"Is this — ?"

"Yes. His name's Peter." They both stared down at the child, just over a year old. His father had been killed in action five days ago. Lacey unsnapped his Onesie and changed him as gently as she could. Felicia sat on the bed and sang a little "shh shh shh," stroking the top of his head with one finger. Aimee had wanted to bring Peter to the service, but her worried relatives convinced her to leave him with the FRG child care volunteers back at the house. Lacey wasn't sure what she would have done. It was the older kids and the littlest babies who were at the church now with their parents; most of the toddlers, the hardest to mind in church, had been left at Aimee's house. But Lacey thought she knew what Aimee had wanted as she sat through the hymns and the eulogy and the prayers: the solid weight of this baby on her lap. An anchor to life.

The news about Staff Sergeant Devon Richards had ripped through the circle of wives and girlfriends and set in motion the wide waves of protocol that surrounded an army service member casualty. Two women from the FRG group, the "care team," showed up here — at Aimee and Devon's home in Hunts Point — within minutes of the official notification, and stayed with Aimee while she called her parents and his, while she attended to the details, while she broke down. Other women — Anne Mackay was one of them — fielded everyone's panicked phone calls about the IED that had hit Richards's unit. No, no one else had been killed or injured. Yes, they were sure. Most of these calls had Aimee as their ostensible purpose (How is she holding up? What can I do?), but the true subtext had been: *Tell me again that my guy is okay.* Lacey knew this, because hers had been one of them.

"Was he one of yours?" The phone woke Lacey up at 3:00 a.m. two nights ago; she'd been expecting Eddie to call from base on a VoIP, and this was the first thing out of her mouth.

"No. Alpha Company."

"Thank God." Eddie was silent, but this was more than the hum and delay following each person's words. Lacey came up on her elbow in bed. "I didn't mean it that way. What's going on? You okay?"

"Yeah, I'm okay. I'm just tired and . . . really pissed. I'm just so fucking pissed."

"I know. I know."

"Such a stupid goddamn waste . . . I can't get into it, but so many dumb little mistakes, all added up together. And now this."

"It's so hard, honey."

"I'm fine! I'm just pissed! Lots of stupid shit went wrong, and we're better than that."

"I know, I just —"

"Lace, I gotta go. Everything's okay. Hi to Otis."

"Wait — Eddie? Eddie!"

For a long time Lacey lay awake holding her cell phone, wishing the whole call could get a do-over.

Now Felicia wrapped baby Peter up in his blanket and carried him off to his nursery. Lacey tidied the changing room and washed her hands. Out in the living room, women were pushing aside furniture to make room for the reception; people would begin to arrive in about an hour. Little kids careened around, getting in the way. Lacey threaded through the chaos to the kitchen.

"What do you need?"

"Here," Dina said, handing her a bread

knife. "Can you slice up the hoagies?"

"Mom!" Otis burst into the kitchen doorway, trailed closely by his buddy Rich. "I just unlocked, like, a whole other level on Mario Go-Kart! We've never even seen it! Can I use their computer to go online and find out what to do?"

"I think you know the answer to that," Lacey said. Dina laughed. "Now scat, unless you want to be put to work." The boys fled.

"How's Otis doing with it?" Dina asked. "Mary's too little to understand, thank God."

"Hard to say. We had a 'talk' and I told him how Eddie was nowhere near where that kind of stuff happens" — the two women exchanged a look — "but he's been pretty poker-faced about the whole thing. Would have helped if Eddie could have gotten him on the phone, but . . ."

"Right. Don't hold your breath on that, yeah?" Lacey sliced without answering. She kept the fact of Eddie's late-night call to herself; as an officer, he had more access to the phone banks than the enlisted guys like Dina's husband. That sliver of guilty relief was drowned out, though, by the bad memory of how they'd ended things. Maybe it would have been better if she *hadn't* heard from him.

"You guys. Holy shit. Holy shit." Another woman burst into the kitchen, staring at them wild-eyed. "Have you seen this?" Others crowded in behind her, Felicia among them.

Dina whispered, "Is it — ? Did something happen?"

"Give me that," Lacey said. She took the electronic reader out of the woman's hands. "How do you work this?" Someone reached over and enlarged the screen.

> AP news: A photo of at least two unidentified U.S. Marines purports to show the men desecrating the bodies of Iraqi insurgents. Photographer unknown. Follow link for photos — *Warning: Graphic.*

"Is this a joke?" Lacey said. The others' faces mirrored her horror. She hit the link; as soon as the first image loaded, all four women recoiled. A row of portable johns, with their doors open. Two soldiers standing, backs turned to the camera, as if urinating. They were looking over their shoulders, in sunglasses, laughing. One waved at the camera. Between them, a slumped figure wearing keffiyeh and robes, propped up and sitting on a toilet. A slumped figure who was dead. There were other photos.

"How could they?" Felicia breathed.

"Which fucking genius took these pictures?" Dina said. "There's your problem. What did he do, put them on Facebook?"

"Jarheads are unbelievable. They are so up shit's creek, it's not even funny."

"You know what this is going to do for the jihadis, right? Give them every excuse in the world to suicide-bomb our guys."

"These photos make it seem like we're asking for it!"

Some other women wandered in from the living room; they too had heard about the photos. Texts were zinging all over. "ABC News is doing a 'breaking news' on it right now. CNN has it all over the home page."

"If I got my hands on those assholes it'd make the Hajjis look friendly."

"I can't wait for them to be identified, and run out of the service. Hi, dishonorable discharge. Not a penny of benefits."

"Please. They'll get beers on the house everywhere they go."

"What sucks is that no one sees what probably happened two minutes before this picture — those dead towel-heads killing one of their buddies. Or trying to. CNN should run a photo of *that.*"

Lacey saw Felicia slip away from the

group. She would hate this kind of talk. And to tell the truth, Lacey felt queasy also: the crowded kitchen, the slumped sitting body, the slices of turkey and ham sandwiches. "Who's in with the kids?" she asked, and several women hurried back to check on them.

"Aimee can't hear *any* of this," someone whispered. "Not now, in the state she's in." They all nodded, faces echoing fright and determination.

In the kitchen, Lacey plated sandwiches and covered them with plastic wrap. Dina loaded the dishwasher.

"They think they're all that," Dina said. "The Marines. So tough, so above it all. Well, where's that discipline now?"

"Yeah."

"Which is the worst, do you think?" Lacey turned to Dina at the sink. "If you had to pick one."

"What do you mean?"

Dina lowered her voice to a whisper. "You know. Between your guy doing *that* . . . and what Aimee has to go through."

"Jesus. Neither."

"If you had to." Dina, in soapy pink gloves, didn't budge. "Gun to your head, which one."

"The — the — pissing thing." Lacey

flushed with anger for having been made to say it.

Dina blew hair out of her face, relieved. “Yeah, obviously. Do them before they do you.”

The rest of the afternoon passed in a sad whirl. When Aimee came back from the service, she was ensconced on a couch, with a wiggly Peter on her lap, ringed by relatives. Lacey didn’t know her well and kept a respectful distance. She rotated plates from table to kitchen to table, and kept an eye on Otis — shushing him when she heard him laugh, but glad that he was, in fact, laughing — and waited for the time until they could leave. She longed to talk to Eddie, just to shoot the shit with him about anything except all this. She wanted to tell him about the Others on *Lost,* she wanted to hear what he thought about Joe Torre’s prostate cancer — would he resign? — she wanted to ask his opinion on skinny jeans. Could she pull them off? Although Eddie would think all of that irrelevant, silly. She could picture the way he’d dismiss it and make her feel embarrassed.

“Hi. Mrs. Diaz?”

It was one of her group members! The youngest one, this girl who came off as thinking she was all-that, but who was probably just shy, Lacey had realized. What was her *name*?

"Oh! You can call me Lacey. How did you — ?"

"My parents used to go to church with his parents. Corpus Christi." The girl nodded toward Aimee on the couch. "I brought cookies. I didn't know what to bring."

"No, cookies are good. Go on and put them on a plate. There's stuff in the kitchen."

But the girl didn't move. She hung back, nearly behind Lacey, eyes darting around the room full of people. "Do I have to . . . should I go say something to her?"

"Not right now. Later." Lacey studied her, remembering what she'd said in the group about her husband making them go three nights in a row to his favorite ribs place right before he shipped out. "Come with me."

In the kitchen, she handed the girl a paper plate and showed her how to fan the cookies out so they looked nice. A woman bagged up garbage and said hello before moving past them. One of the few men present was in there too, on the phone, scribbling notes in a small pad. When he got off, Lacey said, "Colonel Robbins? I'd like you to meet someone."

"Hi. I'm, um, Bailey Reese." Then she whispered, "My fiancé is in Third Cav Bravo."

Bailey. That was it, Bailey.

The rear detachment commander shook her hand gravely. He thanked her for coming. He asked where she was living, how she was handling deployment, how communication was with her fiancé. Lacey lingered for a few minutes, wiping counters, listening as she spoke politely to tired Colonel Robbins, who had spent a hellish week nailing down details related to this funeral. She'd guessed this girl's charm came out around men, and she'd been right.

"Mom! Mom!" Otis collided with her in the hallway. "Can I sleep over at Rich's?"

"What does his —"

"It's fine with me," Rich's mom said, following them into the hall. "We'll get pizza on the way home — can you get him before noon tomorrow? We're going to head out now, though — these heels are killing me."

"That's — sure, okay." Otis and Rich: *Yessssss.* Lacey and the other mom exchanged address info via their phones. Otis skidded out to the elevator; she had to call him back to get a hug. Then they were gone.

Most people not in Aimee's family were

on their way out also. Children were wrestled into coats, cleaned Pyrex dishes were sorted and collected. The funeral's earlier hush gave way to a higher noise level, made up of relief and practical actions and leave-taking. Lacey wandered from room to room, giving good-bye hugs, not sure what to do. At last it seemed awkward for her to stay any longer.

"I just wanted to say —"

Aimee jumped. She'd been checking her phone and Lacey had come up next to her too quickly.

"Sorry!"

"That's okay."

"I mean, I wanted to say: I'm really sorry."

"Oh. Thank you."

Lacey held still, coat over her arm. Aimee looked fried, not even that sad, just — out of it. She seemed like she was waiting for Lacey to go so she could keep scrolling through messages.

"If you need anything . . ." How would Anne Mackay do this? Lacey had thought this moment would have more weight. But in the end, Aimee merely thanked her again, and Lacey left, feeling unsatisfied.

She piled her Tupperware and bag of serving spoons into the backseat, but when she got in the car she swung her key chain around her finger, waiting. Why had everyone left so quickly? You'd think the girls would want to go out for a drink afterward, at least at someplace they could all bring their kids. Lacey realized she'd been counting on it. Why was Martine in Florida with her in-laws this weekend of all weekends? Why had she said yes to Otis's sleepover?

In the early summer dusk, Lacey drove. She went up and down Westchester Avenue, she did the triangle around Crotona Park. Mexican men hoisted giant bouquets of blue and pink cotton candy; packs of kids gathered on street corners, and sometimes under the freeway overpasses. Families held cookouts on any patch of grass, hibachis and folding chairs. Everyone played Jay-Z. Everyone played Rick Ross.

She told herself to get on the BQE, but didn't. She told herself she wanted to see the water, but then she got on the Bruckner and let it lead her to I-95. Lacey skirted the wide expanse of Pelham Bay Park, and told herself that she was going in to check on Lolo —

Give it up already. Conning herself only made it worse. She was going to the Snug. She was going to see if that guy Jim was bartending, and there may or may not be different ways to view that, but at least she could stop pretending. Shore Road to the Pelham bridge to City Island Avenue to the bar. Lacey parked across the street and fumbled her way out of the car with her bag and keys. Whether or not Jim Leahy was working tonight, the truest thing she knew was that she needed a drink.

But he was there.

And he gave her a sidelong smile when she entered, his hands busy underneath the bar. Lacey wavered, and then took one of the tall stools by the window at the bar. On the long side were a couple and a few single men. The door was propped open so that puffs of summer night air blew in, bringing a sense of ease and relief — *you can go anytime* — and the sounds of motorcycles idling at the stoplight. Guys walking by leaned in the doorway to call something to the regulars; make a smart-ass joke and get waved away with a laugh.

"Where's the big guy at?" Jim laid a napkin in front of her.

"Ditched his mom for a sleepover. Maker's Mark neat, if you have that. Double. And a —"

"Yeah?"

"No, that's good."

"You want a beer back?" He whispered, making fun of her reticence.

Lacey laughed. "What, I didn't know if we were too chichi in here for that."

Jim straightened up and gave her a *you're-crazy* look. "I'll take care of you."

So she settled in, shrugged off her jacket, watched some ESPN highlights. Lacey felt a deep comfort in knowing these next few hours were booked for her; a session of time, a frame she could relax into and fill with the rhythms of rounds and buy-backs, talk and silence, a buzzy walk to the bathroom and the sweet knowledge of her barstool to return to. *You make yourself a little home,* she thought stupidly, half a drink in. *You can be anyone you —*

No, she couldn't. Not here. Jim rang up the couple and waited until they finished a sloppy kiss before putting down the check. Did she remember him from school? Lacey squinted, trying to take the gray out of his bushy black hair, the paunch from his frame.

"What did you look like, back then? Do you have a photo?"

"Well, yeah — I keep one on me at all times." He wiped his hands and took out his phone. "Who doesn't? Here." Jim handed it to her. Lacey held it close: against a blue backdrop, Jim, one baby on his lap, two girls in identical dresses lined up in front of him.

She ran her finger along the arm of an unidentified woman who had been cropped out of the picture. "Your ex?"

"What can I say, the rest of us look good."

Lacey gave his phone back. "My husband's in the service. He's in Iraq now, on his second deployment." It seemed important to get this out there on the table too, with her drink.

"That's tough," Jim said. "How long till he gets back?"

"A while. Did you play football, in school?" Lacey didn't want to talk about Eddie or Iraq, didn't want to explain that the reason she was in these black pants and subdued heels was because she'd been at a soldier's funeral all day.

"Six-foot fat Irish kid from Long Island? Nah, I was a figure skater."

"You did, didn't you." Lacey had a blurry image of the blue-and-yellow uniform tops, white helmets. "Did you hang out in the lunch courtyard?" This was where the kids cut class and smoked cigarettes until a monitor would bust them.

"No, but I bet you did."

"Well, I wasn't a total loser."

"But kind of a hell-raiser. Am I right?"

Lacey tipped the liquid around in her glass and half smiled, hiding behind her long bangs. "Remember the fire in the auditorium my senior year? The one that went up the curtains after that play?"

"Oh, Jesus. You set that? So, what, that makes me like an accessory now?"

"I didn't *set* it. But maybe I knew more about it than I should. I hung around with some real meatheads."

"Yeah." Jim wandered off to take care of a customer, and Lacey tried to slow down her pulse. She never alluded to the Asshole in this way; why now?

The Asshole. When she got pregnant by him the first time, summer after high school, Lacey had wanted to keep it. She loved him, she loved him through the craziness of the desperate fights and the other girls, the way he humiliated her in front of her friends and the way he could always get her to come back to him. It was a sweet-sourness in her blood, the way she loved him. She spun a story: a baby to make them real, forever, a baby who could help them rise above midnight drama and police visits and all the mean phone calls. He had a job, she'd get one, and they'd make it work. But the Asshole wouldn't go for it. He made her get the abortion, he even drove her there. (But somehow it was Lacey who got stuck with the bill.) In the week she was recovering he slept with a girl they both knew and didn't bother to come up with a good lie.

Then came the early 1990s, Lacey barely making the grade for her associate's at Nassau in the sports management program, drinking too much. She lived between her mother's and the Asshole's place way out in Suffolk — switching it up whenever the fighting got too bad at either. He began to hit her. Once bad enough to break a tooth and puff up the side of her eye green and yellow. She let him go, she let him back. She lost friends over him; she swore him off and then relapsed. Years passed in this way.

She got pregnant again. It was right after she'd passed her exams and got a good job at a health clinic, doing group classes for obese senior citizens. She threw up at work and took a test on her lunch hour. But this time — it would never stop haunting Lacey — *she* wanted the abortion. They weren't in high school anymore. When he was mean or cheap there was less charm or youth to cover up those moments of ugliness. She couldn't pretend to ignore the blinking danger sign, right in her face. Using up the last bit of good judgment, Lacey made herself an appointment. She might be a lost cause, but no way would she bring a kid into this mess. And then she got drunk, got weepy, called the night before to let him know . . . and caught the Asshole in a rare moment of deluded decency, of imitative chivalry. *I'm going to make this right,* he told her. *This is our chance to be better, Lace, I won't let you throw it away.* (Later she learned there were several other women's "chances" he was supporting — or not — to some degree.)

So she delayed. She wanted it to be true. She missed one deadline after another and then it was too late. He started bailing on her. One morning at 6:00 a.m. she drove to some girl's Levittown apartment and leaned on the horn until he ran out wild-eyed, pants barely on, screaming at her. Another time they fought and he shoved her and she went down hard, seven months pregnant. The afternoon she gave birth to Otis, Lacey gripped her mom's hand and knew he wouldn't make it. *He won't be here.* She went six hours before an epidural. *He won't.* She had been pushing for ninety minutes when they saw the cord around his neck. *He's not coming.* They cut Lacey open and lifted Otis above the curtain so she could see her baby: red, wet, umbilical dangling down.

"My mom was glad. She never liked him,

not that she's any great judge about stuff. And everyone, all my friends, they told me it was for the best, when he just — poof —" Lacey blew out her fingers into star shapes. "Disappeared. This time for good."

She and Jim were the only ones left at the bar. He'd cleaned up, closed up, and was sitting on the cooler with a beer. "They were right," he said. "People usually are."

"Well, I sure as hell think so now. If he ever thought to show his face around me or Otis these days . . ."

"Like to see him try. So your husband can teach him how Marines take care of things."

"Army," Lacey said, mostly to herself. She was disconcerted by the mention of Eddie, but too drunk to let herself worry about it much. Though, was he bringing it up as a test, to see how she'd respond? "I should get going."

"Let me take you somewhere." Jim put her glass and his bottle in the sink. As he came around the bar, jacket in hand, Lacey felt afraid.

"I shouldn't have kept you late — I'm a mess, I know, but I hate to act like some kind of tease —"

"Hey. Hey." Jim came to stand in front of her in the darkened bar, streetlights catching his face. "That's not my game. I like you. I like you, Lacey Reed."

"And that's it. You liking me."

He ran both hands through his hair. "What I want to do right now? Yeah. No. But I can keep that to myself. If I have to." Jim gave her a half smile that hit Lacey low, deep in her belly. They hung there inside the long moment where she was supposed to slide off her chair, put her hand on his wrist, make him drop his jacket on the floor. Instead, he held the door open for her. "Come on. I want to show you something."

He drove them farther out on the island, down the only avenue until it ended in a clutch of seafood restaurants and chain-link fences, pilings and broken rocks sticking up out of the black water. Lacey rested her head on the back of his car seat and wondered aloud whether her mother-in-law ever went to any of these places.

"No one on the island does," Jim said, peering out the side window. "All the seafood places, they're overpriced, they get business from tourists and that's it. But here, this is it." He swerved down a side street, cut the lights, and parked with the passenger side wheels up on the curb. "Shh," he told her as she stumbled out of the tilted-up truck. "There's a guard sometimes."

"For what?" A chain-link fence blocked off entrance to the water, on which was raised a high metal ramp like a kind of boat launch. "A ferry?"

"It goes to Hart Island." When this didn't prompt any response from Lacey, Jim went on. "Potter's field, you know what that is? Mass burials for anyone in the city who doesn't get IDed, all the babies who die in the hospital —"

"Stop."

"I know, it's — yeah, it'll break your heart. And it's right here, but no one knows about it. Biggest public cemetery in the world. They send prison labor out there every day, you see the gray corrections bus riding down the avenue just like the Bx29."

Lacey strained to see the island off the coast but got nothing. Then the very thought of what was on there, within sight and possibly smell of her own woozy self, clanged through her: thousands and thousands of decomposed bodies, of people stacked on top of each other, of the kids . . .

She ran back to Jim's car. Fucking fuck, it was locked. He was right behind her, with apologies, with the keys, and she tried to yell at him — *why on God's earth would he* — when all of it converged: the dead Iraqi sprawled on the toilet, Aimee's husband, the city's nameless bodies stacked in trenches, and her own bad sick flirtatious soul — and Lacey bent over to retch violently onto the curb, hanging on first to the car handle and then Jim. Grateful, angry, and finally exhausted, she let him lead her into the front seat. She let him bring her napkins and a warm beer he'd fished out of the trunk. She rinsed, spat, and then took a long shaky drink.

Jim stood in front of her, leaning down on the other side of the open car door. "I didn't think it's possible, but I am, in fact, even dumber than I look."

"I'll say."

"Jesus. I want to kick my own ass so bad." He scrubbed his face with a hand. "It's been so long since I've been around a woman like you and now —"

Lacey put her hand on his thick wrist. He helped her stand, eyes wide. She kissed him once, a trial, and then again, for real. The car door was between them. Jim pushed her hair away and held the sides of her face.

She was bad, she was bad. It was wrong and desperate and a relief, such a sad relief.

9

Dear Michael, When you say tuna packs, what do you mean? Not actual cans of tuna? I found beef jerky and the protein bars. I told Wes how worried I am that they're not giving you enough to eat but he said you *never* got enough to eat, so there's that.

Dear Michael, If you have any time at all to read, I think you might like *Slaughterhouse Five.* There's a scene where —

Dear Michael, It's hard to know what to say at a time like this, when the news here is —

For the past day or two Ellen had abandoned each attempt at a letter to Michael, feeling that she had better keep her mouth shut. And if everyone else would too, she might find a way to recover from yesterday's news. But it was everywhere, on every computer, every radio: *Investigators have determined the identities of at least four Marines said to have been part of the desecration of several corpses of Iraqi insurgents . . . Names have not been released, although all Marines are said to have enlisted . . . General Casey orders a top-down review of the incident . . . Insurgent violence continues to be on the rise in Anbar Province, where the incident took place . . .*

There was no avoiding the horror. Dressing for a colleague's baby shower, it took Ellen three tries to button her blouse the right way. On the drive across the city, she thought about the most recent letter from Michael. No inkling of the atrocities that everyone was talking about; it was almost as if he was describing an entirely different war in an entirely different place. Or, Ellen thought, though she knew it had been written before that shameful incident (or had it?), as if Mike wanted to deliberately withhold the worst from her.

Dear Ellen, I'll try to describe what I'm doing right now. I am sitting outside trying to stay in the holes of shade a cammy net provides above me. It is a break from standing watch in the bunker. I am in my cammy pants and a T-shirt it is noon and already about 115 degrees. I can look out and see the Euphrates river 200m to my east with the small lane of Palm Trees on both sides. People might say this is a beautiful place but all I see is on the outskirts of this "city" is a place no humans should have to live. So there's my little snapshot. Thanks for the letters and stuff. Tell Wes no more candy 'cause I'm trying not to get fat! Hi again — I am now finishing this letter a week later. Love, Mike

In the car, Ellen put on WORT for classical — but stayed alert, for on breaks the announcer still read out the headlines, melding his honeyed bass around words like *toilet, corpses,* and *retaliation.* When that happened, she had to lunge to turn down the dial. She left the windows down; it was thick and muggy, with the threat of rain. On the one hand, it was touching the way Mike's last letter painstakingly tried to paint a verbal picture of his surroundings, something he must have guessed she would appreciate. On the other, it was a detail-filled document that conspicuously avoided the main subject. All windup and no pitch. Then those ominous casual references to standing watch in bunkers and a place no humans should live! Ellen took University west, the traffic so much less bothersome in the summer. She had scoured the letter so many times it wasn't hard to reconstruct it in her mind's eye, even if it wasn't tucked into the purse now riding on the passenger seat next to a badly wrapped baby present.

"Finishing this a week later," she said aloud. "Why? And why say it?" And what had happened to break off his descriptive letter writing that suffocating day, in the paltry shade of a cammy net, whatever that was. " 'Hi again'?" What had he done between that day and a week later? If they read it in Intro to Literary Theory she would have led the students to a discussion of caesura, that fracture in a sentence or text where breakage provokes emotion, a jarring. Or she would have nudged them toward Derrida, where absence points up and undermines our traditional expectation of presence.

Did she expect him to tell her about what he was really doing there in western Iraq? About whatever those "missions" involved? About the split-second decisions and acts of self-defense and perpetrations of a plan made so far away from his own day-to-day reality, his own single human agency? Did she want to know whether a man pissing next to the corpse of another man was now something Michael could understand?

Ellen turned onto Shorewood, wound her way toward Lake Mendota. There was another absence in that letter, she realized. Jane. Michael hadn't mentioned Jane, at all.

Here in one of Madison's upscale suburbs, the trees were older, leafier. There were fewer sidewalks and more double garages. The homes were graceful, large but not ostentatious. Ellen checked the address and dutifully parked last in the string of cars lining the street. She gathered purse and present but wobbled briefly, closing the car door. She hadn't eaten yet today, or had she? Recently she'd been keeping odd hours, snacking at random, kept at her desk until late at night.

Her colleague Debbie Masterson was a second-year assistant professor they were all trying to rally around. She'd been on a streak of bad luck: her husband, a scientist at UW, had lost his funding and then his job; she'd been on bed rest since May; they'd had to give up their apartment and move in here with her mother. Not to mention she'd be going up for tenure next year, with infant twins and a job-hunting husband. Ellen breathed deeply and paused for a moment on the paved entrance path, trying to clear her head. *You're not the only one in pain,* she told herself. *Snap out of it.*

"You look wonderful," she told Debbie, who was laid out regally on a living room couch, surrounded by friends and plates of food. A quick glance let her know that most of those attending were young women she didn't know, probably friends of Debbie's from grad school. One or two familiar faces from UW looked up and waved.

"I feel like a pasha greeting her minions. A pasha in nude compression stockings."

"Here, let me take that for you." Debbie's mother relieved her of the present and gave her a cup of punch. Ellen tried not to notice that the woman was only a few years older than she herself was. That would only lead her to think about . . .

"Just the person I was looking for." Mark Carroll, department chair. *Damn.* Wasn't a baby shower supposed to be for women only? "You've been hard to get ahold of this summer, Professor. Is your e-mail on the fritz?"

"Really? I don't think —"

"College Committee on Retention?" Mark leaned back against a sofa armrest. "Dean Welter says she hasn't seen you at either of the meetings so far."

Ellen took a big drink of sugary punch.

"It's very difficult to align people's schedules over the summer. And some research has recently taken up a lot of my time."

"Hmm." Mark considered the excuse, tilting his head up to the ceiling. He was such an officious prick. In a department that was 90 percent women, they'd been stuck with this micromanager as chair for the past four years. (Not, Ellen shuddered, that she would want the job.)

"When you agreed to serve on the committee, I was under the impression —"

"I'll be at the next one for sure, Mark." The man had once published a book on 1980s sitcoms, Ellen consoled herself.

"That would be great. So what's this new project? Another Edith exposé? I have to say, I really admire you for sticking to your guns — refusing to branch out to any other subject, you know. It's so deliciously old-fashioned."

"Let's not talk shop at Debbie's party," Ellen said, smiling tightly. "I'll catch you around the office and fill you in."

"Yes! Actually, Jim and I are off to Beaver Island next week — irony noted — but you could just e-mail me your notes and any updates from that next Retention meeting. And someday I'd love to hear how things are with good old Edith."

Ellen threaded her way to a chair off to the side. Debbie began opening presents that were carried to her, one by one. *It's just Mark,* she told herself, sliding a Danish onto a paper plate. *He's annoyed; he's being petty.*

Meanwhile, women of all ages were advising Debbie on baby care. Don't let them sleep in your bed, you'll never get them out. Join a multiples group. Steal all the free stuff they'll let you take in the hospital. Then, when it was clear the few men in attendance had drifted off to the dining room, hushed and triumphant, the real war stories began.

"Twenty hours in, and they've been measuring me at seven centimeters. Then this one resident barges in, snaps on a glove, and sticks his hand up me. No kidding. He says, and I quote, 'You're only at six centimeters, and if you don't progress I'll need to section you in the next hour.' I'm like, what are you talking about, *six.* I'm at seven, everyone else says so! He gets all, 'measuring the cervix is obviously subjective,' and I shout EXACTLY SO WHAT MAKES YOUR FAT FINGERS THE ONES THAT ARE GOING TO DETERMINE A C-SECTION OR NOT."

"Apparently when they're inverted you're supposed to draw them out. Yeah. So they give you these 'shields,' and there I am, getting stitched up after a thirty-hour labor, holding the baby and frankly just trying not to pass out, and the nurse is like, I'm just going to put these pieces of plastic on your breasts because your nipples are the wrong shape."

"She screamed from six to twelve, every single night. Up every two hours for nine months. Literally nine months. The first week I was on the phone with the pediatrician, I'm sobbing of course, and I'm holding this screaming baby, and they start giving me that routine about colic and I'm like, well no shit but would you *listen to this*?"

Could she tape this and replay it for Jane? Ellen caught a pained expression from Debbie's mother, upright in a side chair. Even Debbie looked unsettled, behind her mock-dismay.

The rest of the night at the movies, after Jane had whispered that she was pregnant, was now a bad blur Ellen tried not to bring into focus. At first Ellen, in shock, continued to watch Batman flirt with a saucy brunette and fight a pale-eyed villain called Scarecrow. Then she picked up her coat and left the theater, Jane hurrying behind. And so it was on the edge of a giant parking lot, Ellen having no idea where her car was, that she had to have an unthinkable scene with her daughter. How could you tell me something like that, like that? In the middle of a *movie? Is that really the main issue, Mom?* How do you know . . . are you sure? When did you — ? *I took a test, all right? I took two of them. Jesus, can you dial it down?* But — who's the father? *I don't want to get into that.*

It was Jane's demeanor there on the curb in the shadows under the theater awning, sullen and secretive, insistently casual, *selfish,* that sent Ellen into a panicked diatribe. She hated to think of how she reacted: she lectured her daughter, she used words like *irresponsible* and *self-destructive.* The more Jane withdrew, staring off to the side and chewing on a shirt cuff, the more vehement Ellen got. She tried to staunch her disappointment, she tried to be more sensitive, to modulate her tone of voice. But it was too late. Jane said she had to go, she *couldn't deal with this right now.* When am I going to see you again? We need to figure out what's next, have you made an appointment, of course I want to be there — and I know it must be expensive, that's nothing you have to worry about . . .

"You don't know what I'm going to do about it!" Jane burst out. "I might be *keep-*

ing it!" At that she ran off while Ellen called after her, and passersby stared.

Since then, she had called Jane almost daily, leaving countless messages but had received nothing back except for the occasional grudging texts. *It's fine. Not in the mood to talk.*

Ellen had fought to manage her worry, her dismay — *keep it?! "Keep" "it"?? Where would she "keep" a baby, in that firetrap co-op? On a part-time receptionist's pay?* She had done such a good job of managing, in fact, that it wasn't until she was at a coworker's *baby shower* that Jane's infuriating situation truly hit her. These women, the ones competing to outdo each other's birth drama, they were all women. Not girls — women. They had educations, life experience, husbands. And still they had been knocked flat by how hard it all was. What was Jane thinking? Obviously she couldn't have a baby. She could barely put together a coherent life for herself, let alone be responsible for a child. The absolute impossibility of it reassured Ellen. She remembered the advice given in a "parenting your spirited teen" workshop she'd attended once, during the tempest of Jane's high school years: push them and they'll run the other way. Jane would have to believe that getting an abortion was Jane's idea. Ellen could wait it out.

"Everyone always talks about, you know, pooping while giving birth —" This from a young woman to her friend, both sitting just behind Ellen. Slices of cake had been handed around; conversation broke into smaller pockets. "But that's nothing. I swear I peed every time I stood up, for at least a year after Jackson. There were two of us in diapers."

Ellen ate tiny bites of her cake, an unwilling eavesdropper. She wanted to be in favor of women's openness and honesty around the birth experiences — if woman-positive Serena were here she'd be urging them all on, cheering every bodily disclosure, the messier the better, even though Serena herself had not the least personal interest in pregnancy and children — but really, wasn't enough enough?

"Speaking of bathroom stuff," the other woman said. "You saw those headlines, right?"

Ellen froze.

"I know. So disgusting, so absolutely despicable. If this alone isn't an indictment against us for this war, I don't know what could be. Those men are *laughing.* You can tell, you can see it."

"What I want to know is, which one of them decided to take the pictures? Like, how did that even cross his mind?"

"Which one decided to do it first? How did it start? Did they just" — the woman's voice dropped — "kill that guy and then need to take a leak? And put the two things together and think, hey why not —"

"Inhuman. They're thugs, plain and simple. Bloodthirsty thugs. No better than any terrorist. Do you ever wonder, when something like this comes up, what we *aren't* seeing? What we don't know about? As if there are a dozen other incidents like this every month."

"Massacres. Taking My Lai into the digital age."

"The thing is, the Pentagon, all those old men in charge, they know this is what happens in war. They've probably seen it a thousand times. The only reason they're flipping out is because it got *out,* not because it happened. Because it might threaten their budgets, not because it's morally abominable. *A-bomb-in-able.* I always have trouble pronouncing that."

"I hate this fucking 'support the troops' no-matter-what mentality. No. I won't be co-opted into pretending it isn't our guys doing *this.* We train them to be like that. We tell them it's okay to kill children and defile human bodies. Just as long as —"

"They get the oil for us."

The too-sweet, powdery frosting curdled in Ellen's mouth. The women behind her were on to another subject, but she had a paranoid sense they'd wanted her to overhear, that they had been whispering just for her benefit. *Did they know?* Did they know about Mike being a Marine, that he was there? Had anyone seen that service flag — stuffed in a bottom drawer for weeks but recently attached to a kitchen window in a stupid moment of superstition that it would bring him back safe? Its blue star burned her now, a flagrant sign of her complicity . . . one that she'd hung out herself! Ellen's vision wavered, and the group of women gathered together in the room strung out as if they were all far away from her; their voices shrunk to a thin stream of babble. She wanted to put her plate down but she couldn't reach the coffee table.

It's all right, she heard herself think. *These people don't really know you. They don't know him. Not to mention, he's not even your real —*

The shock of this half thought brought her up short. The others at the party snapped back into view, their chatter roared. It was as if Ellen didn't exist.

"She never learned to crawl, not really. She'd just line up a spot across the room and then roll her way across the rug to get there."

"Oh, totally. Mine did the wounded soldier crawl." Ellen stared. The woman talking mimicked movement with her bent arms held up in front of her, her face distorted to show pain and effort. "You know, on his stomach, dragging his body behind him like dead weight. *Got — to make it — under — this barbed wire fence.*"

The room laughed appreciatively.

Ellen stood and dropped her plate onto the seat of her chair. Snaking through chairs and love seats, she made her way quickly and quietly to the kitchen, where whatever expression she must have had on her face caused the startled caterer to point to the hallway without Ellen even needing to ask. If she could only have a moment alone, and some cold water for her face, she could fight down this rising upsurge of horror and nausea.

With a perfunctory knock, Ellen pulled open the door. Mark Carroll, stunned, legs spread, facing the toilet. His shout and hers overlapped. She closed the door again, mortified, repelled, the echoing thunder of his streaming urine still in her ears. She dropped all pretense and fled. Down the hallway, through the front hall, up the stairs. Vaguely aware of someone calling her name. Ellen's only thought was to get to a bathroom before . . . She tried one room, and then the next, making it safely into the right one, and even had a few seconds to spare in order to ensure this door was shut and locked, open both sink faucets, and kneel carefully on the clean blue-tiled floor before throwing up, twice, neatly, into Debbie Masterson's mother's toilet.

"Just a splash. It settles the stomach."

"The ginger ale will settle my stomach. The rum will do something else."

Serena shrugged, tipping a healthy portion of brown liquid into her own glass. Ellen had her shoes off, was curled up on their couch, after it had been cleared of newspapers and shooed of cats. Serena had spread a light cotton blanket over Ellen's legs and put a pillow behind her head. The open windows behind her let in occasional gusts of damp wind, but that felt good on Ellen's head. Being here felt good, in general. The rain and the early evening darkness lent Serena and Jill's messy apartment a cozy safeness. Serena bustled around, switching on lamps and shifting piles of books and papers into new piles of books and papers. Jill passed through with a raincoat over her arm. She whispered hello to Ellen and kissed Serena good-bye. Here were three women, each in her fifties — or older — each with gray hair and progressive-lens eyeglasses and quiet lives.

"I don't understand," Ellen said. "Why now? Why now that we're older? How can war, real war, be a part of life now?"

"How could it not?" Serena said.

"Because our turn's over! We had our war. I walked out of classes in the fall of my sophomore year. I cried when they showed footage after Tet. There was a boy from my hometown who never came back, was never even found. Their house had a POW/MIA flag up for years afterward, even during Reagan, my mom said. What was their name . . ."

"There was a woman holding this sign at our last action — wait, let me get the photo — it was genius, you have to see . . ." Serena clicked around on her laptop and brought the computer over to Ellen. A photo of a grandmotherly type, covered in PEACE & JUSTICE and NOT IN MY NAME buttons, with a sign that read I CAN'T BELIEVE I *STILL* HAVE TO PROTEST THIS SHIT.

Ellen smiled wanly. "It's a good one."

"So you don't want to play this part." Serena sat in the armchair across from her, feet up on the coffee table. "It's not what you'd planned on."

"No, it's not! I know you're going to disapprove, but I'm okay with the protesting, and I vote and I pay attention and I donate to the right places . . . I just don't see why I have to be tied to it with my heart. Why it has to come into my home, all this fear and —" All this fear. It wasn't just the swooshing wave of inner vertigo whenever she thought of Mike hurt or killed, whenever she remembered how close he was to that possibility. Or her thrumming, irregular pulse, the cold crawliness on her skin. Recently new symptoms appeared, and even though they weren't directly attached to those bursts of dread, Ellen knew where they came from: that twitch in her left eyelid, the one that hadn't gone away in a week. Sleeplessness at night, exhaustion during the day. Sudden bouts of unexplained diarrhea and now, unfortunately, surprise attacks of vomit.

Ellen sighed. An aging woman, complaining about her aches and pains. " 'Why me, why me.' Ignore me."

"Let me think." Serena steepled her hands

against her face, pensive. Ellen was warmed by her concern — that her own devastation should be a worthy problem to be turned around in her mind. "Why do we have this now, why war now, women our age . . ." Serena muttered to herself. "Putting aside the inherent solipsism of the question, and your privileged first-world status, that is."

"Naturally."

"Well, I think I know." Her friend took a deep drink, organizing her thoughts. Ellen waited. "You're given this burden now because you can tell the truth about it."

Ellen laughed. "I can barely stand to admit to people who know and theoretically like me that my — whatever, my *ward* — is a Marine. Is fighting a war I despise. Let alone speak out and make some kind of statement about it all. I'm no Cindy Sherman."

"The photographer? I'm not sure I follow . . ."

"Cindy *Sheehan,* I meant. The mom, the antiwar activist. Oh, God." Ellen covered her face. She'd just compared herself to someone whose son had died.

If Serena noticed her anguish, she didn't mention it. "Well, they both make a kind of sense to me. In any case, think about it. There is a logic for us in having this happen now, when we're old, when we're in typical grandmother position. We have the perspective, the wisdom, the distance to be able to see it clearly, when almost no one else in society can." Serena stood and paced around the room. "The younger men are fighting the war — or avoiding it — and the older men are plotting it, or reliving their own wars. Younger women are caught between the terror of losing a husband there and the raising of children — they have no space in which to think. But we —" Serena sank onto the couch near Ellen's feet. "We're the secret weapon."

"Older women."

"Write about it. Put it into the work."

Ellen studied her old friend, who was nearly vibrating with intellectual force, a lock of silvery hair dipping down her forehead. This wasn't what she wanted, an academic senior-citizen call to arms. It wasn't assuaging her shame at the feelings she'd had earlier at Debbie's party, that instinct to disown Mike. But despite herself, she was drawn into Serena's excitement. It's what she had been doing, in a way, writing to Michael — those pages of stories about his life, with readings selected just for him. A correspondence course he didn't know he'd signed up for.

But first, she had to find something out. "How did it affect you?" she asked Serena, who was lost in thought. Ellen nudged her gently with a foot. "What did you think, when you heard?"

"When I heard?"

"The Marines, that . . . the bodies. What they did." Ellen could barely say the words.

To her shock, Serena's face creased and she began to cry. "Oh — oh, I'm sorry," Ellen said. "I didn't know. I'm —"

"It's unbearable." Serena ignored the tears coursing down. "I've been wrecked about it all weekend. What we do to them."

"Despicable," Ellen whispered. She forced herself to face the shaming that would come.

"They're so young," Serena went on. "So deluded. And what we've done . . . first we ask the unbearable and now we scorn them for submitting. And then we make them live with both." Ellen realized that Serena was talking about the Marines. With sympathy, with real sorrow. She reached over to hold her friend's hand.

They stayed like that for several minutes, a soft steady rain against the window screen, a car swishing by on wet pavement.

"Two of my grad students are building an online archive of citizens' responses to the war." Serena tucked back her loose strand of hair. "Half interactive art site, half journalism project. It has a lot of potential. Would you speak to them? They're doing interviews, and I know it would mean everything for them to have your perspective — a family member's, that is. They haven't found any yet, from what I understand."

"I don't think so, Serena."

"You can be as conflicted as you want. You wouldn't have to do anything other than give your honest expression of what this is like."

If only it were that easy, Ellen thought. "No, I'm sorry. I can't. But . . ." And here she did allow herself to think about Jane (not about her *situation,* which was a matter to be solved soon), Jane the passionate activist, with a heart as big and angry as Serena could ever want. "I think I know someone perfect."

10

"So when they bring the check, I pull out this coupon and hand it to the server. Two minutes later he's back with the host, and they tell us we can't use it."

"Why the hell not?"

"Because, he says, the deal is for a *romantic* dinner for two, and I was with a girlfriend. See, he keeps saying, pointing to the print-out, it clearly states, 'You and your sweet-heart will enjoy a three-course meal,' blah blah blah."

"So how'd he know you weren't lesbos?"

"Don't say that."

"You know what I mean. Anyway, what's it matter? Two dinners is two dinners."

"Right, that's what we kept arguing. But he's like, if we offered this deal to any two people, it wouldn't be worth it to us, and the special was meant to be for couples —"

"And that's when you played the husband-at-war card."

Silence.

"What!" "Why not?" "You're crazy!"

"I don't know . . . everyone was already staring at us, and I cry at the drop of a hat these days. I didn't even want to go there. I was already feeling like an idiot, all dressed up and out for date night with my best friend."

"So you just paid the full damn price? Both of you?"

"Plus the sitter, don't forget."

"Well . . . they did comp one of our desserts . . ."

Groans.

"Okay, but my girlfriend? She went home and wrote a nasty review on Yelp, then she went to town on them on her own blog — now it's getting picked up by all these milwife blogs . . ."

Cheers.

Lacey smiled, but she was looking for a way to steer the group's conversation — well, to where? She wasn't exactly sure but felt vaguely that they should be talking about something else. As usual, though, the women wanted to talk about money. She tipped back in her folding chair to get a view of Otis through the door's plastic pane, on the floor in the hall, playing his Nintendo DS.

Problem was, if she led them to talk about their feelings that would mean, maybe, cracking open the door on some of her own.

On the stairs back at Jim's place, that first night. Because they couldn't make it up to the bedroom in time; her back against the wall, his feet on two different levels, pieces of their clothes tossed over the railing where they drifted down a half flight. His face buried in her neck, his fist pounding the wall.

Lacey drew interlocking circles on the legal pad she'd bought for these meetings. She never actually ended up taking any notes. *Jim* she wrote. *JimJimJimJim.* Under that, she wrote *SLUT* in block letters, shaded them in, and then scribbled over all of it.

Two days later, he came over in the morning as soon as Otis left for camp, and she didn't have to be at the gym until noon. She didn't want to do it in their house, didn't want to deal with a motel, didn't want to waste time driving back through traffic to his place. So they did it in his car, in the neighbors' garage, which Lacey had a key to, since they let Otis stick his bike in there over the winter. The whole time she prayed that garage door wouldn't suddenly rise, if the people next door happened to forget something and came back for it.

If only that fear — that any second, she could have been caught — had been enough to shame her into stopping. But fear made it all the hotter, screwing Jim in his car. Lacey told herself that stopping now wouldn't make any difference to her already degraded state, but if she spent any time thinking about it, she'd know that wasn't the truth. She was crazy about him, but it was a willful craziness. Lacey knew herself, knew she could — she *would*! — pull out as soon as the right time came.

Eddie's last e-mail was upbeat, even more so than usual. He'd forgotten to ask about Otis's nosebleeds, what the doctor had said (allergies, new medicine), and for once he didn't bug Lacey about whether they ran the AC units all day, or how the credit cards were holding up. *These guys might actually be getting the hang of it, believe it or not.* He meant the hapless Iraqi soldiers, the ones his unit was trying to shape into a disciplined fighting force. *No big screwups going on a week now. Freaking miracle. Also the police had a dinner for us, some holiday thing, and it turned out to be pretty fun, as long as you didn't eat much of the food.* Eddie went on to describe the new school being built, the safer roads, even a shocker rainstorm that cooled them for a day or so. He didn't say it in so many words, but you didn't need to be a mind reader. The man loved his job.

Super! That's great for you! Lacey, fighting tears, and for once not thinking at all about Jim. *Maybe you should get your ass back here and see about your wife, though.*

"Lacey?"

What? The whole group was staring at her, waiting for a response. "Oh, um — say that again?"

It was Bailey, the youngest one. Now Lacey noticed the girl's reddened nose, her smeared eyeliner. "We got in a fight. Me and Greg. And it ended real bad. I don't know what to do."

"On the phone? IM?"

"Skype. He works KP, you know, so they get to use the computers more . . . Anyway, he —" Her voice dropped to a whisper. One of the heavier black women nudged her — *go on.* "He saw what I'd written back to his ex on Facebook. She's like, a real nightmare. She's all, I'm thinking about you all the time — she pretends it's about his being over there, but it's not, that's just her sad-ass excuse. So I said back off and get your own husband, and I, you know called her some things . . . Then Greg saw it and he was pissed, he didn't want his family and everyone to see me like that. He says she's just being nice, which is a crock. But I couldn't believe he was, like, standing up for *her* and not me, and —"

"You went off on him." Lacey knew where this was going.

"Yeah." Bailey looked miserable. "He kept telling me to shut up, 'cause the other guys could hear, but I was so . . . you know."

"Yeah." The group nodded. They knew.

"I held my hand up in front of the camera and took off my ring," Bailey said. "I didn't mean to. I didn't mean it. Greg — he just — he just looked at me, total shock, and then he walked away from the computer —"

She was sobbing now, in big *a-huh a-huh* noises. Otis peeked in through the window. One or two of the women reached over to pat Bailey, but the rest fidgeted, or shook their heads.

"How long ago was this?" Lacey waved to Otis, *it's okay.*

"Three *days.* And he won't write me back now, or nothing! I'm freaking out, Lacey. Lacey, what if he gets pulled for a mission and gets hit —"

Instant angry murmurs from the group: *Tshh — why you even — don't say it. Shut up.*

"— And it'll be all my fault! All my fault!

Because he's not gonna be focused and shit, and I can't, I can't even . . ."

Lacey left her chair and went over to Bailey. She squatted in front of the girl. Everyone else watched; she could feel the tension and even hostility, the way they had inched away from this pain, this mess. *Finally, the tissue box she'd been bringing each week!* Lacey handed it to Bailey, waited while she blew and wiped, blew and wiped. Then Lacey took up the girl's purse, pulled out her cosmetic bag. "Here. Fix your face. Go on, I'll tell you what to do. You get fixed up, first." The girl's eyes met hers, wild and scared, and then to herself in the compact mirror. Lacey watched as she dabbed on some cover-up, and a little mascara.

"When you get home, here's what you do. You are going to send him one e-mail — *one.* Short and sweet, and this is what it'll say."

"He's not checking his e-mail! I've sent a million!"

"Oh, he's checking. Here's what you write." Lacey motioned, and one of the other women got up to bring over her pen and pad. She paused, glanced around the chair circle. "What should she write?"

" 'Being away from you made me go a little psycho. I'm normal now.' "

" 'I know you need your space but I am sorry and down for you stronger and truer than before.' "

" 'That Facebook bitch got nothing on —' Okay, okay. 'Nobody can get in between us.' "

" 'Praying for you. Praying for me. Asking God to help me with my faults, take care of you always.' "

" 'I believe in you.' "

Bailey capped her lip gloss and listened. Lacey wrote it all down. She tore off the sheet and handed it to Bailey, who folded it into triangles. "You okay?" The girl nodded. Women stood and stretched; Otis leaned in the door. "I put my phone number on there, you can call me anytime." Bailey nodded again, ready to get out of there. Lacey tapped her bare knee and stood up. "We all screw it up sometimes. Just make it right."

On the way home, she and Otis stopped at the Associated for a rotisserie chicken. Lacey made potato salad and they ate with the back door propped open, swatting at flies who made it through the torn screen, enjoying scraps of car stereo music bumping past. During dinner, Otis read aloud from his weekly book report — this time it was the fourth or fifth of the Percy Jackson series. Lacey couldn't really keep them straight, but if he liked them fine with her. He'd drawn several colored-pencil portraits of the characters, teens and gods fighting dragons and other monsters. That gave him extra points, which Lacey noted in her little spiral notebook near the phone. Each summer assignment — she varied them, sometimes book reports, sometimes math — got Otis points toward a new Wii game. While he scraped the dishes she put one drawing on the fridge, saved the other to mail to Eddie. Wondered if she could sign Otis up for that art class this fall. Why were these places so damn expensive? And getting into one of the free park district classes was harder than getting tickets to Mariah Carey.

After Otis went to bed, Lacey took a long shower and then sat outside on the stoop in a T-shirt and a pair of Eddie's boxer briefs. She drank a beer — drinking only beer at home, a self-improvement step — and read an article on a deadly stampede in Iraq, in one of those weekly newsmagazines she regularly took home from the gym. Apparently a thousand people were killed when rumors of a suicide bomber threw a pilgrim crowd into panic, and they surged over a bridge that collapsed into the Tigris River.

"A thousand people," Lacey said out loud.

Almost impossible to comprehend. She tried to visualize a thousand people, a thousand anythings, in her mind. The death toll for U.S. service members was over a thousand now for sure. Maybe heading toward two. How many potential Hajjis had been killed in that stampede?

The phone rang and she jumped. Martine: "What are you doing? Are you outside or something?"

"On the stoop. Little old lady neighbors giving me stink-eye for not wearing a bra."

"Little old men probably want to give you something else."

"They wish. What're you doing?"

"TV. Nothing. Kids are in bed. You waiting for him to call? Think he's still up?"

Lacey curled the magazine into a tight roll and pressed the sharp edges of the paper against her bare thigh. "Yeah. No. Thought there might be a chance, but probably not until later in the week."

Martine yawned loudly into the phone. "Twenty-one weeks yesterday. For the first time, I forgot to have them cross it off on the calendar. Is that a good sign? Or not?"

"Good if they didn't remember. Not sure about you."

"My girlfriend Sara says they don't start crossing days out until more than halfway.

Also she signed up for some program that'll text her daughter every day with a countdown, and like an inspirational quote."

"Mm." Lacey shifted on the hard stone step. "Listen, could you take Otis some night next week? Maybe Thursday? I can drop him off after my shift."

"Sure." Martine yawned again. "Got a date?"

Lacey glared at two homeboy teens scraping a skateboard against the curb. "I got to get together with a girl from my group. Bailey. She's a real mess."

"Straighten her out, Lace. They give us a bad name, these girls."

"I'm on it." The magazine left a curved red indentation on her thigh.

"Hey, we need to go out sometime. Girls' night. Long as I'm in bed by . . . nine."

Lacey smiled. " 'Night, Mart."

" 'Night. Love you."

"Love you too."

Lacey snapped her phone shut and an echoing pang of self-loathing thwacked within her. Why couldn't she have that: the ability to fall asleep alone on the couch in front of the TV and be content with it? How did other people cope with the bad secret longings, the itchy need for attention, that beautiful burst of adrenaline when you indulged in what was wrong? What was wrong with her? Had she slept through life class the day they taught you how to be a good person and like it?

On cue, her phone went off in her hands. Lacey held it and watched the 914 number blink and repeat, blink and repeat, Jim's number. It rang three, four, five times. From the curb the teens stared.

"You gonna get that already?"

Lacey ignored them. The phone warmed in her hands, and its display changed to MISSED CALL. The ringing stopped. She let out a long shaky exhale.

Oh, now you're proud? The incredulous voice inside her head. *For doing what every decent wife does without a second thought? For pretending you are one?*

The teens were harassing a slow-moving homeless guy. One imitated his junkie lean, the other knocked a plastic bag out of his hand.

They'll all find out what you did. Eddie will find out. Otis. Martine will. All the women in your group, everyone at the gym —

"Hey!" Lacey yelled over their laughter.

The phone clattered onto stone as Lacey stormed down the stairs barefoot. "Get out of here! Leave him alone. Get going now."

She picked up the man's bag and gave it to him with a gentle shove on his way.

"What's your problem," one of the kids said, stepping to her. The friend smiled.

"Don't mess with me," Lacey said. "Not tonight. Get the fuck off my block, or I'll call the police."

"Ooh."

"My kid's asleep up there and if he wakes up because I'm hollering at a couple of fools I will *really* be pissed. Move."

"Maybe we will, maybe we —"

"Mr. Reynolds?" Lacey let out the full force of her voice but didn't take her eyes off the punks. A window opened in the upper floor of a two-flat nearby. "Can you give the station a call about some loitering down here?"

"Shit," muttered one of the teens.

"Cyn already did," Mr. Reynolds called back, weary. "Could everyone shut up now?"

"Shut up!" someone else yelled.

"Fat fucking bitch," one of the teens said. "Ugly old bitch." But they were moving off. Lacey almost wished they weren't; her heart was pounding, amped for more of a fight. Then her energy rushed away. She went slowly back up her stairs, feet sore on the pavement and breasts chafing, alone, alone, lonely and she deserved it.

11

Ellen sat in her car, parked on Denham across the street from the run-down building where Jane lived. Rain poured off the sagging eaves, the rotten wood porch, a quilt someone had left hanging over a plastic chair in the disheveled front yard. Waiting for a break in the downpour, she was also trying to gather her courage. On her lap was a tote bag filled with peace offerings: homemade carrot bread, spirulina-seaweed mix from the health food store, two paperback books on animal activism from A Room of One's Own, the local feminist bookstore.

A sharp knock on the passenger-side window made her start. "No," she called, before fully registering the sodden man peering in at her. He was mumbling something she couldn't hear in the splattering rain, pointing upward and then back at her. "I'm sorry — no," Ellen said, motioning him away. She had to assume he was asking for change, but he just stared at her and repeated what he'd said, pointing up and then back at her car. After a moment he shook his head and moved off down the block, soon dissolving from sight.

As soon as he was gone, Ellen gathered her things and pulled up her raincoat hood. She was spooked, and not just by the panhandler. Why did Jane insist on living here, in cruddy willfulness? Why did she always make things so hard? Most of all, would she listen to reason today? It was Ellen's last chance, if she had gauged the time right.

On her dash across the street she narrowly avoided a giant crack in the road, but she slowed at the rail-less front stairs, no matter the rain, testing each slippery step before she committed. Then Jane was there, bare legged in the storm, grasping her arm, pulling her up and into the house.

"You're barely dressed," Ellen gasped. Water poured off both of them in the dark, humid foyer.

"I was watching you through the window and I thought you were going to drown," Jane said, laughing. "Come on. I'll get us towels." She pointed her mother toward the front room and disappeared into the back of the house. Ellen wiped her eyes and surveyed the crowded, messy hallway. She draped her raincoat over someone's bike and tugged off her rainboots.

Such a shame, what had happened to this house. The front room, which had beautiful bay windows and the shell of a crumbled fireplace, was filled with Salvation Army furniture. The plank wood floors were scraped and warped, and water stains climbed the walls to buckle ripples of plaster up and down. Ellen, in stocking feet, eyed a dark blotch the size of an opened umbrella in the corner of the ceiling.

"You know that might be mold," she said when Jane returned, pointing. Jane now in sweatpants, still bare feet, handed her a damp towel.

"Yep, might be."

Okay. Go carefully. "I brought you a couple of things. The man at Willy Street said to tell you they have the algae back in stock now. I think I heard that right . . . did he mean actual algae?"

Jane seized the bag and held up the spirulina bottle triumphantly. "Lifesaver! But I'm going to have to hide this," she said, glancing back at the stairs. "We've got some sticky fingers around here."

Meanwhile, Ellen scanned as much of her daughter's body as she could without getting caught. No visible signs of her pregnancy, thank God, although the baggy T-shirt and sweatpants would disguise whatever there could be at this point. With her hair tied back and her face scrunched up as she read the ingredients on the back of her expensive vitamin powder, Jane was suddenly *Jane* and Ellen threw both arms around her daughter and pulled her close. Jane wrapped one arm around her mother's back and Ellen felt the prick of tears beginning. Unfortunately, she also smelled the funky towel she'd been given, and it made her recoil.

"Let's go out for lunch," she said. "My treat. You pick where."

"I made tamales," Jane said, frowning. The moment of the hug was over. "It took all morning, but whatever, if you don't want to be here —"

"No — it's fine, fine, of course! I just didn't want you to go to any trouble." *Stop it,* Ellen told herself. She put the towel down on a card table, on top of a copy of the *Isthmus* ("Pentagon Surveillance of Anti-War Groups Extends to Madison") and steeled herself to follow Jane into the kitchen. There looked to be at least six places set at the large Formica table in the middle of the room — but then she saw that these were used, dirty dishes abandoned after previous meals.

"Right here, Mom," Jane said, amusement in her voice. Ellen sat where she was told and laid her napkin in her lap. Jane bustled at the counter and the stove, filling plates, chattering about how great her taping was for Serena's students' project and if only they hadn't had to edit her portion down to fit the program. Almost the whole house had come to support her, and yeah, they'd been pretty rowdy but that was part of taking action. The grad students had wanted her to talk about Mike and stay personal but Jane insisted on bringing in facts from iraqbodycount.org.

They began to eat. Ellen expressed delight at the tamales and salad, she didn't mention the greasiness of her water glass. When a bearded, shirtless man walked in, filled a teakettle, and then left, Jane took no notice and so Ellen pretended not to also.

"When she gets up I want you to meet Melanie," Jane said. "She's going to teach me how to puree all different kinds of things — not just basic fruits and vegetables, but entrées or entire dinners too. Like tamales! Babies can eat actual human food, you don't need to give them that processed slop that comes in pricy little jars." She took a big bite of human food herself, eyes wide and innocent.

Ellen's heart sank. "Oh, Janie. You can't. You need to . . . I want you to think about this. We need to think about what you're planning to do!"

"I have thought about it."

"How can you have a baby? Now, in your life the way it is."

"I'm going to ignore that last part, but, 'how can I have a baby?' Same way billions of women around the planet do, Mom. Not everyone has to have a perfect designer nursery all set up in advance. This is happening, you can stop being in denial now."

"You're not ready! There's so much time for this, later in your life, when you're more settled, after school and finding a real job —"

"Do you think pregnant women in Baghdad are stressing about getting their lives in order, getting some *degree* before they —"

"What does that have to do w—"

"They're too busy worrying about us shelling their homes or raping their sisters —"

Ellen stood up, but where could she go? The rain had stopped. She stacked a bunch of old dirty plates and carried them over to the filthy sink.

"Babies don't need all this stuff, the crib, the plastic toys, a black-and-white mobile so you can train their eyesight . . . they just need love. And breast milk."

Scrubbing viciously at crusted-on food, Ellen blinked away angry tears. "And insurance? Doctor's fees? Diapers, clothes, a car seat?"

"Cloth diapers, duh," Jane said, but quietly. "You don't have to do that."

"Yes, I do!" Ellen nearly shouted. The teakettle whistled, a breathy screech.

"And so now you're kicking me off the medical plan? Now, when I actually need it? Fine. I'm sure there are plenty of clinics downtown —"

"Who is the father?" Ellen went back and sat down, holding a wet sponge. "You can tell me. Sweetheart, please."

"It doesn't matter." Jane's face closed down.

"Is it . . . someone who lives here?" On cue, the bearded man came in to pour his tea. Jane shook her head.

"He's out of the picture," she said.

"From work? From school?"

"No, Mom. It's not — you don't understand. Just forget it."

Could this guy take any longer to make a cup of tea? Ellen sent a glare at his chubby bare back. "So *help* me understand. At the very least he needs —" She dropped her voice. "He needs to contribute! I don't want you to go into this alone."

"Are you kidding? I live with fifteen people. I'd kill for a little alone time." At the counter, the bearded man snorted.

"If you're going to joke about this," Ellen said, and stopped when her voice broke.

"Well how do you think it is for me, Mom? Remember? That it is about me? When I hear you saying you're going to have nothing to do with my baby, with your own grandchild —"

"Stop it. Don't try to make me feel guilty for asking you to think clearly, for once in your life, about what it means to bring a child into the world. You have no sense of reality!"

"Wait a minute, *I* have no sense of reality?" Jane was standing, shaking. The man quietly slipped from the room with his tea. "Do you even know where Michael is right now? And don't say 'Iraq.' Can you say anything specific about the cities or provinces where he's stationed, the missions he's undertaken, the things he's done?"

Ellen open and closed her mouth. Humidity in the soiled kitchen pressed in on her.

"You've written him a thousand letters but

do you even care about what's actually going on over there? Did you know he's been promoted? That he's now —"

"Lance corporal," Ellen finished. "Sit down, Jane. Let's be calm."

"What do you think some grunt has to do to get promoted out there?" her daughter shrieked. "How many kills earns you that?"

Ellen went around the table and tried to hold her, all thoughts of the pregnancy scattered by confusion and concern. Why had she jumped to this, why now? Startled by the girl's feverish vehemence, Ellen only wanted to soothe her. But she was at an odd angle, trying to embrace Jane from the side — her shoulder and upper arm blocked the way. For a moment, Jane let her mother stroke her hair, lean into her, and whisper *it's all right, it will be all right.* But then she jerked away.

"You know more about Edith Wharton's bowel movements than you do about the real world," Jane said coldly. "So don't lecture me." Ellen let go of her daughter's arm. And then she did something she thought she might regret: she left the room. She walked down the long dark hallway, ignoring a few heads above, poked out over the railing in curiosity. Jane followed — *don't overreact, you don't have to go, I'm just say-*

ing what everyone — To tell the truth, Ellen wasn't listening carefully. She put on her raincoat and soggy boots, tripping over the jumbled mess in the foyer.

"Fine," she said, to stop Jane from going on. "Fine, go ahead!"

"Go ahead with what?"

"With your baby, your life — fine. What do I know."

"Mom. Mom!"

Ellen blindly pushed herself outside, taking the rickety porch steps as fast as she dared, nearly running across the street to her car. She was crying from frustration at herself as much as anything else. One or two ugly comments from her sneering, troubled daughter? Was that all it took to unhinge her motherly equanimity? What a poor showing. She should get herself together and go back in. She would get over her own hurt and focus on the real problem: Jane's situation. But the more minutes Ellen sat in the front seat of her car, the more impossible it seemed, to cross that street again, to go back into that crumbled bad-smelling house. To face Jane.

Eventually, she started the engine. A sodden orange envelope obstructed the windshield; Ellen lowered the window to reach it. *Parking violation, maximum fine. $250.* By leaning all the way across the passenger seat it was possible to read the street sign directly above her car, the one she hadn't seen in the downpour, the one that man knocking at the window must have been trying to alert her to. FIRE LANE; EMERGENCY ZONE; NO PARKING ANYTIME.

Weeks went by. Ellen expected a call from Jane; maybe Jane expected a call from her. The worst heat of August had settled low over the city and wouldn't budge. Neighborhood groups formed early-morning water-watches, patrolling for illegal predawn yard sprinklers during the water shortage. Ellen gave up on everything except mowing the grass (a teenager on her block came every two weeks, give or take a week); the lobelia had faded earlier than any other summer, and her favorite patch of wild bergamot never even bloomed. E-mails from Mark Carroll, department chair, went unopened, as did an official-looking one from the assistant dean. It was too hot to cook, too hot to make plans with anyone. Paul called as usual, but Ellen turned down his invitations. She ate little, she slept during the day in fitful naps that left her more tired than before.

One day, visiting her mother in the nursing home out in Maple Grove, Ellen stood up to get a glass of water and the next thing she knew she was flat on her back in the common room, staring up at the faces of aides crowding around. Smelling salts had brought her around; she wanted to get up, but they insisted she lie down until the doctor came. Luckily — in a way — her mother was having a bad day, clarity-wise. Someone had wheeled her back to her room so at least Ellen didn't have to worry about what she might think, seeing her daughter tended to. As it was, several residents clustered close by, excited by the sudden collapse, calling and agitated. The young doctor frowned at her low blood pressure, grilled her on her medications, made her drink two cups of watery orange juice. *I'm fine,* Ellen repeated. She was embarrassed and just wanted to go home.

Dear Michael,

I've been wondering what it is like for you when you are afraid. Hesitating as I write this — not because I know I'm not "supposed" to bring this up, but because I don't want to cause you any more fear by thinking about it. And yet, it seems like it would be an essential aspect of your experience. I wonder if you are allowed to talk much about being afraid, with your friends and fellow soldiers. (I know, I know, "Marines.") Maybe it's a given, and doesn't need to be verbally expressed. Maybe it's something you need to hide, in order to get through your days or to sustain strength. Probably the more highly ranked would never discuss fear in war, or admit to feeling afraid, in — well, in fear of causing doubt in younger men who need to be certain of their commanding officers. But I hope there is a friend there for you, with whom you can be honest, with whom you can share the worst feelings of fear. I think that would make it easier to bear.

It's not shameful to feel afraid. I typed that, deleted it, and typed it again. Who am I to tell you this? How easy for me to offer these pronouncements on your inner state as you undergo an experience that I can never fully understand. And yet, I too am afraid. (Again, I type and delete and type.) So there's that.

Fear. What to write about this. The night I nearly choked to death on a bite of steak while the kids were upstairs asleep, ages nine and six. I staggered around the kitchen, airway blocked, in a panic. Terror — the idea they might come downstairs in the morning to find me dead. To have both parents die on them. I aimed my stomach at a chair-back corner and flung myself down on it: that piece of steak shot out and I gasped for a long time. (I also broke two rib bones and had to drive myself to the ER the next morning after dropping the kids at school.) It can give you incredible strength, to be flooded with fright. But at what cost? For years I never ate after they went to bed.

Here's what I'm thinking about tonight, though. Isn't it the case that being afraid — not the self-directed kind about me choking, but the fear we have of other people, or of ourselves — does involve some measure of shame? And this is why it's such a painful experience, hard to recover fully once you've felt it? Yes, I know that goes against what I wrote above.

About two months after we'd signed those guardian forms, a girl in the class below Wesley's was raped. I don't know if you remember this; I know you and I never discussed it. It happened on the Northside, in that Londonderry apartment complex. A group of kids from our school had gone over to a party there, probably as some kind of rebel move to hang out with the "tougher" kids out by the low-income housing. Where you lived last, where I know your old friends still were. Anyway, I found out about it on a Saturday morning that fall when this woman called me. A neighbor, once a friend. I won't say who she is, except that I stopped speaking to her that day and haven't since. She said the girl had been drinking, flirting with "townie boys" and went into a bedroom with one of them, although her friends tried to stop her. Then the boy brought one of his friends into the room too. This woman said, "There were lots of guys there, laughing about it, guarding the room. They were all in it together." I closed my eyes, full of horror and sadness, thinking of Janey — moping around the house in her pajamas, thank God — thinking about all the children in our community. Then she said, and I'll never forget her singsongy tone, "You're sure Mike wasn't there, right?"

That weekend I fell down into a terrible state of fear. Wesley was out of town for a cross-country training trip. All day Saturday I waited for you to show up, but you didn't come, and you weren't home for dinner. Jane heard about what happened from friends, and was on the phone a lot, hushed and crying. I tried to get her to talk to me about her feelings, but we were both pretty out of it. I didn't let her go out that night, I remember, and she yelled some but eventually went up to her room and at some point went to sleep. I roamed the house late into the night. Many, many times I fought the urge to call you. But we had an understanding about your freedom, that you wouldn't always be around. Still, why were you gone *this* weekend? I was tormented. I knew you couldn't have been part of what had happened in Londonderry. I knew you, I told myself. But then — maybe you've noticed this — fear has a way of insinuating thoughts that seem true. My neighbor's lilting question set off a sliding chain of doubts, I'm sorry to say. *But what if he had been there? What if those were his friends? What if he'd gone along, what if he thought it was funny . . .*

I know. Maybe you have torn this up by now, disgusted by me. Maybe I won't even mail this one. But it's true. I was scared shitless by the possibility that you had been involved. And by the fact that

I was now tied to you, legally and emotionally. That we all were. I berated myself, I barely slept. You didn't show up on Sunday morning and by now even Janey was noticing. Maybe you were hiding. Maybe you couldn't face us, once this news was out. *Had you been there when it happened?* I hid too, stayed in the house all weekend, afraid to face anyone in town. Rumors swirled and news kept coming; there were arrests, with more planned. Each piece of information fed my fears and my shame simultaneously. It's hard to explain why I had to fight so hard to hold on to what I knew: That you were a good person who'd had it tough. That I believed in you. I can blame my sheltered life, snobbery, a failure of character. All I know is how the fear of what *you* might have done rebounded onto me, the fear of what *I* had done. Fear of who you might be. Fear of who I might.

Then Sunday night around ten I heard a noisy car pull up outside, a lot of shouting and laughter. Both you and Wes banged loudly into the house, dropping backpacks and jackets and giant shoes everywhere, pulling open the fridge and cabinets, arguing over who got what food. I just stood and stared. *What?* you asked, glancing up from making a sandwich. *Where were you?* I managed. Cross-country nerds can't time themselves, now, can they? you said. Mom, I told you, Wes said, pouring a second bowl of cereal. Coach said Mike could come on retreat since they needed another assistant manager for the trip. Fifty bucks and a busload of stinky socks, you said. And then, again, seeing my expression: what? I sat down at the kitchen table with you two, who didn't know yet what had happened to the girl from school, watching you eat and eat, and joke.

Had Wes told me you were going with him all weekend? And was it possible I'd forgotten? I wouldn't have thought so, but that's what happened. Not my best mothering on display in any part of that weekend.

And no, it wasn't a "happy ending," discovering that you hadn't been involved. Once you've been touched by that kind of fear, it changes you. I was ashamed of myself. I still am. Partly I write this to ask your forgiveness for imagining who you could have been.

How about some good news? I'm letting you off the hook for this week's reading assignment. I got a little obsessed about finding a text on fear. I had copied Flannery O'Connor's short story masterpiece "A Good Man Is Hard to Find" — which is terrifying on its own, of course, because of the serial killer impeccably named the Misfit — but after writing all this, above, I don't want to add any more. Though someday I need you to read this story, if only for what the grandmother does, in her utter fear, before she is taken into the woods to be killed.

Next time, though, I have a great essay for you. I just learned how to photocopy on both sides so these envelopes won't be as ridiculously thick. I can only guess the mockery I get when you are at mail call.

With love, Ellen

PS: here's a photo of Maisie. Doesn't she look unhappy about the new haircut? I keep telling her it will grow in tangled and shaggy soon enough.

Nine days later, Ellen was on I-88 east to Chicago. Friday late-afternoon traffic was thick, stop and start, giving her lots of time to remember the things she had forgotten to do: arrange for Maisie's care (she left messages with the two neighbors who had keys and prayed that they would be home this weekend); shut down her computer or turn off any lights or radios that were on upstairs; clean the sink of dishes or pick up the living room or maybe even lock the side door. More messages for the neighbors. One thing Ellen didn't think about, though it hovered on the edge of consciousness, was the two-day mandatory department start-of-semester meeting she hadn't gone to, either yesterday or today. At this point, she had — as undergrads put it — blown off just about every possible requisite, short of not showing up for her classes, which would begin next week. Vaguely, she wondered what would happen to her job, her career. With tenure, what could they do? Censure her or put her on some kind of probation, most likely. There had been that case of the Spanish professor who refused to use voice mail; the department had taken a vote.

Serena: *You must make some calls, people are getting worried. Ask for a medical leave.* Ellen: *What kind of medical condition would I claim? Oh, you mean a nervous breakdown. What does HR call that these days?* Serena, gently: *What would you call it?* Ellen, long pause: *Existential malaise.*

The irony, Ellen thought, slowed to a crawl on the two-lane — or rather the paradox — was that for a person slacking off on her job, she was working harder than ever before. That heightened sense of awareness to all forms of meaning, written and otherwise, was one she'd had during the high point of writing her Wharton books. When connections leaped to mind at all hours of the day and night, books open and nested on her desk four and five high, a thousand yellow sticky notes, etc.

A few days ago she'd let Paul West come up (a mistake), when he stopped by to pick her up for a concert date she had meant to get out of. "All this . . ." he said, looking around her study in frank astonishment, "for letters to Michael? Oh, Ellen. Maybe we should —"

"What?" she'd snapped. "I'm ready, let's —"

"But I had no idea. This is . . ."

She steered him out of the study, changing the subject. And after that evening, she hadn't returned his calls.

His expression in her study had startled her into a brief glimpse of what it looked like, her life now, to others. And if she really thought about things, Ellen knew that the fact that she was writing many more letters than she actually mailed to Michael could be considered . . . of concern. But she wasn't thinking about it too much. Ellen felt like she was hanging on in a hurricane wind; if she shifted focus, if she lifted her head even briefly from the work, something bad would happen.

Except Wesley's phone call this morning, almost two weeks since she'd fled Jane's house, startled her into action. He'd been sick, he said, his voice not much above a hoarse whisper. Some kind of infection. He'd been to the doctor twice now, had taken three courses of antibiotics but still wasn't getting better. They wanted to run some new tests. *I didn't want to bother you,* her son said. Ellen almost hung up on Wesley in her urge to get in the car. *Three hours,* she said. *Hang tight.*

But it was going to be four, even four and a half, at this rate. Approaching I-94 the Chicago skyline came into view on her left, which Ellen glanced at frequently, as if it could pull her there faster. One time she had to hit the brakes, just in time; bumper sticker on the SUV she ran up on read MAKE LEVEES NOT WAR.

As she took the stairs up three flights in Wes's Hyde Park apartment, Ellen was thinking hard. *Mononucleosis? Walking pneumonia?* She'd drive him home in the morning, for the appointment Dr. Sherman had shoehorned in as a favor. *Bacterial flu? Allergies?* She was so preoccupied that when Wes opened the door to her it took more time than it should have to see that he was upright, normal color, not wheezing or whispering. Dressed normally. Smiling, but a bit tense.

"Wesley," she puffed. "What are you doing? Are you all right?" Then as he ushered her in, with a one-armed hug, Ellen understood. Jane was in the living room, wearing a UC hoodie of Wes's. She was on the futon, one leg tucked underneath; she gave her mother a sharp little sarcastic wave.

"Don't blame me," Jane said. "I found this out, like, an hour ago."

Ellen shoved her bag at Wesley. "Are you kidding me," she said, still out of breath. "What if I'd gotten in an accident?"

"I told him it was sick. Way to go running to Mom, Wes. Thanks a lot."

"What happened? Are *you* sick? Someone better be in need of medical attention here." Ellen dropped onto the futon. "I can't believe you lied to me. And why are you here, anyway?"

"Because I *thought* I had a place to crash while the house is fumigated for bedbugs.

But apparently I signed up for a family intervention so you all can tell me what to do with my preggo self or my —"

"I don't need this." Ellen threw up her hands. It was so awkward to get *up* from a futon. And how much would that all-day parking lot charge her?

"Stop it." Wes dragged a footstool over and sat in front of both of them. He shook back his bangs, and pointed a finger at Ellen. "She's been calling you, and hanging up, for weeks." Ellen started to respond but was cut off. "She wants help but can't ask for it."

"Hey!"

Wes whirled on Jane. "She pays your insurance, your rent, your tuition —"

"I never asked —"

"Shut it! You're up shit creek, Janey! I'm sorry, but this is not like one of your causes to take up on principle. It's your life, it's a baby's life. And you have no clue."

Jane glared but stayed quiet.

Wes pushed up his glasses. "Nothing's going to get solved by you guys not talking. And we're on the clock here." Ellen felt a rush of trembly warmth for Wes, this cramped and book-filled apartment. "I mean, I don't have the faintest idea, but, like . . . don't we need a plan? She's still a minor, right? Mom?"

For the first time Ellen turned to look at Jane, pulling at loose threads in a throw blanket. A line of small tender pimples ran along her jawline; she had taken out the two rings she usually wore in the top part of her ear. Ellen reached over to touch her sleeve. "How many weeks now?"

Jane sniffed. For a moment it seemed she wouldn't answer. "Ten," she said quietly. "And I'm going to keep it. My decision."

Ellen shook her head, felt tears start.

"Mom," Jane said, her own voice quavery. "Don't. I'm sorry, okay? I'm really sorry."

Ellen leaned over to press her face against the unbearably precious ear of her rash, vexing child. Jane slumped against her. They held close together; a knot of pain unwound itself inside Ellen.

"Well, what about adoption?" she heard Wesley ask. "That's a thing."

"No," Jane said, her voice muffled against Ellen's shoulder. "Mom, I can't. I couldn't."

"But it's all anonymous," Wes persisted. "Or not. She could probably even pick the couple herself, find people who —"

Jane shook her head against Ellen's shoulder.

And Ellen surprised herself by whispering back, "I know." It was true. Having to give away one's own child . . . she felt all the force of Jane's instinctive refusal and, for once, agreed with her. They pulled away and Ellen patted Jane on the leg.

"Let's have you move back home," she said. "For now."

Jane blew out her breath. "It's not that easy, Mom . . . There's stuff going on at the house. I can't just —"

"Yes, you can," Ellen said firmly. She didn't say it, but: *Fumigated for bedbugs.* And Jane just nodded. After that, there seemed little to discuss. Wes ran out to get Indian takeout; the three of them ate curry — just naan for Jane, who was nauseated — while listening to *Sound Opinions.* Wes showed off his latest conference proposal. Ellen got ready to drive back; Jane said she'd rather stay the night and go shopping for vintage the next day. Mother and daughter hugged; *détente.*

Wesley followed her all the way down the stairs, confused by the sudden reversals, mostly unspoken. So that was it? Everything's okay now? How did —

"Naturally! It's all peachy," Ellen said, reaching the lobby.

"Don't do sarcasm, Mom. It doesn't look good on you."

"You're a good brother." She sighed. "But

you owe me eighty dollars in gas money." In a way it was a relief, to face the truth. Janey becoming a mother. Herself, a grandmother. (Serena would have a field day with *that.*) Now she would begin making lists: a crib, a car seat, an ob-gyn. All the pregnancy books, maybe a counselor or program for Jane to help with the transition. Who could she talk to at the university about part-time classes? Even continuing ed? Because Ellen would *not,* she swore, give up on a degree for Jane no matter how long it took.

"One thing. Did you . . . you haven't told Mike about Jane, have you? Mom?"

"Hmm?" In the moment, her letters to Michael seemed to Ellen like a mirage on the horizon. She'd lost the thread. "No, of course not."

"Yeah. Um, I'm just wondering if you should. Since she's not going to. So he can be, like, prepared."

"What do you mean?"

"Because he's the father." Wesley studied her carefully, to see if she could handle this.

Ellen backed up until the row of ridged steel mailboxes stopped her. "How do you know that? Did she tell you?"

"She doesn't have to say it — she won't, even. I think she wants to convince herself that it doesn't matter, or maybe that she won't say anything until after he's back. But it's him. I'm sure. I mean, I'm pretty sure."

12

She quit him, cold. And the worst part was how easy Jim made it for her, because he was a good person. He didn't make a play for her, a pitch for "them." No guilt trip, no wheedling. He bowed out with grace. On the phone he cut off her stumbling apology: "It's a good call, Lace. We'll walk away intact. I don't want to be the guy who makes your life any harder."

Over the next few weeks she went crazy with need and longing.

Was Eddie thinking about her? No. No, and she shouldn't expect it. She was a good Army Reserve wife, she knew what he was up against when he was out there. Lacey loathed these high-maintenance new girls who demanded Skypes and iChats, who laid into their tired guys with complaints about bills or the kids. Or just feeling neglected. Hell no: Lacey would rather staple her mouth shut than distract Eddie, or drag him down into the petty details of home life. That was her domain and she would die before letting him know, for example, how bad things were getting with money.

But there were other reasons Lacey knew Eddie wasn't craving her, aching for her during their time apart, no matter what his situation was. And it was only now, during this second deployment, that she began to understand more. Yes, they weren't newlyweds anymore, and yes, they'd both been around the block — too old for drama. But Eddie wasn't the kind of man to waste a lot of time on endearments or tender emotional talk. Even before they married, Lacey noticed that he was into her only when it was leading to sex . . . and then of course the sex itself dropped off big-time once the wedding and moving in were finished. She'd told herself to get with the program: this was big-girl life, time to grow up and act like it. And then the army only solidified their growing formality, a distancing . . . nothing about this organization promoted impulsive romantic gestures.

She had so much more than she'd hoped for. Lacey was ashamed, but that didn't change the fact that she couldn't find contentment the way other people apparently did. How to admit that you're missing something big and basic out of life? How to say it to another person? *I want to be touched more.*

It was a Sunday afternoon midway through September. Lacey pulled into the parking lot in the shopping center in Yonkers, just north of Van Cortlandt Park. She idled there for a moment, studying the row of storefronts through her sunglasses. Vacuum sales and repair, HairCuttery, Payless Shoes. Squeezed between them was a smaller business, no awning out front, no big sign. But the flag and 9/11 NEVER FORGET poster let her know this was the one: *U.S. Service Recruiting Center.*

"Can I stay in the car?"

Otis was slumped low in the passenger seat, heaving long sighs to announce his displeasure. For a moment she wished he didn't have to come on this particular errand, but then a harder part of her thought, *He's not a baby, he needs to know what's up.*

"No, you can't stay in the car. And I told you not to bring that outside the house." A friend had loaned Otis some repellent video game full of screeching women's voices and *blam blam* gun sounds. "Give me that. Otis, *give* it to me. Jesus." She shoved the handheld player into the glove box and slammed it shut. Otis went *tcch* under his breath and Lacey told herself to ignore it. They'd been having a rough time. Ever since school started, Otis had been pushing back at her — arguing about TV time, putting off his homework until the last minute and then rushing through it, sloppy. Twice already his teacher had e-mailed Lacey with concerns: he wasn't listening, he'd been digging pen tracks on the side of his desk.

Lacey wasn't handling it well, either. Her patience was low; she was stressed about her cut work hours and trying to get a grip on the money situation. She didn't need preteen bullshit on top of all that. And she had given up Jim! That was for Otis, though he didn't know it, and his blithe ignorance of her sacrifices pissed her off even more.

"Well, are we going to go in, or what?"

"You better cut that attitude."

"I'm just *saying.*"

Lacey killed the engine and swung out of the car, slamming her door. She tugged her jacket down. Striding across the lot her heeled boots clopped loudly on the pavement and her purse swung. She shook her hair back behind her shoulders. Otis dragged behind, and when she got to the door she waited pointedly while he caught up. *What?* Lacey pushed sunglasses up into her hair and stared at the door handle until he held it open for her.

"Thank you," she said clearly, walking past him. She almost felt sorry for the guy at the front desk, eyes on his computer screen, unaware of her mood, but she let her inner bitch out nonetheless — clattering down her bag and keys in front of him, snapping out her words: "So, are there forms to fill out? For the food and gas cards?"

Lacey made lists, dozens of lists — in her organizer, on her phone, on the whiteboard in the kitchen — where she racked up the different bills and fees and what they owed and what she couldn't pay. The monthly mortgage was covered, okay, but after that things got chaotic. Car payments and insurance (including Eddie's jeep, sitting in the garage untouched) got alternated, her college loan was mostly ignored until the Sallie Mae calls grew aggressive, and the training courses Eddie'd had to take for his last promotion were coming due. These could all be juggled and delayed, to some extent. But then: utilities and food, two credit cards at their limit (one with a 26 percent interest rate), Little League for Otis (cleats, glove, travel fees) . . . and last week she'd bounced two checks, one to the exterminator (ants), one to the ophthalmologist for Otis's school-required vision exam.

With Eddie's income cut by a third when he went from civilian to reserve pay, and the reduced schedule Lacey had to take on in order to be around for Otis, they'd been just barely managing. But last month her boss called a meeting and said due to how slow it had been at the gym they would all be taking mandatory unpaid furloughs every three weeks. Then she'd asked Lacey to stay behind and said she'd need to work the second shift from September through November: 3:00 p.m. to 11:00 p.m.

Lacey almost laughed. "There's no way," she said. "I don't have anyone who can take my kid until that late." Or her whole paycheck would have to go to a sitter.

The supervisor shrugged. "It's all I have until after the holidays. It'll pick up then."

So she'd had to stay on the part-time schedule she'd worked all summer, and now the pileup of delayed bills and payments reached a breaking point. Last week she'd put off buying groceries day after day, waiting for money to come in, and that meant they ate out at fast-food places on her bursting credit cards. Then on Friday some screwup happened with the auto-deposit for

Eddie's check and she hadn't been able to get a live human on the phone all day, with the result that she'd had to borrow forty bucks from Otis's small stash in order to buy pasta, sandwich stuff, and toilet paper. She made one last list, people she might ask for a loan: Lolo, Martine . . . and then slowly crossed them out. Late last night Lacey thought *fuck it,* and went online to figure out where to go.

"Um, does Eddie know you're doing this?"

Lacey shot Otis a sideways look. "What's that supposed to mean?" They were on chairs in the tiny waiting area by the window. She was whipping through the clipboard forms the desk clerk had given her. Lots of programs donated goods or money for military families, which then got funneled through churches or recruiter stations. Lacey had chosen this one because it wasn't too close to home, but not far enough away to require much gas.

"Nothing."

"No, say it."

"It's just that, I don't think it's the officers' families who are supposed to be, like, getting charity."

Lacey put her pen down and sat back. "You're worried about ranking protocol, huh? Or are you just ashamed of your mom, who's accepting help when she needs it?" She let her voice carry around the dingy office, whose workers glanced up and then away. It was unfair, making Otis squirm in the heat of her reply, which wasn't only about him. She'd cried earlier this morning in the shower, imagining what it would be like to come here. To hell with taking on more guilt about his embarrassment.

Otis shook his head, mumbled something that might have been *sorry.* Lacey blew out a long breath at the pocked ceiling tiles. She went back to filling out forms: *resources, earned income, dependent costs.*

"You don't have to say anything, though," she said, a few minutes later. "To Eddie. We don't need to bother him, is all."

The only man she'd ever been faithful to was the Asshole, and look how that had turned out. Growing up in Great Neck, Lacey's boyfriends were mostly of the petty thief and vandalism variety, guys who were big men only among their crowd of friends, sweet at first but lazy at heart. She went through them like changes of clothes — those tight jeans and off-the-shoulder tops and fake-leather boots she would kick off at the end of the day and discard, a tangled pile in the corner of her closet. She wasn't so different in this. Her girlfriends weren't choosy either; they all rotated boys around according to complicated algorithms of reputation, cuteness, availability, or the chance to get back at some bitch who'd made out with your ex. Lacey's boyfriends shaded into each other, overlapping. She'd officially call it quits with one only after securing her next position — that was the way they all did it, cycling through the halls and malls of adolescence, just marking time until real life began.

Her father had died of a heart attack when she was nineteen. He was a thick-waisted, red-faced man with a deceptively mild expression. He'd worked for Con Ed as a lineman for twenty years before getting laid off, and then took a series of lesser-paying jobs in electrical support. The drinking increased during those years, as did the ugly fights with Lacey's mother, who had to go back to work as a secretary and made no secret of her bitter disappointment. Mostly, her dad went after her brother, Bob — police got called to their house several times — in epic screaming and shoving matches over the car, the late nights, grades, any excuse either could find. One night when she was fourteen Lacey dodged a jar of pickles one of them hurled at the other, yanked her head to the side one millisecond in time, so that the weight and heft of the glass jar blew by her ear, brushing it with coolness before exploding against the kitchen wall. With Lacey, her dad was less physical and restricted himself to heated diatribes about her slutty clothes and friends. That was when he was sober. When he was drunk he slurred weepy expressions of regret about how little she'd accomplish in her life, due to his mistakes.

Lacey and Bob took every job they could find, and ate out every meal they were invited to, not to mention some they weren't. And they had a tacit pact to keep their mouths shut when well-meaning teachers, parents of friends, or other adults asked about how things were at home. After she left, Lacey used to wonder why she hadn't confided in anyone and let that old bastard reap the consequences. But it occurred to her that many, if not all, of the kids they knew were in similar situations. The bad shit in their house wasn't so unique, and everyone seemed to accept that growing up and getting out were the only solutions.

That, and making out with boys. Lacey loved it. She knew it wasn't something a girl was supposed to admit, and she only rarely went all the way, but those long kissing sessions meant everything to her. With someone's clothed body mashed against hers, in a thick fug of cheap cologne and cigarette smoke, she could shut her eyes and let go. Escape.

"Buona sera!" Felicia tried again, when the weary but tolerant waiter brought them another bottle of red. "Am I getting it now?"

"Buona sera, signora bella," he said. The three of them applauded and he smiled tiredly to himself and pulled out the cork.

The restaurant — Buona Sera Ristorante, a newish place on Gramatan up in Fleetwood — had been chosen to convince Felicia to come out. It was closest to her place, where her mom was with the kids. Lacey had picked up Martine, and girls' night out was in full effect, Italian-style: fried calamari and tri-colore salad first, now chicken caprese and seafood risotto. As soon as Eddie's October check cleared, Lacey withdrew more cash than she should have for tonight, including a sitter and a blowout at that cheap place near the gym, but she wasn't going to worry about money tonight. She needed this.

No kid talk, no war talk, was the original rule. Only fun stuff. But it was impossible to stick to: Martine's fight with a snotty mom at the preschool led to how she wrote a late-night three-screen e-mail about it to her husband, only to delete it at the last moment thank God. Felicia had taken on two bathroom rehabs that were cratering, and John better not pull an early homecoming because their place was a wreck. Lacey told Lolo stories, amping up her Latina accent ("Why hasn't anyone called me back? I left that message an hour ago. What happened. Did something happen?") until they were laughing to the point of tears.

"It even got Ed to crack a smile," Lacey said, helping herself to some of Martine's potatoes. "He said I'm the one taking a bullet, dealing with her so much."

"Did you get him on iChat? No luck for me in weeks."

"It was a quick video call. They were about to go out." Lacey didn't say that Eddie essentially confirmed what she asked him about — a rise in suicide bombings around his area. As usual, he kept it low-key, brushing off most of her questions and treating the subject as slightly off topic, nothing that important. Was this how he spoke to the younger men under his command? Did it work for them, did they think the danger wasn't increased at all? They didn't have Lacey's knowledge: the way Eddie had of dropping eye contact when he was tense, his gaze roving up and around, as if searching for assistance or a distraction. She'd seen it when he wasn't happy with her — for being too loud, too haphazard — the effect was casual, tricking her into thinking not much was at stake. But then his eyes would be one step ahead of hers, all around the room, and she'd know.

"So he shaved," she said. "The whole thing" — Lacey swiped a finger across her upper lip — "totally gone. Clean-faced as a baby now."

"Good idea, Eddie." Martine, who never made a secret of her preferences in the mustache department.

"Oh, wow," Felicia said. "I bet you didn't recognize him at first. Why'd he do that, I wonder."

" 'Cause the early eighties called and wanted their look back."

"He didn't want to be mistaken for an Iraqi, with that Saddam Hussein look. Worried he'll get strung up by mistake." Lacey tried to join in.

Felicia made a disapproving *tch* sound, so they dropped it. In truth, it rattled her, Eddie's shaving. When she yelped at the sight he pretended at first not to know why. Then he shrugged it off, saying it saved time and he was sick of dealing with it. But his face looked so bare, so much smaller, paler. What if it was some kind of omen? What if it was a way to punish her for cheating, make her more afraid for him, more aware of his vulnerability?

Lacey took a long drink of wine. *Stop it.* Tonight was supposed to be fun.

"You want to tell her about what happened?" Martine said, pointing her fork first at Lacey, then Felicia. "In your little support group? Not-so-support group, that is."

"Uh-oh."

Lacey sighed. She still wasn't happy with the way she'd handled things. "Well, last week this one girl comes in, she doesn't come every week so I was —"

"Tell her about — she was wearing a T-shirt that says WAR IS BAD FOR CHILDREN AND OTHER LIVING THINGS. I mean, fuck you," Martine said, more tipsy than they'd noticed.

"— So I was glad," Lacey went on. "At first. I don't care about the shirt. But then she blurts out she's leaving the group because her parents are convinced that what we do is brainwash her with right-wing propaganda."

"Say *what*? How old is this girl? She can't

think for herself?"

"Well, that's what everyone jumped in saying. And that if she's doing whatever her parents say on the issue then *they're* the ones doing the brainwashing."

"Right?"

"I tried to get her to talk more but I guess she felt like we were all jumping down her throat so she got all, you know, crossing her arms like they do and not saying anything." Lacey mimed the young woman leaning way back in her chair, chin tucked. "I was freaking out, thinking I'd done something wrong, I mean — I'm not a shrink or anything, maybe she'd complained to Anne Mackay or whatever. Also, right-wing what? We hardly talk politics! They spend the whole hour bitching about the pay grade. God, if anything that group bashes on the army more than the liberal media does!"

"Now tell her the worst part," Martine said, rattling her empty water glass. "Did they turn off the air? Why's it so hot in here?"

"Do I want to know?" Felicia said.

"Well, she goes on to say that her parents are in MFSO, and that they've been bringing her to some of their meetings, and she's starting to see the light." Lacey sighed. Their prix fixe dessert course arrived, but she wasn't hungry anymore.

"MFSO." Felicia spelled it out slowly, thinking. "Military something something —"

"Military Families Speak Out," Lacey said.

"Military Families So Fucking Cowardly," Martine spat. "The enemy among us."

"Mart," Lacey said. "They're a legit organization. I looked it up after. It's an antiwar group," she told Felicia. "Support our troops by bringing them home now, et cetera. You know."

"And for every wife they get on board, they get a spike in traffic I'm sure. I mean, it's no big deal to get some parents out there holding up signs and talking shit about Bush. They don't care, they're old now and used to pissing off their kids. But a soldier's pretty all-American wife turning Benedict Arnold? Oh, that's good."

"What did she say about all of it? Is she against the war now, or what?" Felicia was working her way around the three desserts methodically, one bite from each. "And what does her guy say?"

"Well, yeah, that's what everyone was asking her. I don't know if she's told him or what. No one would let her speak much, really." The wine had lulled Lacey into a tired spaciness. They needed to switch to beer soon. Or something harder. The women in the group had been merciless: *All you're gonna do is put him in more danger, and our men too. Get right and shut up, nobody asked for your opinions on politics and shit. How do you think this is going to make him feel, out there, knowing you've given up on him, humiliated in front of his brothers.*

"I can imagine. What did —"

"Anyone like that is dead to me." Martine waved for the check. "It's hard to be alone, and the news can look really bad, but . . . come on, girls. Do what you gotta do on the down low but for God's sake don't make our misery into a weapon against our own troops. You know?"

Felicia was shaking her head. "If John ever *pictured* me holding up some kind of NOT IN MY NAME sign, or whatever . . . I just can't even."

"I'm not sure I handled it all that well," Lacey said. "I feel like I'm supposed to let everyone have their say in there. As a safe space. But on the other hand —"

"You don't want to let traitors get away with shit! What if she caught some of those other ditsy young wives at a bad moment?"

"What did you say, Lace?"

"I kind of . . . I let them all freak out for a while, and then I — well I told her that the politics part of being in Iraq or Afghanistan didn't matter. That it was separate from what our guys were doing, and so she should keep it separate."

"Sounds right to me. They don't get to choose which battles they fight." Felicia nodded.

Lacey counted out bills for her part of the tab. She didn't disagree, but there was a moment at the end of the meeting that kept coming back to her. *What would you do?* This girl had asked Lacey directly as she was leaving, probably for the last time. *If you came to believe, with your heart and your head, that it was all a mistake, us being there. Would you speak up, or not?*

What had happened was that her immediate answer, deep inside, was *yes.* Lacey had never once backed down from a fight. She suddenly saw the flip side of her own convictions about the rightness of this war — cultivated through pride, close attachment, and lots of Internet research — and got it, in a flash, how she would be acting if what she thought was the exact opposite. She'd go at it with the same energy now poured into this FRG group and all their other activities. *Bet your ass I'd speak up. No mat-*

ter what Eddie thought.

So who was she to tell this person otherwise?

"Let's get out of here," Martine said, sliding herself out of the banquette. "Too. Much. Food."

"Buona sera!" Felicia sang out, to their waiter, to the room at large.

An hour later, Lacey and Martine were cruising around, not ready to go home after Felicia left. They got Big Gulps from a 7-Eleven and took the Cross County Parkway, singing Christina Aguilera with the windows down. They took the Bronx River up through Westchester, going past the darkened golf courses and wooded pockets. On the way back south, Martine announced it was time for another drink. Also, she had to pee. Lacey's buzz had worn off by then but she was game, so when Martine stuck a hand out into the night and said, *So turn off here already,* it struck her as fate that the next exit happened to be Pelham, and her car seemed to take them, of its own accord, to Wolf's Lane and Chap's Bar and Grill, where Jim just happened to be on as manager that night.

Martine barely noticed the venue when they parked outside. She ran in ahead to get to the ladies' room. Lacey followed slowly, glad for the cover of a late-night crowd standing at the bar, noisy music, some game on the TVs. She kept her head down and took an occupied table by the window.

"Hey. I know you." He was there, before she was ready, before she'd figured out what it was that she was doing. Jim smiled down at her, puzzled, touched her hair. " 'Of all the bars in all the . . .' something something."

"Yeah, well," Lacey said. She couldn't look directly at him. The warmth coming off his body was almost too much. "My friend needed to pee."

"Of course she did. No better place to pee in the tristate area."

"Can I take this chair?" someone asked, reaching for the other one.

"It's taken," Jim said, a firm hand on its back. "You look good," he said, bending low to her ear. "You're killing me right now, but you look good."

"Is it crazy that maybe I could eat something?" Martine said, arriving. "What should we drink, Lace? And can I get a glass of water first," she said to Jim, who held out her chair.

"Maybe a couple shots," Lacey mumbled. "We can always cab home from here."

"I'll send a waitress over," Jim said. Behind Martine, he held Lacey's gaze.

They had two Jägermeisters, on the house, then an order of mozzarella sticks. Then two beers, and another round of shots. Martine commandeered the jukebox with a stack of quarters Jim fed her, the two of them arguing the merits of Journey and Chicago. Lacey's babysitter texted back to say she could stay late. The crowd thinned, a couple people were dancing, Lacey took off her jacket to bare her arms in a tight tanktop. She watched Martine dance, sweaty and oblivious to the two guys checking her out. She watched Jim at the end of the bar, directing the waitstaff and conferring with the bartender. He never seemed to look over, but once when he came by to fiddle with the TV above her he stood close behind and she could feel him waiting. They didn't speak. Lacey hooked an elbow over her chair and dangled her hand into the space between them. His hand met hers, rubbing her palm with his thumb, and Lacey felt a deep recognition, like hearing a song she'd loved long ago.

Martine was happy drunk and happily belligerent with the guys who gravitated toward their table as the night got late and most people had cleared out. "Oh, you support the troops? You want to buy me a drink, save my husband a few dollars? Whyn't you buy my kids a new bike, howaboutthat?" Lacey watched and laughed. Jim came and went, touching her every time he passed by.

But then the lights went on and it was time to go, as much as Lacey didn't want to. A waiter called them a cab and they waited shivering together outside on the curb, Martine babbling on about maybe they should go dancing or something, like a real club, God was this hangover going to hurt tomorrow or what. Lacey said, *Just a sec okay,* and went back inside. She walked straight to the back, where Jim was turning chairs upside down on tabletops.

"I don't know," she said fast. "I don't know what I'm doing. And it's like a joke or something, because you can't want me, if this is who I am. There is nothing good in me, Jim. There's nothing —"

He pulled her in hard, no more soft hidden touches. He kissed her and held her shoulders and she cried some even while she was kissing him, but then they were laughing at all of it and then —

Lacey saw her out of the corner of her eye: Martine. Just inside the door. Stock-still and staring.

"The cab's here."

"Mart—"

But she turned away from Lacey and walked out. "Fuck," Jim whispered. "What do you want me to do? I'll go say it was me, that you didn't want to . . ."

"It's okay." But it wasn't. Lacey bit her lip and looked out at the street. At least the cab was waiting, so Martine was waiting. She started to leave and Jim caught her hand.

"Leave your car key," he said. "I'll bring it back later, after I close up."

"I can't . . . not tonight."

"No, I meant — I'll just drop the key through your mail slot. So you can take Otis tomorrow."

Lacey dug the key off the ring and put it in his hand. "I . . ."

"Go talk to her. Just let me know you got home okay."

When she got in the cab, Martine was staring out the opposite window. "Don't tell me anything," she said before Lacey even shut the door. "First stop is my house," and she gave the driver the address.

They were quiet all along Martin Luther King Boulevard, and on E. Third, but when the cab turned onto Fulton and hit a red light Lacey said, "I'm sorry."

Martine chewed the inside of her lips and

shook her head. "Don't."

"I keep it all separate, Mart. You know I would never do anything to hurt Eddie. Not while he's there. I'll be upfront when the time is right. It hasn't been so great for us recently, you know? Maybe I got into it too fast —"

The more she spoke, the more plausible it sounded — to herself, that is. All the things she said were true. Eddie wasn't going to be the love of her life, and on some level Lacey had always known that. She'd needed someone, and Otis needed someone, and it all fell into line. Even the army fit in — gave her respectability, a cause to fight for. In fact, Lacey went on, in a way FRG and the group and the army had come to mean more to her than —

"Stop!" Martine cried. The cab came to a fishtail halt. *"I. Don't. Want. To know!"*

"But —"

"Make all the justifications you want, Lacey. Make it all okay in your head, spin it the way you got to spin it. Just leave me out of it." She opened the door and got out, still many blocks from her house, ignoring Lacey's sputtering and the cabdriver's impatient curses. She wouldn't turn around and when Lacey leaned out of the open door calling her she started running unevenly down the Mount Vernon sidewalk, her tiny purse bumping against her hip.

"You gonna give me another address, or what?"

She told him in a low voice.

"All this sitting around and waiting," the cabdriver said. *Tch.* "Meter's on for that too."

"I know, all right? I know!" And then Lacey burst into tears, head down on her knees.

"I'm just sayin' there's a charge for all of it. That's all."

13

Ellen's fall honors seminar was reassigned to a junior faculty member. This, she knew, was to punish her for many failings over the spring and summer — ignoring the retention committee, skipping the semester planning meeting. She accepted the change without comment and taught two standard courses, Intro to Literary Theory (although by rights she was due a break from this one) and Twentieth-Century Women Writers. Mark was still incredibly pissed off; she could tell by his ferocious cheer whenever they met in the mailroom. Whether anyone else was gossiping or speculating about her Ellen didn't know and mostly didn't care. She had regained a kind of numb equilibrium and wanted nothing more than for it to sustain. She met her classes and gave her lectures. She graded essays and assigned tests. She mentored two grad TAs, and even showed up, briefly, at the cake-cutting for an assistant dean's retirement party.

It was strange to be at work and not in the middle of a years-long book project. The teaching part of her job had been a second priority for so long that occasionally she was confused by the extra time at the end of each day, each week. *What am I supposed to be doing now?* Ellen would think, stilled at her desk. It was the sensation of having forgotten something important. She only felt the weight of all those hours of research and writing once they had receded from her life.

As if in answer to that absence, Ellen's feverish letter-writing to Michael also fell away. She still wrote him, but they were letters now of a conventional format, or so she guessed. Weather, Maisie, Wes and Janey news (minus any of Jane's *real* news, that is), little stories about her day, innocuous questions about how he was faring. These Ellen handwrote instead of typed. She stopped scouring texts for a way to understand, a way to help him. It made her feel scared to think about those thousands of words she had written on fear and shame and death and what it means to be a human caught in war. She never opened those files on her computer. A brush with madness.

Jane was living at home. They found a good ob-gyn and a comfortable routine. At the last checkup, Ellen read a P. D. James novel in the waiting room, which she tucked away when Jane came out. "Soon I do the ultrasound thingie," Jane said, waving a piece of paper. "They'll be able to tell whether it's a boy or a girl. But I don't know if I want to know yet." She waited, as if Ellen would tell her what to do. But Ellen merely smiled and nodded, and gathered their coats. On the way out, Jane said, "Will you come with me? Into the room, when they do it, I mean?" Ellen had had to use all her strength to hold back her surprise and delight, *of course.*

Jane had even picked up a part-time job, thanks to Debbie Masterson, who paid her to help out with her new twins twice a week. Ellen had awkwardly offered to pay for this, had wanted to give Debbie the money to give to Jane, but Debbie refused. She was grateful for any chance to rest, she said, and Jane was gentle and good with the babies. But Ellen knew that Jane was getting more out of the arrangement, in real-life lessons of what was to come.

Even Ellen's stomach turmoil had lessened, the sudden inner lurches, the rush for a bathroom. She still avoided the international news, but it was easier now. "Maybe I've acclimated," she said to Maisie one morning, who had no clear reply.

Only the fact of her coming grandchild could shock Ellen awake, every once in a while, a looming life change for her, for Jane. And for Mike. *Jane was having Michael Cacciarelli's baby.* It would wake her up at night, this tacit knowledge, confounding and new each time, and Ellen would press her hands against her eyes and shake her head, *no, no,* which did nothing to dispel all her disbelief and betrayal, not to mention the truth of the pregnancy itself. But every time she confronted Jane — *How did this happen?* When *did it happen*? — she was met by such a withering stay-out-of-it response from her daughter that all she could do was recede. Eventually, on the subject of Mike as father, they built up a wary silence. Luckily, she and Jane had plenty of practice with that habit.

Ellen always included a ten-minute break in every class that met for two hours or more; often students praised her for this in their course evaluations, but the truth was she needed it mostly for herself. A few minutes of quiet, a stroll around the halls, a drink of water. Then, recharged, she could continue the discussion or take a new direction as needed. As a younger teacher, she had considered any kind of pause a waste but now she knew enough to pace herself.

One drawback: occasionally a student tried to corner her for a one-on-one during the break, with "just a quick question" about a grade or an assignment, a wishy-washy substitute for making an actual appointment or just stopping by office hours (something they resolutely avoided). With a hidden sigh, one Thursday afternoon in October, Ellen sat next to Kim Watkins on a bench in the hall of the Helen C. White Building, going over the girl's essay on Jacques Lacan and "The Agency of the Letter in the Unconscious."

"It's not 'the unconscious is a language,' it's 'the unconscious is structured *like* a language.' " Ellen swiftly circled the offending phrase and wrote in the correction. "Do you remember what that means to Lacan's idea about no central point of reference, for the self?"

"Um . . ." Kim squinted at the page, trying to figure out whether she was being asked a real or rhetorical question.

Deep within Ellen's leather briefcase, at her feet, her phone rang. With one hand she reached in for it, then stopped. "About returning to the self, after a trauma, for example?" she prompted. Kim's work so far was dutiful but low on insight.

"That there's . . . no way back? After? Because of . . ."

Ellen nodded encouragingly. The phone continued to ring, but she withdrew her hand.

"Everything changing?"

"Kind of." Ellen wrote in the margins of the paper as she spoke. "Language exists as a system of relations — remember Saussure from last week? — so when Lacan talks about self-recognition as a system of relations . . . here, you begin to touch on this but it needs to be developed much more clearly . . . . what he's arguing is that there can't be any central point of reference for the self, and that's noticed most after some kind of change or —"

"Looking in the mirror!"

The phone stopped. Kim was so pleased with her connection that Ellen let it go. They all loved the mirror theory best — probably because of their own high levels of self-absorption — dropping it in even when not relevant.

She walked back to the classroom with Kim, who was visibly relieved their talk was over. "I *like* the psychoanalytic theories," she confided. "I mean, they do a good job at *some* things."

"Well, I'm glad," Ellen said, amused.

"I just don't always get what they have to do with, like, *literature.*" Luckily this was Kim's form of rhetorical question, and Ellen wouldn't have to answer. She too wondered why so many of these older theories needed to be part of the survey course, but her current M.O. was to go along and get along, so she tried not to engage in long defenses or explanations.

Students were still trickling in with soda cans, or texting; there was at least a minute or two left. Ellen found her phone at the bottom of her bag, but she didn't recognize the MISSED CALL number. NEW VOICE MAIL the screen flashed. Ellen almost put the phone away but decided to check, in case Jane needed something. She walked back out into the hall, listening, until the first crackly seconds of the recording stopped everything.

"Hold it up some? — can't hear her —"

Michael's voice. Barely audible, broken up by static and pauses. Other voices, sounds, in the background.

"You want to — okay, now or —"

This time the pause was so long Ellen thought the call was over. When his voice returned, closer now to the receiver, she folded forward into a shaking crouch at the front of the classroom.

"Hi, it's me. All right, just, it's not as bad as they've told you. I'm okay, I'm fine. We took a hit — I don't —" The sound broke off, unintelligible. Students were kneeling next to her, standing over her; she jerked away from them.

"One's all right, one's . . . well, I don't." Michael's voice slurred away. He was gone.

Clattering, then a new voice, clear and serious. "Mrs. Silverman. This is a message for Mrs. Ellen Silverman. Please stand by this number. You will receive a phone call at approximately" — pause, mumble — "hundred U.S. Central Standard Time. Please stand by for the phone call."

"What? What time?" she cried, into the phone. But the connection was broken. She couldn't make her fingers work, they were numb and shaky. "Call that back," she said, pushing the phone into the hands of the nearest student: Robbie Wenner. "That — that number. Call it back."

The class was silent. Robbie touched the screen a few times and listened briefly. "Okay, I think it's —"

"Give it to me." Ellen listened as hard as she could, but the call wouldn't go through.

What had he said, that male voice? Something at hundred o'clock, that military time. But what did it mean? When? Where was *Michael*?

"Professor, are you okay?"

She held out a hand, and Robbie helped her up from the floor. Ellen patted him briefly on the arm. She could barely see. The phone was a live thing in her palm. She walked out of the room and then back in.

"Can you — I'm sorry, but I . . ."

They nodded, worried, urging her out. "Go, it's okay." "Sure." "Hang in there, Professor!"

Ellen fled, without her books or briefcase or coat. She held only her phone, cupped in front of her.

Down the elevator, mercifully empty, across the lobby and out into the windy fall afternoon. Ellen went as fast as she dared without taking her eyes off the phone. She took the path up to Park and went past the Union, past Bascom Mall and the parking lots, across the grass and into the back entrance of Humanities.

The first classroom she tried was wrong; a startled instructor looked up from passing out photocopies. Ellen went up one floor — yes, this must be it. Without knocking she pulled open the door into a darkened lecture room.

Serena was midlecture, clicking through images on a digital screen. When she caught sight of Ellen she cut across the stage, still speaking to the class, flooded by the blinding projector light.

"What's wrong?" Serena said, covering the microphone clipped to her lapel.

"I think . . . I think Michael must be hurt." She said it in a rush, full of wonder.

Serena uncovered her mike. "Class dismissed. Check your e-mail later tonight."

Now they were in Serena's office, a narrow, high-ceilinged space with tall windows, staring at the phone on a table between them. Six replays of the message had convinced Serena that the man said "sixteen hundred" U.S. Central Standard Time, that is, 4:00 p.m. It was a few minutes after four, and Ellen was alternately numb and crazed.

A burst of adrenaline shot through her. "This is good, right? He was speaking to me. He's — This is good, right? They'll send him home. He'll come back to me, it'll be like nothing happened."

Serena tipped her head, *maybe.* Earlier, at her desk she had googled "military time," "sixteen hundred," "phone calls from Iraq" while Ellen huddled on a chair, and now they could only wait.

"I should call Wes and Jane. Or —"

"Let's get all the information first."

"He said, 'One's all right, one's . . .' " Ellen gripped the hem of her sweater. "What does it mean? One of them? One of his . . . friends? 'We took a hit.' "

"I don't know."

"It can't be that bad, if he called me himself! How could he possibly call me if . . . ?"

"Ellen."

"I can't believe I didn't pick up. He was right there. He was right on the phone and I let it ring. And now he could be dead."

"Stop."

"At least they're with him. Someone's with him, they're taking care of him."

"Yes. Now be calm. When they call, you need to —"

The phone rang. Area code 910. Ellen's breath drained away and she answered, staring straight ahead.

"Yes?"

"Is this Mrs. Ellen Silverman of Madison, Wisconsin?"

"Yes it is."

"Please verify your date of birth and address, ma'am?" She did. Serena slid over a pen and pad of paper.

"Mrs. Silverman, this is Rear Detachment Colonel Balton. I am calling about Lance Corporal Mic—"

"Is he alive?" Ellen shouted. "Is he all right? He just called, though I didn't get to talk to him. But he was talking! What happened? Can you put him on the phone?"

"Ma'am. Yes, he is alive. I'm calling from Camp Lejeune, in North Carolina. The information I have states that Lance Corporal Cacciarelli sustained injuries yesterday morning in the field and has been medevaced to Baghdad for evaluation and treatment. He —"

"Can I talk to someone there? In Iraq, I mean? I'm sorry, I know you have things set up this way but he literally just called here, and I —"

"Mrs. Silverman. I am your contact for all communications. The area medics have determined that once stable Lance Corporal Cacciarelli will be transported to Walter Reed via Ramstein base in Germany. As soon as I have the timeline I will call with his arrival date and your transportation options."

Ellen looked at Serena, lost and frightened. "You said, 'once stable.' What is his exact condition now?" Serena nodded, *good.*

Short pause on the other end. " 'Your

Marine has primary injuries in the following systems: skeletal, skin/muscle, cardio, vestibular, and neurological. The full extent of the injuries is not known at this time. Lance Corporal Cacciarelli is responding to treatment and will be transported as soon as stable.' "

Serena saw what this did to Ellen and scooted her chair as close as it would go. She touched her head to Ellen's, the phone between them, and wrote rapidly, copying down the information, sketching out questions.

"Is he going to live?" It was all she could do to manage this question. The man's careful response evaporated Ellen's strength.

"Ma'am, I can promise he is getting the absolute best care possible. Now I have some information and forms to send you about traveling to Walter Reed. Is there an e-mail address you have access to right now?"

Ellen sank back from the table. Serena took over the call, identifying herself and giving the needed address. She went on to ask several clarifying questions, ones Ellen herself should have thought to ask. Calm and taking notes, Serena pressed the man: *When will we know more? Who can we call after this, to follow up? How soon until she travels to Washington? How do we make arrangements to . . . ?*

There was a hot burble inside her, a nauseated melting. Ellen stood in a panic, groped around. There was no way she could make it to the restroom, even if she knew where it was in this building. She couldn't even talk. In the corner of the office, behind Serena's desk, she pulled down her pants and squatted over the plastic-lined garbage can, sweating and shaking as a toxic mess poured out of her.

Serena, still on the phone, found a box of tissues and pushed it near Ellen. Then she locked her office door and continued with her crisp, precise questions to the man on the other end. Ellen hung on to the side of the desk, half naked but without shame. There was only a basic primal relief. And, in the last moment before facing what she had to, gratitude for the luck of Serena, elegant and unflustered and bearing this moment with her: the terror, the shit, the unknown.

14

"Mom! Someone's at the door!"

Lacey stuck her head out of the shower. "What?" Couldn't Otis get off his butt and come tell her whatever he was yelling about from the living room? And why did anything need her attention now, during the ten minutes before the hot water inevitably conked out?

She wrapped herself in a towel and came out, giving Otis the stink-eye as the doorbell rang again. "You couldn't get off the couch and answer it?"

"I'm *reading.*"

"Uh-huh." A computer game catalog.

Cold October air leaked under the front door to swirl around Lacey's wet legs. "Yes?"

"Lacey?"

She checked the peephole. Shit. *Anne Mackay,* right there on the doorstep. "Hi! Oh, hi, Anne. You know, I just got out of the shower. Give me one —" No, she couldn't leave her out there in the cold. Lacey opened the door, cursing herself for not owning a robe. "Come on in."

"I am *so* sorry," Anne said. "I would have called but I was actually running errands in the neighborhood —"

"No, it's fine," Lacey insisted. "Just let me throw something on." She led Anne into the living room, swatted Otis's feet so that he would sit up and make room on the couch. Then she ran into the bedroom as Anne greeted Otis and began to ask cheerful questions to which he responded mostly in half phrases or single words. Lacey pulled on jeans and dug around for a clean top. She combed out her wet hair and tried to picture how messy her place looked through Anne's eyes. Not much she could do about it now; did she even have any decent snacks to offer?

Back in the living room, Otis was unwillingly showing his catalog to an enthusiastic Anne, whose trim slacks and crisp white blouse made Lacey want to rewind the entire morning. What was she doing here on a Saturday morning at 10:00 a.m.? What was she doing here at all?

"I was just going to make some coffee, I don't know if you —"

"That would be perfect!"

"Right. Okay. Otis, maybe you can help me in the kitchen for a sec?"

"Help you make coffee?" But he shuffled in after her.

Lacey pushed a brown paper bag at him. "Look," she whispered. "We need to clean up the place some. But without her noticing. So just go around and pick up stuff, all right?"

"What stuff?"

"Clothes, toys, anything lying around. But don't do it so it *looks* like you're cleaning up. Oh, crap. Is there still a pile of laundry on the chair out there?"

Otis shrugged. "Why are you freaking out? You never care about cleaning."

"She's like my boss, all right, so cut the 'tude and help your mom. Don't tell me we're out of milk." Luckily she did have a new can of Chock full o'Nuts, so Lacey was able to bring out two decent mugs with sugar and powdered creamer on the side.

Once they were settled, Anne launched into a long funny story that Lacey could only partially follow; it had to do with Anne having *thought* she signed her daughter Isabella up for basic ballet lessons but somehow mixed up the class descriptions and got her nine-year-old into an advanced toe-shoes and barre class, which the teacher seemed to think was perfectly okay even though Isabella was in way above her head, and started *arguing* with Anne when she tried to switch the girl into an easier lesson.

"So she's, you know, this classic hair-scraped-back ballet teacher, not an ounce of fat on her, and she just goes off on me in this ridiculous French accent! With all these little bun-heads standing around and snickering! I mean, I don't even think the woman *is* French. It's the role she feels she has to play. Anyway, she goes —" Here Anne put her nose up and let out a trill of Frenchy-sounding words interspersed with English.

"So I'm a little ticked, right? Bella is practically in tears and this woman is insisting she has to stay in this class if she wants to be in their program. Well, maybe it wasn't nice of me but I pull out *my* college French — I spent two semesters in Paris — and I go, *Eh bien, excusez-moi, mais je pense que je connais ma fille mieux que vous!*"

Lacey kept a smile on her face, wondering whether she was supposed to pretend she could tell the difference between fake and real French. The caffeine was helping her catch up; there were no errands that could possibly take Anne Mackay around here. So what was it? Maybe it had gotten around that Lacey had been to two different vet agencies for prepaid grocery and gas cards, and a box of freebies she'd been handed and had carried, mortified, to her car and into her house. The roll of toilet paper in the bathroom she prayed Anne wouldn't ask to use was from that very box. Maybe Anne was here to offer some kind of *we're-all-in-this-together* moral support or, worse, an actual loan.

Or what if one of the girls from the group had complained about her? Could you get fired from a job you hadn't even applied for? That someone had *asked* you to do? That didn't pay?

"We had a nice day with Bailey last weekend," she said, testing the waters. "Right, O? At the zoo?"

"Bailey . . ." Anne said, frowning, as if she'd never heard of the person Lacey had e-mailed her about several times, checking that she was saying the right thing to this frustrating girl who was threatening to walk away from all of it.

"When you made us walk around for hours in the cold and all the animals were, like, inside because it was freezing?" Otis said. But he gave her a teasing smile.

"When we took the tram out and back," Lacey countered, "and you got hot chocolate *and* an ice cream?" She'd worked overtime at the gym that Friday, since Otis was at a sleepover, but had rallied as she could, treating Bailey to lunch and a day at the Bronx Zoo she had planned because Anne's handbook suggested including wives, especially ones without children, into fun outings if they seemed depressed.

"I think she had a good time," Lacey said. "But maybe you want to call her? She told me she hasn't talked to Greg — that's her guy — in a while. And the thing is, she didn't seem that upset about it." Huddled in her jean jacket, Bailey had stared at the ibex and shrugged while Lacey kept on with gentle questions about how she was doing.

"Maybe it's not for everyone," she whispered while the long-horned goats shuffled around their feed pen.

"What isn't?" Lacey said. But Bailey hadn't answered, merely moved on to join Otis at the Great Bear Wilderness.

Anne clucked, nodding in concern, but in a general way. What Lacey didn't say was that Bailey most likely had something else going on, someone on the side. The girl was furtive in a new way, smiling to herself, as if Lacey wouldn't notice, was both more cheerful and more stressed. It wasn't hard to tell she was keeping a secret.

Takes one to know one. That old-school

comeback, one of the first Otis had learned to toss around. Lacey used to think it was funny. Now it pierced her. Who did she think she was, showing off her fake perfect life, la la la I'm taking my son to the zoo on two hours of sleep, to someone who was struggling with the same ugliness and failure that she was? Who was she trying to convince?

"Mm-hmm," Anne said, eyes wandering around the room.

"How are things for . . ." Lacey stalled out, forgetting if she'd ever known the name of Anne's husband.

"What? Oh, Roger's good. He says he got eight of our letters on one day, after about a month of nothing. I don't know. Everyone's using MotoMail now, but I guess I'm old-fashioned."

"MotoMail?"

"That service? Where you e-mail a letter and it gets printed out at base and then delivered? You should try it."

"Not very private, though." Lacey glanced at Otis. "Not for *those* kinds of letters, I guess." This kind of joke would be a no-brainer with Martine, but Anne just smiled blankly.

Martine. A pain winched through Lacey. Since that night at Chap's, they'd barely had contact. Next morning, Lacey had called and called, but Martine never picked up. Over the next week, Martine would only text her, not speak directly. *Whatever,* she wrote to Lacey, who was desperate to know if they were in a fight. *I don't want to be involved.* Also, *You're apologizing to ME?!* This after Lacey had left a message saying, *I'm sorry.* Finally: *I don't think so.* Lacey had texted: *Can we get together?*

She was sorry, no lie, a sorry excuse for a soldier's wife. But was she truly sorry for what she'd done with Jim? Sometimes. She thought about calling it off, again. But since they'd resumed, with late-night calls and one feverish lunch hour of kissing in her car, there was calm again in her mind, in her life. She could handle Otis and this crappy new sassing-back of his; she could hold her head up in the checkout line paying for food with charity. She subsisted on coffee and takeout and had cut the drinking down and was as sweet as she'd ever been to Eddie, when they talked.

Lacey wasn't dumb. She knew none of that mattered, balanced against the bad. She'd be honest with herself, if not with anyone else. She didn't make any promises to Jim, and he didn't ask for any. *But just say the word, Lace, and we'll make this right.*

You'll do right by him, when the time comes. We can make a good life out of this.

What she could use most of all was someone to talk to. And yeah, Martine was probably never going to be that person — Lacey bit down on the rush of sadness — but now she'd made sure of that, hadn't she?

A beat of silence stretched out uncomfortably, there in her living room. Martine wouldn't have, would she? No way. Lacey tried to find something to say, any topic, while she spun crazy circles of fear inside. She'd known, of course, that Mart would never tell Eddie — through her husband or any other connection. She would never risk distracting him, over there. It was a code they had never discussed, but Lacey felt it as strongly as if they'd signed a contract in blood. That didn't mean, though, that Martine wouldn't tell Anne.

Who now stood, smoothing her dark pants down slim legs, stepped uneasily around the pile of laundry to a side table where she picked up the digital photo frame Lacey had given Eddie for Christmas last year. Over the woman's shoulder, Lacey saw the images flick by in a tilted slide show: Otis at Orchard Beach, Eddie and Lacey swanked out for a night on the town, Lolo stiff on the front steps in City Island.

"I like this," Anne murmured. Her voice was subdued. Lacey felt a flash of terror.

"It's too bad, but we've got to get going."

Anne set down the frame and studied Lacey. She showed no sign of taking the hint.

"Otis has a game," Lacey said weakly. She prayed he wouldn't contradict her. "But it was really good to see you . . ." Why wasn't she leaving? Would she confront Lacey here, in her own home, in front of her son? Spit on her, curse her out?

From back in the kitchen, her cell rang. Lacey ignored it. "Maybe we can get together sometime, like for a drink — I mean, coffee or something?" She urged Anne toward the door with every inner impulse.

"Why don't you get that. I'll wait."

"That's okay. It's probably my mother-in-law. She's, you know." Lacey made a face. Her armpits pricked.

"Answer the phone, Lacey," Anne said quietly. Otis looked up from his catalog. Lacey went in a daze around the corner to where her phone was lilting on the counter under a pile of mail. Now she knew. Why Anne had come. In her hands, the phone had quieted but almost immediately began to ring again.

She walked slowly back to the living room,

where Anne still stood, her face now broken open by fear. "How bad?" Lacey said.

Anne shook her head, she didn't know.

Lacey nodded. He wasn't dead; that would have been casualty officers at the door. "Hello," she said into the phone. And pointed to Otis, then the back bedroom. Anne bent quickly to the boy and led him out of the room.

In the next few minutes, Lacey learned that Major Diaz had suffered injuries to face, chest, and limbs in a Humvee accident in Baghdad, was receiving treatment at base, expected to be medevaced by Huey within the hour. Routed through Landstuhl, transferred to Walter Reed within the next forty-eight to seventy-two hours. Current status of Major Diaz: stable, though unconscious.

Lacey stayed calm; she drew on all the times she'd heard wives go through this and knew enough not to press the RDO rep for details, answers, that weren't available yet. She didn't write anything down, but she made sure to confirm her eligibility for Travel and Transportation Orders — reimbursement for three people in terms of gas for the car, lodging and food expenses while at the hospital. Once that was cleared, there was nothing else to do except put down the phone and call Otis to her.

She held her baby, she kissed his head and told him Eddie got hurt but he would be okay. Everything was going to be okay. Otis began to cry. Anne knelt in front of the two of them, promising help, crying also. Only Lacey stayed cold and strong. A long list of immediate actions formed in her mind. The first, and hardest, would be to tell Lolo. And she'd need to borrow money from Anne for the trip to D.C.; she could pay her back as soon as the T&TO funds cleared. But for now she rocked Otis and let Anne go on about how she found out only an hour ago and came rushing over as soon as she heard, that Lacey would have every bit of support from the entire FRG, and that she'd get through this, she would, she had them all in her corner.

Inside, though, Lacey listened to a voice calmly explain why this had happened. *You did this to him,* it said. *You made it happen.*

I know, she thought, and braced for what was to come.

Part Two: Away

15

Walter Reed Army Medical Center,
Washington, D.C.
October 2005

By the middle of the fourth day Michael had been in surgical intensive care at Walter Reed, it had been determined that he would probably survive. Probably. Ellen didn't fully understand who had decided this, or by what measurement, since he was still in a coma — light coma, medically induced — and she couldn't see any change in the terrifying condition of his body, but the force of her gratitude kept her from asking too many questions. It was hard to form thoughts or questions here. Yellow curtains pressed closely around Michael and the other four men in their beds. Gowned personnel barreled in to work on him — Ellen roughly ushered aside — in new emergencies she couldn't detect. Digital shrieks came from monitors and equipment attached to unconscious Michael and the men behind the other curtains. The doctors didn't speak much to her, aside from brief updates that left her more confused than before. She got the sense they were hedging their bets.

Yet it wasn't the doctors or the nurses that infuriated Ellen — or the many ranks of half-medical, half-military staff with their jargon and hurry and protocol — it was herself. Why couldn't she find a way to make herself heard, here? Who was this woman, stammering and feeble, passively agreeing to procedures she wasn't clear on? Why did she let that one surgeon cut her off on the question of pain in a coma? She, who could lecture to the back of a two-hundred-seat auditorium without a microphone, who could summarize salient points and counterarguments at the drop of a hat, who was no stranger to the blazing self-importance of young men with highly advanced degrees?

("We can get back to saving the liver and spleen, *or* I can stand here discussing it with you." That's what the impatient surgeon had said when she fumbled around asking about pain levels. In response, what could anyone do but shut up and step aside?)

Mom, they constantly called her here. Too

busy with life-or-death to learn names. "Step outside now, Mom." "Okay, Mom, we're gonna need you to . . ." "Your signature here, Mom, and here . . ." Each time, the word burned her. *But I'm not,* she cried inwardly, afraid she was a fake or fraud, afraid this biological lack would doom his chances somehow. But she moved, she signed, she did what she was told.

It didn't matter what she said or thought, anyway. Michael would survive, or he wouldn't. Whole cadres of people worked around the clock to stabilize him, using every effort and technique at hand. There wasn't a lot of critical abstraction involved. Maybe this was the time that people who could, prayed.

If it hadn't been for the wife of the man in the bed two down from Michael, Ellen might have continued in this confounding meek state. But the woman she overheard yesterday afternoon — they all did, no one could escape that New York accent — was anything but meek.

"You gotta be kidding me! No. No way. Still on dialysis, still with the balloon pump, and . . . you see this? Look at that color. I showed you people that yesterday, *Jesus.* That's plasma leaking from the vent, so don't —"

Ellen had stayed rock-still, shocked and a little thrilled to hear this torrent unleash. From where she was huddled on a plastic chair, in the back corner of the SICU — Michael was having another round of lab draws — she couldn't see the owner of that indignant voice. It was coming from somewhere inside the warren of yellow-curtained rooms.

"No. He's not ready. No way in hell. Just 'cause you need the space doesn't mean I'm gonna roll over —"

A murmuring voice, or two, in response, trying to calm her.

"Maybe you think I don't know the rate of death for patients moved out of Intensive before fully stable. Or the risks of cranial swelling. They go crazy, they pull their own tubes out! I've read about it, you've seen it —"

At this, Ellen's attention sharpened. Michael was scheduled to be moved to one of the wards, later today or tonight. But . . . that was a good thing. She'd been told he was better, he was ready . . . wasn't he?

As the woman's voice rose higher, stubbornly refuting every doctor's murmur, Ellen suddenly realized there wasn't just insistence in her words, there was also logic.

And informed experience. And the distinct sense that there were more perspectives to consider aside from the hospital's authority.

Ellen bent forward on her chair and pressed her torso close to her thighs. She craned her head farther down and peered under the curtains. At first she could see nothing but the rolling wheels of crash carts and the movable levers of the hospital beds. Nurse and staff clogs, moving steadily around the beds and the equipment. Chair legs where other visitors sat by the beds, perhaps also listening in silence. And then Ellen found what she was looking for; she knew.

Facing two sets of sea green pant leg scrubs were shoes that could only be worn by the owner of that voice. Even in the requisite blue shoe covers that Ellen herself had on, the stacked heels were high on that pair of peeling black leather boots. Pushing herself upright, Ellen glanced down at herself: an oversize gown made of some material that was a cross between paper and cloth, plastic gloves that made her hands sweat and itch. Under that, plain slacks, a simple blouse, a light wool cardigan; and under the shoe covers, a pair of flats. Some variety of the same clothes she'd been wearing since she arrived in Washington, D.C., three days ago. A few more sets of each hung in the closet of her room in the Marriott in downtown Silver Spring. What would it be like to stride these floors with the height of such boots?

The woman's voice had gone quiet. Some agreement had been reached. But now Ellen was alight with urgency. She had to be back with Michael, but as soon as she could she went out into the bright spaceship-like hallways outside their room. Past the soiled linen containers, more crash carts, the hand sanitizer boxes affixed to each doorway. She caught a glimpse of tight jeans under a visitor gown and — yes, those black boots — disappearing into the women's restroom by the elevator banks.

"Excuse me," Ellen said, pushing in after her. "Why shouldn't he be moved? My — well, my son is scheduled for later today." Ellen glanced down the row of stalls — empty. "I heard you back in there, and . . . Please. Do you know something?"

The woman turned from the mirror to face Ellen. She was tall and strong, maybe forty. Her smeared black eye makeup looked like it hadn't been washed off in days. Ellen tried to smile, tried to regulate her ragged voice, aware that she was far away from a normal social interaction. Suddenly afraid this woman would simply shrug, and dismiss her.

"How long have they had him in the coma? He's got TBI, right?"

Ellen nearly swooned with relief. "It's been three days. The last X-ray showed less swelling, but —"

The woman narrowed her eyes. "Propofol, right?"

"Yes."

"All I know is, better to be in SICU when they bring them out to check function. It can get rough." The woman twisted her long blond hair up and tied it into a knot. There were faint pockmarks on her cheeks, and her lips were chapped.

Ellen swallowed. "Rough how?"

"Psychosis, delirium. They get wild, in a nightmare you can't calm them out of. And they can do a lot of damage before they're sedated again. They can't talk, they think they've been kidnapped and shit, they want to fight you. My girlfriend's husband vaulted out of bed, and this woman told me —"

"Are you a doctor?"

The woman turned and gave herself a rueful smile in the mirror. "No. So don't listen to me. Ask his care manager, or whatever they're called." She tousled her bangs this way and that, pushing them out of her eyes.

"I didn't mean —"

"It's fine." She went briskly into a stall. Ellen started to speak, but the rushing stream of urine covered up her words. When the woman came out a moment later, she looked surprised to see Ellen still waiting there.

"I apologize, that came out wrong. I can tell you know a lot about this, and I don't and . . . I just don't know if I'm getting the full picture — in there." Ellen nodded in the direction of their room, brimming with tears of shame. "I don't want to make any mistakes," she whispered. She leaned back against the cool concrete wall and watched the woman push up the elastic sleeves of her gown and wash her hands, slowly and thoroughly.

"What I did was, I got them to agree to Eddie staying one more night and one more day in SICU. Also that they have to bring him up from the coma, at least for the first time, here and not on the ward." They made eye contact in the mirror, ghosts in matching translucent gowns. "Try that. He'll get a better shot."

Thank you. Ellen breathed. And then she was gone in a rush of new energy, walk-racing as fast as she could down the achy-bright hallway to find Michael's doctors, already organizing persuasive sentences in her mind.

That was awkward. Lacey skidded getting out of the elevator, nearly went down flat on her ass in the front lobby, had to hop around to get those booties off. She'd been bitchy to that woman, the gray-haired teacher type, but it was just auto-bitch, spill-over from having to ream out the doctors. Not to mention the mother-in-law night-mare waiting for her back at Mologne, in the single room she, Lolo, and Otis were crammed into. Or the fact that Eddie had lost an eye, most of his sight, and an unclear but possibly significant amount of brain capacity. Or her negative bank account; the unpaid vacation days she was using up; those ten hours of sleep she'd gotten, in total, over the last three days.

Or the unmentionable, the unthinkable: Jim.

Wind whipped her hair and flattened her thin shirt against her body as Lacey crossed the hospital campus. Set far back from the entry gates on Georgia Avenue, the main building was called Heaton — an ugly 1970s-era behemoth, with tall thin pillars that appeared to struggle to hold up the flat bulk of the structure. You could use an underground tunnel to get places, but she went instead along the interior road that wound around the front of the Old Hospital. Why she liked to take this route, past the fountain and the great lawn and the white pillared grandeur of a building not even in medical use anymore, Lacey wasn't sure. Even though it pissed her off, this "ye olde hospital" false face of Walter Reed — the one in the postcard photos at the gift shop — she was drawn to it as well. In the short space between the shit she'd left in Eddie's room and the shit that awaited in her own, it was good to have these moments of walking, fast, in the wide silence of this open space.

Mologne House, where they were staying, had its own weirdness. As if insisting on its usefulness today, they'd slapped a giant futuristic awning on this red brick Georgian with a porthole up top. Automatic entry doors slid open and two guys in wheelchairs passed Lacey coming in. Her "hey guys" — tired but obligatory flirty tone — went unnoticed. More wheelchairs clustered at the bar in the lobby, where the implacable servers knew when to put a lid and straw on the beer glass, and how to cut someone off after the third time his mom called down to insist.

On the way up to the fifth floor Lacey bit her inner cheek: *Be cool, be cool, be cool.*

"And he just *look* at me like I'm not speaking *English* or like he's a robot man —" When Lacey unlocked the room and came in, Lolo continued her diatribe, merely shifting it in a different direction. " 'What are we suppose to do about a sink that won't drain?' He don't know. And the ones above us? All night long. All night, Lacey! With the music, it's going *bump bump bumpa bump* right above my head."

At Lolo's imitation of house music Otis snickered, on the couch with his DS player.

"Right above my *head,*" Lolo insisted, and her voice shook.

"At least your head was in a bed," Lacey muttered. Otis was sitting on what was her bed, a saggy pullout. She flopped down next to him and pulled him in for a hug, let him squirm away, back to the game.

"I'm hungry, Mom."

"You just had lunch! And did anyone pick me up something?"

"We didn't go."

Lacey stared at Lolo, who shrugged defensively. "It's crowded and the food is bad. Pasta, lasagna, every day. And the meat was off."

"It's subsidized! We can't —"

"You could smell it! Bad, like it was sitting out for hours. I'm not feeding him that. What I could cook is —"

"You can't cook here, Mom! There's nowhere to cook! And we can't keep ordering in, all right?" The army lodging advance was $150 a day, eaten up quickly by their room charge and service fees. Then she was supposed to get $64 a day for incidentals — i.e., food — but for some reason the actual disbursement turned out to be 80 percent of that (no one explained why), so that was $51.20, which was rounded down to $50 a day. Didn't go far for three people. Especially when one of them needed a drink or three at the end of the day so badly she started counting down the hours before noon.

"I will pay for my own lunch," Lolo announced stiffly. "And Otis too. But I will not allow my grandson to be sitting there with the hooligans, the way they drink and talk —"

"All *right,* Mom." Lacey dug her wallet out of her bag and handed over a twenty-dollar bill. Ten left. "Get something from the chicken place. But save me at least one piece."

Otis pumped his fist and reached for the phone. He let Lacey press her mouth and nose to his head while he ordered the food, and she breathed in his warm familiar boy-scent. Was he doing okay? He said so, but the one time they'd let him in to glimpse Eddie he'd gotten shaky and later pitched a fit about nothing, like a toddler. Also he was having bad dreams, Lacey could hear him moan and cry out from her couch in the next room. She'd go in to soothe him — Lolo in a deep sleep, flat on her back — and in the morning, he'd never remember, or admit to, what he'd been dreaming about. It's what brought her closest to crumbling, this fear of how damaged Otis might become, by everything here.

Which is why she was sending him home tomorrow. Lacey took a deep breath. "Mom?"

"It still won't drain. Come look at this. This is unacceptable!"

This is unacceptable? Still, she dragged herself into the small, worn bathroom. Lolo was gesturing wildly at a filmy inch of water in the sink, talking so fast Lacey could barely break in.

"So. You gotta take Otis back tomorrow. I'll keep the car, and they think there's a flight sometime in the afternoon." Greyhound, is actually what the social worker had said to Lacey, but fat chance of that.

Lolo was still going on about the sink. *"Mom."*

"Leave him here? In the coma, with all the tubes, with . . ." The older woman faded out but Lacey heard what she didn't say: *With YOU?*

"You'll come back, in a week. In a few days, once I figure things out."

"When he wakes up, he's going to want me."

"If he wakes up."

"How dare you!" Lolo threw up her arms in the small space, to push away what had been uttered. "If that's how you think, if that is your attitude —"

"Doesn't matter what kind of attitude anyone has! And if you think that, you might as well go home and pray from there, all right?"

"But —"

"I can't do all of it, I can't. Be over there all night with him, then back here to take care of you and Otis, and then go stand in line at Benefits, and then call insurance for hours, and then back to Eddie . . ."

"So I do the papers. Give me the phone numbers and —"

"Also, Otis can't miss any more school —"

"*Tst.* He's a smart boy. He won't —"

"You think it's good for him to be here?" Lacey hissed. "I don't want him just sitting around while we wait to see. Until we know which way it's going to go."

Lolo sucked in her breath. "Don't."

"All right." Lacey had more — the worst part was still to come, didn't she understand? — but she subsided. The toll had been taken: when she'd gone over to tell her mother-in-law about Eddie, Lolo had collapsed. And a couple of times over the next few days, she'd cried so hard she'd made herself faint. After that, Lolo's breakdowns weren't as severe, but they were still intense. Staff in ICU tried to restrict her to short visits with Eddie after the first time her sobs rocked the floor and she'd needed oxygen to recover. Now Lacey saw, in the harsh yellow bathroom light, the trauma's reverberations in Eddie's mother's elegant face. A broken capillary snaked red lightning across one eye; flaky patches of skin ran down her jawline; sunken skin fell down around her eyes.

Lacey reached to gently brush back a tuft of her hair, only for Lolo to lurch back in a scowl. "Let's do your face," Lacey said, not reacting. "After lunch, we'll go to him."

Her mother-in-law glanced into the mirror above the plugged sink. Lacey could see her struggling to be nice. The dark bags under her eyes did it. "Yes." She sighed. "He can't see me like this."

Lacey found her makeup bag, and neither woman commented on the words left hanging in the air. *He can't see me.*

That night Ellen and Lacey seemed to be the only ones in SICU, aside from the staff, aside from Eddie and Michael. Each was aware of the other, in soft movements or noises from the other side of the room, or the occasional rustle of a yellow curtain. The men's monitors beeped in low-toned counterpoint. Sometimes a nurse would speak to one of the women, and then she would step outside to the achingly bright hall, stretch her sore legs with a short walk, and then return to her chair.

Without discussing it, both Ellen and Lacey were determined to stay all night, this last night in SICU, in case through error someone tried to move either of the men. The three other soldiers that had been in this room were gone, moved up to one of the wards earlier today. Ellen felt the quiet emptiness of the room to be a reprieve, although she imagined the extra spaces, with their curtains drawn sharply back on the rods, would be filled with new arrivals at any hour. For now, though, there was a bit more peace.

Michael's unmoving face was swollen and streaked reddish white. Catheter lines came out of each of his shoulders, and one threaded into an artery on his right thigh. A thin tube ran up his nose and a larger one was taped to his mouth. He wore a blue gown, stained in yellow patches from the iodine, which bunched up around his waist.

As she did several times a day, Ellen reached in carefully among the tubes and gently, slowly, tugged the gown down so it covered his genitals. In doing so, she avoided looking at the giant swaddled lump of bandages wrapped around where his left foot had been. Gone. It was gone.

In the shattered hours when she first arrived here, when they wouldn't let her in for more than a few minutes at a time and the doctors said he might not live, the loss of one foot hardly registered with Ellen. It barely seemed to matter then. But tonight it was hard to face, the full contours of Michael's body — uneven, unbalanced. Slightly but sickeningly out of order, like a broken toy.

On the phone that first day with Jane and Wes, they had all cried about his foot.

"Does he know yet?" Jane had said.

"Mom, who's going to tell him?"

One of the doctors would, Ellen supposed, once he was awake. Or, maybe, she'd have to. She wiped her face; a person waved at her through the glass panel on the door. Outside, she was surprised to see one of the volunteers with a cart; it was late for them.

"Saw you in here," the man whispered, in his seventies maybe, smiling at Ellen and nearly bowing. "Take something, it will help pass the time." Uncomprehending at first, she followed his gesture to the cart, where rows of books were neatly arranged.

"Oh. Well . . ."

"Do you like mysteries?" The old man whispered. He had a large button pinned to his shirtfront: *I WORK FOR SMILES.* "How about . . ." He tapped his fingers lightly along the creased spines. "This one, and — oh yes, this one. And one more. Here." Ellen turned over the worn books he had put into her hands. *Sin and a White Sand Beach. Lady Merley's Secret.* And, improbably, *Northanger Abbey.* She felt a slight flush of indignation on poor Jane Austen's behalf, lumped together with the bodice rippers. Ellen handed the books right back; she couldn't imagine reading here, now. But the little old man was persistent, pulling out another choice. "I'll find you something,

now let me see — Oh. No. Not this."
Vaguely curious at what he dismissed, Ellen glanced at the book he had quickly reshelved: red hardcover, no dust jacket.

"May I see that?" Astonished, she reached for the book. Yes, it was: *A Son at the Front* by Edith Wharton. Ellen laughed shortly. The chances of this particular book — one of Wharton's least-known, worst-selling novels, published at a time when the public was eager to be rid of reminders of the Great War, rarely in print — appearing with these dusty hospital giveaways, to her of all people . . . it was a surreal shot-in-a-million. Though of course it made sense. Down the line someone made a well-intentioned mistake, thought from the title it might be rousing, inspiring, to a parent trapped in today's version of war's hell. Promptly discarded.

"I'll keep this. Thank you." Ellen brushed off the old man's entreaties to try something else, something lighter. When he left at last, she pushed the book away in her bag. She wouldn't read it, though. Reading itself was like a country she'd left, oceans away.

Meanwhile, on the other side of their shared SICU room, Lacey tried to pray. Eddie would expect it, everyone would expect it, and hadn't she done it so many times before, in church and at every FRG meeting? Whenever bad news came about other women's husbands? Well, now it was her turn, so she bent her head and mouthed the words printed on the tiny booklet:

Watch, O Lord, with those who wake, or watch, or weep tonight, and give your angels charge over those who sleep. Tend your sick ones, O Lord Christ. Rest your weary ones. Bless your dying ones. Soothe your suffering ones. Pity your afflicted ones. Shield your joyous ones. And for all your love's sake. Amen.

She crossed herself and put the booklet back into its plastic bag with the rosary, under no illusions that Jesus or God or any higher power would listen to what she had to say. Because even if she'd had no contact with Jim after sending him one text — *Eddie hurt bad. Going to D.C. Don't call* — he was still in her mind. Somehow, bits and pieces of remembered happiness could float to Lacey's awareness, during odd moments, like losing a dollar in a vending machine, or walking in the dark back to Mologne for a few hours' sleep. What he'd say. His sideways smile. The way they just fit each other. Amid fear and chaos a small fierceness inside Lacey would sometimes assert: *So I did find it, the real thing.*

But. She touched Eddie's warm wrist, her own eyes hot and dry. "Ah, babe," Lacey whispered. "You deserve better, that is for fucking sure." His head was almost entirely bandaged, with a steel halo fitted into the top of his skull after the craniotomy. White cotton was packed into the left eye socket, the one he'd lost immediately. The right eye was covered by what looked like a pink plastic soap dish. Three little stuffed animals, two bears and one kitty, were tucked in next to Eddie under his PIC lines and pressed against the bed bars. One held a sign that read ARMY TOUGH. Lacey plucked them out and tossed them on the radiator. She had no idea where these came from; every time she turned her damn back someone put another in his bed.

There was a chance his right eye could be saved. That there would be some amount of sight coaxed back by multiple operations after he was stable. *If* he became stable, off the vents and out of the coma. One of the residents had told her as much, probably just to get Lacey to stop haranguing him with what she knew. Then he tried to walk it back; most likely the eye would never function normally, and even if Eddie had some sight later, it might be just flashes or pinpricks of light, nothing usable. For all intents and purposes, he was blind. And she should resign herself to that, prepare for it, amid all the other injuries he had sustained.

"Yeah, okay," Lacey had said, cutting off the standard cautions. She knew they didn't want to raise patients' hopes — and especially not the families' hopes. But she couldn't help it. If Eddie could just see a little . . . if he'd only get a tiny bit of vision, enough to walk around or avoid big obstacles or handle stairs . . .

Then what? Lacey couldn't shake this secret inner wish. Did she think she'd get a pass on her sins, if Eddie could see? Would that make up for how wronged he'd been? It was stupid, but that didn't matter, of course. *If only, if only,* she found herself thinking, whenever she caught sight of the pink soap dish.

There was no such thing as time in the SICU. Work continued around the clock, and there were few windows and no fresh air. Nor was there any change in lighting — fluorescent tubes ran the length of each ceiling, perpetually on, surgical spotlights rolled from room to room, and even the automatic glare of the bathroom fixtures whirred to life each time the door was opened, day or night. The only sign Ellen and Lacey had that it was 3:00 or 4:00 a.m. was the unfamiliar faces of the nurses and staff on shift. Every few hours they ate some version of the same foods — vending machine granola bars, instant cups of soup, endless coffee — and the wired bodily exhaustion was constant, not noticeably different now from the middle of the day.

Even the arrival of a young aide to bathe and change Michael in the predawn, the one who kindly offered his hand to help Ellen struggle up, stiff and slow, from the chair at his side — even that seemed right on time, appropriate in this never-ending loop of awakeness.

In this world only Michael was asleep. But not for much longer. She'd been told he would be brought out of the coma soon — 6:00 or 7:00 a.m. — and kept on observation in SICU for several hours, before being moved, if all went well, to one of the wards. So this was it, Ellen thought. She had to leave the room, and she did, refusing to allow herself to look back, although dread — *What if he . . . ? What if this is the last . . . ?* — sloshed through each unsteady step she took down the hallway.

The waiting room, painfully bright with flowery vinyl-covered furniture, had magazines and a coffee machine. Ellen wanted neither. She sat, hands empty, and only then noticed her in the room's opposite corner — the woman who'd told her to keep Michael in SICU, the woman with the boots (kicked off now, her bare feet propped up on a coffee table). She was texting, Ellen noticed, and when she glanced up Ellen called across the room, "Are you allowed to do that?"

"What?"

"All the signs out in the hall — no cell phones on this floor."

"So?" Lacey kept scrolling her messages — Anne, Bailey, a couple work friends, Felicia, several other FRG women. She only ever wrote to Otis but read them all. Thank God Lolo barely knew how to use her cell phone.

"So maybe it causes problems with the machines. Interferes with the signal, like on an airplane."

At this, Lacey looked up and studied the woman. Back straight, short simple hairstyle, quiet but with a definite no-bullshit aura. *Teacher for sure,* she thought. *Must be her son in there.* "It doesn't work like that. The only reason they have those signs is so we're not all zoned out by talking on the phone, clogging up the hallways and getting in the way. Ordering pizza."

"Oh."

"That was a joke. The pizza."

"Yes, I know."

Lacey went back to texting and Ellen pulled out her own phone and turned it on. Listening to all her new messages — Serena, Wes, Paul, Serena again — took some time, so she sneaked looks at the woman across the room. Slumped down on her couch, chin on chest, blond hair pulled up in a messy bun revealing darker roots underneath. Every few minutes she took a sip from a giant soda cup, or chewed its straw. Her face, though haggard and not quite clean, was intelligent . . . *Must be her eyes,* Ellen thought. They were a rich aquamarine. Stunning, actually.

But the last message drew Ellen's immediate attention. Jane, pissed off. "I know you said to wait, but that's not going to happen. That's ridiculous, Mom. I need to see him. I gotta talk to him, as soon as he's awake. Wes says . . . whatever. So I got a flight —" Ellen raised her hand and dropped it into her lap. Arriving at National at the end of the week, late at night apparently. No mention of where she'd be staying or who would be picking her up. Ellen herself, obviously. She hung up and thrust the phone back into her bag with a little more force than needed, causing Lacey to look over.

"Everything okay?"

"Yes. No, not really."

"That's the truth."

"It's just — My daughter's coming. In a few days. Without asking, without even checking if it's the right time for him to have people here . . . She has no idea what it's like here. I told them, just wait until he's more stable, when we know if . . . You know."

Lacey nodded. She knew.

"This is just like her. Swoop in, no concern for what other people need." *No concern for* me, Ellen thought. She should stop talking but once she'd started it just felt so good to let it out. "Seeing him like this . . . why? What does she think it will accomplish? Then I'll be taking care of her, and I really don't have the energy. Not to mention, she probably shouldn't be traveling all around anyway."

"Is she at school or something?"

Ellen let out a big sigh and shook her head. "Do you have kids?" she asked, trying to regain polite conventions.

"A twelve-year-old. My son, Otis. It's not his son." Lacey tilted her head back in the direction of the men's room. *Why did I say that?* "We've only been married for a few years. But he was always a career army guy, so — 'what did you expect,' right? Happens on my watch."

"No one expects this."

"I expected worse. The other thing. I didn't think too much about this happening, about how it would go."

"Yes," Ellen exclaimed. "Me too!" She leaned forward. "When I first heard, I thought . . . I had this feeling that it was my fault, that I'd caused it."

"How could you have caused it?" Lacey's heart thumped. She'd felt, of course, the exact same thing.

"I realized that I'd spent so much time being afraid that he'd get — you know — that I didn't worry enough about this. About just getting injured. 'Just.' " At this, both grunted. "Magical thinking, I think it's called."

"What's so freaking magical about it? If it was magic, we'd hardly be *here.*"

"Well, I meant — never mind."

"I know what you're saying. It's like you forgot to picture all this" — Lacey swirled a hand at the flowered plastic chairs, the hallway, SICU, all of Walter Reed itself — "and so it happened. And you're here."

Ellen sat back. Yes. That was it exactly. The experience of being understood, to have someone speak aloud the deep inchoate belief so troubling that she hadn't found words for it herself, rushed through her like a warm, salty ocean. Overcome by relief, she felt the sudden shakiness of having carried this burden so long.

The two women smiled at each other.

"I'm Lacey."

"Ellen."

"How did it happen to him. IED?"

Ellen nodded. Yes, she needed to focus. "A grenade, they told me. Michael was on a patrol, in Anbar somewhere, I don't know exactly —" Lacey leaned forward. "He'd been outside a building, with his partner. And then — someone threw it into the road where they stood."

"Ah, shit. And the other guy . . . ?"

"He wasn't hurt badly. So he was able to get Michael to safety, before he —" Before he could bleed out. Ellen heard herself speak the facts, but it felt as if they were someone else's words. "What about yours?" She made herself ask, because this must be what one did.

"Still don't know much. His Humvee was in some kind of explosion." It made Lacey jittery, how little they were telling her. She cut off Ellen's polite sympathy. "What time did they tell you they'd bring him up?

Morning sometime?"

"Yes. I tried to get her to be more specific, but it was that head nurse at the desk, Ms. Jameson, and —"

"God, what a cunt."

Ellen laughed. "Sometimes, yes. Did you hear the way she yelled at that poor woman who pressed the wrong call button? The one whose husband, both his hands were —"

"*Yeah,* I heard her." Lacey thunked down her soda cup. "She told me I was going through too many gowns and if I wanted more spit cups to *ask* for them, not help myself from the cart. As if I'm not saving them time and effort. I've worked with bitches like that. Ones with the stick so far up their . . ."

"I know," Ellen said. She was shivering with exhaustion.

"Like the details outweigh the big picture." Now Lacey was striding back and forth. "Like she wins if she goes home at night having policed every tiny breach of procedure. Goes home solo to her sad cats in her sad one-bedroom —"

"Well —"

"Eats a low-cal dinner, and then gives herself an enema. For fun. What's wrong?"

Ellen had slipped sideways on the vinyl love seat, and was trying to find a way to rest her head on her arm that wasn't so painful. "I'm so — I can't sleep but I just can't be . . . All these lights, and it's so cold . . ."

Lacey came over and sat in the adjoining couch. "Where are you staying? Mologne?"

"No — no, at the Marriott."

"What?"

"The one in Silver Spring."

"You've been there the whole time?" How rich was she?

Ellen sighed. "I'll have to figure something else out. With Jane coming, for who knows how long . . . and also it's just too much, all the highway intersections. I hate that drive, especially at night."

"You should try the Mologne House. Better commute. Especially once they move him to Prosthetics." Lacey stopped herself from saying *and it's real nice.* Who knew what "nice" meant to someone with Marriott tastes?

"Oh, but I . . ." *But I won't be here* that *long,* is what Ellen almost said, confused. But she'd have to be here, somehow — wouldn't she? Who else? She raised her head an inch — it did feel better, lying down. "Is that where you are, the Mologne House?"

"For now," Lacey said darkly. The truth was, she couldn't afford it. Yes, it was covered, but being reimbursed was not the same as taken care of. She already owed one week back, and even if she moved to a smaller room now that Lolo and Otis went home — which, frankly, she didn't have the energy for — there was no way. The social worker had mentioned something ominous about Building 18, a lower-cost option farther back in the hospital campus. Lacey knew nothing more except she was certainly headed for a downgrade.

Ellen pushed herself back upright, head pounding. She felt nauseated.

"You don't look good. You should take a nap."

"I can't! What if they come and —"

"So, set an alarm. You've got your phone." Lacey had been considering the same thing for herself, in fact.

But Ellen looked so out of it, greenish around the mouth and silvery hair smooshed up on one side, that Lacey didn't push it. "All right. We'll take shifts. You go first, and I'll wake you up in thirty, forty-five max."

"You don't have to do that." Voice wobbly. "I can't —"

"Ellen. I won't let them move him. I'll get you up, if they come."

The woman's blue eyes were steady,

determined. Ellen lay down again, grateful. She could trust a person with eyes like that. A soft poof of fabric fell down over her head; Lacey's jacket.

"For a pillow. Or use it to block the light. I've got a sweatshirt back in the room," Lacey said.

"Thank you. Just for a few minutes." The jacket's mingled scents: perfume, tobacco, and a faint, not-unpleasant body odor. Ellen let her eyes swoon closed. "Your turn next," she murmured, as she heard the door open.

"My turn next," Lacey agreed. Back down the hallway that led to Eddie, that led to whatever might come next.

16

The process of coming up was terrifying for both women.

As the hold of the medicine dropped away from Michael, he began to snort and huff like an animal, eyes wild beneath his closed lids. *Talk to him,* Ellen was commanded, and so she did — her own strung-out, blurted sentences sounding inane in those tense moments, with the yellow curtains pressing in. But obviously what she said meant little, so she went on and on, describing the hospital and the windy autumn day outside (oh, Ellen — the weather?) and all the e-mails she was receiving, every day, from his friends, and all the calls from Wes and Jane, and how he was going to be fine, just fine, and she was here with him — it was Ellen, did he know that? — and yes, it would feel scary but it was okay, he was okay, and —

Then Michael roared up and knocked a

monitor over. Aides jumped in quickly, shoving Ellen aside. She watched him thrash, she shouted, she almost went to her knees when a thin spurt of blood whipped across the room — he had ripped the line out of a shoulder — and she wept, creeping forward and then cringing back. Still, when she could she kept talking, saying anything and everything, in hopes that her voice might find its way into his wild bucking. The doctor adjusted the drip, the aides held him down, and finally Michael opened his eyes.

Ellen made herself come into his view, *it's okay, it's okay, I'm here.* He hissed and babbled, nothing intelligible, and he stared at her as if he'd never seen her before. Without a shred of recognition. And then he bared his teeth and howled, a scream that made her cry out.

"It's not working! Put him back under," she begged.

"It'll take a little while," the doctor grunted while he and the aides struggled to restrain Michael. He pounded his legs against the bed, his wrapped-up stump. "It's all right."

It was anything but all right. But after several minutes, they gave him some of another kind of sedative and his dumb fury died away.

It was a kind of progress, they explained to Ellen later. His vitals were functioning, and the dementia would lessen the more he became used to being awake. It could take some time, she was warned. They'd try again, and again, and soon he'd adjust.

That night back in the hotel Ellen was so wrung out she climbed into bed in her clothes. Unable to sleep, she made herself write down a few important pieces of information in the notebook that she'd begun a few days earlier, to keep track of the constant medicines and procedures. "Disinhibited" is what the doctor had called Michael's thrashing. "Emotionally labile." She copied these terms down, amazed by a world where such cool phrases were used to describe the purely animal pain and fear rocketing through Michael's every nerve as he was pinned down in a strange bed by three men.

And what about me? Ellen thought. Why did my voice do nothing to calm him? His bulging eyes, his whole body shaking. She felt as if he might bite her, or put his hands around her neck. Curled up under the covers, unwashed and hungry, Ellen trembled. Why should he be calmed? What was she to him? Their connection was so precarious, so short-lived. Compared to the trauma of war and injury, wasn't it likely that everything about them had been obliterated? And did that mean she was even more useless here than she felt? Ellen pictured Lacey calmly and competently handling her husband's awakening — how reassured he'd be to find her there, to hear her familiar voice, their years of marriage stabilizing him even in the confusion. A thousand previous memories rushing in to align him with reality. With life.

But she could do this. Mike needed her; she'd saved him before, hadn't she? No, her letters hadn't worked — she shook her head in bed, disgusted — all those pages, all that reading: worthless. All right, but she could do better. It might be a technicality that brought her to Walter Reed, mere guardian in a world of real moms, but that didn't mean she couldn't bring him back, couldn't find their connection again. She'd find a way.

To get herself to sleep, Ellen clung to a memory: the two of them, on the couch in the basement. The TV on mute, a late-night talk show. Mike had two weeks to make up a dozen incomplete assignments — including a ten-page research essay — in order for him to graduate high school. Ellen, in her bathrobe, knew a dire situation when she saw one, and sorted quickly through a pile of half-written reports and mediocre paperbacks — dog-eared and underlined for decades. *Death = theme. Green light = symbolism!! Danny R sux cox.* "This first," she said. "No, this one. If you read two chapters I'll tell you about the rest. No, Wikipedia doesn't count for a source. Because I say it doesn't. Now look, for the research essay you'll want to set it up like —" She took his pen and swiftly sketched out an outline, muttering about remedial teachers who couldn't bother to write up clear directions or a rubric, when she felt his gaze on her. "What?"

"Nothing," Mike had said. Sheepish, grateful.

Ellen went back to writing. "Don't know what I would have done," he said then, quietly, almost to himself.

Eddie Diaz came up smoothly and without incident. Lacey gripped the rosary in one hand and his in another, but no bad dreams shook him, no terror swept through his placid body. In fact, it was so easy that the attending congratulated herself, in pointed response to Lacey's insistence that the procedure be done in SICU.

Eddie slowly swung his head back and forth against the raised back of the bed. Lacey spoke to him, but he didn't seem interested in what she was saying. Instead, he pursed his mouth and flickered his tongue in and out, searching. She held the straw to his lips, ignoring the doctor's *not too much at first* — and felt him pull deep, until the ice rattled at the bottom of the Styrofoam cup. The doctor began to say something, but was cut short by what happened next.

Eddie laughed. He set his head lightly back on the bed and laughed a long, fluty trill. Lacey dropped his cup and ice slid around on the floor. "Ed, Ed," she murmured. "It's okay."

But her husband let out a long moaning sigh that turned into another laugh. A laugh she'd never heard from him before. Light and breathy, carefree.

One of the aides in the room chuckled until Lacey shut him up with a look.

"It's just the Versed," the doctor said. She flipped back a few pages on his chart. "It'll sometimes cause —"

"I know what Versed does," Lacey hissed. "And he's not on it."

"He's not? Oh, right. Well, there's bound to be some emotional disinhib—"

"Hi," Eddie said softly. "Hi, hi."

"Hi, hon," Lacey said, leaning across him on the bed. "You're in Walter Reed. You can't see because there was an accident, in the Humvee. But you're okay, and all the guys who were in there with you are okay —" His men, she knew, would be his top concern.

"Hi, hi, hiiiiiii . . ." Eddie giggled. He reached up to gently pat the contours of the covered eye.

"Captain Diaz," the doctor said loudly. "I'm Dr. Renard. We are protecting your eye with a shield. Can you tell me where you are? Do you know why you're here?"

"Of course he can't," Lacey snapped. "He's been out for a week. Ask him —"

"Here, I'm here," Eddie began, in nearly a whisper. With a tiny smile flickering. "Ha. Aha ha." He turned his blind face her way, sweetly. Lacey edged back, throat full of nausea. The aide went *awww.* Eddie made a smoochie face and she almost bolted. But he just wanted water again, so she filled another cup and put the straw to his lips. After he drank, he swooned backward: asleep again?

Dr. Renard turned to one of the nurses. "Do you have the rotation schedule? For pressure wounds?" She went on to discuss raising his heels for bedsore prevention, and gave orders about his drip and TPN feed.

All the while Lacey fought her dismay. And — yes — her disgust. Who *was* this simpering stranger? With the cutesy-pie voice and the tee-hees? Where was Eddie? Twenty minutes later, he was still giggling as if he had a secret, while drifting in and out of consciousness.

She followed Renard into the hall. "What's that about?" Lacey demanded. "He's not like that. Why is he *laughing,* for God's sake?"

"I know it's disconcerting. But you have to give it time. We don't know the extent of the closed-head injury, and until —"

"Is it permanent?"

Renard studied Lacey. "If it is, it's not the worst. Sometimes a personality shift can go the other way. They become angry all the time, flying off the handle at whatever. Or there can be constant crying . . ."

Lacey gaped at this bitch. Who quickly covered her ass. "But that's jumping the gun by quite a bit. We're set to do a CAT scan as soon as Ocular gives the okay. Most likely, it's a temporary reaction to one of the meds, and will wear off." Then she hurried away.

For a long time Lacey lingered outside in

the hall. Eddie was scheduled to be moved to Ward 58 tomorrow morning; Ellen's Michael would be in 57 of course — everyone knew about 57, infamous from the sheer numbers of lost limbs from the war. Lacey found herself glad to know that Ellen would be nearby. The professor — she'd been right about that! — had a steeliness that was impressive. She wasn't some scared bunny, like some of the other moms . . . or one of those who raised loud and confused complaints to anyone who would listen. Plus, Lacey could use a friend here.

No, she couldn't call Anne or the other girls back; most of those calls had been trickling away in any case as the days went on. They couldn't understand. Lacey herself wouldn't have understood, before this, what it was like here. The FRG women who had meant everything to her — all seemed a long way away now.

She took out her phone and stared at it. Too early to call Otis — he wouldn't be home from school until five. She'd already spoken to her mother-in-law twice today, anyway, for updates on Eddie and to answer the million questions Lolo had about Lacey's apartment, where she was staying with Otis: *Was this all the towels Lacey had? Why no DustBuster, that vacuum canister was much too heavy? How to work the TV remote (again)? I don't like this coffeepot, I put it out for the trashman.*

But here was yet another message from Lolo; as Lacey listened, prepared to be annoyed, she grew very still instead. Could she possibly be hearing this right? "— And also, that man just came for the bills. He said you said it's okay, so I gave him the envelopes and those papers by the phone. Also he left an envelope with the money, he says for the groceries? Must be from the army. So I already put the order to Big Apple but they don't deliver until tonight. Otis needs a new set of uniforms and you need to call me back right away because of his homeworks, I don't know this math and he says he don't have to —"

Lacey strode away from Eddie's room, hands shaking as she pressed buttons on the phone. Jim answered right away and she didn't wait. "What are you doing? What. You go to my *house*? You talked to his *mom*? What the *fuck*?"

A long breath exhale. "I didn't do it to get in your way. You didn't have to call me or anything. I just wanted to help out. As a friend."

"Help out by what? Hanging around my mother-in-law?" A man in BDUs turned the corner and gave Lacey a crisp nod; she tried to bring her voice down. "Getting her all confused? And what is this — about papers, something you took?"

"Nothing! A couple utility bills and I took care of them, okay? Also a few other things. Those ones that went to collections, Lace — that's not good."

"That's not your business! I don't need any help! Just stay out of it, all right?"

"Okay. Okay."

She held the phone tightly so that she wouldn't cry. "You gave her money?"

"Just a few bucks. For Otis, for whatever. I won't do it again. If you say. Lacey. Hey, Lace."

"What?"

"Don't hang up. I won't call you, I won't do anything more . . . Just don't go yet."

She touched a corner of the framed poster on the wall: *Family. Community. Country. Together we can save lives! Wounded Warriors* ARE *America.* This was bad. Every second she stayed on this call her resolve buckled. How to fight it, the spreading belief that this was a good man? And that this love mattered, somehow, even amid it all?

"He's not right, Jim," she whispered. "I could tell right off the bat. He's awake but . . . I think something's broken in there, even if they can't see it. More than the eyes, I mean."

"Oh, Christ. That's messed up. And it's gotta be so hard on you."

"Yeah. Well. Like it should be."

Long sigh, *shhhhh.* "It doesn't work like that. Even if we hadn't been . . . what we were, this still would've happened."

So if she tried to be a good wife now, it didn't count? It wouldn't make Eddie better? His eye, though . . . there was still a chance. *Just a little light,* Lacey thought. *Let him have that. Give me that much.*

"Tell me something about your girls," she said. "Are they liking school? Did Jenny get braces on?"

"Ah, she cut a deal with her mom. Braces can wait until after cheering season, if she keeps a B average. Not how I would've done it, but who am I? Just the guy who pays for braces."

"What about the other ones?" Lacey glanced down the hall. No one came in or out of Eddie's room, but she knew she'd have to go back there soon. A memory of Eddie's soft, wandering laughter pierced her, and she recoiled. Give her anything else: blood spurting, vomit, protruding bone. But that laugh . . .

So she held back for a few more minutes.

She traced the letters on *Wounded Warriors* and listened to Jim tell her about his daughters, his voice bright with love for them. She didn't thank him for the money, or for paying her bills. They didn't mention it again. His stories about home, about the restaurant and what she was missing in New York, let her hang there a little longer, suspended between two worlds, until it was time to go back down the SICU hall.

17

Away from the SICU, there was limited space for privacy. The fifth floor was ringed with wards around the building, two to each side. Inside that were the nurses' stations and waiting rooms; behind that layer, in the innermost part of the floor, were closed-door offices Ellen was never invited into. Supply closets, equipment rooms, and janitor services were tucked into each hallway's corner. Luckily Ward 57, the amputee ward, where Michael had been moved yesterday into one half of a double room, was next to an interior courtyard called the Healing Garden. Ellen had only noticed it in passing, in the business of Michael getting settled into this new space, and she was surprised when Dr. Grant suggested they go in there to talk over what he needed to explain to her.

"Pretend we're actually outside," he said, in apology. The young doctor, Ellen's favorite so far on Michael's team, dragged a metal chair over with an echoing scrape and held the back while she sat. Milky light from the ceiling's plastic skylight panes fell down over the two of them, tucked in a corner of the stone-paved garden between two giant potted ferns. He held a folder on one knee — the business at hand — but didn't open it yet.

"I'm sure you have questions. I'll answer everything I can about the process for his leg, and then we'll make sure Neuro gets back to you on anything related to the TBI."

Ellen straightened and opened her own notebook. She might be new, but she understood how rare this one-on-one moment was with the head of a surgical team. "One of the other doctors was telling me Michael needs another cleaning-out surgery?"

"Debridement, we call it. Yes. There are bits of foreign matter, dirt, and shrapnel still in Michael's tissues and we go in to clean it out, essentially. It's how we stay on top of any infection that might arise, but then again we don't want to cut too much or damage the remaining tissue any more than we have to at one time, so we go in periodically, not all at once. He's had three of these, and will need maybe, I'm thinking, two more, unless . . . Well, that's what we can discuss." Dr. Grant tapped his folder. He was in his middle thirties, Ellen guessed, with a boyish flip of hair that reminded her of Wes.

"An infection that starts in the, in the stump" — that word — "is dangerous because . . ."

"Even if infection originates there, it could spread rapidly — inflammation, fever, pus — up the rest of his leg, threatening major arteries in the thigh. And of course then there is the fear of other body systems becoming compromised, when they're already overstressed from the trauma. Neural, muscular, or cardio."

"But he's on antibiotics, just in case." Since the fury and trauma of his coming out of the coma, Michael had been in a twilight state for the past day and a half. He would flutter his eyes open, and could take sips of fluid. He made gestures and guttural sounds, but no words. Mostly, he slept, flushed and quivering.

"Yes. And debriding the wound site does let us get inside the damaged area to be extra sure nothing has started to devolve."

"But you don't think that's enough. In the long term."

Dr. Grant smiled at her. "No, I don't. My opinion at this point is that we need to amputate farther up his leg. I'm sorry. I know that's not easy to hear."

Ellen was struggling under the kindness of his gaze; she almost couldn't work through the meaning of the words because of how self-conscious she was about her horror. "But — cut off more of his leg? Isn't that — isn't that the opposite of what we want?" Stupid, irrelevant, but exactly what came to mind.

"I know. But there are —"

"You said his injury was a good one! Because it was so far down, and that having his knee still would mean he'd have —"

"I don't believe I ever —"

"Well, someone did." Ellen tried to rein in her voice, bouncing off the cold stones of the Healing Garden.

Dr. Grant took a deep breath. "I wanted to save his knee, yes." Past tense. "Transtibial prostheses give a much more normal movement than an above-the-knee amputation. But here's what I wanted to show you." He took a sheet of paper out and put it on top of the folder. A diagram of a leg in profile, unmarked. Dr. Grant moved his chair closer to Ellen's so she could see; with his blue-inked pen, he drew a line across the diagram, a few inches up from the ankle. "This is where Michael is now. But because of the way his injury occurred, the impact from the explosion went upward, like this —" Sharp lines pushed up, the pen making a *scritch* noise against the paper. "And the force drove against the front of his knee, which caused it to degrade."

"This prefix," Ellen said, studying the sheet, "is starting to wear on me. Debride, devolve, degrade . . ."

"So while Michael technically retained his knee, the MRIs show bad damage to its structural integrity."

"Won't it heal? Eventually?"

"Maybe, over a long period of time, with rehab, and luck. But what might happen, what I think is more likely, is the combined pressure of supporting his body weight on a prosthesis, on a damaged knee, would hamper his walking and standing to a point where . . . well, where he might have trouble walking much at all."

Ellen looked away. In the middle of the Healing Garden was a rectangular pond. A young woman with a baby strapped to her chest squatted low to the pool, pointing into it. The baby kicked its feet against her body and sucked on the fabric sling.

"If we do a transfemoral amputation, we'll know what we're dealing with. We won't have to worry about remaining shrapnel causing infection, or how bad his knee might be. He'll be fitted for a C-leg as soon as he's recovered."

"How much?" The baby let out a shout of delight; there must be fish in the pool. "How much would you have to take off?"

"About nine inches. Up to here." The blue pen — *swish* — made a swift and inexorable mark across the diagram.

"But that's —" She couldn't say it out loud: Michael wasn't supposed to lose his *leg*! Just his foot. That's what had happened over there. And you'd barely notice if someone was missing a foot. But this — that firm blue line sliced above the joint of the knee, forsaking every bit of leg below it, the way it made even the anonymous *diagram* look wrong and off balance — this was something else! Another person's body, not Michael's.

"Maybe a little less, depending on what we find when we go in. I have several fact sheets prepared for you — here — so that when we meet tomorrow, post-op, I'll need your decision."

Ellen was startled by Dr. Grant's handing her the file, his beginning to rise. "But we need to talk it over with him! We have to wait until he understands, until he's awake enough —"

Dr. Grant was shaking his head. "I've consulted with Neuro; he won't be clear-headed by the time we'd have to move on this. Legally, it's your call. But as you'll see in there, I don't think the decision should be a hard one. This is the right thing for Michael."

The young mother walked her baby around the pool, singing softly. Ellen stared at the pavement stones underneath Dr. Grant's empty chair. *It's your call.* Because of a twenty-minute appointment in County Court four years ago. Because she signed a document promising to make good decisions on his behalf. "But that was supposed to be for school," she said, not realizing until the words echoed that she had spoken aloud. Dr. Grant's diagram of the bisected leg quivered in her hand. She didn't sign up for this.

"I'd do it," Lacey said, eating another French fry from Ellen's plate. "If the choice is between having a knee and a lifetime of pain versus no knee and no pain —"

"It's not exactly that simple," Ellen said. She picked up another section of turkey club and stared at it.

Lacey shrugged. "If it's just the idea of adding another surgery — I mean, you know he'll be having dozens, right? Not to mention what he's already had. Colostomy, skin grafts . . ."

"What I want to know is why they can't go in to put pins in the knee — stabilize it somehow, rather than just —" Ellen put down the sandwich, although she knew she had to eat something. Rather than just cutting it off.

They were on the ground floor of her new home for now, Mologne House, where Lacey had helped to bring up her bags and then offered to show her around.

It was the strangest hotel in existence. In the lobby was a bar, decorated in dark woods with a red-and-green Oriental print on floors and furniture. The walls were cream, paneled, filled with muted paintings of fruit and birds. A bit shabby, a bit old-fashioned; if you glanced quickly you might mistake it for a business traveler's midrange staple. But on the love seat nearby, on his phone, was a man with his jeans leg pinned up over a thigh stump; his pretty girlfriend held his crutches between her legs and listened in to the call. Portable oxygen tanks took up room under a table. Men with metal prosthetic arms, bandaged heads, colostomy bags tucked discreetly under sweatshirts, milled around the bar area, waiting for family members, talking with friends. Orange crepe-paper pumpkins and black pipe-cleaner spiders spun slowly, hung from fishing line. Older men in uniforms strode through with purpose, and women in dark pantsuits adorned with badges spoke clearly, helping, managing. A pleasant-faced Asian woman sat behind a grand piano and played "I Get a Kick Out of You."

These women, Ellen thought. The wives, the mothers. She took a bite of turkey club and scanned the room. How were they so at ease here? Waving, calling out with delight when they spotted someone familiar. At the table behind Lacey, there was a woman with a beautiful chignon wearing an oversize gray hooded sweatshirt with raised puffy letters that read: AMERICA'S HEROES CANDLE WALK 2004. Red, white, and blue, of course. She was speaking rapidly, heatedly, about something — Ellen couldn't catch the words — to another woman at the table; occasionally they would break out into matching peals of laughter. Every so often the woman in chignon and sweatshirt would reach over to break off a small piece of pizza for her son, immobilized from neck to waist in a plastic corset, tipped back in his full-body wheelchair. It had to be a show, how stagy and loud and comfortable she was. *A show put on just for me,* Ellen couldn't help thinking. She shuddered; she would never become that. For a moment, she felt a pang for the Marriott, which had been an escape from Walter Reed, she saw now.

Lacey debated whether a third rum and Coke was going to freak Ellen out. When it was what, 3:00 p.m.? She shouldn't have had this second one. Stopping after one drink was a thousand times easier than reining it in after two. Two meant the gates were open, and she was less satisfied than before she'd had the first sip.

"Everyone else seems to think it's the right thing to do — my friend Serena, my son, even my, well, Paul — my friend," Ellen said. "I called them all, and it's unanimous." Only she hadn't called *everyone.* Because how could Jane see outside her own entanglements with Mike, whatever they might be, to be helpful in this? Impossible.

"Anyway, I just wish it didn't have to be me, making this decision. Alone, I mean. I wish he —"

"Because you're his guardian, you mean? Not the mom?" Uh-oh. Ellen's quick freeze was tiny, but real. Lacey remembered now how carefully the woman had explained this, a distinction she herself didn't find so important, but . . . "I mean — not that it would be easier that way. But I get why you're having doubts. Except you shouldn't be! Not because of that, I mean." Shit. Couldn't she shut up for one second? "Excuse me?" She held up the empty glass so that the waiter could see.

Ellen smiled to herself. *Not the mom.* In a way, it helped to hear it spoken out loud like that, so flat and blunt.

"The thing is," Lacey went on, determined to get this right. "Saying yes to someone else's transfemoral amputation is not ever going to feel right, or easy or whatever. It *is* a big deal. And you're right: It sucks. It sucks that you have to be the one."

"Thank you," Ellen said, and bit her sandwich to cover the surge of grateful tears. Lacey hadn't said it but the implication was clear: no matter if you're the real mother or not. "Who are you looking for?" Because Lacey's gaze was roaming the room now.

"These guys from Eddie's unit. They're gonna visit him."

"That's nice. How did you get in touch? Michael's commander has sent me a few e-mails, but I haven't written back yet."

Lacey frowned. How did she get in touch? What kind of question was that? Apart from constant back-and-forth e-mails ever since the news about Eddie's injury, Skype-ing from the computer room at Heaton, and updates she wrote each day to the rear commander? These were the guys who'd been with Eddie out there; they were his lifeline. "Uh, you should probably write him back."

"How is Eddie's . . . how's his demeanor?"

"The maniacal laughing? Yeah, still there." Lacey drank once, twice, and one more time to get toward the bottom of the glass. Jesus, these were short pours. "But he went around the room twice using just a cane, and used the bathroom on his own, so . . ."

"That's good. That's wonderful."

"But the surgeon is giving me the runaround about his optic nerve surgery. All they want to talk about is his physical therapy." Speaking of which, her gym had called twice in the past two days, not that she'd answered. Lacey guessed the honeymoon period was wearing off — the flowers they'd sent, the card signed by everyone, the *How are you?* texts from Gwen. Now it was *When are you coming back?*

"I should run, because —"

"If you want, I can get a list of some audiobooks. For Eddie. If you let me know what his tastes are, maybe . . ."

"His tastes?" Lacey was trying to remember if she had any cash in her wallet. Just then, she glimpsed the bright blue braid of a shoulder cord on a dark green Army Reserve uniform. The man crossing the lobby had clipped gray hair, and two or three underlings hurrying behind him. That had to be who she wanted. "I better run. Meeting those guys from Eddie's unit . . ."

"In reading, I mean."

"What?" Lacey's purse had slipped off the back of her chair, and now all her shit was rolling around, lipstick, coins. Come on, come *on* — if she could just grab a minute with the brigadier general. Because that's who it had to be. "Oh. Eddie's not exactly a big reader or anything. Maybe if he needs something to help him fall asleep. Ha. Okay, gotta run, I'll text you later." Her drinks were on Ellen's tab, right? Lacey kept her head down as she left the bar, hot with shame but still hoping no one would flag her down to pay.

Ellen gave up on the sandwich, allowed a busboy to collect her plate. She folded her arms, tucking hands against her body; at least it wasn't freezing in here, the way it was on the wards, or had been at the Marriott. What would Jane, arriving day after tomorrow, think of this place? Of the young man hopping easily around the love seat, waiting for his girl to bring around the crutches? Of Michael . . .

And here the images came so fast and thick — the baby on its way, Jane's stubborn silence, Michael hurt and howling — that they clogged up her mind and shut down any kind of real response. So for a while she just sat there, in the lobby bar with the war-broken men and their women. The late-afternoon milling around; desultory talk and dark wood; the melancholy piano background music. It was almost like the Rathskeller on a weekday. As if she had a pack of student essays to read and an extra hour before her seminar. As if Serena were on her way for coffee, and the war were nothing more than muted images on the TV in the corner of the taproom.

The waiter brought the check and she paid it, not caring that Lacey had forgotten to give her money. She stood up, hands empty, and slowly walked back to the ward.

Lacey stalked the hallway outside some guy's room, a double-leg amputee over in Ward 57. Peered in through the door whenever she could risk it without drawing attention. The soldier in there was receiving a Purple Heart. She'd been right — those guys in the uniforms back at Mologne were the ones awarding it. She could glimpse their solemn faces as they read the citation, the still circle of dark green uniforms crowding the hospital room. This was probably last of a series of rooms they'd hit today.

The only woman in the room — Indian-looking, older, probably the mom — glanced up and caught Lacey peeking in. But then she was distracted by one of the officers and Lacey hurried away.

It was late and she should get back to Eddie. The shift change would be in an hour, and she wouldn't trust those night nurses with changing a diaper, let alone the dressing on his left eye. No room for error if there was going to be any chance of saving it.

Earlier, two guys from Eddie's unit — they'd served together last deployment, and were stationed now in D.C. — stopped by. Lacey had been hoping for a miracle, but no luck. Eddie lolled his head, laughed softly, and barely spoke. The guys betrayed nothing, no shock or shakiness at their onetime commanding officer now sightless and witless. They did a better job than she did, to be honest, at actually staying with the conversation. They craned close to hear his giggly whispers, they tried to respond and keep it going, and they saluted on their way out as sharp as you could ask. "You got this, Major. Give 'em hell." "You're looking good, sir. You'll be out of here soon." But Lacey could only imagine what they were saying now, on the drive back out to base. Shaking their heads: *Is that fucked up or what?* But to her, nothing but respect, correctness.

She'd tried, at the beginning of the visit, to get them talking. Why was it taking so long to win over the Iraqi people? When they'd seen how much safer they were now? She even referenced a building project boondoggle, some Jalibah plumbing project the locals had totally effed up, that she'd read about weeks ago on *Power Line.* But both soldiers had politely rebuffed her. It was like she'd made an ugly mistake by even bringing it up, the war. They told Eddie about the Ravens game instead.

Why, she wondered now, pacing outside this stranger's room. Because her intel was so out-of-date? Out of their concern for Eddie, who was kicked out of it irrevocably now — his guys, that shithole, the work he'd loved? Or maybe because — this thought chilled Lacey — it didn't matter here, of all places. The stuff she'd fixated on, all those blogs, all that data. It shrunk down to nothingness. On the ward, it was all beside the point.

Suddenly the door opened, and conversation spilled into the hallway. Uniforms, hand-shaking, nurses and doctors and photos and hugs for the wife. Lacey waited and when the cluster of men headed for the elevators, she made her move.

"Excuse me? General? Can I talk to you for a sec?"

The bristly white-haired man gave her only a sideways smile, and didn't slow his pace. He was handed a phone and began talking on it immediately.

"It's about my husband, Major Edgardo Diaz? If you could just take a quick look at his file?"

"I'm sorry, ma'am, but you'll need to make an appointment to —"

"We're in room five-eight-four-oh, which is right around the —"

"Ma'am. All queries related to the review process need to be channeled —"

"All *right.* Jesus." She swiped away the business card this underling was waving in her face. Elevator doors closed on the brigadier general and his party, and Lacey was left alone in the foyer.

Or so she thought. One last young guy in uniform, bringing up the rear. He held a cardboard box and gave Lacey a once-over before flicking his gaze away.

"Hey," she said, drawing it out. In the way she knew exactly how to. "Do you have a sec? Just a quick question about the Purple Heart process. I know, I know, you can't tell me anything official. Promise I won't beg." When he hesitated, she pointed toward the Healing Garden. And gave him a tilted head smile, *please*?

While Staff Sergeant Jerry Miller scanned through Eddie's injury file next to her on a stone bench, Lacey jiggled her foot and swatted away a tiny spider dangling from its long invisible thread. Healing Garden, what a load. It was stuffy in here, even at night, like a greenhouse with wilting and possibly fake plants. Across the reflecting pool was a woman with two kids who were using their bench as a desk, writing with pencils in workbooks. Every so often she would point at a place on their pages and they'd erase furiously. The rest of the time she was scrolling her phone.

"That's all you got for the injury report?"

"Yeah. Why, should there be more?"

"It's just that they've classified it as VINA — see?" Sergeant Miller pointed to a blurry acronym stamped on Eddie's papers. "What was it, a rollover?"

"All I know was, he was driving back to

base and had to swerve, then went into a ditch, and yeah — it flipped. He's blind in one eye, you saw that, right? And, well, there's significant concussion damage."

Don't make me describe the laughter.

But the sergeant was shaking his head. "Vehicle Incident: Non Applicable. That means, well. That it was an accident. Not enemy combat."

"An *accident*? Only in the sense that he *accidentally* swerved off the road to avoid the *accident* of getting blown sky-high by an IED. Put on the road by some Hajji. By accident. Fuck." The mom across the pool gave her a sour look: *Language.*

"Doesn't say anything about IED. You got documentation on that?"

Lacey blew out her breath. "Look. Obviously he wouldn't have rolled his Humvee on purpose, so . . . There had to have been a reason he swerved! He saw something, or . . . You know, there had been two other explosions in that quadrant in that past month! One of his buddies told me on IM. Wait — wait, where are you going?"

"I'm sorry," the sergeant said, handing her back the file. He must have been all of twenty-three years old; sweet and chubby, dark black skin. "Doesn't qualify. It's not a file they're going to consider for award."

"But — so — that's it?"

"What a lot of people do is" — he dropped his tone, as if sliding her a secret — "write their representative."

Lacey couldn't speak.

"You know, like your congressperson. From your home state. Shoot them an e-mail, get them involved. Sometimes a big name can put on the pressure, and . . ." Sergeant Miller fluttered his hand up toward the filmy dark skylights. After a moment, when he got nothing back from Lacey — no flirtiness now — he left.

She wanted to rip the leaves off all these plants, these tasteful goddamn *healing* plants. An accident. Of course, it was only too perfect — a dumbass solo rollover on a sandy road without a shred of cause or glory . . . that could only be the reason why Eddie had lost his eyes, his mind, his dignity without even knowing it. They were dropping Purple Hearts on the chests of boys almost half his age! For losing a finger or two!

"Do you know what time it is?" Speaking to her. The mom across the pool. "My phone just died."

"Yeah . . ." Lacey checked her phone. "Nine-fifteen."

"Oh boy. Bedtime, guys. Let's go. Quick

kiss for Daddy, don't wake him up." No protest from the kids, who stacked up their worksheets. One little boy kicked a pebble into the pool and then followed his mom out.

Lacey wanted Otis, bad. She wanted to be checking his homework and giving him shit about playing his DS past bedtime. She wanted her sense of purpose back, her FRG phone tree, Anne and Felicia and Martine . . .

She wanted Jim.

If only she could get moving now, to check on Eddie and then hurry back to Mologne where with luck she could get in before last call at the bar. Secret shots behind the cover beer she'd sip slowly. But what was this falling feeling? A slipping, blank-faced freeze. It was, Lacey realized, with more wonder than anything else, fear. She was afraid. She probed at it, turned it over and over, couldn't find a way out — yes, she was. Not when Eddie deployed or seeing pictures of those sick losers pissing near corpses. Not hearing that he got hit or the first time she saw his missing eye. Not even when Martine caught her with Jim — well, okay, some then.

But here, now, in the Healing Garden. Lacey was afraid.

18

Once when the children were in grade school, Ellen and Don took them along on an early-fall weekend trip to Chicago. Don had a conference, so Ellen made lunch plans with friends and afterward took the children to the Lincoln Park Zoo. It began to drizzle, so they went inside a building in the Children's Zoo, where the main attraction was a giant play structure made of steel cables and built to look like a spiderweb surrounding a tree.

Or something. Ellen, tired and ready to meet Don back at the hotel, thought the whole thing looked menacing — narrow crawl spaces tunneled around and around, nearly up to the ceiling, filled with children. The noise was shattering. Jane, naturally, kicked off her Keds and dove right in, climbing much higher than Ellen wished a five-year-old would. Wes hesitated, so she followed him around as he peered at curled snakes and little turtles in their glass-front habitats.

Ellen, craning her neck, could barely locate Jane amid the humid scrum of shouting children. So she didn't pay as much attention as she should have when Wesley quietly said he would give it a try. Sure enough, her sweet unathletic Wes got stuck halfway through; she heard him crying, saw his little hands holding on to the wires. Ellen tried to call up directions, encouragement, but panic kept him in a tight corner high above the ground, not budging. So she dumped her purse and shoes and tried to go after him, scraping her knees on the rubber flooring, neck and back painfully torqued in the tight, wired-in tunnel.

But Ellen too became stuck, having taken a wrong turn — she could see Wesley trapped in a tunnel directly across from her, but was unable to reach him. Backed-up kids were calling at him — *go, already!* — and wrestling their way past Ellen. Parents below shouted that she was going the wrong way. She had a dire moment of breathlessness.

"Wes! Wes! Mommy's right here!" But he showed no sign of hearing her.

Suddenly Ellen saw Jane, wriggling through the tunnels. She scooted on hands and knees, past much bigger kids, and swung herself up to the platform where Wesley clung to his corner. Ellen saw their heads close together. Jane tugged at Wesley's pant leg, and again, until he edged away from his corner. Step by step, he followed Jane: around a curving wire tunnel, down a drop hole, across a long skinny platform. It took Ellen much more work to get herself out.

When they were all three on the ground again, she hugged both and then took Jane's round little face in both hands. "You. You!" Jane had danced away from her, on to the next thing, but with a sly smile — *I am awesome . . . when I want to be.*

Ellen should have been thinking of that moment, the tucked-in smile on her daughter's face, as Jane approached Michael in his hospital bed, two days postamputation. Each sight of his heart-shreddingly now-shorter leg, wrapped in white bandages, still made her gasp internally. But this was the first time Jane had seen him, so Ellen didn't know how she would react. In fact, she was tensed for . . . what? Crying, screaming, some form of Jane's emotional outbursts. She wouldn't be so uncharitable, Ellen told herself, if she weren't so scraped out from lack of sleep. Michael had been sunk down deep again into anesthetized sleep ever since the operation, in order for his body to process this new trauma. Ellen had spent most of the past two nights in the chair next to him, just in case. She wasn't sure she had it in her to soothe someone else right now.

But Jane went quietly into the room with none of the hesitation Ellen felt. She slipped off her shoes and dropped her coat on the floor. For a moment she stood still at the foot of his bed, the hem of her long paisley dress quivering. Ellen held herself back, in the doorway.

"Can he hear us?"

"I don't know, sweetie. They tell me to talk to him, but . . . I just don't know."

Jane nodded, slowly. And then she went to him and put her hands on his arm. She fit them gently, so gently, under the PICC lines, and walked them, one by one, up his body. She fluttered over his stomach and chest, over the faded green-print gown. She touched his jaw and cheek, she touched the top of his head and his still-strong shoulders.

Ellen opened her mouth — *be careful* — but said nothing. Jane's face was wet, but calm. Her sock feet stepped silently, the loose dress that covered her swelling belly moved with her soft motions. She murmured things Ellen could only half hear: *Oh. Oh, no. Oh, Mike. Mike.* She didn't stop touching him.

And then in a swift easy motion, she climbed into bed next to him. Held her body close to his, on the other side from his damaged leg, put her arms around him and her face close to his neck. Ellen backed outside and let the door close quietly.

In the hallway, she leaned against the wall and cried. A nurse passing by touched her shoulder briefly but didn't stop. How had she missed this? That rich, flowing intimacy in her youngest child's touch. It was almost too much to bear. And how Jane went right for what he needed, what she must have known he needed these past weeks, more than anything — that kind of loving touch, body to body.

But how could they not have told her! What they were to each other — how could she not have known? Ellen's tears slowed to a stop. She found a tissue in a pocket and blew her nose. She should go back in. Jane really shouldn't be in bed with him and if a nurse saw . . .

But for now she left them alone, together. Apart from her.

The peace didn't last. Back in Mologne,

Jane surveyed the room in distaste.

"What, we both sleep in the same bed? It's a double, not even a queen!"

"Unless you want the couch, honey. It's not exactly easy to get any room here."

"Hey, question. It's like a regular hospital there too, right? I mean, it's not just for the soldiers." Jane was pulling clumps of clothing out of her backpack.

"I'm not sure, why?"

"Well, I saw online they have an ob-gyn department, so I was going to see if I could, like, make an appointment."

"Why?" Ellen sat down on the edge of the bed. "Are you all right? Is something wrong?"

"No, I'm totally fine, it's nothing. But do you have a directory around here? Oh, and I guess there's the insurance issue. Do you know if they'll take yours?"

"Jane, *what?*"

"Don't freak out. It's just that . . . I realized I'm missing my ultrasound tomorrow and —"

"You're kidding me."

"Whatever, they have those machines everywhere, and it's not like I need to know the gender right now, the way everyone gets all hung up on that —"

"Stop. Just stop. I cannot believe how irresponsible you are! How do you expect to take care of a baby if you can't even —"

And they were off — zero to sixty. Back and forth on the subject of ultrasounds and whether or not they were important, whether they needed to be administered on or near the dates they were scheduled. Then there were the tangents on questions of whether Jane was taking her prenatal vitamins and folic acid pills, the ones Ellen had bought her ("I would, but they make me *nauseated*") and whether she'd called any of the pediatricians on the list, researched car seats, or signed up for the day care waiting list at UW. No, no, and no, with increasingly incredulous reprimands from Ellen and stonewalling shutdowns from Jane in equal, opposite force.

Then Ellen, knowing it was the worst time to bring it up, brought it up. "This is Michael's baby. Isn't it? Let's be honest about it so we can figure out what to do. Wes says —"

"If you already know, then why are you even asking me?" Jane mumbled. While Ellen had been pacing the small room, she had shrunk into a sullen ball on the sagging couch, picking at the ends of her hair.

"I saw you in there! Jane, I saw —"

"Oh, are you the only one who can love

Michael, Mom? You're in charge of how everyone feels and relates to each other, right, I forgot."

"But how long have you two . . . I mean, why didn't you even tell me?"

Jane snorted, a sound programmed to light up every one of the frustration clusters in Ellen's brain.

"Was it . . . serious? Did you have plans . . . ?"

"Mom. Be real. Plans for what? Dumbass Mike losing his leg and me getting knocked up? That'd be like the worst reality show ever."

"So it is his."

"*God.* Would you just give it a rest? But yeah, so back at home we were . . ."

"What?"

"It's not like it had a *name* or anything. It was just . . . You know . . ." Jane flipped her hands vaguely around and Ellen had to restrain herself from shaking her. She felt so stupid, imagining Mike and Jane sneaking off to various rooms in the house — in her house! — and laughing at her, how little she knew. Clueless Ellen, such a do-gooder. She wished she could have it out with Mike too.

"A fling?"

Jane glared at her. And then retreated into a private showy smirk. "Sure, okay. Yep, call it a *fling*. Whatever label works for you."

"I'm just trying to understand. There are more factors at work here than you're thinking about. First of all, you're not even a legal adult yet. And I'm the one supporting you. So —"

"So you deserve to know all my business, is that it? You pay, I tell?"

"Would you please focus on something other than yourself for once?"

"This is about me!"

"What about Mike? What is he supposed to do about it? How much can he be involved? Do you have any idea what his life is going to be like, once he recovers from this? How are you even going to tell him? When?" Jane was crying now, but Ellen couldn't stop herself. "How can he possibly handle all of what he's been through, and learn he's a father on top of that?"

"I didn't even say it *was* him!"

"You need to —"

"Shut up, Mom! Just shut up, okay?"

They were so loud and livid that neither heard Lacey knock on the door, if she even did knock. But there she was, astonished, and calling them both out.

"Hey. Hey! What's going on?"

Ellen, instantly ashamed, grew quiet and tried to calm her red face, her thumping pulse. Jane was on her feet, still shouting.

Lacey came in and quickly shut the door. "Wait a minute. Don't you shout at your mother like that!"

"It's all right, Lacey. We're just —"

"Take a breath. Take a full breath." Lacey was at Jane's side, Jane who was gasping with tears and fury. "That kind of screaming makes you hyperventilate, and it's not good for mom, and it's not good for baby. Plenty of time to hash it out later."

"But she —"

"I know, I know. Long breath out. Like that, yeah."

"I feel dizzy."

"Honey —"

"Let's get her some water. You drinking enough water, sweetie? No, you're not." Ellen rushed back with a glass from the bathroom tap, contrite. Jane did look woozy, and she hung on to Lacey's arm as she was guided back down to the couch. She drank the entire cup without protest.

"When's the last time she ate?"

"Oh my God, I don't even know — we went right to SICU after I picked her up and —"

"I had cereal this morning before the plane," Jane mumbled. She laid her head back on the couch. "Who are you?"

"Nothing since this morning?" Ellen exclaimed. "Why on earth didn't you say something? We could have —"

"So let's figure out where you're ordering from," Lacey said, cutting her off. "Chinese or pizza, Chinese's faster."

"Pizza," Ellen and Jane said, at the same time. Jane smiled at her mother, and held out her empty glass for more.

Sometime later, the box of pizza was empty except for discarded crusts. Lacey was finishing her fourth beer, Ellen still on her first, and Lacey was just light enough to feel she could legitimately help herself to the last one in the six-pack. After all, Ellen just had one to be sociable, clearly. Did she ever dress down? Even at 10:00 p.m., after a knock-down-drag-out with her teen — now that girl had issues — the woman looked ready to pour tea at church. Gray wool slacks, soft sweater, small gold hoop earrings . . . and stocking feet. Yes, Ellen had slipped off her nice leather flats, but she was wearing stockings or knee-highs underneath.

Lacey sighed. Everything was packed up in her room, except the clothes she had on — these too-short jean cutoffs and a holey ARMY STRONG T-shirt of Eddie's. No bra.

And that chipped purple polish on her toes . . . well it wasn't like she'd planned to stick around for dinner.

Jane was asleep in the bed across the room, snoring intermittently. She was still in her clothes, but Ellen had pulled the covers up over and smoothed her dreadlocks off her face. So, Ellen's teenage daughter was a hot pregnant mess! Lacey felt bad, but she couldn't help liking this new development. It made Professor Ellen just a little more approachable.

"Who's the dad?" she whispered. "She's not going to marry him or anything dumb like that, right?"

Ellen shook her head.

"Well, you better get his parents involved. Square away the money stuff right off the bat. They'll make him contribute, even if he doesn't have it himself. They'll be so pissed at him, it'll help your cause, believe me. They'll pay up."

"That's not really — never mind."

"Let's face it, she'll be better off on her own. I mean, I practically have a degree in this. You don't want some deadbeat around. That'll hold her back more than the baby."

But why was Ellen so silent, so serious? Avoiding a straight look at her? Oh, *wait.*

"It's not . . . ?" Lacey pointed toward the

door, in the general direction of Heaton Pavilion. Ellen kept twisting her paper napkin around a finger. "It's his? Whoa. Holy shit."

"Holy shit indeed," Ellen said. "She won't say one way or the other, which means it probably is."

"And you knew nothing? That they were . . . ? Huh. Well, that is some crazy incestuous shit there."

"They're not related! For God's sake, Lacey!"

"I know, I know. I said *incestuous,* not incest."

"Stop! Would you keep it down?"

Lacey went to the minifridge, cracked open the last beer, and brought it to Ellen. Who took it, to her surprise. Over the next hour, she got Ellen to talk about all of it: Jane's history of drama with school, partying, cops (which Lacey could have guessed anyway). Michael's shit-box aunt and bad situation. Their family's taking him in when — not that Ellen said this outright — they should have been paying more attention to Jane. Ellen's (naive) assumption that there'd be no hanky-panky. And why was it somehow *worse* to know that it had been nothing more than "friends with benefits" — Lacey was impressed Ellen even knew that phrase — rather than some big love affair. Why did it make her feel even more stupid and left out . . .

Then there was a long last weepy part, which Lacey couldn't really follow, a lot about good and bad neighborhoods in Madison and no one went to college except Wesley (who's Wesley?) and reading lots of books against the war and now she didn't want to read any books at all, but she missed them, but they seemed so pointless now and what was she going to do about Jane? And the baby? What was she going to do about Michael?

Jane slept on, even while the thumping bass from the wall behind the bed increased in volume. Lacey and Ellen peered into the hall and saw a gathering of others, mostly women in bathrobes or sweats, out to investigate. One of them, a tired-looking woman with big hair, pounded on the door in question and unleashed on the occupants as soon as it was opened. She held her ground — *totally unacceptable, gonna call the front desk, turn it off or I'll* — even when guys in wheelchairs kept rolling out of the room to argue with her. Chair after chair — "how do they all fit?" Ellen murmured — of shaved-head wounded soldiers maneuvered their way outside to protest they'd already turned down Jeezy twice so get over it. They were drunk, laughing, and after a while the woman just gave up and left. One by one, everyone wandered back to their rooms. A few little kids, up too late, danced around the hall in pajamas before being shooed back in.

Inside Ellen's, Lacey said, "Who knows what we're in for over in Building Eighteen."

"When do you move?"

"Tomorrow. That's why I was stopping by, earlier. See if you wanted my extra space heater. I got maintenance to give me an extra. Which is illegal, I'm sure."

"And Eddie . . . how is he?"

Still fucked up. "He's good. Really good in PT. They think he'll go outpatient soon; maybe in the next week. I mean, they're already talking about having him show up for formation."

"And then . . . stay with you? In Building Eighteen?" Ellen's shock proved it to Lacey; this *was* rushed. Sending a blind man off the ward that soon? But then again, she seemed to have no energy to fight it. The process, a dozen different entities setting Eddie's course of treatment, was like a huge bulldozer. She could only lie down.

But the thought of him there with her, in whatever shabby room she'd been shunted off to, them together and alone and that soft crazy laughing, the two of them in bed together . . . Lacey wasn't sure she could bear it.

"So what do I do?" Ellen whispered. She was staring at Jane in the bed.

"You don't tell him," Lacey said. Here was one thing, at least, that was clear. "Do what you have to do. But don't let her put that on him. Not here."

Ellen nodded. She knew.

19

"If one more person tries to give us a damn dog . . ." Lacey slapped the "PAWS for Patriots" brochure back onto the counter. The staff sergeant in the PT Annex barely reacted as she swept it into the garbage.

"I just hand out what they tell me. Fill out top part of this one, initial six places where I flagged, then fill out last page of this one —"

Lacey stared at the clipboards stacked in front of her. "I did those already."

"When?"

"Monday!"

"Today's Wednesday." The staff sergeant turned away, uninterested in the sheer amount of crazy-making these endless forms brought about. By now, Lacey could rattle off Eddie's Social Security number, service ID code, treatment code, and TriCare ID number in her sleep. Everywhere she went people made her fill out forms. Often, the forms contradicted one another: She'd be told to sign off on an MRI that Eddie wasn't scheduled to have — yet. She'd enter home information on one benefit sheet but base info on another, with no idea which was right. Every time she saw a printout of his medicines it was out-of-date, and she stopped carefully correcting it — crossing out and writing in the dozen different drugs — because there was no sign any human was reading these anyway.

"Do they not think we have anything else to do?" she muttered, taking a seat next to a heavyset mom bent over her own set of clipboards. "Half my life with these forms."

"Pff. Think it'll keep our minds off of what's really going on," the woman replied, pointing with her pen toward the gym. "They're wrong." Her soldier must be one of the guys out there on the blue mats, lifting medicine balls or pushing weight machine levers, wearing gray T-shirts and black shorts, using whichever limbs they had left. Or maybe the woman in a back brace and tight bun, an eagle tattoo on her shoulder, doing standing toe raises on a box.

There was a good vibe in here — the familiar get-'er-done aura of men working out — although for Lacey it was weird being off on the sideline. She was so used to being the one calling out reps and correcting form. Some of the guys even looked like they were doing her Rudy's Gym boot camp routine, only with prosthetics: squats, plank, lunge, plank, scissor abs, repeat. They spun the arm bikes and balanced on a wobble board. It couldn't be much different, Lacey thought, working from a PT angle.

Eddie was happy too; so far, he loved his OT days. He'd mastered walking with a cane so well that they had him doing spatial drills and PT without much accommodation. If led to the right equipment, he could bench-press, leg-lift, and stretch out with the rest of the guys. After all, many of them had head or eye bandages too. Once in a while, though, Eddie let out a shrill bark, like a seal on a rock. It was his new sound, meant to signal delight, maybe. The therapists didn't startle. They were used to it by now, even if it drew side-eye from a couple of the other guys. But to Lacey on her plastic molded seat all the way across the gym, the sound pierced the big room and sent a sliver of despair, each time, right through her stomach.

There he went again: *Errrrrooof!* "Huh," the heavy woman said, not looking up from her form. Lacey burned.

Her phone buzzed: her own gym. Which

was only minimally more appealing than Eddie's bark, so she actually answered, for the first time in over a week.

"Mrs. Diaz?" An unknown voice, young and hesitant. Lacey left her bag and clipboards on her seat and went to stand in the foyer. This couldn't be good.

"Yeah, who's this?"

"Oh, good. I'm calling for Regina Morgan, in staffing? She wanted to make sure you —"

"Wait. I'm on leave — my husband's been injured, he's . . ."

"I'm very sorry, Mrs. Diaz. Well, but Ms. Morgan wanted to make sure you got the letter —"

"Did you talk to Pat Simmons?" Patty would sort it out. True, all the phone messages had been getting more dire, and Lacey had assumed her third extension for leave would be approved, but . . .

"Patricia Simmons is no longer with the organization. Did you have questions for Ms. Morgan about the letter?"

Lacey stared at the darkening afternoon outside; it was beginning to snow. "What letter? I told you, I'm not home. My husband —"

"You were sent a contract notification by registered mail. I see here that it was signed for by L. Diaz, last Thursday? Um . . . Ms. Morgan says, um, the thing is we have to have it signed and back here by the end of the week."

Goddamn it, Lolo.

Under the fluorescent lights, snow glittered and vanished. Barely even November, and there's snow? It was going to be hell walking him back in this. Building 18 was on the other side of the campus and the damn shuttle never showed up on time.

"So what's it say," Lacey asked, in a low voice.

"I shouldn't actually —"

"What."

"I can't — you know, I'm not supposed to . . ." The young woman's voice came closer to the phone, whispering. "But they won't give you any more paid leave. It's all vacation days after this week."

"Yeah. Uh-huh."

Lacey hung up. When she finally turned away from the snow, one of the PT staffers was waving at her to come. Eddie, at a table full of blocks and cups and dials, was twisting in his seat. His bandaged head tipped back and as she crossed the cavernous room Lacey could hear his yodel call.

"I'm here, I'm here," she murmured, squeezing his arm. Eddie's head-waggling slowed to a stop. The therapist guided his hands to the objects on the table and he began to sort through them, fitting piece into piece. Standing at his side, Lacey looked at his tanned neck, his shoulders under the gray T-shirt, his straight back. That was Eddie in there, in a wordless disguise. Swamped with emotion, Lacey felt as cut off from him as she ever had.

"Can I — I'm just going to —" Screw it. Lacey pulled off her shoes and dropped her jacket onto a mat table. She reached the pull-up bar with one light jump up, and yeah, she had to rock her hips hard to get those first ones in but then the right muscles were firing. Three, four, fiiiiiiive. A few PT guys whistled. Then she hung from the bar and closed her eyes. Untucked shirt, belly exposed. Brought her knees up to her chest, and down. Up, and down. One more pull-up, barely. The burn wiped her mind clean.

"I don't *want* any, okay? Just leave me alone." Mike swatted at Ellen's arm as she once again tried to bring the straw to his mouth.

"But this is the berry flavor. Completely different from that chocolate you hated — just try a few sips." Mike had healed enough to be moved back to Ward 57. Nausea from his meds kept him from eating or drinking much of anything, and last night a nurse had given them a stern speech about his needing to take in more nutrients on his own. So here was Ellen with a thick pink shake full of TPN, coaxing as best she could. Her theory, half remembered from when the kids were babies, was to tap the straw at his lips and move it away. He needed to make the effort himself if they were to get anywhere.

"One sip. Or I'll turn on the Bach and Beethoven." Mike, loath to complain about anything at their home in Madison, was known to subtly shut off the classical music channel Ellen left on in various rooms. She would switch it on, and an hour later he'd walk by and just happen to switch it off. "All those . . . violins," he'd say, face squinched, if confronted. Oh, what she would give to see his guilty-as-charged smile right now.

"Mom, give it a rest already! He said he doesn't want it." Jane paced around the hospital bed, agitated. She was wearing a loose flannel shirt and baggy jeans that almost hid her growing middle.

Mike groaned, a stifled cry, and pushed his head back into the pillow, eyes closed. Jane froze. "Are you okay?" she asked at the same moment that Ellen said, "Does it hurt?"

His eyes opened to the ceiling and he huffed out two breaths and then laughed, or tried to. "Yeah, it hurts! It fucking kills!" Mike arched his back, straining up, and then collapsed back down. He looked from Ellen to Jane and back again. "I can't even believe it, being here." His voice was high, on the verge of tears. Ellen felt the pulse thumping in her throat.

She couldn't look at his eyes. She couldn't look at the tightly wrapped stump of his shortened thigh, so she stared at his hands. Mike's hands. One gripping the metal rail of the bed, the other tapping restlessly against the mattress. Strong fingers with pronounced knuckles, and a few dark hairs. Fingernails short and blunt. These hands had no desert tan, showed no sign of having carried a weapon, of having been in Iraq a month ago. They were a healthy young man's hands, lying against faded green checked hospital linens. Ellen let go of the shake and put her hand over his, the one holding tight to the railing.

"Dr. Grant said the nerve pain in your — in your leg would be worst today and tomorrow, but then should —"

"Where's the thing, I gotta push the —"

Mike shook off her hand to fumble in the bedsheets at his side.

"Here, here." Jane handed him the Dilaudid pump with its clicker button.

"It's too early," Ellen said quietly. "Another twenty minutes."

"Push it anyway," Jane advised. "Maybe you'll get a little something."

Mike clicked and clicked the button and then flung it away with a cry.

"I'll go get the nurse."

"Wait, let's wait. You can do this." Ellen daubed sweat from Mike's forehead and cheeks. She held up the straw and this time he drank. "Let's talk about something. It'll pass the time. And maybe there's only fifteen or so —"

"Small talk, Mom? Seriously? 'Oh hey, Mike, how you been? What's new?' "

He gritted a short laugh between his teeth.

"Jane, why don't you tell him about . . ." Ellen went blank. Jane stared at her. A warning. "That concert you went to," she finished lamely. "What's that band?"

Instead, Jane spoke to Mike. "Do you remember anything — about getting hit, I mean?"

"Jane! Don't make him think about that. He needs to focus on recovering."

"Don't make him think about it, or don't

make *you*? It already happened, Mom. It's not like talking about it will —"

"There's a time and a place. Let him be the one to —"

"Well, he probably blacked it all out, right?" Mike watched Jane stalk back and forth in the small space, knocking down a row of cards Ellen had propped on the radiator — mostly from friends of hers, or the parents of Wes's and Jane's friends, though there was one from Michael's football coach, one signed "best wishes" from the principal of his high school (a short article had run last week on his injury), and one from someone (shakily addressed from FL, an elderly relative?) named Mrs. George Horodner. Wesley, who was splitting his time between Chicago and Madison, had mailed a packet of cards to Mologne House as well as Ellen's own bills and correspondence, which she'd barely glanced through.

"And I say, *good,*" Jane exclaimed, warming to her subject. "I mean, you were only there for a few months! It'll seem like a bad dream, all of it. Except for —" She stopped. They all avoided looking at his stump. This time it was Ellen's turn to signal Jane a warning.

"These kids were throwing rocks," Mike said, staring up at the ceiling. His tone was almost conversational. "Pop out from around the corner, toss them to us on the ground, for fun. Cottle said it was sandbox soccer, so we kicked them back."

"Who's Cottle?"

"They throw, we kick. Throw, kick. They're laughing. Then they . . ." His gaze scraped the room. "They, um."

"It's all right," Ellen murmured. She held up the pink shake, a question, which he ignored. Her own hand was unsteady.

"They all run away. We don't know why. We don't care."

Jane's face, tightened in horror, must reflect Ellen's own. Mike's voice grew flat, disconnected. He didn't look at either of them.

"It's hot, it's quiet in the street. Then it comes, over the wall. Someone threw it. I go to kick — and — and —"

They were silent for a long time. Jane rubbed small light circles on Michael's shoulder. It was as if he'd slipped away, into a dark sullen place all alone. He seemed not to know they were there, seemed to be thinking furiously, gaze averted, stuck on a problem only he knew how to figure.

Ellen reached out with the pink shake and at the instant the straw touched his mouth, Mike exploded. Bursting forward, he back-handed the cup of liquid against Jane, knocking her off the bed. Splattered and shocked, she scrambled quickly out of his range. "Move back," Ellen called, afraid for Jane and for the baby. "Move away!" Hands on his shoulder, Ellen tried to pull him back but he was vibrating from the force of his anger, and his shouting — she now realized he was shouting, at the room, at Jane, who shrunk back, soaked with pink slime.

"Mike. Michael, stop it! You'll hurt yourself! Jane, go get an aide. Get someone!" Jane fled.

In the moments before the aides came rushing in, Ellen tried to wrestle him down, helpless against his garbled vehemence. He was unintelligible, but veins stood out on the side of his reddened throat. As he twisted to get away from her, he slid sideways on the bed and his stump raised into the air, the most she'd ever seen it. Ellen gripped Michael on his shoulders, his back. His wrapped half leg was out in the open and there was his catheter bag and the sour smell of new sweat layered over old. Ellen tucked her head down, away from his fists, and held on.

In the depths of her consciousness, there was a voice calmly noting throughout tumult. *There was something she'd read once, about pain creating reality. Who was it? Yes — Elaine Scarry. This is what she meant: for the person in pain, there is no other moment. It makes and remakes his world.*

> Injuring is the thing every exhausting piece of strategy and every single weapon is designed to bring into being. It is not something inadvertently produced on the way to producing something else, but is the relentless object of all military activity.

Then it comes, over the wall. Someone threw it. *His stump, his stump.* This is exactly the point, Scarry would say. His broken body. "The relentless object of all military activity." It's all led directly to this moment.

Two nurses hurried in, with a burly aide. Ellen relinquished her hold and let them take over. Her damp empty arms slowly cooled, fading patches of warmth left by his thrashing heat. Jane waited on the other side of the door, crying.

In bed with Eddie, Lacey felt most torn. In his silence asleep, he seemed like the Eddie of old — flat on his back, faint rumbled snore-whistle, the same warm smell of his body. But the comfort she'd get from this would ricochet back around as pain, as punishment. And Lacey would tremble next to him, unable to sleep, lie awake and watch the gray light on his eye bandage, the curved plastic shield. She shouldn't be allowed to be relieved by his closeness in bed, by the chance to touch or hold him if she chose to, which she did not. Because let's face it, the biggest source of relief was the break sleep gave from his laughter, that soul-scratching soft giggle that came out of nowhere several times a day. Neurologist said it would go away, maybe. The swollen parts of Eddie's brain made it hard to see what was permanent damage and what would right itself, eventually. But Lacey knew; he could only come back so far from this. It was a secret only she knew, not the doctors. This was a punishment.

When the thoughts came like that, there was no way for her to lie in bed next to her husband. And in this small dirty hole of a room, nowhere else to be. Lacey paced, she drank, she scrolled endlessly through her phone. She didn't know why, but it bothered her that no-name Building 18 was off the Walter Reed campus, even though it was right across the street on Georgia Avenue, a nondescript ugly place stuffed with cheap kitchenette efficiencies. But it did. She felt more alone here than she would if they were on the other side of the city. Lacey pictured Ellen in the warmth and comfort of the Mologne House bar — which was stupid, Ellen never went to the bar unless she, Lacey, dragged her there — making conversation with vets who might have lost body parts but at least had their wits together.

God, she missed Otis. He and Lolo were arriving tomorrow to spend the weekend, and they would try to do a mini-Thanksgiving somewhere around here, probably turkey in the cafeteria. Lacey hoped the four of them could split up for a while, mother and son each, so that she and O could be together, maybe get out of here for a while and pretend they were on a vacation. Except how? Her car, left to rot in the underground parking space, had finally died, and Lacey had no idea what to do about that. And with what? She'd been free-falling without cash for days and weeks now. Luckily, you could scrape by — there was always a breakfast buffet somewhere, or a dinner sponsored by some church group, or (worst-case scenario) a box of packaged snacks left in a hallway. Eddie didn't seem to notice what they ate; his drugs kept his appetite down. Her phone bill was paid, thanks to Jim she assumed. She'd been washing out her panties and Eddie's briefs in the stained plastic sink. And the Services Center came through with small cash loans every once in a while, on top of their pitiful per diem. But Lacey wondered when the bottom would fall through.

Still, while Eddie snored she held on to a stubborn dream: her behind the wheel of a convertible — and why not? — with Otis laughing beside her, the two of them rolling through hills on a sunny day, on their way to a restaurant. Maybe to meet Ellen and her family. So put Lolo and Eddie in the backseat, okay, sure. Maybe his eyesight starts to come back: *There's light coming through!* he exclaims, no laughing. Lolo grabs hold of his hand and gives Lacey a grateful smile through the rearview mirror. And she's okay, she hasn't done anything wrong. There's warm wind in her hair and lots of cash in her purse and she's driving all of them with not a bad thought in her head.

After he grew strong enough, Ellen began to take Michael in a wheelchair to his various appointments around Heaton, the ones that didn't take place in Ward 57. His stump was declared to be healing well, and he started the long process of being fitted for what would be his prosthetic leg. Infectious disease specialists put him on a program of drugs for what they vaguely called "Iraqi bacteria" that soldiers had been found to have floating around in their bodies. He saw a psychiatrist for sessions that left him silent, and angrier than ever. When Ellen caught her in the hall one day the harried woman said, "Post-traumatic," and produced a photocopied list of symptoms and a green pamphlet entitled "Taking Care of Yourself While Caring for Others." The woman on the cover of the pamphlet was staring off into space, much like Michael did most of the day. "Obviously. With paranoia, generalized anxiety, depression, and temporary short-term memory loss." She pointed out the newly prescribed medications and started to turn away.

"What if — ?"

"Yes?"

Ellen hesitated. "If there's a big piece of news for him, a family situation, something that would change his life — which he doesn't know about —"

"Good or bad news?"

"Hard to know."

The therapist shouldered her bag, whose side pocket, Ellen saw, was thick with green pamphlets. "If it can wait, good. If it can be resolved without his involvement, even better. These violent tendencies . . . I'd be concerned about anything that could exacerbate them."

Ellen let her move on to the next room, the next mother. Even though this brief and unsatisfying conversation confirmed what she had already decided to do, it still felt wrong. What she had planned. But that didn't mean much, Ellen reflected, in this place where it all felt wrong, all the time.

20

"It's me, isn't it?" Jane lay on the bed they'd shared for the past week, curled up on her side. "I feel like I'm setting him off, or something."

Ellen was afraid to look up from the pile of mail in her lap. Now was the time. "It's everything, honey. He's not himself. Yet." She had scanned bills and statements until the numbers made no sense, and then simply began to drop them one by one in the wastepaper basket at her side.

"Yeah, but . . ." Jane rolled on her back. She put her boots on the bedspread. "I get the sense that the sight of me makes him crazy. Like he's disgusted by me now." Tears slid down her temples into her hair.

Ellen went over and sat by her side. "You need to focus on taking care of yourself. That's your only job right now, sweetheart. Michael is on a long journey of —"

"Mom: '*journey*'? Really?"

You had to swallow it, the way she ricocheted from vulnerability to this withering sarcasm. Ellen took the opportunity to tap her daughter's giant boots: "Take these off the bed, please. What I mean is, we don't know how long it will take for him to recover. But you're on a very specific timetable." Jane stuck one leg up, then another, and Ellen tugged at the heavy boots.

"It's not like I have anything to do, back home."

"Other than prenatal appointments, setting up the baby's room, filling out all that insurance paperwork I left you, taking the infant care class, the CPR one, the birth one, visiting those four pediatricians we lined up . . ."

"Oh my God."

"And the emotional toll this takes, seeing him like this — well, it isn't good for you. Lacey agrees."

"Please. That would be your dream come true, if I had a spontaneous stress miscarriage."

"I'm not even going to respond to that."

"Do you think he can tell?" Jane rolled to face Ellen. "About the baby?"

"I'll tell you what *I* can tell, which is that this is obviously Michael's baby. And that you and he had a relationship, *some* kind of relationship. I don't know whether it's ongoing, or . . . But you did, in our house, without telling me."

Jane stared up at her, a face full of *you can't make me.*

"Why didn't you tell me?"

"Mom, *please.* I'm talking about what to do *now.*"

Ellen stayed on the bed, Jane's knees resting against her side. She closed her eyes. How could anyone know what to do now? *Was* there anything to do? The combination of Mike's amputation and his PTSD made almost every interaction fraught. Had she pictured this, she would have expected the pain and suffering, but not the thousand ways she was made to feel inadequate, unhelpful, and often simply in the way. Yesterday, when they were in to dress his stump, the group of residents and nurses must have temporarily blocked Mike's view of Ellen, off in the corner. Or he had forgotten she was there. But when they parted and he saw her — fighting to keep her face blank as the raw, purplish, stapled skin was revealed — he let out a yelp of vivid surprise and displeasure, as if she'd burst in on him doing something private. "Get out of here!" he had shouted. And the day before, when she called his room around 9:00 p.m., while

Jane was in the shower. (It was a habit to call and check that everything was okay, even if she'd just left him an hour ago.) "Oh," he said, voice dropping in disappointment. "Thought it was Tom, 'cause he's calling me back. I gotta go." He'd hung up, without another word. It wasn't Jane making it worse for Michael. It was as likely Ellen herself. It was everything, and nothing.

"Mom? Do you think he knows?" Ellen ransacked her memory for the last time Jane had looked to her so trustingly, so in need. Jane, who had slivered Ellen's heart over and over through high school. Jane, who had screamed things in the worst of their fights it was pure misery to recall. Jane, with the underage drinking and most likely drugs and the late nights and the lies and the unerring ability to take the hardest path, always.

"I don't know, honey." *Do it now.* "The doctors say he —"

"The *doctors.*" Jane waved them away, irritated. "Mom, do you think he's reacting against — this?" She touched her belly and for a moment they both looked down at it, covered in a ripped sweatshirt. "Not intentionally, or, like, consciously but . . . is it just one more thing about his situation he can't handle?"

Ellen took Jane's hand. "It's a lot for you to handle. I'm sure it would be for Michael under any circumstances, assuming that . . . he'd be involved."

"He once told me that he —"

"What?"

"Never mind." She scooted to sitting, using Ellen's hand to pull herself up. "Tell me honestly. Do you think I'm making it worse? By being here?"

If she leaves it's best for her. It's best for him. "I don't know," Ellen heard herself say. "It's possible."

Jane stared, nodded once, and then wiped her face hard. "Yeah. Yeah, okay."

"I'll have groceries delivered," Ellen said, desperate. "From Willy Street, or whichever co-op you want. And I'll come home in a few weeks. For next weekend, maybe! Wes will be there, back and forth from Chicago, and for Christmas we can — we can maybe . . . And you know the neighbors, Mrs. Easton? I'll have her check in to see —"

"Okay, Mom. I get it."

"There's plenty of time before the baby gets here. By then maybe —"

"Mom."

No matter how many times she'd heard that word, in that exact tone, meaning *enough already,* Ellen couldn't help but feel that this one was different, worse, more knowing. She'd injured a tender and frail connection. And by doing the right thing, she'd gone wrong. What was it they said about this, the military? Collateral damage.

Lacey would have let Ellen in except for Lolo, how she was acting. It was like she couldn't see how much Eddie had lost, up top. She babied him, she thought his giggle was sweet — *Oh, you think that's funny? What's so funny, baby?* — she was having the time of her life taking care of him. Right now she was trimming his neck on the nasty stained love seat while Eddie lolled his head around and burbled with pleasure. Otis was flopped on the bed with headphones on. And Lacey was going out of her mind.

So she made them stand in Building 18's third-floor hallway when Ellen stopped by, after quickly introducing her to Lolo and pointing out Otis, who could care less.

"Sorry," she said, leaning against the closed door. "But you don't want to be in there, trust me."

Ellen, who'd tripped on the ripped old hallway carpet earlier, wasn't sure she wanted to be out here, either. "It's . . . nice," she said, and Lacey burst out laughing.

"Nice try. But it could be worse. I guess. How did it go, with Jane?"

Ellen touched her glasses lightly. "She'll fly back tomorrow. Apparently she'd bought an open-ended ticket. On my credit card, of course."

"Wow." Lacey had no idea what that cost, but to Ellen it meant only a wry smile. "Well, it's for the best."

"Do you think so? Because I feel terrible."

"Are you kidding? They think they want to be here, but they have no idea what it means, for real." Lacey jerked a thumb backward at the closed door. "For her it's all play time. She's in pretending mode. Like he's five again."

Ellen nodded, unconvinced.

"Plus, do you really want your kid around . . . this?" Lacey pointed to a giant poster of Jessica Simpson taped to the opposite door, breasts spilling out of a tight minidress, and the bumping music from inside the room. Up and down the hall, women went in and out of doors, talking loudly on phones, often wearing nothing more than robes or boxers and T-shirts. Everyone had overflowing garbage cans set out, takeout boxes piled on top. The cafeteria was nearly a mile away and few of the guys could get there without major pain.

Lacey didn't even mention the cockroach situation, in the drains of the kitchenette sink and under the counters. Lolo was going to flip out.

"Gotta love the army," she said, shooting for lightness. "If it's possible to cut corners, they'll find a way." Yesterday, when she'd tried to have Otis tell Eddie about JV basketball tryouts, he'd kept his mouth shut and shook his head. In the bedroom later she started to chastise him and he cut her off with one sentence: *It's not like he was ever my real dad.*

"But —" Ellen looked truly disturbed. "How are you —"

"Did Michael get his rating yet?" Lacey switched topics quickly, not able to bear the direct pity. As usual, Professor Ellen had no idea what she was talking about. "Disability rating? From the P.E. Board? *Physical evaluation.*"

"Oh. No. That is, I don't think so. I could ask —"

For Christ's sake. "Well, you'd know if he did. It's the amount he'll get of his base pay, depending on how bad he is. They sent me to four different offices and I still can't get anyone to give me a ballpark figure. But we're hoping for at least seventy-five."

"Seventy-five . . . ?"

"*Percent,* Ellen. Of his pay? But this doctor requires this test, and then this guy needs something else, and then the file gets sent to the wrong place." This was pointless. What would Ellen care? When it came to money, she had her head stuck in the sand. For a moment, Lacey even felt a surge of connection to Lolo, who at least had been following the rating office debacle with interest and verve. "So I should probably get back —"

"Can I ask a favor?" Ellen said, out of the blue.

"Me? Sure, what?"

"Michael's PT aide says he needs to work on some upper-body strength. He has this bar, you know, above the bed —"

"The trapeze, right."

"Yes. Well, it's meant to be how he can get himself in and out, move from the bed to the chair. And even though he's been doing these arm exercises, for some reason they think he doesn't have enough strength yet overall. I'm not sure why."

"Probably it's a core issue." At Ellen's puzzled look, Lacey patted her own stomach. "His core. You need those ab muscles, and especially in his back, to be able to pull his own body weight up. Eventually" — she was warming to this — "he's going to need to twist himself, right? To sort of swing himself out of the bed and onto the wheelchair? Yeah. That means a torque motion, where his obliques are going to need to take all that load."

"Obliques."

Lacey demonstrated, twisting her torso from side to side.

"Well, he doesn't seem to be getting what he needs from the aide. And I don't know a thing about it, obviously, so . . . what do you charge?"

"Excuse me?"

"What is your hourly rate, for private sessions? Would you have any time this week, and next? Maybe twice a week would be good."

Lacey stared. This was a joke, right? But why did Ellen seem so serious, so straight? "You don't need that. I'm sure the PT guy can —"

"No he can*not.* He specifically told me that Michael needs practice on the whole upper body, above and beyond what they do in therapy. I can't get him to do much of anything, let alone any type of —" Here Ellen tried to mimic Lacey's twisting sit-up move and they both had to laugh.

"But —" Lacey fought her inclination to argue. Could it be true? It wasn't just a handout, was it? Not that she could afford to turn down one of those, either.

"How about one session, to start. You can assess what needs to be done, and then we'll see about going forward. Totally around your schedule with Eddie, of course." Not a glimmer of pity or embarrassment.

"Um . . . my rate is — was — seventy-five. An hour."

"Fine. Let me know what times you have, either tomorrow or Thursday, and we'll set it up." Before Lacey could react, Ellen leaned in and gave her a brisk hug, and then was walking swiftly down the hall, stepping neatly around the garbage cans in her petite loafers. But then she hurried back.

"I almost forgot! The whole reason I came by. Here, take this."

Lacey peeked in the plastic tote bag Ellen handed her. "CDs?"

"Audiobooks. For Eddie, I got two military histories and a new thriller by Michael Connelly. For your son, not as much choice, but there was a mom returning this right when I was checking out and she said it was great."

Lacey held up *The Mark of Athena* by Rick Riordan. "He actually loves this series," she said faintly.

"Perfect," Ellen said, oblivious to Lacey

fighting back tears. "To play them, they loan out that CD player, and there are headphones in there too. Seems strange they haven't upgraded to MP3 players, but . . . Anyway, last one is for you."

"Me? I don't really —"

"I know, I know. But just in case. Sometimes a book can help." Ellen reached over to pull it out of the bag and this time she *did* have a twinkly look, as if she had Lacey's number. It was an actual book, hardcover, called *Birds of America,* by Lorrie Moore.

"Never heard of her."

"That won't be a problem," Ellen called back, on her way down the hall again. "Short stories. Give one a try!"

Damn. Lacey grinned. The English professor couldn't help herself.

•

It was raw and wintry-damp as Ellen hurried across Georgia Avenue, holding up a hand — *sorry, sorry* — to the wailing honks of passing traffic. She was smiling, even though Building 18 had thoroughly upset her. Why hadn't Lacey mentioned the shoddy construction, those moldy panels in the front hall? The damp darkness of the stairwell, and of course the trash everywhere. She couldn't help but feel relieved to be back on the main Walter Reed campus, where there was the relative luxury of Mologne House. Did anyone know? Who was in charge of the housing? Why were injured, recovering soldiers allowed to live in such conditions? Why were their wives and mothers?

But overall, Ellen felt good. She reviewed the moment of spontaneously offering Lacey that work — had it been too obvious? — and judged it successful. Now all she would need to do was smooth things out with the overbearing PT aide, who was determined to get Michael lifting weights through his own orders, barked out military-style of course. Taking things into her own hands. A once-familiar feeling, flooding back.

Ellen stopped at the guard gate to show her identification and stepped quickly onto one of the front paths curving up to Heaton. It was nearly dinnertime, and Michael, who had lost almost thirty pounds since his arrival from Baghdad, had finally started to eat. He'd been promoted to soft foods, and Ellen, taking a tip from another mother on the ward, had stopped by Pediatrics on the first floor and wheedled a box full of baby food jars. She simply opened them — that same twist-pop giving a jolt of body memory stretching back almost thirty years — and scraped into a bowl or cup for him. If Michael knew or suspected, he said nothing. His favorites so far were banana, beef-and-rice, and peach oatmeal. He rejected peas outright. Just like Wes and Jane had!

Jane. They were barely speaking. Ellen squelched the sharp prick of guilt over how she had handled things. Jane was better off at home, focusing on the baby — *oh God, she was going to have a baby!* — and Michael was better off without the knowledge that he was about to become a father. But still: *Jane, Jane.*

Ellen let go of her coat collar inside the spacious dated foyer. A twelve-foot Christmas tree placed at the front windows was glowing with colored lights. Underneath, large boxes designated for troop gifts and charity donations. But what were these nearby draped tables set up for? NO LIMITS ON OPPORTUNITY read a placard, over the black and gold Army star. Three or four people in uniform stood behind the tables, stacking pamphlets into boxes on the floor, chatting and laughing as they broke down their setup. Different placards on the table read: TROOPS TO TEACHERS. TRANSITION STRESS. FINANCIAL COUNSELING. Ellen picked up a flyer.

No degree? No problem! With expert training in over 150 jobs, the U.S. Army can provide you with career services that will make you a top prospect for today's leading industries. If you are a U.S. Citizen or permanent resident alien, between 17 and 35, and within good moral standing, ask about how the U.S. Army can further your career goals . . . *TODAY.*

"What is this?" Ellen said aloud, glancing around the lobby. Behind the security desk, none of the busy staff seemed to notice her. "Excuse me," she called, and one of the service members looked up, a smiling young woman with her hair tightly pinned back under her cover.

"I'm sorry, we're closing up. Back tomorrow at 0800 though."

"No, I — what is this program? What are you doing here?"

Wary of this lady's tone, the young soldier squared off. "It's a career services info table. There are job training opportunities, and stuff like that. When soldiers transition out of —"

"Recruiting," Ellen said loudly. In disbelief. "Right here, in the lobby of Walter Reed. That's what this is!"

"No, what I said is that we provide separation and transition career information for interested parties. If you have a question, we'd be happy to discuss that tomorrow when —"

"Who do you provide this career services info to? Obviously our patients up on the wards are already in the armed services. And so are they —" Ellen gestured to security, to official-looking men walking briskly through the lobby, to the staff at the front desk. "All of them . . . so who are you here for?"

"Ma'am. I'm afraid we don't have time for questions right now."

"I don't have a question, I have a comment. We are not fooled by this rhetoric, this, ah, 'find the right fit for your skills seminar.' It's soliciting, and I'm appalled. Not to mention the fundamental *idiocy* . . . I mean, talk about not knowing your audience. Who are you going to hand these out to? The families who've already donated someone to the cause and are now here to pick up the pieces?"

Underneath her outrage, Ellen felt her dormant authority kick in like a furnace. She welcomed it. That brisk walk across the campus, the deconstruction of the false lingo, even the chance to speak out, loudly and clearly — it all converged into this moment of righteous fury unleashed on some hapless low-level flunkies who didn't ask to be here.

"You're here to get the kids!" Ellen almost shrieked. She could feel the lobby's attention gathering. "Siblings, younger brothers. High school kids. Who walk in here because they've got a parent upstairs, plugged into a ventilator or learning how to walk again . . . How dare you." A little wobbly. "How dare you!" She steadied her voice and said it again. She was right, wasn't she? Even if the tables held, she now noticed, clearly marked forms for "Alumni Programs" and "Post-Service Benefits." By now the young soldiers behind the tables were staring at her without expression.

"Who gave you permission to be here?" Ellen faced the info desk, where the on-duty receptionists shook their heads: *Not me uh-uh I'm staying out of this.* She whirled on others who happened to be walking in or out of the front doors, badges clipped to breast pockets. "Who cleared this? I'd like to speak with whoever said it was okay to be *recruiting* right here in the, in the hospital where they ship all the broken —"

But now she couldn't go on, thinking about Michael. His fast-healing shortened left leg, with its neatly tucked-over flap of skin, a tightly sealed envelope. Ellen's breath left her; she let the flyer drift back down onto the table. The soldiers went back to packing up, conspicuously turning their backs on the crazy lady who'd gone off on them. A few people made eye contact and nodded, perhaps in tune with her point of view, perhaps only glad she'd shut up.

For a moment Ellen was lost. Where was she headed? Right, Michael's, for the baby food dinner hour. But she didn't have the energy needed for the endless elevator banks and the uncertain weather of his mood: gloomy, irritable, silent, or spitting mad, depending on the hour and his medication schedule and whatever else went on inside him, so utterly changed and so far away from her. Spent, she found her way to a lobby bench and sat down heavily, not noticing the woman who had been watching from across the room, who stood now in her line of vision, tactfully waiting for her to look up.

"May I?" She said, gesturing toward a nearby chair. "Wow, that was something. I was wondering if you'd like to talk sometime. About your experiences here at Walter Reed."

Ellen studied her; psychologist or social worker, she guessed. The woman was in her early to mid-forties, with a light cloud of frizzy, black hair. Dressed in wide-leg pants, shrunken blazer, clog-type Mary Janes, chunky silver jewelry. And was gazing at her expectantly, with a quiet curiosity. And admiration?

"I'm fine," Ellen said finally. "I don't need any counseling. At least, not because I find it abhorrent to blatantly recruit here. In the lobby."

"Completely abhorrent," the woman agreed. "Not that they were, technically, recruiting. I don't think. But you made your point, that's for sure." She handed Ellen a business card. Shelby Levine, *New York Times*. "Am I right in thinking you have a . . . son here? Yes. Is he doing all right?"

"You don't work here," Ellen said.

"Oh, I'm working," Shelby said, sticking out her hand. "I bet there are lots of areas here where you see they could do better."

"Yes, well. I'm sorry. I need to get back up to the ward now."

"Ward Fifty-seven? And you're staying in Mologne?"

Ellen nodded. How did she know? "I'd love to buy you coffee, in the next day or two," Shelby Levine said. "To hear what this is like for you, living here, and maybe for other people you know." She cocked her head and smiled. "Off-site coffee, that is. And off the record, if you'd like."

Ellen paused. Then she gave her cell phone number, which Shelby quickly tapped into her own phone. She liked this woman, this reporter. Most likely she was on assignment for a soft piece on how difficult it was to be here, and though she didn't particularly have much to say on that other than the obvious — it was difficult to be here — she would give a quote or two. Shelby reminded her of some of her favorite grad students, or new colleagues, the sharp ones who weren't afraid to show they cared.

They both stood to leave. "So what were you thinking about, back there?" Shelby said, pointing to the now-empty recruiting tables. "You were inspired. You tore into them."

Ellen politely demurred — *oh, I don't know* — and waved good-bye. But in the elevator, she knew the answer to Shelby's question. What had she been thinking of, when she let loose all that indignation and righteousness, when she hadn't cared one bit for what people thought of her, loud and insistent and causing a scene?

Jane. With a heavy heart and a sense of obligation and a desperate confusion, she'd been thinking about, she'd been channeling: Jane.

21

Lacey jerked awake, sweaty and gasping. Where was she? What was that noise? Slowly, it came back: the dusty, overheated room, Eddie's bandaged face on the pillow near hers. The screeching noise was a power generator outside their window; even from four flights up they could hear it whine and thump all night. Now she let her heartbeat slow to its grinding wheeze, and felt around for her phone on the nightstand: only 12:10 a.m. She'd been asleep for less than an hour.

Days had been sliding together, and sleep was a natural casualty. After Otis and Lolo left — God, she missed Otis — there was nothing to make Lacey get up and get dressed. Often she stayed in the same clothes for days, throwing on a coat when she needed to take Eddie across the street for an appointment. She ate here and there, slept for large chunks during the day, and cared less and less about what the nurses, doctors, and staff might think about her greasy hair or limp jeans.

When the ATM wouldn't let her take out another twenty or forty bucks, she waited until it would, getting a check here or there from MedFAC and taking as much free food as she could find. All of Eddie's basic needs were accounted for, of course — meals and clothes and medical. But Lacey once had to sneak a handful of dressing bandages to use as menstrual pads. Though really, all she needed cash for was booze.

In her clearer moments — not that this was one of them, jarred awake, sweaty and disoriented — even Lacey would say that things were getting out of hand in that department. Instead of sitting in on Eddie's therapy sessions or diagnostics or scans, anything that didn't need her presence, she'd begun to go outside to "take a walk" — that is, sneak around in the woodsy areas behind those severe brick buildings to drink vodka from a flask. Right, only vodka during the day, or beer if she was back in their room. Brown liquors were for nighttime only. But making up all these rules, then praising herself for sticking to them — another was that she was allowed to drink more of the cheap stuff on the theory that eight-dollar bourbon wasn't intended to be savored — well, she knew how dumb that was and what it probably meant. *I'm not an idiot,* Lacey told herself. *Not one of those "I don't have a problem" people.* But did owning it make it better or worse?

Frankly, the only time she got it together was when she saw Ellen or Michael. She'd dry out — as much as was possible in a half day or so — shower, find a decent shirt, shoes. And put on a show. The funny thing was that pretending to be okay actually helped her, for a while, feel okay.

She'd gone over to Ward 57 twice so far for training sessions with Michael. If she'd worried that accepting money from Ellen would feel awkward, well, it did — but less so than being broke. It helped that Ellen herself was distracted and nervous around Michael. His sullen grouch routine really got to her, Lacey was surprised to see. She took it too seriously! Too personally. The right way — Lacey had sized that up within a minute of being in his room — was to get on him, not to take any shit, make sure he knew you had his number.

"Oh, is that too tough, Mike?" she'd said, that first day, when he balked at repeating the simple abs-and-arms circuit she ran him through. "Huh. Sure, I'll modify it for you. My girlfriend does four sets of these, but . . ." Soon enough he was fighting her to give the weights back. Also it helped to speak up about his missing leg when he whined. "Off balance? *Yeah,* you're off balance, because you're missing a leg! That's why you need to strengthen the rest. Let's go." It wasn't hard; she could do that flirty-steel routine in her sleep. She and Gwen once did off-season training for a Jersey City arena football team, and this was a lot like that. Except for the bandaged-up half leg.

"He doesn't respond like that," Ellen said afterward. She'd heard all their laughter and banter from outside in the hall. "Not with any of the therapists here —"

"Well, duh. They're part of *this* —" Lacey circled her arm around, meaning: *Walter Reed.* "And I'm not."

"But not with me, either," Ellen had said quietly. To that, Lacey could only nod.

No magic answers is what she told herself now, lying in bed in the dark with Eddie. No magic. Lacey rolled on her side to face him. Under the bandages, relaxed in sleep, his face looked young, unfamiliar. She gently touched his smooth upper lip, still so strange without the mustache. He flinched, twitching his nose, and she took her hand away. Lacey studied his swollen face on the right side. At her insistence — the Ocular guys argued there was so little hope that it was pointless — they'd begun some steroid shots in the nerves around his remaining, damaged eye. From what she'd read online, two surgeries were necessary: one to repair the nerves, and one to remove any debris still in the eyeball itself. But getting the surgeons to agree on, or even to admit to, a plan of treatment was like getting Otis to be excited about fish sticks for dinner. Why were they so opposed? You'd think these guys'd be raring to go when it came to slicing and dicing. If Lacey hadn't been on them all the time — it was really the only thing she still had energy for — she got the sense they would have relegated Eddie to the lost cause file long ago. It was hard enough to stop Rehab from putting him in all these blind-accommodation courses. *He's not completely blind!* she wanted to shout. *Not forever, anyway.* "Little lights," Eddie had said once. That's what he saw. Short flashes of light, which meant there was still a chance.

Carefully Lacey took his heavy arm and laid it across her chest, then waited. When that seemed okay, she scooched closer to his warm body and slid her leg between his. Lacey pulled up her T-shirt and maneuvered

Eddie's hand onto her breast, where it lay heavily, unmoving. She touched herself. Thoughts and memories, present and past, lit up the screen of her closed eyes and Lacey tried to ignore them, tried to get herself to the place where they didn't matter.

Based on his last set of MRIs, and the continued disinhibition, it's likely that we're looking at some level of permanent damage to the prefrontal cortex. Language, emotional lability, memory loss.

The time he told her he didn't like her on top; the time he said she was too loud in bed.

Oh that feels soooo good, doesn't it? Look, he likes it! Eddie getting a sponge bath in SICU, head almost entirely wrapped except for his uncovered mouth, thick and loosened with physical pleasure.

The time he threw out her vibrator, disgusted. The time he said it wasn't normal for the woman to want so much sex, after she'd had kids.

And Jim. Jim, Jim. What if it were Jim's hand on her bare breast, what if it was his warm legs around hers. Lacey's breathing got faster.

Scritch. Scrabble scrabble. Right under the bed! Lacey wheeled up just in time to see a small mouse streak across the room and disappear into the closet.

"Are you *kidding* me?" She flung off Eddie's arm; he mumbled and rolled over the other way. Lacey sat up, filled with horror. A mouse, inches from her face. What if it climbed onto the bed while she slept? Made a nest in her fucking hair?

Right then, her cell phone rang and Lacey pressed ANSWER, too freaked out to take notice of the late hour.

"You're not asleep, are you?" It was Ellen's daughter, Jane, sounding not at all concerned that she might have been. Lacey heaved herself out of the bed and went into the living room. No more beer, which was what she really needed — throat dry, face flushed — but in back of the kitchenette's one cabinet she found the last-resort-only bottle of mulled wine that someone had left on a holiday baked goods table.

"Clearly not," she said, gagging from the sticky sweetness. "Gah. Hang on." In the fridge was a liter of flat lime seltzer, and Lacey chugged just enough to be ready to face the wine again. "What's up? How come you're up?"

"Why go to bed when I'm up four times a night to pee? When does that stop?"

"When you have the baby. Only then,

you'll be getting up four times a night because of *his* peeing. And pooping. And needing to be fed."

"Everyone tells me that like I don't already know it. Anyway, we're going to co-sleep."

"Whatever. You can't co-diaper, or is that a thing now too?" Lacey sat cross-legged on the sagging couch with both bottles nestled on her lap. She listened to Jane launch into another diatribe against Ellen — it had a slight variation but the standard theme, *she doesn't get me* — and kept a worried eye out for any mice movement in the corners of the room.

These phone calls from Jane, meandering late-night talks, probably weren't the smartest idea. Lacey wasn't sure why, but she knew enough not to mention them to Ellen. They'd started a few weeks ago when Lacey, bored one night and half drunk and lonely but pretending to be concerned about Jane after Ellen had sent her away (that's how Jane always put it, "when Mom sent me away"), had sent her a short text. Who knows what it said, something along the lines of *you ok*? But possibly Jane was feeling as bored and lonely because seconds later Lacey's phone rang, and what should have been a short conversation stretched to almost an hour. Neither of them had a lot to do at night. This had continued, off and on, and although Lacey wasn't kidding herself that Jane wanted much more than a willing ear for her to vent about her mom, she sometimes tried to slip in a few pieces of relevant information: *Yesterday Michael got a 95 on one of the cognitive tests, but he's calling it 100 and claiming he's always been color-blind so the color-matching section isn't relevant. He's gonna get another surgery soon, but this is a good one — move some nerves around so his C-leg will work better. Hey, how does your mom get ahold of so many damn books, even out here? I barely finish one and then she's got me into the next.* With typical teenager self-absorption, Jane rarely asked about any of them at Walter Reed, how Lacey was, or how her mom was holding up. Still, Lacey thought she could detect care in there, hidden under the required blasé.

"Four more months," Jane said now, apropos of nothing.

Lacey could barely remember what week it was. "So . . . April something?"

"Yeah."

"You getting scared? About the birth? Don't worry — once the drugs kick in it's really not that bad."

"I would *never* get an epidural," Jane

sniffed. "It stays in the baby for up to a week afterward. They're sleepier, they —"

"Ha! You should be so lucky, 'they're sleepier.' I don't think Otis went down once for a nap longer than thirty minutes until I put him in day care. And even then I don't know what he did, but it wasn't my problem from nine to five."

"Did it . . . was it really bad?"

Lacey drank, first some cough syrupy wine, then flat seltzer. Should she mix them? "Which part?"

"When he . . . came out. The stitches, and all that. I once had to get stitches on my chin and Mom says I almost passed out when I saw the needle. I really, really, really don't like the idea of needles. Down there."

"Yeah, well . . . luckily you can't see any of it; you'll barely notice what they're doing down there. And by that point you'll be holding him. Or her. Think about that. Holding your baby. One moment they're not alive, and then they are, and you're holding them. I mean, it. Him, her, you know."

"Mm."

"Look, it's normal to feel freaked out by it. But Jane, I gotta say —" Or did she? Lacey went ahead anyway. "If that's the biggest fear you have, you'll be fine."

"What do you mean?"

"You know what I mean. Your mom is totally willing to house and feed both you *and* the kid for an indefinite —"

"I didn't ask her to do that! Nobody's making her be all in charge. She just wants to run my life, that's all that is."

"Will you grow up for a second? I know you think you and I have all this in common, like, the single mom thing. But I would have given my right tit for *my* mom to be able to let me and Otis live with her rent-free, not to mention even give a shit how I'd handle everything. I took a cab home from the hospital, with this little baby on my lap. I had no idea."

"Just because we have, like, some money doesn't mean —"

"She *loves* you. You hear me? She isn't here because she's choosing him over you, or some shit like that. She's here because no one else would be. And it sucks, everything —" Lacey had to take a quick chug of sweet wine to cover a sudden fierce wobbliness in her voice. "Everything here sucks. So maybe cut her a little slack."

Jane was quiet. So, maybe that did it. Now this girl would hang up on her, stop calling, go ahead being pissed off. Would Lacey now be forced to *read,* while drinking, until she could sleep again? She eyed Ellen's latest, *Bel Canto* by Ann Patchett, which she was two chapters into and actually kind of enjoying.

Except Jane stayed on the phone. "All right. I mean . . . whatever. Can we change the subject?"

"Definitely." Relief. And in the girl's vulnerable bravado, Lacey suddenly heard echoes of Bailey. Bailey, from her FRG group, a million years ago. What had ever happened with her? Was anyone looking out for her? Lacey pictured her, and then Anne Mackay, and then Martine and Felicia and the women in the group she'd led and Aimee, someone who'd lost her husband, and all the others. They hadn't totally stopped trying to reach out to her — except for Martine — but Lacey's silence to every call or text must have let them know to back off. Or maybe they'd moved on, busy counting down the days until deployment ended and real life resumed.

If she wanted to, she could find a different mil-wife activity to join every hour here at Walter Reed. Flyers abounded; there were prayer groups and errands co-ops, support groups and mentors and volunteer opportunities everywhere she turned. Yet Lacey stayed away.

It was like she was floating alone in outer space, tethered only barely to a life where all of that mattered. How busy she used to be, running from work to FRG meetings and back again, helping out and dragging Otis along for the ride. And all that time, ignoring the fact of Eddie, who he really was and how they were not meant to be. Filling up her days with military stuff, everything and everyone except Eddie.

And now here they were, the two of them. One broken in the head and the other — Lacey let herself think it, go ahead and wallow — broken in the heart. Alone.

"Will you tell me some stuff about, like, the fun parts? When he first walked or . . . cute things he said. I need something to look forward to."

Lacey took a deep breath. "Fun parts, fun parts. There are fun parts?"

"Not cool."

"Yeah, I'm kidding. All right, let me think." Drink. "Okay. One time — there's this book, *Goodnight Moon*? It's like a —"

"Oh my God, Lacey. I know about *Goodnight Moon*!"

"So anyway. I'd read it to him a thousand times, he was about two or something. It's really basic, just good night this and good night that. I used to pray it was going to make him sleep through the night. Wait. 'In the great green room, there was a telephone. And a red balloon. And a picture of —' "

Jane chimed in. " 'The cow jumping over the moon.' "

"That's really weird, now that I'm thinking of it. Why the telephone? Is that the most important thing in the room?"

"This is what my mom would call deconstruction. She'd give you an A."

"Well, this one time, after we'd finished reading, he was in his pajamas, the zip-up footie kind . . ." Lacey closed her eyes, her body vividly remembering the warm weight of Otis then, his wiggly chunk of a body, the softness of his cotton fireman pajamas. "I was carrying him over to his crib, and we had this thing where I had to fly him there, like zoom him around the room before dumping him in. And he was in my arms, facing up to the ceiling and I was . . ." Lacey swayed, on the couch, cupping her arms. "And he was staring up, and he whispered, 'g'night moon, g'night stars.' " She held still, there again with her baby.

"Wow. That's adorable. Was that, like, his first words?"

Lacey opened her eyes. "No. He'd been yakking for a while." She wouldn't explain more, about the magic of that moment, what it was like to be there when little O sent up his own whisper-prayer to the moon and stars. It was okay if Jane didn't get it.

Jane yawned. "One more thing. I don't know how else to do this, but . . . do you think you could tell Mike a couple of things for me? Or, you know, let him know some stuff?"

"What stuff?" The thick gooey wine kept Lacey from being as alarmed by this request as she maybe should have been.

"Oh . . . Just some things. I'll figure out how to get it to you. Like a letter for him, or something you can tell him from me. When *she's* not around, obviously."

"Look, I don't think I should get between —"

"It's nothing serious, I promise. I just want some privacy without her all in my business. You know?"

Lacey did know. Maybe she should have refused, but she couldn't help it. She knew about being young and messed up and in love. Fuck, she knew about being *older* and messed up and in love too.

22

"If you need to squeeze your balls, go ahead," the petite, polished social worker said to Mike. "Sorry — I mean —" She gestured at the two purple latex globes on his lap, each labeled GRIPPER HAND STRENGTH PLUS. These were meant to relieve stress, they'd been told. To head off a meltdown. To get Mike some kind of physical outlet.

But if he noticed the double entendre, he didn't show it. "It's okay," Ellen said, and offered the flustered young therapist a smile. She was desperate for any help with how to talk to him. Almost everything she said was wrong, set him off. Ellen knew the cause was his PTSD, but before this she'd stupidly assumed that would have meant flinching at loud noises — Vietnam-era shell shock. But no, all the psych people assured her: this anger of Michael's was a primary symptom of what they were seeing now from combat trauma. If it seemed directed specifically at Ellen, well, then either that was her own paranoia, or it was reality — in either case, not much to be done. They were constantly tweaking his doses; they had to wait it out.

This was a first "family session" meant to draw Mike out, encourage him to share more about the bottled-up thoughts and feelings that were clearly tormenting him. Gently, for the past thirty minutes, the therapist had asked questions about what she called *the incident* — what did he remember from the street, the Baghdad CASH, the transport to Walter Reed? — while Mike sweated and dodged and answered in short vague phrases. That's when she gestured at the stress balls. Mike picked up one now and the three of them stared at it, purple and round, on his open palm. Then he arced a perfect three-pointer across the room and — *thunk* — into the wastepaper basket.

"Good shot," Ellen murmured. "Mike was a wonderful athlete," she told the therapist. "In high school, he played —"

"Oh my God she doesn't *care*! What are you, going to give her my highlight reel?" Ellen pressed her lips together. "Fuck's sake," Mike muttered.

"Let's try something different," the therapist said. "Can I ask each of you to close your eyes?" Briefly, Ellen and Mike met glances, and then did as they were told. "Now picture yourself in a safe space . . . Actually —" Ellen could hear the sound of papers shuffling. "Right. Bring to mind a happy memory. One that makes you smile. It can be from anytime in your life, just recall it in as much detail as possible: where you were, what was happening, what was so wonderful about it."

Ellen straightened in her chair. She fought down critical thoughts — *what was the theoretical background of this approach?* — and hoped against the odds that Michael wouldn't find this stupid or cheesy. Certainly there were dozens of happy memories of the four of them, back home in Madison. It was only a matter of his being comfortable enough to share one. Now, which would she choose? The time they took Wes out for a birthday dinner and Mike joined the mariachi band when it came around to their table, singing full-out in made-up Spanish?

"Michael, do you want to go first? What kind of happy memory are you thinking about."

"Um. Okay. It's not a big — just this time we took this boat, and — anyway."

"No, that's great." Ellen heard pleasure and encouragement in the therapist's voice. Behind her closed lids she was sorting through memories, confused. When had they been out on a boat? "Tell us more. Where were you?"

"Well, it was my buddies Troy and Benny, also this guy Tagger . . . we were at this pond one night behind Benny's uncle's place. Benny said his uncle had a boat tied up, we were gonna use it, but then there were these locks all over, like on the tarp and stuff?" Ellen listened in disbelief. There was a smile in Mike's voice. "We'd had a bunch to drink — anyway, Troy swims out and unhooks this other boat, we don't know who the fu . . . we don't know whose. And we take it out, trying to be quiet but loud as hell probably. Laughing and stuff. Then we just . . . floated around, out in the middle of the pond. With a couple of bottles and some beef jerky." He chuckled. "On some random guy's boat, probably his pride and joy."

Ellen held it in, how much this hurt her, and how angry she was at herself for being caught off guard and selfish. Why shouldn't he remember a fun night with his friends? That had nothing to do with her, or Jane, or Wesley? *Of course* he wouldn't think to include her in his choice of a memory, just because she was here; it was absurd, this disappointment. She held it in while the therapist praised Mike and told him to return to this memory, that night on the boat, anytime he felt overwhelmed by pain or anger.

But there must have been a remnant on her face, as the session ended, because she'd kept her eyes closed too long and when she did open them the therapist seemed surprised and Mike said *what?* when he happened to look over to where she was.

Mostly, they watched TV. A lot of TV. TV pretty much all day long and into the evening after his dinner, when Ellen would usually say good night and go back to her room at Mologne. She supposed he watched it all night too, or at least had it on while he slept in fitful stretches. Often she'd be back at the ward before he awoke, and the set would still be on. Mostly Animal Planet: he liked the shows where "animal cops" — Ellen still wasn't sure what their exact authority was — investigate pet abuse and then bring the perpetrators to justice. "Soon as the camera's off, I hope they beat those people to a pulp," Michael muttered. Also ESPN, NFL Classic, and every live sports event, including golf, which she'd never thought he liked but she saw how it riveted him now: the pale green hills and flats of a Florida course, the hushed announcers and pressed polo shirts, and the barrage of unfathomable terms: bogey, under par, eagles and handicaps and scratches.

On this bleary afternoon, a dull-white winter day, they were watching a bad murder mystery from the 1980s, a TV movie with endless commercials for cat food, medical call buttons for elderly people, and toilet-scrubbing bubbles. Ellen sat in the one chair, no book or pens or anything, and Michael shifted around endlessly in bed — nearly every position made him ache, especially sitting upright — and they watched in near silence, although Ellen counted it a triumph the rare times they happened to chuckle at the same time, or even make a dull sound of recognition. *The investigator's daughter is part of the drug smuggling ring?* Hm. Mm.

For once they had a break from prosthetic prep; over the past few days Michael had had constant visits from technicians at the Gait Lab. They made him wear shrink socks, which caused bleeding and itching on his stump, and tested out several custom-molded thigh sockets. All of this would lead soon — no one could say when — to the actual fitting of his new leg, to being upright, to the next phase. Ellen wanted to be excited about that, but instead she felt sleepy, disconnected from it all, as she sensed Michael did too.

As sometimes happened in these long stretches of TV time, she found herself carrying on an inner dialogue with Mike, even as they physically occupied the same space in silence. The heartache of not being able to talk to him, of trying to convince herself that it wasn't true that he couldn't stand her around, led to long stretches of giving free rein to all the things she had to say, which she couldn't say.

How could you not use a condom? *With my* daughter? *I let you into my house, I trusted you with everything . . . and this is how I'm repaid?*

Why didn't anyone tell me? Why was I left in the dark? All those times we talked, every one of those nights on the couch in the basement, watching TV or having a snack . . . you never once thought you should let me know that you and Jane were . . .

Well, so what were you? What are *you two, to each other? God knows she won't tell me. And I suppose you both laughed about it, sneaking around to be together right under my nose. What made it so hard to talk to me?*

"Ugh, this is killing me. Where's the Sonadryl? I didn't take it yet. I gotta take it."

"Don't scratch," Ellen said automatically. "You took the Sonadryl this morning, with the others. They'll give you another tonight."

"I don't *need* it tonight, I need it *now*! Look at this!" Michael lifted his T-shirt — he was now wearing mostly regular clothes on top, with extra-large shorts below, to fit over his bandaged stump. Along the left side of his torso was a thick, bright red rash, laced with white streaks where he'd given in to desperate scratching. The burn was a reaction to a set of meds earlier in the week designed to relieve pressure in his bowels and urinary tract. Now he needed more medicine to counteract what they'd given him.

"Here's the cream." He wouldn't let her put it on, so Ellen merely handed over the tube. Michael muttered about how fucking cream doesn't do jack shit, which she silently agreed with, but he slabbed some of it on anyway. They returned to the show.

And now, a baby. She's going to have a baby! What are we going to do about this, Michael? Because if the two of you weren't exactly the best candidates for parenthood before this, how can you and she possibly manage now? How can you be a father? You barely made it back alive. But then what is it going to do to my beautiful stubborn girl when she has to raise this child, your child, on her own?

"What?" he said irritably. She must have made a sound, a kind of quiet moan, out loud.

"Nothing. I'm going to take a little walk." Damn. Why did she have to use that phrase? Once she even said, *stretch my legs.* "Need anything?" He shook his head once, eyes on the screen up in the corner of the room.

In the hallway, Ellen said hello to the woman who stuttered, the one whose brother was also an above-the-knee. She peeked into the room on the corner as she passed, where a really young-looking soldier missing an arm sometimes fought loud and long with his teenage wife. Rosalie was at the nurses' station, accepting a delivery from FedEx; she'd just become a grandmother for the third time, although Ellen guessed she was barely in her fifties.

A teenage boy, asleep in one of the waiting rooms with his headphones on. Too old for the Ward 57 family room, which was stocked with donated toys, art supplies, board games. Ellen always wondered how older kids made it work when they had to live here for some time. Did they try to keep up with the class? Did their teachers extend deadlines, accept late work? Could this boy even care about homework when his father had come home wrecked from war? Was his mother able to make arrangements with the school, did she worry about the effect on his grades, his education . . . or was she so overwhelmed she simply had to let it go?

Ellen quietly took a seat on the opposite side of the room. She scrolled through phone messages; it looked like Paul had called her back after she left him a message last night but she deleted his now. Their relationship, so easy back in Madison, was strained. Conversations were flat and low on meaning. He said the right things, he asked about Michael and her own self, but . . . something was missing. Ellen found herself unable to tell him what it was really like. Most likely, she had to admit, what they'd had wasn't built to sustain an experience like this. They were turning away from each other.

But she needed to throw a line outside, to know that the world still continued. A brief longing for quiet, routine Madison in winter: the warmth of the reading room in Helen White; Maisie's favorite snow-covered trail along Lake Monona; sun pouring through the windows of her south-facing bedroom, melting icicles. She made a call.

"I don't believe it." Serena's voice rushed in before Ellen was ready. "I was about to call you."

"I didn't know if you'd be in class —"

"It's Saturday, darling. We're about to go meet Louise and Dan for a matinee and then early dinner on State Street somewhere. But I have a few minutes. Did you get the last box? I hope you don't have to carry these anywhere yourself. Maybe I should lighten the load."

"No, they're fine. Very thoughtful. And thank you — I'm sorry I didn't call." Ellen couldn't tell Serena that her weekly boxes of books were stacked unused in the corner of her room. When she looked through their contents, she felt nothing, even though it was apparent Serena was choosing them with care, with an eye toward what she imagined Ellen might want — might *need.* Novels mostly, heavy on the Victorian period. Collections of stories by cotemporary writers, mostly African or Latin American. New issues of *MLA, PMLA, The New Yorker,* and any moronic interdepartment memos she thought Ellen might chuckle at, with infelicitous phrases circled and marked "!" *Department Staff: Please attend today's*

MANDATORY meeting about ID policies. If you cannot attend, please review the attached document. A sign it was Serena packing these kind, useless boxes: each one came with a notably leftist book or magazine, included without comment. *To keep me honest,* Ellen thought. Every few days she carried an armful of books to the giveaway shelves, except for the few she saved for Lacey.

Should she tell Serena to stop sending them? No, because it was the only way that Serena could believe she was helping. It was surely what Ellen would have been doing herself, if their situations were reversed. And no, because it would mean saying aloud the troubling, bewildering, but incontrovertible fact that she had lost all desire to read.

"Oh, stop. I'll take any chance you have to talk, and don't worry about calling. Now tell me the latest." So Ellen did, as quietly as she could, although the sleeping teen's music was up so loud it came through his headphones. She gave the facts about Michael's most recent progress and setbacks: the nerve-recalibrating operation that went well, the gut blockages and treatment which hadn't. She did her best to describe his mood swings, and did appreciate, if not fully connect with, Serena's murmurs of sympathy. She tried not to fall back on automatic cheerfulness, or dip down too far into actual horror.

"And you don't have any timeline for coming back?"

"Yes and no. I've talked to Jane and Wes about flying home for a few days as soon as Michael can handle things better. My friend Lacey said she'll check on him as much as she can." Ellen hurried on, afraid Serena would ask about Jane. Who she hadn't spoken to since she left Walter Reed. Who was ignoring her calls, once again. "I don't know when I can, though."

"There's got to be someone else who can stay with him. You can't do this all by yourself!"

"Who? I sent a registered letter to his aunt, no response. I've tried to call her — nothing. Anyway, I hate to think what he'd do if she actually showed up here. His cousins have texted him . . . all the old girlfriends too. Cards and gifts come in, but . . . no, there's no one else."

"And what are the prospects for him going home? For leaving there, for good?"

The teenager tried to roll to his side, became tangled in his cord, and wrestled his way out with an exasperated huff. She flashed on what Michael would go home to:

a rehabbed room on their first floor, no job and no leg, and Jane with their baby. "Too early to say," Ellen said, covering her mouth with a hand. "We're in true limbo here." *Limb-o,* her ever-linguistic brain chimed in, obnoxiously.

"Well . . . I don't know what to say. That you're trapped there, that you have to go through this . . ."

"Tell me about school. How many dissertators?"

"Oh, you don't want to hear about that. Really, I want to know about *you.*" Ellen opened her mouth but Serena went on. "What are you *eating*?"

She laughed. "Well, it's a far cry from Jill's famous spinach and quinoa gratin. In fact, the pickings are so slim that I've started drinking TPN shakes. There's a nurse who took pity on me when she saw my lunch. Now she slips me one almost every day."

"Do I even want to know? TP . . . what shakes?"

"Total Parenteral Nutrition. Michael hated them, but I have to say, the vanilla blend isn't bad." She wouldn't mention they were the only thing she could keep down. Remembering all the dinners at Serena and Jill's, all the times she'd had them over, Ellen missed her own kitchen with a fierce thump. She missed any form of cooking, big complicated messy menus or even the chance to boil a small pot of spaghetti and top it with a single fried egg, some toasted bread crumbs and parsley, a few red pepper flakes. Her longtime favorite solo meal, to be savored slowly at her kitchen counter with a glass of Beaujolais and a thick *New York Times* best seller checked out from the library that day . . .

"Oh, I know what I can tell you about. Shelby."

"The reporter?" Serena's voice perked up. "So what's the story? Are you a whistle-blower?"

"I think I'd have to be an employee to be a whistle-blower, wouldn't I? Anyway, I'm not even officially on the record yet. It's strange . . . so far I'm still not sure *what* she's reporting on, but it's not a puff piece, that I can tell."

"Absolutely. So listen. After you told me her name, I googled Shelby Levine. Ellen? She's done front-page work from all over. Sierra Leone, Afghanistan, Chechnya. What is she like? I feel sure she's on to something big, related to the war."

"What is she like? Well, she's like . . . the best grad students or new colleagues you've ever had. Those once-in-a-lifetime, dedicated, brilliant women. The ones you know will get the fellowship, the TT job at Stanford. In fact, Shelby went there for her PhD in poli-sci." So far Ellen had met with the reporter twice, once for coffee and once for lunch at Charlie's Diner, one of the handful of businesses on Georgia Avenue one block north of Walter Reed. Each time she had tried to ask about the project, Shelby neatly deflected her questions and turned them back on her own experience, and Michael's, and what it was like for them being thrown into this military hospital environment, all at once, for an unknown period of time. It seemed like, above all, she wanted to get to know her. And Ellen, quite frankly, basked in the attention. She hadn't realized how much she had been missing that particular blend of warm conversation, rich with bookish ideas and allusions, the winding elegant dependent clauses, the expectancy of understanding.

"So she's using you for access," Serena mused. "To the administration, to some kind of higher-ups involved in Michael's care. Maybe that gets her closer to whatever decisions were made to prosecute that blasted war. Or a cover-up! Something to do with how we never *see* these injuries, these deaths."

Ellen rolled her eyes at *using you.* And at Serena, typically as blunt as ever. "Maybe. Although frankly she seems much more interested in who I've met here than who works here. My friend Lacey, for example." Yes, Shelby asked a lot of questions about the women living at Mologne but soon zeroed in on Lacey when Ellen told her — maybe she shouldn't have — what Building 18 looked like on the inside. Still, she rarely if ever wrote anything down, and as far as Ellen knew she wasn't taping it. But at the end of lunch Shelby had asked if Ellen thought Lacey would be "amenable" to meeting her.

She wasn't sure. Lacey would shift her eyes if Shelby went into raptures again about the most recently published journal of Susan Sontag, and she might storm out if the two of them disparaged all of Bush's cabinet members as vigorously as they had. The image of Lacey even at that table in Charlie's — in her too-tight jeans and too-blond highlights — made Ellen uncomfortable. Would Shelby perceive how funny and unique she was? Would she love her feistiness and New York attitude and staunch loyalty as much as Ellen did? And why was she so interested in her, anyway?

"I wish you were here," Serena said. "I

wish I could beam you here, even just for dinner. And I hate to run, but —"

"No, go. Of course. I'll call again, sooner this time."

"Happy New Year, darling."

They hung up. Ellen sat in the waiting room a moment longer. New Year? She supposed that was right. Though how many days into 2006 they were now, she couldn't say.

But then Ellen had an idea. The perfect way to have Lacey meet Shelby, and best of all, it could involve food, home-cooked food. The teenager started up in the sudden silence, as if her voice had kept him asleep. He was startled, suspicious; she gave him a small wave and saw recognition awaken in his pimpled face: *Ah, fuck. I'm still here.*

Now she hurried through the hallways back to Michael, buoyant with thoughts about her new plan and how to carry it out.

But even several doors down from Michael's room she could hear the commotion from within. Others passing by stopped to peer in the window. Ellen's heart lurched and she began to run.

"I don't fucking care! You can't tell me what I don't know! Don't touch me, don't *fucking touch me*!" Michael yelled. His voice skittered up to a high range, and when she came in she saw he was backed up as far as he could go on the bed, using both hands to shove himself up higher on the backrest. He pushed with his only bare foot, fighting to get away. A man in blue nurse scrubs, hands raised, was trying to be heard above him, calling for him to calm down.

"What's going on?"

"Get him out of here! Get out!" Michael seized a water bottle off his movable tray and fired it across the room; it slammed the wall, missing the nurse by inches. He grabbed for something else and knocked over the tray. Ellen came in as close as she dared. He was spitting and red-faced. She spoke a rush of low steady words, and his terrified eyes went from her to the man and back again.

"All I am trying to say is —"

"He was choking me. Had his fucking sand-nigger hands on my throat!"

Ellen whirled between Michael and the nurse, who was now backing out of the room. Others came in, including an aide named Rob Beers, one of the only guys Mike really liked, whose name was a never-ending source of delight. They helped Ellen talk him down, they sent a sedative into his drip. Mike sobbed, sometimes rearing up again in outrage. No one knew what he was talking about. Rob Beers agreed with everything he said, matter-of-factly, and retaped the catheter bag that had torn away. Ellen stroked Mike's sweaty head, told him over and over that he was safe, he was all right, no one would hurt him now. As soon as he sank down into longer periods of quiet, Ellen slipped out into the hallway.

Several people looked up as she came out; one of them pointed to the nurses' station. And there was the man in blue scrubs, leaning over the counter and using Rosalie's phone. When he saw her approach he hung up.

"Look, it's happened to me before. It's all right. You don't have to apologize."

Ellen stared. "I came to ask you what happened. What made him so agitated?"

"Isn't it obvious?" The man pointed to his name tag. MOHAMMED JEET. "He was asleep; I went in to do a vitals check, and he suddenly woke up and shoved me away."

"I don't know what to say." Ellen studied the man's smooth olive skin, his dark hair bundled into a topknot.

"My parents are Sikh from Punjab, but I consider myself only culturally so." He seemed to expect some kind of response from Ellen. "In fact, I grew up in Austin, of all places. Texas."

"He must have been having a bad dream," she said stupidly. "Or a flashback . . ."

"Nah," Mohammed said. "Just the usual; lots of guys react that way, at first. Not many go all the way into a total rage spiral like that, but hey! It's better than depression and lethargy."

"I know he doesn't think that way. What he said. I mean, he wouldn't ever speak like that if he hadn't —"

"I get it. Anyway, I gotta go. I just stuck around to make sure you were okay. And tell you that you didn't need to apologize, or whatever."

"Thank you," Ellen said, automatically. She wanted to ask if this was his usual route; he wouldn't be back in their room anytime soon, would he? But Mohammed pushed away from the counter and sauntered off. Surely he wasn't pleased to have provoked another Marine?

In the short time it took to return to Michael, Ellen fumed. Well, so what if this man was ethnically Indian, as opposed to Middle Eastern, was Sikh instead of Muslim? Was it such a good idea to send in guys named *Mohammed* to draw blood from Iraq vets with PTSD? Wouldn't Lacey have a field day with this one. And how smug he was, carefully explaining to another clueless-mom-type his *Texas* origins, as if to rub it in more, the ugly racism from her son. Well, at least most of the other nurses and aides, the ones they usually saw, were white.

She froze in midstep. Shame coursed through her. What was happening to them here? Ellen made herself go back into the room.

23

Two pounds, eight ounces. Two pounds, thirteen ounces. Three pounds, four ounces — oops, too much. Lacey watched the mom in a puffy fur-lined winter coat and skintight yoga pants scoop green beans back out of the scale and into their bin. Then she twisted the bag with a neat knot and tossed it in her cart behind a toddler playing with her phone. *HAND-TRIMMED ORGANIC HARICOTS VERTS* read the sign. *$6.99 PER POUND.*

"Over twenty bucks," Lacey said. "For a pile of beans." But no one was listening to her in this suburban Whole Foods. All over the produce section, people were weighing, fingering, sniffing. Slanted wood bins spilled over with multicolored fruits and vegetables. Six kinds of pears. Tomatoes on the vine, off the vine, heirloom, conventional, organic. Peaches from Ecuador, peaches from Colombia, peaches from Nepal. Carrots that were $2 a pound and bananas that were

$4.99 a pound.

A cold mist spurted out over the lettuce section, wetting the arm of Lacey's jacket. She yelped and moved away, rubbing at the leather. She pulled a few grapes off a nearby display and ate them, staring blatantly at one of the cheerful green-aproned stock girls, who only grinned as if to say, *Eat more! Eat as much as you can hold! Aren't they juicy and delicious?*

"This place is freaking me out," she said to Ellen, who was studying her grocery list. "Why don't I wait in the car. I mean taxi. I mean, whoops, we have no taxi now, so how the hell are we gonna get back?"

"Don't be dramatic. Here, what does this say?"

"How'm I supposed to know? Didn't you write that?"

"Yes, but — did I mean two pounds of eggplant, total? Or two-pound eggplants, quantity unknown?"

Eggplant, gross. Lacey fidgeted away, one eye on the only person in this chilly room who was as out of place here as she was. Eddie. The chubby Latina aide who'd come with them was carefully leading him around displays, occasionally stopping to hand him a sample of overpriced exotic fruit. She talked quietly and steadily to him, even when he made those twisting movements with his head or let out a sharp half laugh, half bark. Basically, all the things that Lacey herself should be doing. From across the produce section, Lacey watched as other shoppers noticed Eddie, took in his cane and the aide and his gray army sweatsuit, the bandages on his face and the way he lolled his head. They stepped nervously out of his way, or ostentatiously made room for the aide to bring him through. She saw a wife elbow her husband and whisper.

Why couldn't he be an amputee, like Mike? How much simpler that would have been — then, he'd be treated with deference and respect, the meaning of that outward injury so clear and immediate. *And I'd be able to understand him,* Lacey thought. It'd be *Eddie,* minus a leg, giving orders, being uptight. Finding fault with her. So what was she really wishing for, here?

It was ridiculous that he was even here on this outing. Lacey could barely bring herself to be near him, so thank God for the aide. When Ellen had come over a few days ago, burbling about a dinner party and the need to get some of the other women together, as a kind of morale booster — and how she desperately missed *cooking,* the dumbest thing of all in Lacey's opinion — but there was nowhere else to have it other than Lacey and Eddie's room, they were the only ones she knew who had a kitchen, well, "kitchen" . . . she must've caught Lacey in a rare good mood. After all, a dinner to boost morale was just what she and the FRG girls used to put together, except for them it meant Wednesday's free wings night at Warwick's on North, whereas apparently to Ellen it meant a four-course feast that took a million hours of pre-planning and shopping. Where were all these other women going to sit, down on the nasty floor with the mice poop? So why had she agreed to this? That was easy: because of Ellen, of course. Because it was the first time in a long while that the professor had looked excited and happy about something, and Lacey didn't have it in her to say no, even though she dreaded people seeing the shit-hole they lived in.

A more confusing question: Why had she gone along when Ellen suggested that Eddie come with them to this suburban Whole Foods, in a special taxi-van the hospital had arranged, happy to have him practice "real world" interaction? Why had she brought his barking and blindness and innocence out here in the Friday afternoon pricey-grocery-shopping madness of the real world?

Because I want to be who Ellen thinks I am. Devoted wife. No bad thoughts. Immune to the humiliation of Eddie, of me.

Now Ellen was consulting with the aide about her list, the two of them nodding and pointing and sorting out what had to be purchased. Eddie spoke and they both turned to him, Ellen tipping her face up, careful, listening. He'd started saying some two-word sentences now, *It's gone* (about lunch), *I'm done* (after a haircut). This was celebrated in Neuro; apparently putting together a verb and a word was a big deal in terms of his brain regluing parts of itself together. Of course, no one would say whether he'd ever progress further, they never committed to an actual educated guess. They seemed to think that this two-word development, plus the fact that Eddie — aside from blindness — was remarkably okay in his physical movements and spatial awareness, rarely knocked into something and could dress himself, do all the bathroom stuff on his own . . . that this was all pretty good. *But it's not enough!* Lacey raged. Were they going to leave him like that, and her with him? Was this going to be their *life*?

Ellen answered Eddie, or responded to

him. She didn't look like she wanted to jump out of her skin when he did one of his high-pitched laughs next. She and the aide kept talking to him, and each other, and Lacey watched the three of them go around a corner and into the next aisle. Then she took out her phone.

"Hello?" Jim said, wary, incredulous. He'd picked up before the second ring.

"Yeah. Can you talk for a sec? Everything's all right, I mean."

"Oh man, I was gonna say. I thought something had happened, or something." Neither of them said aloud what that might be. "So, how are you? What's going on? This is me being cool, by the way. You like it? My heart's revved up over sixty, though."

"Yeah, it's stupid." Lacey picked up a box of sea salt–crusted oat crackers and set it down. "I went with an urge, but . . ."

"Go with it! Always, always go with the urge."

She laughed. "You have to tell *me* that? So where are you? You got the girls?"

"Yeah. One of them has a party to go to so we're gonna drop her off and then go to the mall. 'Cause I'm a sucker."

"Daddy treats them right."

"Can't help it. They're getting so big. So beautiful, you know? You should see Marissa in her winter dance picture. She's a knockout. Except for this loser standing next to her."

"What, you?"

"Very funny. No, some skinny piece of shit who makes her cry and who she texts all hours of the day and night but who somehow knows better than to show up around here."

Lacey smiled at the vehemence. She trailed Ellen, Eddie, and the aide by an aisle's length, holding the phone close.

"How'm I doing?" he said. "Do I sound natural? Is this okay, is this what you want?"

"I want everything and nothing. Don't go down that road."

"So tell me how he is. But mostly how you are."

Lacey told him about the special night-vision goggles Eddie now wore for optics treatment. They were building up his sight reaction times, testing him for any responses to light and darkness. Maybe it was just her, but it seemed like the doctors were now a little more interested in working on his eye. They had either started listening to her, or were impressed with her dedication (the notebook where she wrote down every day and time Eddie mentioned the flashing in his eye), or they wanted to get rid of her by actually working on it. But there was movement there, more so than in the past weeks.

She told him about Ellen and this crazy dinner party plan; about Jane who kept calling her every few nights; about how beat-down she felt. How she missed music, all her music, driving around listening to her CDs or Z100 or the time she made Otis listen to both Pink albums and got him to dance around the house with her. That hearing half a Bruce Springsteen song on the shuttle bus driver's radio yesterday had brought tears to her eyes.

"But you probably think Bruce is corny."

Jim answered gravely. "Lady, you have no idea how many Springsteen shows I've been to. This is not a matter to be joked about."

"Hey, can you do me a favor?" They'd reached the frozen section. Ellen was motioning for her, and Lacey held up a finger: *One sec.*

"You bet. I'll get in the car now." A smile in his voice.

"A favor for there."

"That kind's a lot less fun."

She let it hang in the air between them, the sweet ache of wanting each other. A gay couple pushed their cart past her; six bottles of fizzy water and a bunch of flowers.

"Will you go see Otis? I'll tell his grandma.

You can say you're a friend, whatever. He can't come down again until next weekend and I just want . . . someone to check in on him. Like, take him out to eat or something."

" 'Course I will. I'll go over there tomorrow! I could have done that a lot earlier, if you'd — if we hadn't —"

"I know. Listen, Jim?" Eddie was shaking his head at the aide. She kept a hand on his elbow but he didn't want to go any farther. Lacey hung back near the canned soups. "It doesn't mean . . . whatever it could mean. This call, you seeing Otis. Don't think I'm going to be all over you for stuff."

"Look. When it comes to you, I'm a pro at not letting things mean what they really mean. All right? So don't even think about it."

"Thank you. You can tell Otis I miss him like crazy. Text me how he looks, how he's doing. Tell him I been e-mailing his teacher and — never mind. Never mind." The aide was craning her head around for Lacey, so she spoke fast. "Also one night after I'd had a few I started feeling like I wanted to call you so bad I pulled the battery out of my phone and put it in a bag of water in the freezer."

"Lacey. I —"

"I gotta go. Thanks."

She ran to catch up with them. "What's the matter?" Eddie was stuck still in the middle of the aisle; a backup of shoppers from both directions waited to go around him.

"He tired of the crowds, maybe? *Que pasa, papi?*"

"Let's go, Ed." Lacey tugged on his sweat-shirt. "We gotta get out of the way here."

He turned away from her, frowning. It was an expression she knew minutely and she almost expected him to come out with a quick and scornful reply. "Push bar," he muttered to the shelves of body lotions and vitamins. "Push hand."

"You can hold my hand," Lacey said. "Here, right here."

But that wasn't it. He batted at the shelves, her hands, the aide's. By now the blockage of carts was causing murmurs and audible frustration. Eddie stepped in small circles, left and right, saying his two-word sentences over and over. *Like Rain Man,* Lacey thought. Then he started to yelp and she got desperate.

"Maybe he wasn't ready," the aide whis-pered.

"Oh, that's really fucking helpful now, thank you," she hissed back. "C'mon, Eddie. Let's go, we can go outside. All done, okay? All done."

"Can we get through here already?" someone called from a cart back in the aisle. "What's the problem?"

Lacey whirled to face a train of shopping carts. "What's the problem? You want to know about our *problem*? Okay, let's see. The problem of the bomb-filled road in Iraq where my husband's Humvee flipped? Or the one where his head got bashed in and he lost an eye and has dents in his skull because he was over there fighting to protect your right to buy organic shampoo!"

People glanced away; the carts began to back up awkwardly.

"Anyone else want to hear a problem?" *Oh lord,* the aide whispered. "How about the problem of my bosses and how they decided to stop holding my job for me? Or the one about my dead car that got towed out of the hospital garage and now I'm getting charged a hundred forty bucks for the privilege of going to get it?"

Barely anyone was left now but Lacey stared them all down, the retreating carts. She was just getting warmed up, she was ready to roll. Then Ellen came back, eyes wide. "What happened? I could hear you all the way over in the bakery!"

Eddie was still turning around in tight half circles, making popping and peeping sounds with his mouth.

"He's done," the aide said. But Ellen was asking Eddie himself, *Are you all right? What do you want?* In a tone of such naturalness, as if she were asking anybody else in the store, that Lacey about fell over. How did she do that? "Push bar," Eddie told her.

"Like this?" Ellen brought his hands to the cart handle. "He was touching it before," she explained. "I said he could take over pushing." Lacey and the aide were silent, flabbergasted. Eddie lit up, expertly swiveled the cart to and fro. "So, great. This way I can focus on finding fresh bread crumbs. This way, Eddie. Thank you. Why do you think they would only have the dried kind? They taste like sawdust."

When Lacey tried to go with them, Ellen gently shouldered her away. "We've got this." She smiled up at Lacey and whispered, "You do this all the time; why don't you take a little break, get something at the coffee bar."

"I'm fine! What, do you think I'm losing my grip? None of these people get it. They have no clue what we're going through! You think I'm gonna back down from letting them have it once in a while?"

"I would never think otherwise. But look how well this is going." And it was. With only one of Ellen's hands lightly guiding the cart, and the aide walking alongside to block any oncoming traffic, Eddie was utterly focused on pushing. No laughing or barking. No more circles.

"All right. Thanks. How much more do we have to get?"

Ellen went back to the list. "Damn, I knew I'd forgotten something. Can you run back to produce and get four — no, better make that five — pomegranates? Make sure they're the heavy ones, those will have the most seeds. We'll meet you at checkout."

"But —"

"Don't worry, we're fine!" And around a corner into the next aisle went the three of them.

Lacey walked slowly back to the giant room of fruits and vegetables, all the rows of food products flowing past her. She was tingly, in a daze, as all this energy left over from shouting at strangers leaked away. And Jim. Talking to Jim. Heat rose up through her stomach and chest, and she replayed every moment of the call in her mind.

"Excuse me?" A girl in a green apron, holding out a tray. "Would you like a sample of our new German-style lager?"

"Sure." Lacey picked up the paper cup, half full. And then she set it back down. "Actually, no. I'm good."

This fizzy hunger inside was all she needed right now. So Lacey went around and around the produce section, past peppers and clementines and clear plastic boxes of strawberries. She hugged herself, smiling.

Now what the hell had Ellen wanted her to get?

24

Two nights later, fifteen people crammed into Lacey's one-bedroom apartment in Building 18, and Ellen thought she must have been mad to arrange this. Shelby still hadn't arrived, thank God, because the spaghetti sauce had to finish cooking and there wasn't enough room on the stove top to boil the water at the same time. So she'd have to finish the sauce, store it somewhere (not in the minifridge, not on the non-existent counter, maybe on the coffee table?) while she used both burners to try to heat up water — a giant pot borrowed from the Mologne House restaurant — for the noodles. She could only hope the two big bowls of salad, stacked on top of each other on the floor, weren't wilting too badly. Lacey had solved the problem of drinks by emptying hers and all her neighbors' trash cans and filling them with ice, soda, and beer. There were also bottles of wine teetering on every available surface, including the small radiator cover. Eddie had helped her strip the bed, push it to the wall (which only gained a foot or two of space, but still), and then cover it with a plain sheet. So now women were lounging on that, laughing and talking.

People don't turn their noses up at a party, Ellen told a worried Lacey. Especially not here, not now.

What was Lacey so nervous about, anyway? She was drinking even more than usual, which wasn't good. Ellen kept giving her little tasks to try to take her away from the beer, but Lacey eventually snapped at her: *This was your idea and I'm not the help.* Yes, it was a cramped, ugly place. But everyone knew it wasn't *hers.* And since when did Lacey care what other people thought, Ellen told herself, wiping perspiration off her forehead with a paper towel, awkwardly aware that she was springing Shelby on her friend without warning.

People kept coming in. Some Ellen recognized from Mologne and Ward 57. Others she didn't. The word had spread, as she'd wanted it to. Women came bearing boxes of Dunkin' Donuts, liters of Sprite, a pizza from the place up on Georgia Avenue. One plunked a giant can of cheese dip in the middle of Ellen's carefully trimmed crudités. Several of them shed coats and immediately pitched in to help out in the kitchen, sizing up its limitations and adjusting seamlessly. They hand-washed pans and dishes, they wiped up spills. They set out napkins and plastic forks and paper bowls.

A few injured soldiers turned up. One man missing a hand was demonstrating how he could spin his electronic prosthetic 360 degrees. A few others poked their heads in but lingered in a group just outside in the hallway. Eddie was there, of course, in a seat of honor — one of the only available chairs — and he was quiet, maybe taken aback by all the new voices, all the motion around him.

The rest of the partygoers were women. Moms, sisters, wives, girlfriends, daughters, cousins, aunts. They didn't seem to care that it was standing room only or that dinner wasn't nearly ready. They didn't bother to introduce themselves or find the host. Coats and bags were piled in Lacey's small closet, and the drinks were flowing. Ellen caught snatches of cross-talk as she balanced the sauce pot onto the sink — *Yeah, I've seen you on Fifty-seven; how's he doing? Anyone else see a red-tail fox in the woods out by PT? You mean a fox like an actual animal?*

Who goes outside? — but she'd forgotten to fill the pasta pot with water first. An older woman, no English, picked up the sauce using her sleeves as oven mitts and nodded at her to go ahead; *I'll hold this.*

As soon as the water was set to boil — it might take an hour — Ellen saw Shelby in the doorway, holding her coat and a bottle of wine. She waved her over and gave her a one-armed hug, mindful of her spattered apron.

Shelby's eyes were roving the crowd. "I owe you my firstborn."

"Sure, go mingle," Ellen said. "I'm afraid dinner will be on hold —"

"Is everyone here from Building Eighteen?"

"Some. Some stay in Mologne House, like me . . . I suppose you want to go cultivate some contacts."

"Yes, but first —" Shelby took out her phone. "Do you think your friend would mind if I gave myself a little self-tour? Nothing personal of course. Just to get a sense of the —" She took a photo of the buckled linoleum under their feet, the rolling hills that Ellen kept tripping on.

"Well there's not much more than you're already seeing, and there are people in the bedroom, so . . ."

"Great, thanks."

"Wait." Ellen held Shelby back by the arm. "I can't feel right about this, entirely, if I don't know what's going on. What is the story? Please tell me."

Shelby nodded. "It's about the conditions here at Walter Reed."

"Conditions? You mean the treatment for the soldiers?"

"No. Nothing to do with the medical side. It's conditions *here.* The ones *she's* living in, and others like her." With that, the reporter aimed her phone at a cabinet door half off its hinges.

Before she could think this through, someone knocked over the salad bowls and spilled lettuce that needed to be scooped up off the floor and thrown away. Ellen decided to set out the salad for serving, and that involved finding room on the sole coffee table, not having any serving utensils and deciding to pick up the bowls and essentially dump out salad onto whoever held a paper plate out for her. The Pyrex mixing cup of her homemade vinaigrette was passed from hand to hand. (She noticed more than one person flicking pomegranate seeds out of the lettuce to the side of their plates.) Meanwhile, the pot boiled, the spaghetti needed to be stirred — where was the long-handled spoon? — and it was foggy and hot in this room where the windows couldn't be raised more than two inches.

"Have you seen Lacey?" she asked two women in the bedroom doorway.

"Who's Lacey?"

Eventually the spaghetti with sauce was dished out to anyone who wanted it, or to those who hadn't already filled up on pizza and doughnuts. Ellen perched on the side of Eddie's chair, after asking him if it was all right. Conversation loosely ranged around the room before coalescing into the one topic they all had something to say about.

"Remember that day last month when they actually held formation, out by the old Red Cross building, with the snow?"

"I remember the temperature. Negative fourteen, they said on TV."

"Sorriest-looking bunch of soldiers ever, not even any snow gear. *That* can't help morale."

"What would happen if the army couldn't actually give some dumb orders one day?"

"How many documents have you filed this month? I did fourteen at, like, four different commands."

"Ha. Try twenty-two."

"Four different commands? I been to that

many this *week.*"

"Did you hear about that family, you know — the mom is from Tennessee, she's got that real cute accent? — she was telling folks that Processing II couldn't find any record of her boy having been to Iraq. Not one thing in the computer. She was like, 'C'mon up to Heaton and he can prove it to you pretty fast.' "

"But they've got a new system now — or is that Processing III? We got a visit from a Staff Sergeant Michaels who —"

"The one with the burns on his neck? He's a patient too! He lives in Mologne with his mom! The two of them decided to take matters into their own hands, and God bless. They made up an Excel document, and we're on their e-mail list now. You should too."

"Someone's doing that on our ward too. After one of the young Marines went postal at Processing I."

"Yeah, I heard that."

"Don't blame him. And my son's headaches are so bad when he moves around. With the lights, you know? I hate having to bring him to all those different offices. Once we had to leave before they even saw us, and we were waiting at least an hour."

"At least you knew when your appointment was. Jared says he keeps getting calls and stuff about where he's supposed to go and when, but he forgets. One time we were here for over a week without talking to *one person* other than the nurses. Not one doctor, not one admin, no social services, nothing. I thought I was going to go crazy."

"Like Kafka."

"Like you're here but they don't even know it."

"How many times have y'all seen some poor young boy wandering around by the Fisher House looking for a building he can't find? I help one of them every other day it seems. And they are out of it, I'm telling you."

"Yes! That area is ridiculous. How does it go? There's Building Twenty-nine and Twenty-five over on that one side . . . and then, what? Nineteen and . . ."

"Thirty-four next to it."

"No, Thirty-five!"

"Yes, Thirty-five, and then the ones in a row on the south side are, um, Building Thirty, where we went for uniform req— twice, because they lost our form — and then Twenty-six next to it, and Twenty-two next to that."

"Whose genius idea was it to name them with numbers, huh? Building Eighteen. I mean, really."

"Who do you think? Same guys who probably signed off on the 'pre-existing condition' of my brother's ulcers that he gets. *Now* they're finding ulcers. Guess what that's gonna do to his chances for disability?"

"But he was good enough to send over there. Damn."

"Did anyone get to meet Miranda Lambert? She came onto the ward last week. She's real sweet. Signed all this stuff for Freddie. And climbed onto his lap for a photo! He was in heaven."

"Miranda who? We got that guy from *Seinfeld.* And John Stamos."

"Jerry Seinfeld was here?!"

"No, one of the other guys."

"Oh."

"We don't get anyone in Fifty-two. They all go to Fifty-seven."

"Gotta get that promo shot with a real live amputee!"

"Don't you love when the cameraperson subtly tries to get you out of the frame?"

"Keith Urban, the guy from *Top Chef,* that woman from *Sopranos,* and a couple of football players. He was asleep each time. They left signed photos. And T-shirts, of course."

"God, I'm tired of all those T-shirts. I'd give them away, but they say shit like 'They Bleed Red, So We Wear Red.' Who the hell wants that?"

"There's this place where they can turn them into quilts —"

"No one wants another damn quilt! These are young men, not some old grammas!"

"So, did you all hear about that mom who was so freaking tired of being late to PT because of the shuttle schedule that she, like, commandeered one that had the keys in it and drove a whole bunch of people around on the route, dropping them off and making pickups? And then just left the van outside PT when she and her boy went in there."

"She's my hero. That shuttle is the bane of our existence."

"Who else was in Mologne for the fire drill that time?"

"Was that a drill? I heard one of the guys pulled it. Drunk, obviously."

"Well, either way it was a scene. Whoever could had to fireman-carry the guys down who can't walk, three flights, and then there was this line of moms passing down their wheelchairs."

"Yup. We was on that brigade. My shoulders were sore for a week afterward."

Ellen hung on every word. Lacey reappeared in the doorway, listening in with a few other younger wives. She pointed at Eddie once: *Is he okay?* And Ellen rubbed Eddie on the back and nodded. Throughout the main conversation hovering around the living room couch, Shelby wove in and out, talking quietly with women one-on-one while always keeping one careful ear on the conversation. Ellen didn't see her take any notes, although she handed out several business cards, writing something on them.

She wished Serena could be here. She wished *Jane* could be here. Both of them would love this group of women naming, solving, and laughing together about all these problems, large and small. The visual of all of their men, back at Heaton right now or in PT or thickly asleep from their medicine — as happened to Michael, a scarily deep sleep more like unconsciousness than real rest — affected her deeply, that each woman was tethered to pain and injury and loss with a loved one, even while they forked up soggy salad and glutinous pasta. (Ellen could admit she'd been bested by that abominable kitchenette.) All those times Serena had made her attend town hall forums against the war. All those animal activist meetings Jane went to. Ellen never felt she could fit in. Life on the page is where she'd felt at home. In fact, there was barely any occasion she could remember, outside time with Jane and Wesley, where, if she wasn't wishing she was off alone to read, she was comparing life to a book, or remembering a book, or making a mental note of a book to read in the future. Until now.

I made this happen, she thought to herself. Looking around at the animated faces of women talking. *Me.*

"You got another spray cleaner?" Someone called to her. Ellen touched Eddie briefly, then went to join the two women who were valiantly attempting to wipe down the greasy sink and counters. They were grimacing at the ineffectiveness of Ellen's all-natural eco-product. "Anyway," the first woman went on. "All a sudden he can't *stand* to be around me. Nuh-uh. Oh, I'm fine when there's something he needs done but other than that . . . *Tch.*"

Her friend laughed in agreement. "Mine gets real shifty-looking, with his eyes? Here I am saying something to him, and he's looking all around the room like there might be someone else he could talk to instead." She mimicked the darting desperate eye movements. "Sorry! No one else in your room but me." They cracked up.

Ellen eagerly joined in. "Are these your — what ward are they on? And do you think it's related to PTSD? Because mine's been going through the same thing, sounds like —"

"Ha. No, these are some at-home kids we talking about. My nephew, her younger boy. Two of a kind, sounds like — God love them."

"Oh." Ellen was confused. "I thought . . ."

"Teenagers," the second woman said, putting a sympathetic hand on Ellen's arm. "There's no cure for it."

After some time, most of the older women left and it became a primarily younger, noisier crowd. Bottles of liquor had appeared, and the women got louder and rowdier. Luckily Ellen had plenty of help clearing places and bagging up trash. There was nowhere to put these bags except out in the hallway, where she unwillingly lined them up against the wall. On one trip out there, Lacey appeared and grabbed her hand.

"The goddamn toilet is plugged and I can't fix it!" Her face was lightly coated with sweat — so was Ellen's — and puffs of warm alcohol blew out with her breath. "What am I going to do?"

"Did you plunge it?"

"With what plunger? And I called Building Services but of course no one answered. Ellen, it's about to overflow!"

"All right. Let me think. Did you try jiggling the handle?"

"That's what you do when it keeps running, not when it's disgusting and backlogged!"

" 'Scuse me?" Someone stuck her head out into the hall. "Kind of seems like your toilet isn't working?"

Lacey looked stricken. Then a teenager came out, leading four or five people down the hall. "Mom says they can use our bathroom. 3G. Stay in line, no cutting!"

"See? Problem solved." But Lacey wasn't comforted. If anything, she looked angrier.

"Listen. What were you doing, inviting that reporter here?" she blazed. "Without asking me? Huh? I mean, we don't know her. She's not part of . . . *this.*" She circled her arm around, at the hallway, the garbage bags, the line for another bathroom.

"I did tell you, remember I said I'd been meeting with this woman and she was really interested in learning about —"

"She's a snoop! And she's in there right now, taking notes about how banged-up my husband is. What is she, gonna make a little article about how cuckoo he sounds when he barks like a seal? So everyone can read about us?"

"Oh, Lacey. That's not it, not at all." She hated how trembly Lacey was, arms crossed over her chest. And wished to God she hadn't drunk so much. "No one would think that way. But that's not what she's —"

"I'm sorry . . . Mrs. Diaz?" This was Shelby, now appearing in the hall. "Is there a problem?"

"I was just explaining that what you're working on isn't about the actual injuries of our — of the soldiers." Ellen prayed that this was right. "We're not sure we want any coverage of how they are, right now. They're still recovering, after all."

"There won't be any coverage of anything, unless you agree." Shelby's glance shifted from Ellen to Lacey and back again. "This is me trying to understand what living here is like for you."

"Oh yeah? It's not some gotcha journalism where you're gonna try to get Eddie to say bad things about the army? He's on ten different drugs! I don't know if he knows where he is!"

"Absolutely not," Shelby said. "Mrs. Diaz —"

"Christ. It's Lacey."

"Lacey," Shelby said, smoothly restarting, "we are not asking you for anything you wouldn't want to tell us. Outpatients like your husband outnumber inpatients at Walter Reed twelve to one. There is a literal overflow of men being warehoused in substandard buildings like this one. Why should you and Major Diaz have to stay in a place with mold on the walls and broken fixtures? What about when your son comes to visit?"

Lacey shook her head, not buying it. "You know how much Mike's prosthetic leg costs?" She pointed at Ellen. "It's top-of-the-line shit! Plus, all the refitting and adjustments and therapy and . . . All of it, taken care of. Forever! For all of them! How about she does a story on that?"

"No one's saying —"

"Thing is, you're not the only one having trouble," Shelby added. "You heard everyone in there. The endless bureaucracy, the disorganization . . ."

"Whining about the army. That's original."

"Maybe your story, of what it's like to live here . . . maybe it could help other families who are in your shoes. You deserve better, and we want to tell that story."

"I deserve better. I deserve better." Lacey tipped sideways in her heeled boots and Ellen caught her elbow, which she yanked away. "Look, maybe you two never had to live in a place with roaches and mice before. Right? 'Oh, this is awful, this is terrible, we better put this in the newspapers.' Don't come into my place and start telling me how shitty it is. I know *exactly* how shitty it is. Go find someone else to be your patsy."

"Lacey. I'm —" Ellen reached out to her.

"You don't know me. You don't know about us!" she shrieked, backing away. Pointing at them. "How do you know what I fucking *deserve.* Get out of here!"

Before either of them could stop her, she ran back into her apartment and slammed the door. And Ellen stood there, in her sauce-stained apron, wrecked.

"Well, that could have gone better," Shelby said, sighing. Then she took a picture of the garbage stacked along the wall.

25

There was almost nothing for Lacey to do on the Internet anymore. Where had she used to spend all that time? Facebook was particularly painful. Every other post was an FRG friend putting up a link about remembering the troops on Presidents' Day — *while you get a day off they're fighting for our freedom* — or reminding everyone about a blood drive or showing off photos of recent get-togethers. Lacey scrolled through as fast as she could, willing herself to not click on any of the smiling women, arms around each other, the kids she recognized, the parties she'd missed. There were a few private messages to her but she barely read them. *Thinking of you. How is he? Praying for your soldier.* She started to type Martine's name in the search bar and then quickly closed the window. No, it was no good to spy on Martine, even though missing her could come on like a gale-force wind. How good it would have been to be able to go through this, even long-distance, with Martine. None of that "praying for your soldier" from Mart. No, she would have had some choice words about this whole situation, would have made Lacey laugh, would have let Lacey bitch about all of it here at Walter Reed, no judgment. Well. So much for that.

She was killing time in one of the computer labs in the Evaluation Board building. They were doing some tests on Eddie, Neuro this time. Memory games, language assessment, large and small motor movements. She hoped with all her heart he would fail them definitively. In the mammoth hive-mind that was the Benefits Admin, all these tests and decisions would add up to dollars someday, and they needed every one they could get, assuming that Eddie would never work again. Problem was, he was so damn good at these tests — he aced them in PT over and over again, and clearly he loved the praise from the aides when he did. How messed up was it that his success could be such a huge liability? Lacey didn't trust those dopes in Benefits to have any common sense. With her luck, they'd probably rate him high just because he could walk an obstacle course using nothing but a cane and his superhero proprioception . . . never acknowledging that the man was now, essentially, retarded.

She listlessly checked the news, but her heart wasn't in it. A bomb in Karbala kills four service members. Coalition forces announce a new curfew for M.A.M.s in Baghdad. Bush vetoes $124 billion spending bill by Congress because it includes a timetable for withdrawal by U.S. forces.

It floated far away from her, the significance of these facts. She was four floors underground in the belly of Walter Reed, surrounded by thousands of injured soldiers and on-duty soldiers and yet Lacey felt less connected to news about the war than she'd been in her kitchen in Mount Vernon, streaming Coldplay in the background.

Probably she was just jittery about Ellen. They'd pretty much ignored each other since the dinner party disaster last week. Not that Lacey missed her appointment with Mike yesterday. When she showed up at the right time, carrying two foam rollers, an exercise band, and a Dr Pepper (his favorite), Ellen had calmly stood up from her chair and ceded the room to her. The two of them had actually nodded to each other, like snooty royals passing in the castle hallway! Even Mike thought it was weird.

"What'd she do to you?" he said. Lacey mumbled *nothing* and got him started on wrist rotations. She wasn't about to bail on him, just because his mom, or whatever she was, had been such a bitch.

Mike was looking good these days, about to get his new leg. His doctors were happy with her work with him; they liked the increased mobility in his shoulders, his built-up core. When she teased him that girls were going to go crazy for a cute guy like him with a fancy new digital limb he got all blushy and grinning before he remembered to be all crabby and *whatever, I don't care, what do you know.* It made Lacey wish she had a photo of him just then, boyish and carefree, to send to Jane.

Lacey swiveled side to side in the computer chair, clicking around aimlessly. The movement eased her pounding headache because it echoed it, matching the pain in her temples with the *creak-crak* sound of the chair's squeaky axis. A guard in the front looked over with a sour face. Lacey ignored him. She was dully hungover from leftover wine from the party, the air in here was dry and cold, and no one else was at the computers.

It would soon be Otis's winter break and he and Lolo would take the train down, to stay a whole week. It was too much: the ferocious need to hug her boy, hear his voice, coupled with the nerves and dread about dealing with Lolo. Eddie's devotion to her may have driven Lacey nuts, but at least when he was all there upstairs she could share that duty with him. Now it was just her and Lolo as the only functioning adults. And her mother-in-law sounded practically perky these days when they spoke. She was going to all kinds of new support groups — Wounded Warrior Moms, Mothers for TBI Hope — and she was raring to go on taking care of Eddie.

Swivel, swivel, swivel. What else? Lacey guessed she could check e-mail, though she rarely did anymore. As expected, it was a depressing list of FRG events she wasn't going to go to and didn't care about, notices about Otis's school stuff that she couldn't attend, and one abrupt e-mail from her boss in reply to Lacey's last week. She'd told him she wouldn't be back "for the foreseeable future" (a phrase Ellen had recommended) and asked him to hold her job for her, based on seven years of good reviews (Ellen, again). His response, which Lacey had read without a shred of surprise, said basically, *I don't think so.* The economy was tight (*no shit*) and since business was down it looked like Gwen could cover the cutback classes and walk-ins (*thanks a lot, Gwen*). So they were probably going to do away with her position eventually. So, in fact, she was doing him a favor by being off on her busted-husband hospital vacation! (He didn't say that part.) Her private client e-mails had also fallen off, after a surge of initial "of course I'll wait for you!'s." Now they'd found other trainers, ones she'd recommended.

Work-wise, she was a free woman.

Lacey was about to log out when she glimpsed two blue unread messages at the top of the screen from an address at first she didn't recognize. And when she did, it was as if someone had plucked her hard from within, down in the deepest part of her body. *Leahy2005@aol.com.*

The first was a photo of Otis, a full-color big file that took several seconds to unroll down her screen. Jim must have taken it when they went out to eat together. She put her hand to her mouth, stifling a short laugh, and a pinwheel of emotions. Otis was making a scrunched-up, *whatchyou doing that for* face, but there was a hidden smile blended in. She studied every minute feature: he was outside, it looked like the boardwalk at Orchard Beach; sunny, patches of snow on the ground behind him. He had his green parka on, and some new blue scarf that Lolo must have gotten him. His cheeks were pink, his hair was a little long, he looked bigger and older than she could have imagined, and Lacey rocked herself on the computer chair, eyes filling up. Her boy, her boy. What was she missing in his life while the days unspooled here in blank sameness? Why wasn't she there with him, goddamn it all to hell. Fuck Eddie, fuck her promises to him that he couldn't even remember now anyway. She wanted her boy.

Lacey wanted to know everything. It took all she had not to call Jim immediately — she hadn't since that time in Whole Foods — to demand all the details. Where did they go? What did they do? What did he say? Does he miss me? What did he eat?

But then she clicked open his second e-mail and Otis slipped from her mind. The subject line read, *Because I had to.* And the e-mail had nothing, no message, only an audio file. A short line with a play button next to it. Lacey looked around the room, cheeks aflame. No one but the guard up front.

"Hey, um . . . do you have any headphones? Like, to borrow?"

"Say what now?"

"Never mind."

Lacey clicked play. Warm, quick-thrumming chords came through the PC's small speakers. They almost knocked her out of her chair. It was a Springsteen song and yes, he'd had to. Because even before the lyrics, the restrained urgency of this music — now, in this chilly room, filling her aching brain — sung every part of her ache and how tightly she'd been fencing it in. Maybe the singer was Bruce but it was Jim, and it was her own self too.

Lacey, with her eyes closed, drank the music in through her skin and every nerve ending. Let it all out when her favorite part came up, about *staying hungry,* about *starving tonight.* And when the guard mumbled a caution she sang louder. As it ended she held her breath as Clarence Clemons played them out on his sax, the rising tones lifting up, lifting higher. Blowing holy energy straight back into her bones.

"Sorry about that," she called breezily, passing the guard on her way out. "But it's the Boss."

Now back to Eddie. And weirdly, that love song from Jim — if that's what it was — gave her strength to tackle Benefits once again: the numbing forms, the redundancies, the mindless bureaucratic maze of offices spread out miles apart. Her phone buzzed with a text: *My name is Lorna and we're in Wd 57 w my son. Got your info from Ellen today and she says you do phys training? Jack is AK too and wants to work on his arms and abs. Your rate is fine, can you come this week? Also I know three other guys who are interested. Text me back ASAP pls.*

Lacey had to read it twice. More work, actual money coming in? Ellen . . . who had recommended her? She had to break into a jog on the way to the elevator bank, slipping around the waxed hallway floor in her boots. What if . . . Maybe she could create a small group boot camp for guys on 57? Get the doctors' buy-in, sweet-talk the nurses, charge a lower rate for a package of classes. Maybe they could use one of the conference rooms? Or what about the Healing Garden? High on ideas for what that money could do, and on Bruce, and on her sweet Otis arriving in a few days, Lacey was full up in her heart. She wanted a drink so bad; she didn't need any kind of drink, ever again. Humming and planning and hurrying back to Eddie.

26

The third time Ellen got up to vomit, she didn't bother going back to bed. The tile floor of the bathroom cooled her bare legs as she waited for the next bout, but after a few minutes she was shaking all over. So she crawled on hands and knees back out to the carpeted floor in the small entrance hallway between the outer door and the bathroom. She was shivering there half asleep when the knock came, the one she'd been expecting. With difficulty, Ellen got herself upright and opened the door a crack.

"Thank you, Marietta." The day maid handed her a stack of folded, warm fresh towels and sheets. "I have another, if you can possibly manage." In a pillowcase, this morning's soiled load. Ellen gave the girl a twenty-dollar bill.

"You sure I don't call doctor?"

"No, I'll be all right. Now excuse me, I need to — oh, oh —" Ellen could barely push the door shut before she had to rush back into the bathroom.

She must have fallen asleep on the floor, because she woke there sometime later curled up under the sink, sore and chilled but without the violent stomach cramps. Slowly, Ellen washed her face and hands with warm, soapy water. One glance in the mirror made her shudder: pale, tightly drawn, bruised under-eyes. Back to bed. She made herself take three sips of water before inching back under the covers. Every motion spiked a nauseating crackle of pain through her head.

It had come on full strength over the weekend, this flu or virus or whatever it was — GI distress with fever, plus cough — but in truth Ellen had sensed its approach a day or two before then. She'd tried to ignore the wooziness, the aches, and the crippling exhaustion, and had made herself keep to the routine: arrival at Heaton by 7:00 a.m. for rounds and Mike's breakfast; a full day of following him to appointments; TV; his dinner and tidying his room; evening preparation ("meds and bed"); back to Mologne around nine. But on Saturday the first appearance of a dry, barking cough drew ire from the weekend shift in the nurses' station.

"You turn right around and get that checked out," they told her, barring her way to Michael's room.

"I'm fine," Ellen said, irritated. Her mistake was to think their concern was for *her.* Didn't she have enough to do around here besides run to the clinic for a simple head cold?

Uh-uh, they said. *No infectious conditions on the ward.* Period. Ellen protested; a set of regulations were produced (rules and regs abounded in this place, of course). An attending was pulled into the argument and made the final call. A digital thermometer was promptly inserted into her ear and the verdict read aloud: 101.3. She was sent packing with a photocopy of the clinic hours, a box of Emergen-C, and a guarantee that she could return twenty-four hours after she hit 98.7 with no symptoms.

The hotel phone rang, once, and stopped. A few seconds later, her cell phone rang. This was Wesley's code to pick up, so she fumbled a hand out of the covers to find her cell.

"Hi," she said, which triggered a thirty-second coughing fit.

"Jesus, Mom. You okay?"

"Fine. Wait a minute." She coughed a wad of mucus into a tissue. "How is he? What's happening?"

"It's amazing. It's literally amazing. They had him up on the track thing, you know, the one between the bars. And he just killed it, Mom. I mean, first time with the real prosthesis on, and Mike looked like he'd been wearing it his whole life. The aides were, like, literally laughing at how sick it was the way he went through all these exercises. He barely had to touch the bars."

Ellen moved her head away from the phone to cough as quietly as she could.

"He did their first test strength routine, so that was, um, okay yeah I wrote it down like you asked — leg swings, heel strikes, grid work, and, uh . . . a couple others. What's incredible is that even though what everyone hears about is the leg, the leg, this amazing C-leg that's been invented, the *real* innovation is the knee. It's called a PK, which stands for —"

"Power knee. I know," Ellen said irritably. Who was the one who'd already been to a dozen appointments in the Gait Lab?

"Yeah, I was talking to one of the technicians, and he was saying that Mike's going to be able to go up and down stairs pretty much the way you and I do. Like, step over step. Not, step, together, step, together. You know what I mean?"

Ellen did. She couldn't believe she wasn't there today, of all days, when Michael got his leg. What she wanted was to be wholly grateful to Wesley for snapping into action, for his excitement and all the calls and updates, for taking her place, but frankly it was hard to take, being instantly cut out of the action. *Has he asked about me?* She wondered fretfully. *Does he even notice I'm not there?*

The day of her quarantine from the ward, from the Gait Lab, from anywhere Michael or other recovering soldiers might be, Ellen had tried to persuade his team leader to reschedule or at least push it back a few days until she was well enough to accompany Mike to the lab. How else would he get there? *We'll take care of everything,* she was assured. They were on a very specific schedule due to his suction measurements and the availability of the technicians. Ellen couldn't imagine him there by himself, though, so as soon as she gave up on the doctors she got on the phone to Wesley. It was all arranged within hours: his flight the next morning, a rental car, his hotel room in Silver Spring. Whatever misgivings she had about Michael's moodiness and how he and Wesley would do were put to rest that first day when they called together. Basically, they made fun of her; the first target was the notes and charts she had all over the room, still tracking his food and liquid intake long after the nurses asked her to.

"Mom, really? 'Urine, volume and color'?" Wesley had hooted. "What do you do, take a good look after he goes?"

"Ask her what she did one time after I took an especially good shit," she heard Michael say, laughing.

"Oh, God." Wes groaned. "What's been going on over here, you guys?"

"Tell him, Ellen!"

"Well, I . . ." There was no escaping it. "I put a smiley face next to the date, in the chart." Couldn't they let her collapse back in bed? "Now listen, if you see Dr. Rombardy, remind him about the swelling on his —"

But Wesley was laughing too loudly. "Mikey, you got an A! In pooping! Is that your first A ever?"

She hung up on them.

As she almost did now, with Wesley. But instead she forced herself to be cogent for the rest of the update about Michael in the Gait Lab, although she did hold the phone away from her ear when he described the hoagies they'd ordered for dinner with a couple of other guys on the ward. No, she didn't need anything. Yes, she would call if she did. Fine, he could stop by tomorrow on his way to the ward. Drive carefully, etc. etc. Wait! Make sure the night shift had his cell number as well as hers.

In a few minutes Ellen felt herself tugged back down into the clenched state of dozing; not asleep and not awake, her body tightened with flu and her mind raced with images and memories.

Like the bitterly cold Saturday afternoon they'd sat in the frozen metal stands to watch one of Michael's football games his senior year. To Ellen, everything about this giant public school seemed unfriendly — the ugly one-story buildings, the ragged fields, the rowdy teens in the stands, and even the few people her age, unsmiling parents who spat disparagement at the referees. But for Wes's and Jane's sake, she put a good face on it. She shushed their scornful privileged comments — about the cheerleaders' sprayed and teased hair, or the way the announcer kept mispronouncing *Realtor* (for one of the team's sponsors) — and tried to figure out which player was their Mike. None of them knew his number, and the boys all looked the same in their dingy white jerseys and white helmets. This was supposed to be the one area of his success, the one arena where Mike hadn't screwed up or burned bridges. And yet as each quarter inexorably ticked down there was no action that distinguished one player over another, as far as Ellen could see. The cold wind took away the coaches' screams before they reached the sparse crowd. All they could hear over the squealing PA system were the rattling metal stands and the satisfying *click-crunch* of helmets and pads crashing into one another, again and again.

Jane fled to wait in the car. Wes elbowed Ellen: "Aren't you glad I never wanted to play?" he shouted, scarf over his mouth. And what had she said, cold and frustrated with this useless outing, what had she said without thinking? "Luckily, you never would have made it past tryouts," maybe. Whatever it had been, her words made him turn away, visibly stung.

Meanwhile, all around them a chant rose up from the home stands: *YOUUUU SUCK! YOUUUUU SUCK! YOUUUUU SUCK!* Ellen was amazed by the hearty vehemence full-grown adults brought to it, hurling the words down vaguely toward the other team, or simply out into the gray windy day.

After the game, trying to salvage some

part of this, she'd hurried down the unsteady riser to try to catch Michael as the players jogged off the muddy field toward the gym.

"Mike! Mike!" Ellen had called as the sweaty boys ran past, her voice high and desperate with need. None of the helmeted horde noticed or recognized or acknowledged her there, leaning over a railing. Did he hear her? Did he ignore her? *Great game,* she would have said. And claimed due credit for being there — wasn't that what this was all about, after all?

"Exit on the other side," a beefy security guard told her. All the players were gone.

Ellen coughed and coughed again. She squinted back up in the stands, mostly empty now. There he was, Wesley. Crutches propped alongside. Waiting for her, furious and ashamed, his half leg jutting out. *How can he wear those shorts in this cold?* A coughing fit winded her; she could never make it back up all those steps; she was stranded down here, far away from him. Wes held his shiny-pink stump in both hands and shook it at her — *See this? See?* — and he was laughing in a terrible way, laughing and shaking that misshapen chunk of bare thigh . . .

No! No, no. Ellen fought her way awake

in her darkened Mologne House room. Coughing helped; she had to push herself upright to make it stop. At least the nausea had abated, for now. Sweaty, she wiped her mouth with a cloth. What a miserable nightmare. Not Wesley. It didn't happen to Wesley.

What was worse than the dream (the half dream, for the football game had been real, and never seeing Mike, and her mean comment to Wes) was her waking relief, this unforgivable and utter elation that swelled within her every cell, as she realized anew — *say it* — that at least it wasn't her *real son,* amputated, broken inside, trapped in this new lifelong hell, up there in Heaton.

Ellen put the side of her head to the wall and cried. The force of the shame and the relief. No, she'd never had to worry about gentle, brainy Wesley coming to this. At once it all seemed false and guilt-filled, every minute she'd spent at Mike's side — every baby food jar, therapy session, PT trip. Was that why he was so prickly, so apt to pop off? Could he sense it too, that she was here on a technicality?

But that wasn't right. She tried to think clearly, huddled in pain, sensing a new awareness pounding at the door of her illness. What about all that agony while he was gone? What about those months of wrenching anxiety, the unsent, unhinged letters? Had that been optional? A kind of made-up existential crisis she forced on herself in lieu of a real mother's fear, a real mother's pain?

All right, then. Reframe this. Consider the context. (Things she'd scribbled, a thousand times, in student paper margins.)

They'd faced the judge, across his enormous desk, that morning Ellen became Michael's legal guardian. It was October, less than a year until he turned eighteen. The forms were reviewed and stamped; the two of them signed where they were told. Then a clerk was summoned, to be a second witness as Ellen read the oath out loud. It was a moment of surprising solemnity, amid the bureaucracy, compared to the nervous joking she and Mike had done in the car on the way over. *After this I'm gonna call you Ma. Don't you dare.*

"I, Ellen Silverman, will faithfully and completely fill my duties as Guardian. I promise to, at all times, protect my ward's interests and to make all decisions based on the best interest of my ward."

Did that awkward repetition, my ward's interests, best interest of my ward, bother her then? Had she broken the mood with a slight frown, always needing to assert her readerly superiority, if only to herself? Ellen pressed the damp washcloth to her mouth, tried to see herself back through the years in that judge's office.

What had she known then about protecting Michael? That Ellen, in the courthouse, the one in the pressed skirt and good shoes. What did she even know about the phrase "transfemoral amputation"?

"But what if," she said aloud into her room at Mologne. A sting of acid down her throat. What if the oath had said more? "Furthermore, I, Ellen Silverman, promise to tacitly support the war in Iraq and all U.S. military intervention thereof, including my ward's voluntary participation in activities designed to maim, kill, and otherwise perform duties as per the orders of Commander in Chief George W. Bush. I promise to accept fear and terror for an unknown duration of time related to the following: the possibility my ward will be killed during war; the possibility he will kill during war; the possibility he will be kidnapped, tortured, and executed; the possibility that he will suffer. I promise to bear the fact that he will lose a limb. I promise to leave my job, home, family, and friends, to stay with him for an unknown duration of time while he heals. I promise to accept, if not understand, that my very presence will not ease and may even trigger my ward's anger, frustration, and other symptoms. I promise . . ."

She fell back to sleep.

Sometime later, Ellen lurched out of bed, instantly dizzy. She felt her way to the bathroom, resigned to another bout of vomiting. But two thoughts blazed through her nauseated fog and she held them tight, understanding what had been shown to her. Now all the struggle to understand her place here fell away, all those questions about Michael and what if and if only . . . Guardianship, motherhood, these distinctions fell away because it was love, just love, its own reward. How could she not have seen? In the face of it, this simple love for Mike, she felt wordless, lightened.

And also wretched, weak. But there was Jane. Think about Jane. A bad mistake, her leaving. *Ellen's* mistake. But she would fix things as soon as she survived this flu, or even survived these next few minutes. They would go to him together, and tell him. They would rise up and make the best of it. Because what you chose and what you were given made up a life.

And, oh, she needed her daughter. Jane, Jane. Come back.

27

It was Wild Turkey doubles, and she'd had four or five, lost track. Lacey was alone at the bar in the Mologne lobby with that burn-it-all-to-the-ground feeling, and she didn't care. Not caring was part of the feeling: dangerous, on-the-edge. For the past few hours, she'd been trading jokes and buy-backs with a nearby table full of guys, but things were devolving, she could tell. Flirting had taken on a bad tinge, as if they were daring her to go further. She knew they were talking about her. Fuck 'em.

Lacey had been broke for so long that she'd forgotten how to do this, drink with actual money in her wallet. Maybe she'd never known how, come to think of it. Her training sessions were a huge hit over in Ward 57. The doctors were all for it, as long as she cleared the exercises with them first, and she was up to three weekly group boot camps with four or five guys in each. Thing is, what she was having the guys do was pretty much basic strength stuff they should have been working on themselves; she provided the incentive and the discipline, not any new techniques. The moms and wives all paid in cash, $30 per, though Lacey knew she could get more if she wanted to. Last week she'd caught a ride with another Building 18er to a Western Union where she paid off collections for two credit card bills and caught up on utilities. When Lolo arrived with Otis the day before yesterday, Lacey was proud to hand her mother-in-law a hundred bucks, although of course the woman put up a big show of not wanting to take it before she finally did.

"But he's doing so good now." Lolo couldn't take her eyes off her son's face. She just kept stroking it and admiring the new eighteen-dollar shades Lacey had bought at Sunglass Hut. "Why let them cut things in the brain when they don't have to?"

"Because light," Eddie had said firmly, and Lacey had wanted to cheer.

"Mom, I know it's scary. But if there's a chance they can get some sight back in his eye, then . . ."

"What about getting some thinking back in his head?" Otis had muttered, and both women shot him a look to kill.

But what then? What now? With the optic nerve surgery tentatively set for Thursday next week and another week or two of recovery, Eddie was going to be released soon. They would be set free, sent home. For a while, both here and at home, Lacey could keep busy chasing the money with forms. While they waited for MEB to make a final decision on his rating, she could figure out whether he'd be medically discharged or retired: one got you severance pay, one got you nada. Then again, would VA rating money be enough to cover them without any other army income — no ID card, no TriCare, no post privileges? Add to this equation that disability dollars got deducted from retirement pay, *but* they were nontaxable. And the fact that some flunky had let it slip that the rules about concurrent receipt were changing next year anyway. So would they be able to collect both retirement and disability, based on his twenty years of service? Only for a time, it appeared. And those benefits might cancel each other out. Not to mention Social Security disability, which she hadn't even looked into — apparently it had nothing to do with retirement or disability pay, but might disqualify you from either. Or both.

Fine, so that was enough crazy to keep her distracted for a while. But what would happen when the noise and action died down, and the thirty phone calls and the nine trips to Kinkos and the follow-up appointments and the PT and social services and driving Eddie everywhere he ever had to go, again, ever. What was she going to do then?

Her and Eddie, alone in their place all day. Not talking, not touching, not fucking. No job at the gym, no group to lead, no Martine. Otis grows up, goes off to college, her looks melt away and no one notices. And Eddie's slow high-pitched dribble of a laugh echoes through the house.

Lacey killed her drink in two eye-watering gulps. " 'M ready," she called to the big-momma-type bartender, squelching a wince.

Bonk. One of the guys swung his wheelchair against her tall-legged stool. "Can't be that bad, girl," he said, looking up at her. Southern accent, maybe nineteen. Had both his legs, but they hung limp on the metal front-rigging. He backed up and rammed her chair again.

"What? Did they dare you?" She nodded at the table he'd come from.

"You should come on over there, we don't bite. Less you want me to." This was offered up in a nervously questioning tone, *am I doing this right?* Lacey granted him a smile — a real one. These guys. It could break your heart.

"Hey, Jensen, she wants a guy that brought his dick back from the sandbox."

"Ignore them," Lacey said.

"Look, it's all here. Working order." The young guy, Jensen, hiccupped. "Unlike some people I could mention!" he shouted back over his shoulder. Hoots and retorts from the table.

"Go on," Lacey urged him back to his friends. She swiveled around to the bar and a fresh drink. The clock over the bar said 10:20. Two more, maybe three? Have to bear down before closing. Lacey checked her phone; no messages. Earlier, she'd thought about calling Ellen to see if she wanted to join, sip that endless single glass of wine she sometimes liked to have. She really should talk to Ellen. There was something she needed to tell her, even though she wasn't supposed to. But they'd barely had contact since the horrible night of the dinner party when Lacey had screamed like a crazy person at her only friend. So now she just had to hope Ellen wouldn't pass through the lobby and see her like this.

■ ■ ■ ■

Three days ago Lacey went out for a run. A jog, to be more precise. Half walk, let's be real. Working out those guys in 57 made it all too clear how far she'd let things slip in that department, though she'd lost about ten pounds, probably all muscle. She was wearing somebody's cast-off trainers (from a lost-and-found box) and a pair of Eddie's gray sweatpants that were too heavy for the day — melting pockets of dirty snow, puffs of cold spring air. Lacey was puffing too, cursing the many months of nothing that had led to this sorry state of affairs. She had always prided herself on staying in shape even during a partying phase. At Rudy's Gym they were used to her bathroom-dash for a quick hangover vomit and then back out there to keep lifting. Boot and rally! But this, this was pathetic.

She made it about a mile into Rock Creek Park and had to rest, winded, on a bench. But then a few tri-dip sets later, she was back at it, dragging herself out toward Walter Reed.

Jogging in place at the corner of Sixteenth and Alaska, waiting to cross, Lacey idly noticed the white Pontiac G8 on the other side, with its flashers on. *Just like mine,* she thought.

Wait a minute.

Because now the woman was getting out of the driver's seat and waving to Lacey. Was it — ?

"Is that my car?" Traffic separated them and the black-haired woman didn't hear her, only waved again. "That's my car, dammit. Hey!"

Horns blared as Lacey charged across the street. She ignored whatever the grinning reporter was saying and went around to check the license plate: XLJ 314.

"How'd you get this? Why are you driving my car?"

"You set some kind of record at the pound, apparently. They thought it was an abandoned vehicle."

"Yeah, well." Lacey tightened her ponytail, acutely aware of the other woman's skinny jeans and cool tunic-type sweater thing. "It's probably worth more in parts, anyway."

The reporter laughed. "I stopped by for you at Building Eighteen, but someone told me you'd be out here. It wasn't locked by the way. Front entrance. I just went right in."

"Yeah. The buzzer's broken again. First floor's pissed. There's been two break-ins, and one woman had her . . . never mind."

Behind them, a tall wrought iron fence barred off the south side of Walter Reed, the nicer part. Rolling lawns and dense trees; through them you could only partially glimpse the older buildings, red brick with white cupolas and curlicue trim on the eaves. Lacey sometimes hid out back near here when she drank during the day. Like a servant creeping around the mansion and its grounds. The reporter tossed her the keys in a long silvery arc. "Want to give me a ride home?"

Lacey studied them. The key ring with its plastic tab advertising Sip N Bowl out on White Plains Road, one of Otis's favorites. House keys to their place, which she hadn't touched in months, hadn't even thought about. She traced one of the nicked metal squares, still warm from the other woman's hands.

Lacey was no fool: this was a quid pro quo. She'd paid off her car in exchange for . . . what? Some dirt on this place. Some truths. Well, maybe it was time.

"I'm not a squealer," she said, looking up. "That's not who I am."

The reporter held up both hands. "Just a ride," she said. "We'll talk, and you decide. Promise."

"All right." The door handle clunking up, the squeak of the driver's seat, curved to the shape of her ass, the touch of the steering wheel worn shiny at four and eight . . . sense memories so strong it felt like Lacey had climbed back into her old life. She'd had to blink her eyes a lot, sweat and tears mingling, as she leaned over to call to this reporter lady still standing outside. "So get in."

Now in the bathroom in Mologne's lobby Lacey lost her balance while squatting to pee and fell forward against the stall's door.

"Whoa," someone out at the sinks said, with a half laugh.

"Shut up." Both hands on the door, she braced herself to try again. Also, she could rest her forehead there for a moment. C'mon, Lace. *O can't see me like this. Or Lolo. Lolo and O, O Lo. O no o no . . .*

She flicked water on her face and then on the mirror to break up her image in the reflection. Drops zigzagged down, mesmerizing.

Back at the bar, she called for the check, which had been set in front of her place already. Her glass was gone, even though it'd had at least one last melted-ice sip. Bitch. Her jacket was on the ground. Fine, now where the fuck was her purse?

Laughter behind her. Intentional laughter, meant to be heard. Lacey whirled and saw her bag on the soldiers' table, contents dumped out and spread around.

"You shits. Give me my stuff."

"We were gonna pay your tab but" — laughter — "nobody's got that much money, so —"

"Uh-oh, tampon." It was pinched between the metal fingers of a prosthetic hook. "Is this a bad time of the month?"

"Lemme see the lipstick again." Burp.

"Is this really your phone? Oh man, now I feel better."

A fury rose up inside her. She scrabbled to corral all her embarrassing crap back into her bag, but they kept snatching things back. And nothing replaced that drunken fury, no shame or self-preservation, when finally one of them unfolded and smoothed out the picture of Jim. It was actually a computer printout from Facebook, the only photograph she could find without obviously stalking him. Jim, baseball cap on backward, cup in hand, mid-laugh. Outside on someone's patio, a barbecue she hadn't gone to with him, a button-up shirt she'd never seen and probably never would.

"Who the fuck is this," one of the vets

said, flatly.

"It's not her man, that I know. I seen him, blind guy, Mexican. Right?"

"Give it back to her." This was Jensen, not looking at Lacey. Not smiling.

"No, I wanna know who this fat fuck is and why *he's* in here."

"Wouldn't you like to know," Lacey hissed, and made a swipe for the photo, which was neatly whipped out of her reach. "Maybe it's her brother, all right?"

"Is it your brother?" the soldier holding the photo said to her. Taunting, a test.

"Sure. Sure, it's my brother. We're BFF, so I carry a fucking photo around. Of my brother."

Cold stares from all of them, with their patchy-shaved heads and missing limbs; their busted insides and messed-up brains. These sullen young faces. Resentful like Bailey's, or Martine's, just like anyone who'd been disappointed by Lacey. How could anyone mistake *her* for someone to admire? What had she done, letting herself be a part of this military world with its belief in things like honor and duty and courage? She was a sham and she couldn't bear it one more instant, these broken boys looking up at her for reassurance.

"You think we sit home the whole time

waiting for you to get back?" she cried. "Your perfect virgin angels, right? Sewing flags and staring at your photos. You don't know. You don't know anything about people like me."

She gripped the handle of a nearby wheelchair as the floor tilted. The poison of her bad self and the drinks rushed upward.

"Yeah, I cheated on him. There. I'll fucking announce it right here in the Mologne House for American Heroes and their Saintly Wives. Okay? Is that what you want to hear? That I'm a slut and so is your girlfriend and yours and yours —"

"Shut up, bitch."

"This girl's crazy."

"I'm here, aren't I? This slut is the one who takes him to every appointment, PT, MBI . . . Okay? For a man who I don't even think I ever loved! Lost my job, never see my kid, live in a fucking hovel with mold that gives me nosebleeds but that's not enough, right?"

There was shouting now. From the guys, from the bartender, from others in the lobby who had drifted over to see what the commotion was. A roar of disgust turned on her like a firehose. But Lacey couldn't stop.

"Because I'm supposed to offer up my *soul* too! It's not enough that this whore actually showed up and stayed here and is in the shit with him every day, every month . . . no! Because we've gotta *love* it too!"

Someone was pulling on her arm. Lacey ripped it away. People were pointing, yelling, demanding she leave.

"I'm a drunk but not a hypocrite! Say what you want about me, but I know the deal. All right? I know the deal. People usually do, when the — What? Get *off* me!"

Ellen. In a soft wool robe. "Let's go. Lacey. Come with me."

Now the growing mob included Ellen in their vitriol, but she stayed calm and quiet, murmuring to Lacey, guiding her back and away. She swept up Lacey's things, she spoke to the bartender, she put distance between Lacey and the soldiers at the table. Little by little, Ellen drew the two of them toward the elevators, waving off people who stared. Lacey was weeping hysterically now: *I didn't mean it, I didn't mean it.* But fuck those guys. *Go away, Ellen, just leave me alone . . . I'm so, I'm so . . .*

An hour later she wasn't sober yet, but she was quiet. Ellen made her take a hot shower and drink a cold glass of water. Literally. She stood in front of Lacey and wouldn't let her stop until she finished glugging it.

Each time Lacey tried to collapse into a sobbing pile, Ellen put on her stern-professor face and gave her another task, like, open this bottle of Advil and blow your nose. Tough love. Right now she was supposed to be pulling Ellen's comb through her own wet and tangled hair, but the world kept collapsing in on her — what she'd become, how much she missed Jim, and what Ellen must think of her now . . .

"I can't. I just can't."

"Stop that." Ellen tugged her back up from flopping sideways on the bed. "Give me the comb."

Lacey held still, shivering in a towel on the edge of the bed. Ellen combed her hair a handful at a time, from the ends up, the way she'd probably learned from dealing with Jane's over the years. Oh, Jane . . . Lacey needed to tell Ellen about Jane.

"Listen, Ellen?" But something caught her eye before she could finish. Shrugging off the comb she went to the dresser and picked up a thick leather folding envelope. Lacey struggled to swallow. "Is this . . . ?"

Yes. It was the actual emblem she'd imagined, she'd tried to conjure, for Eddie from almost the minute she'd heard he'd been hit. In her hands, right now. She had even thought of how they'd display it at home, somewhere subtle but noticeable. Classy. Where people's eyes might fall on it and they'd know what he had gone through, what she had. It would be the tangible proof, signed and dated, of how much they both had lost. And it would have been what carried Lacey through, alone in the apartment with Eddie-but-not-Eddie.

"I don't believe you. Were you going to tell me?"

"About what? Oh, that? I don't —"

" 'Oh, that?' Jesus. Does getting a Purple Heart happen to you every week or something? So it just slipped your mind?"

"It's not *my* Purple Heart. Now come over here, let me finish."

But Lacey couldn't stop staring at the medal, smaller than she thought it'd be, mounted in a plastic box-type thing, and the fancy script on the citation: *To Michael B. Cacciarelli, Lance Corporal . . . For Wounds Received in Action on October 11, 2005, in Iraq, Given Under My Hand.* Signed by the secretary of the navy and the adjutant general.

She hugged Mike's award to her chest, reeling with the unfairness of it all. To compose herself, Lacey gazed around the dresser Ellen had apparently repurposed as a workstation. What were all these notes and lists, covered over with the same miniature forceful script?

"Is it killing you not to have a desk, or what?"

Ellen went *hmph.*

"I bet this is the longest you've ever gone without a desk in your life. Since you were a kid. What is all this, teaching stuff?" Lacey fingered one of the many scraps of paper taped to the wall above the dresser. But she was wrong: these were names of people, women, that she half recognized from the hospital, or from Mologne or Building 18. Lists of women and their soldiers, with notes jotted next to each about where they were from, what they were like, whether they might be willing to talk to the reporter. Copies of articles titled "Minimum Safety Requirements in VA Hospitals: The Engineering Perspective." Sketched-out ideas for meetings, dates, facts.

"You think it's all a crock, don't you." Lacey set the award carefully back down on the neat dresser. "The military. You hate it." She sat down and felt Ellen's careful hands on her head again.

"I don't know," Ellen admitted. "I never had to think much about it, before."

Lacey struggled with all the sharp things to say, the retorts that came automatically to mind anytime she encountered a head-in-the-sand liberal who probably didn't know the difference between Kirkuk and Mosul and worse: didn't care. She and Martine and Felicia and the others . . . they used to store up and trade put-downs for people just like Ellen, the ones who didn't get it, didn't know or respect or appreciate all the work that was being done to keep us safe here in America. But now Lacey was silent on all of that.

"What was it like?" she finally asked. Ellen was rubbing her head with the towel, squeezing excess water out of her hair. She never wanted it to stop. "When they gave it to him."

"It happened early on, while he was still under. In and out. I don't think he really knew what was happening."

"What was it like for you, I mean?"

"Oh." The towel stopped. "Confusing. I was . . . proud. I'd never seen him get an award. The formality, the deference, the ceremony. I'm susceptible to all that, I guess. Later on, I scrutinized how meekly I accepted it all — them sweeping in to give him this *thing,* the way we were all so hushed and deferential about a piece of metal, but nobody even mentioned him losing his leg. I can only imagine what Jane would have done, if she'd been there."

Lacey snorted. She had an idea.

"But no, I didn't feel as disgusted as I would have thought. Before."

"Well, that's something."

"Let's go to bed. Should you call your room to let them know?"

"Nah, I don't want to wake them. I sent Otis a text, and I'll be back over there early."

Tell her, Lacey, she cried inwardly. But she couldn't; it felt too good to be here, coming down from the hysterical shit show she'd put on downstairs, like this was a cozy haven, away from Eddie, away from the little piles of mice shit in the corners of their room, away from all of it. It even smelled fresh in here, like a goddamn Mologne cologne. It felt too good to be with Ellen again.

For the first time that night, Ellen looked uncertain. She held up a potential nightgown for Lacey to borrow — as if Lacey had worn a nightgown since she was ten! — and they both glanced from it, size two, to Lacey, size twelve.

"Lucky you." Lacey dropped her towel and scrambled under the covers. "Getting me in all my glory."

Ellen picked up the wet towel and hung it over a chair. "Oo-rah," she said.

■ ■ ■ ■

For a long time they lay together in bed, face-to-face in the dark, talking. Lacey couldn't believe how sick Ellen had been and she was overcome with guilt about their stupid fight. But she was better now, and would even be allowed back on the ward starting tomorrow. Or the next day, depending on how strict they were. Someone had told her three full days after the fever and vomiting was gone, but someone else had said, just use common sense.

At first, afraid to upset her, Lacey didn't mention seeing Mike at last week's training session — with this guy who was Ellen's other son, the sweet nerdy guy hanging around! — or how great he was doing on the new leg. But strangely, Ellen was pretty chill about having had to miss all that. She wanted to know how he was, she asked all about Lacey's new boot camps on the ward. She seemed happy to hear that Lacey had agreed to meet with Shelby for lunch sometime next week, but she didn't bug her or plead or try to convince her that cooperating was essential to the nation's right to a free press or whatever.

"Are you sleepy?" Lacey asked.

"Not yet."

"Okay, well . . . about all that, downstairs. What you probably heard."

"You don't have to tell me. Only if you want to."

Lacey took a deep breath. And then she whispered it all, told everything about Eddie and how he'd gotten mean on her right after the wedding but she told herself it was part of the army thing and he was so stable, and he was kind of okay with Otis . . . and it didn't hurt he'd be gone for long stretches. She whispered about the Asshole, about the bad choices, while tears slid down the side of her nose, how probably they had something to do with her shitty dad, as did the drinking — it didn't take Dr. Freud — and she knew she could be better than this but it was just so hard. Finally, she told Ellen about Jim. What she'd done and why and how she'd stopped but couldn't really.

"It was cheating but it didn't *feel* like cheating. And I know about how cheating feels. This was different."

"Mm."

Lacey cast her gaze wildly around in the dark, as if she could find evidence to help her prove it. "Sometimes it's enough for me that he's out there. Even though we can't be together, *obviously.* Just to know that I found it once. A good guy who's crazy about me. I feel all settled and at peace with it. Sometimes. That's what real love is, right?"

Ellen's face was only a few inches away on the next pillow but it was impossible to tell what she was thinking. The older woman was studying her, was listening closely.

"It's okay if you're judging me. You can say it. I won't get —" Lacey's voice wobbled briefly. "I won't get mad. Aren't you going to tell me I'm a bad person?"

"No."

"You're not?"

"No."

"Did you sleep through what I just said?"

Ellen laughed softly. "No."

"Well, Jesus, Ellen." Lacey rolled on her back and blew out her breath. Wild Turkey, ugh. "Can't you at least tell me what to do, then? About this big ol' mess of a life?"

First she felt a small warm hand on her arm, sliding its way into her own hand. Then she heard Ellen say, quietly, "No."

They lay like that for a long time, hand in hand. Ellen fell asleep; her breathing changed, became deeper, with long pauses between. Lacey watched shadows on the ceiling and thought about all the different things that had brought her here. She sobered up but stayed awake; it felt like being on watch, like she had to protect this small gray-headed woman in bed next to her. Lacey wanted to rescue her too, and as the night passed she sorted through all the ways she could do that, could throw Ellen a lifeline.

In the end, before she drifted off, Lacey came up with two, for starters. First, she would spill it all to the reporter. Give her everything she needed about the conditions of her building, all the gory details, even pictures if she wanted. Why not? Not like Lacey had that much to lose — what was the army to her now, or even to Eddie? — and anyway, if Ellen thought it was important then she must have her reasons. So that was the easy one.

Next up, and it would have to happen quickly — there was a lot she'd have to finesse . . . but Lacey was going to solve the Jane problem for Ellen. Bring mother and daughter back together, get them talking again, move them past this divide. It wouldn't be simple, knowing those two. But it was going to happen immediately, that was for sure. Because Jane — who'd showed up at Walter Reed unannounced only a few hours ago, who'd begged Lacey to find her a few moments alone with Mike, who swore her to secrecy — was right this very minute asleep in the sleeping bag she'd brought from Wisconsin, on the floor of Lacey and Eddie's room, with Lolo and Otis crammed in there too, in Building 18.

28

That morning, arriving at Heaton, Ellen walked briskly through security and held the elevator for an aide wheeling a cart full of cellophane-wrapped baskets holding teddy bears and candy. The two of them exchanged a roll of the eyes, knowing both the inanity of these gifts and that their incoming flood would never stop.

She was impatient — late — it was almost noon. When she woke this morning she was startled and annoyed to see that it was ten o'clock. How late had she and Lacey stayed up talking? And where was Lacey now? No sign of her; she must have slipped out early. Ellen rushed through a shower, dressed, and sat on the edge of her for-once unmade bed to make several phone calls, to the airline and taxi services and so on. Then she spoke to a woman at an agency called Children and Family First, out near the intersection of Wisconsin 151 and 94, by the big office park, and made an appointment for twelve-thirty on Friday.

Two nights ago, in the aftermath of that terrible flu, Ellen had hit on the solution. They had dismissed adoption without really considering it, she had realized in a rush. But it was perfect for Jane! It fit right into her devotion to service and helping others!

My fault, Ellen thought, waiting for the slow ding of each elevator floor on its way to floor five. She had let the pain of the idea cloud her better judgment. Yes, it would be hard on Jane. But raising a baby would be harder.

Now if she could only get Jane on the phone. She'd left several messages but no response of course. Still, that was expected. Michael would never have to know, and what a relief for Jane, not having to put this on him. And she'd be free, Ellen thought, slightly bouncing up onto her toes. Free to go on to college and a career . . . fine, even free to have a relationship with Michael, if that's what they both wanted! She'd never said it was his baby, and so giving it up didn't have to mean it would be a secret from him. It could be the way forward. Okay, so Jane being Jane it would mean a trickily elegant convincing process with the eventual goal that she, Jane, be the one to come up with the idea. Fine. None of that mattered if it would save her daughter's future.

Well, maybe it was better that Jane hadn't picked up the phone. (When did Jane ever pick up her phone?) *Ding.* The elevator opened onto five and Ellen turned automatically toward Ward 57. This was a conversation best had in person, and she would be home the day after tomorrow, in any case. Jane would just have to be surprised by her arrival.

The hard part, Ellen thought, waving to Dr. Pritzker, would be telling Michael she needed to go home for a few days. He should be all right with that, though. He'd survived with her being gone for the flu; he'd probably jump at the chance for more. But for now, oh God, she couldn't wait to see him on that new leg!

She was caught off guard by how crowded Michael's room was. There was Lacey, there was Wes, and most of all — when she could finally take it in — there was Michael, with his sweatpants pulled up on one side to reveal the metal tubes and black cord disappearing into a white sock and brand-new sneaker. They were all talking rapidly over one another, so they didn't notice Ellen at first when she came in. One at a time they fell silent and she realized that although Michael was standing upright, there was a figure in his bed.

Jane.

Propped up against the raised back of the bed, hair splayed against the messy sheets, knees bent and skirt falling up her bare thighs, barefoot. And in the middle of all that, at the center of Jane and of the hospital bed and of the entire room it seemed, was the high curve of her belly. A T-shirt stretched thinly over it, and her round navel strained even against that, a miniecho of the pregnancy.

Ellen did as good a job as she could manage, to cover her shock and surprise. She went first to her daughter and gave her a dry kiss on the forehead. Then she went to Michael and gave him a long hug. Then, she shot a dirty look in the general direction of Wesley and Lacey.

"Well," she said. "I can't tell if this is a party I'm late to, or one to which I haven't been invited." Her chair, the one she'd sat on for months while they watched TV, was heaped with coats and bags.

Jane opened her mouth but Lacey hurriedly said, "Give her the show, Mike. The full demonstration."

"You mean my robo-leg? My next-gen

Terminator parts? Your all's tax dollars bought it." He beckoned her close. Ellen bent down to admire the brushed blue-and-gray fiberglass shell and watch as Mike tugged up the black carbon fiber leg socket they'd fit to his exact specifications. She listened to him explain how the knee microprocessor worked, instantly converting reads and settings to adjust the swing of the knee joint. At his urging, she reached into his cotton sock to touch the rubber foot-shaped sock he pulled on over the metal blade. Each part of this she'd known about for months, had taken notes on, had a stack of photocopies about. But Ellen, rejoicing in Mike's energy and enthusiasm, let him explain it all, and asked lots of questions to which she knew the answers.

It bought her time too. But the fact of Jane, the presence of Jane, burned behind her. Finally, she couldn't wait any longer.

"Honey, why didn't you tell me you were coming? I would have picked you up."

"He knows, Mom. About the baby. So you can drop the whole pretend-everything's-okay act."

"It would be hard *not* to know at this point, now that you're here. So why don't we take a moment to talk about how we can —"

"No. Uh-uh. First, how about you tell Mike that you basically lied to him, and to me, so you could hide me away and not even let the two of us *deal* with this —"

"Jane!" This was Lacey. "You promised."

"Lacey, maybe it would be best if you could give us a little time alone, as family."

"She's here because *she's* the only one being honest! If it weren't for her, Mike would still be thinking that I, like, didn't even care about him anymore. Because you twisted it all around, Mom! You never even gave him a chance to make his own decision."

Michael was clicking a small remote that caused a whirr-buzz in the ankle area of his C-leg. Toggling between two modes; *bzzz* click, *bzzz* click.

"We don't need the whole ward to hear all this," Wesley mumbled. "Drama."

"Oh, it's nothing out of the ordinary," Ellen said. She scooped the coats off her chair and dumped them on the radiator. "You should have been here the time a National Guard soldier two rooms over mixed up the dates and had both his girlfriends visit at the same time."

Mike snorted, and that one sound filled her with hope and energy. She sat down and tried to look calmly at Jane. "So why don't you tell me what the two of you have decided. About this baby."

Everyone began talking at once. It was only Mike and Jane's business; it was the whole family's business. Ellen should butt out; Ellen had every right to know what the deal was. They should give this some time; they should air it all out now.

"Are the two of you . . ." Ellen managed to say. "Together?"

Jane made a whooshing noise, as if this had nothing to do with anything. Michael looked uneasily from Jane to Ellen to the remote in his hand.

"Obviously, I'm going to do what's right," he said, in a low voice. And then, directly to Ellen. "I should've told you. I'm sorry." He flashed a grimace at Wes.

Before she could respond, Jane erupted. "*You're* sorry? What about her telling me that you hated me!"

"I did *not* do that!"

"You made me leave by saying he'd be better off without me around. That he'd never want me or this baby in his life." Tears streamed down both sides of Jane's plump cheeks.

"What I — what I wanted was for you both to have some time to —"

"Lacey says all you ever did here was

scheme up ways to make sure he never knew about me being pregnant. Like you wanted to spare him the fucked-up life that I have."

"It was me. My idea." This was Lacey. "So just leave off on your mom, all right? There's no way he could've handled that news a month ago. Mike knows it. Right?" They all stared at Lacey except Mike, who watched his new foot raise one inch and tap, raise and tap. "It's not like it's been a picnic in this room, you know. You should have seen what he put your mom through and you'd be glad you weren't around!"

Mike's gaze flew up to Ellen and she saw a flash of confusion. *Really?* "Careful," she said, as he wobbled.

"Your idea?" Jane said softly. "But you — I thought you were on my side."

"There's no *sides,*" Lacey cried in exasperation. "I never said I had any magic answers, either."

"But you felt entitled to get in my business," Jane said, heating up again. "In our business —" she gestured at Mike. "And make decisions for people you don't even know."

"That's enough, Jane," Ellen said.

"Yeah, can we all just —" Wesley made a tamping-down motion with both hands.

"And who put you in charge, Mom?" Jane

gripped the plastic bed railing. "Of everyone's bodies. How come you know what's best? For everyone!"

If it weren't all so horrible, Ellen would have had to laugh at the phrasing, and Jane's hysterical generalizing: *Everyone's bodies.* "Well, I hardly thought I needed your permission —"

"Not me, Mike! Did you even ask him what he would have wanted, about his leg?"

"That is fucking ridiculous," Wesley said. "Stop it."

Ellen could barely speak. "It was — he wasn't able to understand what was going on . . ." Her voice petered out. Michael's attentive silence, just to her left.

"Not then. *Now.* Do you even know what he thinks about it getting amputated? What he would have done? Did you ever even ask him?"

At this, the small crowded room went quiet. Jane's desperate questions hung in the air and drifted downward like ash, legitimate, scorching.

All those eyes, waiting for her answer. No, she hadn't asked Michael's permission. She hadn't asked his forgiveness. For that's what Jane meant, right? She hadn't had one real moment of connection with him since he arrived at Walter Reed unconscious. He used to practically bite her head off when she reminded him to take his midday antibiotic! What could he possibly say about going from missing a foot to being a full-blown AK? *Sure, no biggie?*

That's when Ellen did what she promised herself she would never do. She left.

The real failure, Ellen knew, lay in her leaving. Which Jane called her on, even as she was doing it. *Fine, go ahead and walk out, like you always do. Mom, come back and face reality!* Wesley ran to catch her in the hall and she brushed him off as kindly as she could: *I'm fine, I just can't be here right now.* On the walk from Heaton to Mologne, Lacey called three times, no message. The heat of Ellen's anger carried her back to her room, stayed while she packed, and made the phone calls to rearrange her travel. *Fine. Go ahead. Do what you want.*

But it had dissipated by the time she was going through security at Reagan National and by the time she had boarded her plane all Ellen felt was emptiness, regret, tiredness. They would go on to have this baby no matter what she did or didn't do. And there was no place for her.

Back in Madison, Maisie sniffed the cold water lapping against a muddy slush of a shore, and leaped back to Ellen, howling with excitement. Apparently Wisconsin's snowfall this year had been a record low, especially compared to last year, and Ellen wondered if this lake had even frozen over once. It was certainly in full early-spring high tide now, the waterline farther up the small dirt and sand beach than she could remember seeing.

Picnic Point was a mile-long peninsula into Lake Mendota, a beckoning finger jutting out into the blob-shaped body of water that bordered the university on its north side. Originally private property before the U acquired it midcentury, the narrow spit was lined with trails and studded with marshes and swamps. It was a favorite with dogs and their owners as well as students desperate for a make-out session in the woods. More than once Maisie's barking had flushed out undergraduates from the bushes and Ellen would apologize except that really, they never looked quite as embarrassed as they should.

"Well, go on. Get wet."

But Maisie was torn. She kept nudging at the gray water and then wheeling back to Ellen.

"I'm sorry. I'm sorry, sweet girl." She picked twigs out of the dog's fur and took off a glove to rub her behind the ears. "No, we haven't been here in so long. Yes, too long. Too long, right? How about a stick." Pressing up from achy knees, she found a stick and flung it way out into the water. Maisie tensed, and then took the plunge. For a while they went through the dog's favorite routine: fling, swim, fetch. The trickiest part was to get out of the way when Maisie, having dumped the stick triumphantly at Ellen's feet, vigorously shook her fur with a spray of wet droplets.

On her last joyful charge, Maisie swam past the floating stick.

"Hey, you missed it, silly," Ellen called, but the dog paddled on without turning back. A pair of ducks had drifted in toward shore and were now paddling away from the dog, who had spotted them. "Maisie, come," Ellen said. *"Come."* She called again and again, with increasing volume. Maisie went farther into the lake, farther than she'd ever gone, her chin held bravely above the water. Those damn ducks were drawing her out into the middle of the lake! By now she probably couldn't even hear Ellen's frantic cries. Ellen, who was ankle deep in the water, promising treats, shouting, *"Come back, come here! Maisie! What are you doing?"*

She can't stay afloat much longer, Ellen realized, as it hit her what a dire situation they were in. No one else was on the shore; there were no boats. She tried a step farther in, and another, wincing as the icy water surged over her boots and soaked her pants. Every time she glanced up Maisie's head was smaller, a bobbing brown lump way out on the lake. Ellen began to panic. What if she goes under? I can't just stand here!

Then she was shedding her coat, pulling off her boots and throwing them to shore. She did it all so fast, that first flailing into the water, that she gained several yards before it shocked her, hard. The mind-choking cold. Ellen tried to shout, but had no breath. As soon as the water enveloped most of her body she knew it had been a mistake. Gasping, she thrashed for air, for life. Her feet lifted off the muddy bottom and she thought it was over. The dog was forgotten. She fought for herself.

But when Ellen staggered back onto the beach, Maisie trotted up after her. Her noisy half swim must have drawn the dog's attention. When Ellen could breathe again, she patted the dog blindly and said, *"We have to hurry."* The mile back to the car was a blur of pain and cold. Ellen's hands were so stiff she could barely turn on the ignition, and she had to use her forearms on the steering wheel. Maisie lay on the backseat, not even raising her head. Ellen thought about driving straight to the vet but in the end went back to their house. She managed to half drag, half carry Maisie inside and throw a towel on her. Her own warm shower made her cry out as her hands and feet burned bright red, but she stayed under the spray as long as she could.

"We're okay. We're okay," she kept saying. To the dog, to herself. She opened the radiator full throttle and got into bed, with Maisie, both of them under the covers. But it took a long time to stop shaking. What had almost happened, and what she'd almost lost, and where she failed. So even when she found a stretch of uneasy sleep, Ellen felt cold deep inside, where the warmth and safety couldn't reach.

That was her second day back. On the third, Ellen had sorted months of mail, paid a dozen bills, and sent thirty e-mails before her second cup of coffee. She filled boxes of unread magazines to donate to the local hospital (*The New Yorker, Gourmet, Vogue*) and to the department (*MLA, Victorian News,* various lit quarterlies). She ordered thank-you bouquets and fruit baskets for neighbors who had helped to take care of Maisie, kept an eye on Jane, and supervised things like tree maintenance and electric meter readings. She scrubbed the fridge and surveyed the pantry and made a list for the market. She made appointments to get her hair done, her teeth cleaned, and her eyes checked. She left messages for the house cleaner, the roofer, and the lawn care company.

And when it was 10:00 a.m., she rinsed out her coffee cup, gave Maisie two extra biscuits, and walked out the door in her Italian light wool trouser suit, brown leather pumps, favorite bag. On the drive to campus she remembered a host of to-dos related to the car — EPA testing, tune-up, city parking sticker — and added them mentally to her growing list.

At Helen C. White, she didn't technically *avoid* the secretary or the mailbox area, she just came up the other set of elevators. Yes, she would at some point need to stop in and have some inevitable discussions — with Mark Carroll above all — about the status of her leave and what would happen in the fall. She would call Serena. But for now, she'd fly under the radar. For a moment Ellen wondered if she'd been blockaded out of her own office; she had to shove the door hard to get it to open and then step over months of mail, review copies, and schedules that apparently had been dumped right inside the threshold. But sorting through this was even easier than the papers at home; most of it went straight to recycling with barely a second glance.

"Professor Silverman?" It was Lynne, tapping gingerly. "I might be a little early, so if you want . . ."

"No, this is fine. Come in and — oh, let me clear off that chair. Sorry about the mess."

"Please! I'm just so grateful you can find the time. You definitely didn't have to do this. Switching advisers in the fall wasn't actually that bad, and —"

"It must have been very disruptive, and I couldn't be sorrier. But you're doing some very good work here, Lynne." She paused to let this sink in, gratified by the proud and nervous expression on the young woman's face. "I'm so pleased to get a chance to read it in progress. Well, let's get started. As you can see, I jotted comments throughout, on the margins, but I also typed up some global suggestions for each of the chapters. Here. Why don't you take a moment to read, and then we can discuss."

But the girl didn't open the folder in her

lap, the one holding the pages Ellen had printed out and carefully critiqued for most of yesterday morning.

"Professor Silverman, I was —"

"You can call me Ellen by now, Lynne."

"Um. Ellen, I wanted to say that I know what you've been going through must have been so hard — I mean, that it is so hard . . . And I don't know the details or whatever, so I hope this isn't intruding or anything. But I'm really, really sorry about your . . . son. Not son, that is — or, maybe, your . . ." Lynne glanced around in panic, boxed into a corner.

" 'Son' is fine, Lynne," Ellen said quickly. "And thank you," she added. The torrent of emotion that rose up caught her off guard. The girl's uneasy speech, her obvious relief at it being over, the way she'd overcome the what-to-say obstacle that people twice her age mostly fumbled . . . Someone had raised her right, Ellen thought, discreetly pressing the inner corners of her eyes.

"Do you want to read that," Ellen said gently, and Lynne opened the folder eagerly, ready to talk dissertation.

The quiet of her house unsettled her. Five months in Mologne's dorm-like hotel, where people went up and down the hall outside her room all hours, and car doors slammed in the parking lot, and walls were thin, letting in muffled sounds of music and anguish, on both sides, had her skittish and uneasy in the wide oasis of calm at night in her century-old two-story home on Chamberlain Street. Also, what were all the things she used to do, here? Her third night back, Ellen wandered from room to room, switching on a light and then switching it off again. She stood on the threshold of Jane's room for a long time, silently observing the usual mess, a tangle of clothes and bedsheets and books and bags, as well as the few newer items shoved together in a corner: a worn blue cloth-covered bouncy seat, a pack of toddler-size diapers, some kind of pillow labeled MY BREAST FRIEND. She thought about cleaning up, organizing, making better choices for this baby's arrival, but stepped back and closed the door on the room.

Ellen couldn't relax. She puttered around the dark house, at first enjoyably, then with an edge. A hot bath, her favorite white cotton nightgown, and a small glass of bourbon: no help.

"Don't even suggest TV," she told Maisie, who followed her everywhere. "Quite enough of that."

Eventually she ended up back in the kitchen staring at the UPS box that had arrived that morning. Inside was a stack of books and a letter from Lacey. When she unfolded it, a brochure fell out. Ellen only skimmed the first part where her friend wrote the expected things in a handwriting that was tightly looped and even. *I didn't know she was coming she just showed up. I'm sorry. I didn't mean to get in your business and I wish I never kept talking to her when she called me. She misses you, but you know a girl like that can't say it straight. I'm sorry. I miss you a lot. I'll do whatever you want, like to check in on them here or stay totally out of it.*

More interesting was the brochure: "For Those Who Have Served." On the front, a blurry photo of two women in uniform pressing PLAY on a recording machine, with the white curves of the Capitol out the window behind them. Skipping down, Lacey's letter said, *After you brought those books on tape he went through them so fast. I tried to find more around here but you know what a junk pile it can be. Shelby the reporter got this guy to call me and he works at the Library of Congress do you know about that place? I didn't have to but I drove over there and it is amazing. So this guy signed Ed up for a program where they just gave us all this stuff, a player where he can do a kind of digital bookmark and make it go faster or slower (slower being good for Ed, obviously), and speakers that are in a pillow, it's wild. He gets all these books, I mean like dozens at a time I think he likes the history ones best and Lolo and he found out you can get Spanish too. It's called the NLS. He never does the crazy laugh thing when he's listening to them and it gets him calm. He's thinking about the books, later, I can tell. Anyway it's the first goddamn freebie here that actually makes sense for us and I had to tell you because you started it and also because the Congress library is really something I wish you and I would have gone there together.*

Ellen did know the Library of Congress. She had been there several times. On her first visit, in the late 1970s, she'd been a newly minted assistant professor at her first job at a small school in upper Michigan. She traveled to D.C. for a spring conference, and took the tour with four other people and a chatty senior citizen docent: in the Great Hall they marveled at the Bible of Mainz, and the Gutenberg Bible, facing each other under bulletproof glass. When their group came to the Main Reading Room, Ellen slipped away from the tour to wander that golden-domed space, a heaven to her. On a whim she filled out a slip of paper to request a book and waited at a curved oak desk until it was brought to her, under the marble statues of female muses. Then it was there in her hands, in a pebbled dark-green binding: *Solitude and Safety: Representations of Female Space in Wharton's Early Stories,* by Ellen Silverman, PhD.

What had she thought then, in her only suit and new heels and wedge haircut? With Don still alive and the kids so young — Jane not even walking yet — holding her own book, her first book, in this temple to written art? *This is just the beginning,* probably. *So much more to say.*

In the box Lacey had mailed Ellen recognized the stack of books as the small pile she kept in her room at Mologne, the few she hadn't given away from the many Serena had mailed. A Post-it: *Jane let me in and I just thought you'd want these.*

Ellen poked at them with distaste. "She might have sent my phone charger." Maisie put her chin on Ellen's thigh.

Still, Ellen took Wharton's *A Son at the Front* from the stack. The copy she'd so improbably found that first week in SICU, on a candy-striper giveaway cart. She flipped it open and read the introduction. Not bad.

Quite excellent, in fact, this short text by an Iowa-based scholar Ellen recognized from a feminist lit conference several years ago. Maisie looked up at her with surprise.

"Well, all right, it's late. Let's go read in bed." Ellen put the Library of Congress brochure in as a bookmark, and petted her old dog.

29

"G-what? I don't think you pronounce it like that, Mom."

"Global War on Terrorism," Lolo said proudly, enunciating. "G-WoT. It means the whole operation — including political and legal things. Also the UK. Not just USA."

Lacey bit her tongue. It was tiring to constantly acknowledge Lolo's admittedly impressive gains in veteran and military knowledge. All those Sundays that we could have been actually discussing something, Lacey thought, remembering those endless afternoons in her dry City Island parlor. But they'd passed each other with no overlap, for Lacey herself now had very little interest in, or maybe it was energy for, the military world. Occasionally she would realize how strange that was, to lose the connection *here* of all places, surrounded 24-7 by the full complement of patriotism and bureaucracy that made up a working military base. Back in her mil-wife FRG days, this would have seemed like it was made for her, a place to finally fit in. *Mil-world,* is what she and Martine used to call it.

"He's going to be hungry," she said, standing up. "What did he have? Cereal or something?"

Lolo remained placid in her waiting room chair. "I got him a Burger King before the bus. Plus they gonna have lunch, the lady told me."

"You know, he's gotta stop eating all that fast-food crap. Kid's pudgy enough as it is."

"I cook when there's a kitchen." Lolo turned a page in her magazine. "A *private* kitchen."

Lacey had to concede the point, as much as she was in the itchy mood for a fight. She wouldn't eat anything that came from Building 18's dirty common area either; the place was crawling with bugs.

Anyway, Otis's eating habits weren't the issue. Not the main issue, that is. Kid could lose a few, for sure. Why had she agreed to Otis going off to a full-day tour of D.C. on the day Eddie had his big surgery? Right, right, it would obviously not have been ideal to have *him* sitting around for six hours, the way she and Lolo were doing, wired with hopes and fears. Which is why the social services lady pushed so hard to include him on this kids' "fun day" activity. And maybe there was part of her that just didn't want to deal with Otis today, the day she'd been waiting for so long. The day Eddie was going to get his sight back.

She didn't love thinking about yesterday's meeting with the psychotherapist. Otis, she was told, was demonstrating "significant behavioral shifts" related to stress about his father's injuries. "He's not his father," Lacey had snapped, and that got them off on the wrong foot. But really, was she supposed to listen to some twenty-one-year-old tell her about her son's behavior? After meeting with him, like, three times total since they'd arrived at Walter Reed? No one had to tell her Otis was giving off more attitude. This very morning when she told him to go put on a collar shirt for the field trip he actually said, "Better check yourself first." Fine, she wasn't winning any fashion prizes around here but that kind of sassing was not the norm. Although, what was the norm? Which baseline should she use to measure his behavior? Before Eddie got injured? Before she started cheating on Eddie, or before she married him? Before Lolo took over as the main *caregiver*? That's what they called it in social services. What could you expect, when the kid was dragged from home to hospital and back again, missing school, missing his mom (she hoped)? Did they really have to give her yet another damn pamphlet to read?

Of course they did. This place ran on pamphlets.

"Listen to this," she said to Lolo. " 'How Can I Explain Moderate or Severe TBI to a Child?' " She thwacked the shiny brochure against her hand. " 'Teens and preteens may be self-conscious about visible changes in their returning parent. Rehearse what to say if others remark on tics, outbursts, or other unusual behaviors.' "

"Fine. I'll tell him what to say if you embarrass him."

"Oh, that's really funny, Mom. How about this: 'You are going through a difficult period. Take time for yourself to recharge your batteries. Massages can feel good and relieve stress. Check the phone book in your area for licensed massage therapists and make an appointment.' I mean . . ." Lacey shook her head and left her mouth open, as if there was anyone else in the operating waiting area for her to perform disbelief to. "Well, of course! Why didn't I think of that? I'll get a ninety-dollar massage! I better find a phone book."

"Why you so mad at the massage? One

day they give us free back massages after chair yoga and I loooooved it."

Lacey gave up and sat down again in a *whoosh.* Lolo was wearing an off-white pantsuit with a cheetah-print scarf. Her reading glasses were tinted rose and she had on a full face of makeup, matching gold earrings and bracelet, though her shoes were the sturdy slip-on kind with a wide, flat heel. This is what she'd packed to come to Walter Reed? Ten to one she thought the surgeon wouldn't put in a good effort if she didn't get all decked out. Lacey, on the other hand, was in the hooded sweatshirt she'd slept in, and a pair of saggy-ass jeans. "How much longer till we get an update?"

"They say not until halfway."

"Well, when the fuck is that?"

"Tst."

"Sorry."

This last week of preparing to leave had the feeling of school before summer break — from what Lacey could remember of that. The simultaneous sense that she had tons to do, and nothing at all. She'd be alternately excited (*let's get the hell out of Building 18*) and paralyzed by dread (*what were they going to do at home?*). But the time here was coming to a close, no two ways about it. The Evaluation Board was set to make their ruling on Eddie's benefits in the next few months, so they wouldn't hear about it until after they were gone. (*How convenient for them,* Lacey thought — *less chance to be bombarded by angry wives in person.*) She closed out accounts at the PX, the cafeteria, and TriCare. She gave away all the good stuff she'd hoarded: extra space heater, pillows, ice trays, Drano, mice traps, roach spray. They had appointments and exit interviews with everyone from Psych to Building Services to Housing and the Travel Service.

And as Shelby had instructed, Lacey made no mention of details about the falling-down dump that was Building 18, that had been her and Eddie's home for the past five months and two weeks. They were building a case, and if the cat got out of the bag the army would have a chance to cover their ass before the story went to print.

In the past week, Lacey had hosted three evening get-togethers for Shelby to do her thing from her nasty couch. She was all in now. But it wasn't like she had to close the deal; her job was to provide drinks (*just soda . . . well, okay, with the occasional bonus vodka shot, but only if things got really heated*) and coax the other women to come hear the reporter out. It worked. Of course it did. Lacey was mostly a mess but she knew this about herself, knew it from her years in FRG: people tended to follow her lead. So when she vouched for the reporter, and then the camera crew, when people heard she'd let them interview her — on camera! Having actually done her bangs with the flat-iron, not just clip them back like she did every other day — with Eddie, and let them film every inch of her crappy place, they felt okay about talking. Most did, that is. A few mil-wives gave Lacey the *are-you-kidding-me* routine with a hot vehemence that would have been familiar to her even a few weeks ago.

The real question was how had she come to the place where she felt okay about this . . . not only about breaking the *we-take-care-of-our-own* code, some silent agreement about upholding the army at all costs that she never remembered signing anyway — but about letting herself be seen. As she was now. With Eddie at her side, quietly mumbling and only letting out one high-pitched giggle. Fine, maybe she was going to come off as white trash on national TV but so what? That didn't mean it was right, the way they'd been treated here.

There was only a twinge when she pictured what someone like Anne Mackay would think, if and when she saw what Lacey had done. Too bad if delicate-flower Anne had to look at photos of Lacey's backed-up toilet or found her weak enough to complain about it in public.

Although last week Lacey got an update from Bailey — not directly to her, but a part of a mass-e-mail she'd sent out. It was a wedding announcement: *We did it!* in hot-pink cursive font, with several photos of Bailey and Greg from their ceremony and reception at what looked like the Palisade Plaza in Yonkers. And in the background of one of them, dwarfed by massive up-dos of Bailey's twelve bridesmaids in blinding violet taffeta, was Anne Mackay. Smiling, clapping, on the sidelines of the dance floor where a shiny-faced Bailey was deep into a tongue kiss with young Greg. Lacey wanted to lay bets on their first dance song: "Can You Feel the Love Tonight"? Or "Have You Ever Really Loved a Woman?" In any case, she was glad to know that Anne had stepped up to be there for Bailey, for real. Maybe there was more to her than Lacey knew.

It wasn't just that she was cut loose from Mil-World, or that her car was back and there was a steady source of incoming boot camp cash — though that all helped; it was a sense Lacey had that she needed to make an offering.

For Ellen. All she wanted was for Ellen to be proud of her . . . and look how that had turned out. It was stupid, but Lacey felt like if she kept on with helping the reporters, it could somehow make things right. Look, Ellen was the one who got her into this whole project! So even if she was now hiding out in Wisconsin not taking anyone's calls, including Shelby's — *whatever,* Jane said about this, *it's her M.O.* — it had to mean something that Lacey stepped up to take her place. Didn't it? And what should Lacey do about the situation over in Mike's room?

She should stay out of it. And she was, mostly — even though Jane was apparently over it, those things she'd shouted about Lacey feeling entitled to get in her business were never far from mind. But damn if things weren't going downhill, and she didn't only mean the unholy mess in the room — empty cups and takeout boxes, clothes everywhere, a sweaty unwashed smell in the unaired room. Plus, the kids were fighting. Nothing major, but both times she'd stopped by to pick up Mike for boot camp she got the sense that she'd interrupted an argument. Lacey was uneasy;

Jane looked like she was going to pop that baby out any day, though apparently she had six weeks to go. And though Mike never showed that side to her, Lacey kept remembering all the times he'd exploded at Ellen.

Two days ago she ran into a Ward 57 nurse in the Heaton cafeteria line and the woman made a point of asking, "So when's she coming back? Your friend, the AK's mom? Something going on there?" Lacey played dumb, but she was worried too. And she missed Ellen, she really did.

Now, in the windowed corner area off Ward 65, where Ophthalmology was located — it felt weird and wrong to be up this high in Heaton — Lacey resigned herself to another chapter of *Mrs. Dalloway,* an Ellen loaner from last month that she'd pretended to have finished (and enjoyed!). She was now forcing herself to make good on the lie. Even if she'd be the only one who knew. *Oh for God's sake,* she thought while reading, *can you get on with this party already?*

"Lacey," Lolo said. "Edgardo gonna come home with me."

"What are you talking about, Ma?" Lacey reread the same paragraph for the third time. Was this part another flashback or actually happening? No wonder you had to study these kinds of books with a professor.

"The stairs won't be a problem for him. Some people from the Fort Hamilton came to look at the house, and they say it's okay."

Lacey looked up from the book. Her mother-in-law was staring straight ahead, hands folded on top of the closed magazine. "What do you mean, it's okay?"

"He can come live with me." Lolo punctuated each word with a nod of her head.

"I don't —"

"The Transition office, they set up all the in-home care, they in charge of arrangements for what he needs in his rooms, and how often he gets to the doctor on base, and —"

"I know," Lacey said. "I've got an appointment there next, I don't know, Monday or something. After he's out of recovery from this."

"*I* had the appointment," Lolo said, with a sliver-flash of vehemence. "Two days ago. When you do the exercises."

"What?" Lacey tried to make her mind work. Lolo went to Transition? Without her? Who was watching Otis? "How did you know which building to go to?" To this, Lolo tilted down her head and glared over her sparkly dime-store reading glasses. "Mom, I'm glad you're involved and all that, but —

you don't have to deal with this stuff. I'm taking care of it. You don't have to worry about it."

"I'm taking care of *Ed,*" Lolo said. "Here." She pulled a folded sheaf of stapled printouts out of her purse.

Lacey scanned them, caught off guard by the conversation taking shape. What did Lolo know about her fears for the future? *Discharge Plan: Edgardo Diaz. Next Steps in Home Care. Approved Funding: Medication, Equipment, Mobility Retrofit.*

Wow. "You got weekly transportation to the base? That's . . . incredible." Lacey had been stymied at every turn for even a monthly ride for Eddie. Full-time transitional care nursing during the week, overnights when needed, pharmacy delivery. "This is . . . this is incredible, Mom. How did you get all this?" About half the items on here, already approved, were ones Lacey had given up on weeks ago after her every request was denied. And she wasn't alone! Nobody in Building 18, as far as she knew, had gotten this much from Transition.

"I know how an office works," Lolo said. *Don't forget,* her virtuous smile said, *you're looking at a senior secretary for Bronx Borough President Fernando Ferrer.*

"Well . . ." Lacey struggled to contain all

her frustrated questions. She knew how these offices worked too, dammit! "This is great. It's going to make things a lot easier for Eddie. And me," she went on carefully. "But I don't know why you didn't tell me about this." *Permanent Address,* on one of the forms. Entered neatly in the line next to it: *28 Carroll Street, City Island, New York.*

"Ah, Lacey. You know. We know."

"We know *what,* Mom? Let's just focus on the surgery today, all right? One thing at a time." Her heart was pounding.

"He'll live with me. You can come all you want. But it's all right now. You can let it go."

"Let it go?" Lacey cried. "What are you talking about?"

"We did a special prayer meeting about it, me and Father Dorian. He says it's okay. My baby might never get all better. But God is good, he came home. He came home to me."

"He's getting better, Mom! He's in there right now so they can save his eye!"

"But his brain," Lolo said. "He's not gonna be a full man." She broke down crying, and Lacey did too. "But I — I give thanks for that I can hug him, that I can have my son back. God is good."

"Mom, Mom. Shh, it's okay." They

clasped their hands, all four together in a pile, Lolo's rings pinching Lacey.

Her mother-in-law recovered first, wiping under her sunglasses. "You did all this for him, here. You did everything."

"Of course I did, Mom. What do you mean?"

"Now you can go on." In the silence after she said this, Lolo looked straight at Lacey. "Father Dorian agrees."

"Go . . . on?"

"I know it wasn't so good. I'm not making the judgment, but I have eyes. I didn't think it would last, you know I never did, even before . . . this. I was wrong. You were a good fighter for him, Lacey."

The painful sweetness of Lolo's understanding was too much. Lacey's head dropped down, almost to her knees.

"Sorry," she whispered. "I'm sorry."

"Father D says we can't know about a person's marriage but I think I know. Look at me. Look. Yes?"

Lacey made herself uncover her face, and nod. "But that doesn't mean I want to — that I ever thought of not —" What was happening? What were they saying?

"So. Good." Lolo sniffed with finality. She actually opened her magazine again while Lacey reeled. A thousand images and memories came rushing in while she struggled to understand what it meant to take Lolo up on this. The ways she knew Eddie: How he hated not getting the joke and would google references later that he hadn't understood, even minor ones, that he'd pretended at the time to get. How he yelled at her for buying tissues with lotion because they were a dollar more, but once loaned a guy from work $300 because his wife lost her job. How he loved fireworks, would stare up at them openmouthed, knew all the different kinds: peony, crossette, multibreak shells, cake. How he made her wash before they had sex, how he had to wash after. How he never hit her, not even once, but his suppressed anger was so much worse that she used to wish maybe he would. How he taught Otis card games like spit and slapjack, but once told him Pop Warner was boring as hell and he couldn't stand the games. How he punched a man on the street who was cursing out some girl, how he couldn't bear to hear people slag off their parents. How he slept tightly curled up all the way on the side of the bed, flinching in annoyance if Lacey cuddled behind him. How he was incredibly embarrassed about a chipped incisor but refused to go the dentist — he just made sure to smile thinly, smile less.

"But what about . . . what about Otis?" Lacey blurted.

Lolo snapped her a fierce look. "What about Otis what? You think I won't have my boy over to see his Lolo? Every weekend, every time I want? Every time *he* want."

"Okay." She was trembling.

"You'll drive him to me. When he want. Or I do."

"Yes."

Lacey couldn't say anything more. There was no ground beneath her feet and her mind was clawing around in empty air, trying to find a place to land. What did Lolo know about her affair with Jim? What kind of person would she be, to accept this, to let her damaged husband live with his mother and not with her? The future was torn open, a wild whistling air now blown in to scatter everything she thought she knew.

Several hours later, they crowded into the recovery room where Eddie was coming up from the anesthesia. The surgeon said he was surprised — the procedure was as much of a success as anyone could possibly have hoped. He gave Lacey credit for pushing them to explore the options and admitted he hadn't given today's work much of a chance. But once the remainder of the swelling went down Eddie would have 60 to 70 percent sight in his eye. Even now, they were told, he was seeing clearer shapes and colors.

Lacey and Lolo hovered over him in the bed for at least an hour, while the nurses kept close watch on his vitals. He was pale and twitchy at first but grew increasingly calm once he understood who was there, both women on either side of him. They spoke softly and cheerfully to Eddie as he swung his head back and forth between them. The lid over the socket for his missing eye was neatly sewn down; Lacey wasn't sure if he'd ever understand what he had lost there.

And what he had gained back. Because early the next morning when the bandages were slowly unrolled she watched as her husband's remaining eye opened, and blinked, and slowly tracked its way around the room past every smiling face until it rested on Lolo.

"Mom," Eddie said, in wonder. And then he laughed, slow and sweet.

30

"The worst risk would be septic shock." Lacey's words brought Ellen to a complete stop outside Helen C. White, the phone pressed to her ear. "But that's nothing like what's happening now, I mean. It's a bad infection in his gut, is what they told me, probably started with a urinary tract thing. He's already on two different antibiotics on IV."

"All right." Ellen stayed calm. Michael had had infections before; hardly anyone on Ward 57 escaped them because of all the open wounds and compromised immune systems. "Bacterial, you said?"

"Yes. But not that fucked-up Iraqi kind. What's it called, acino-something?"

"Acinetobacter, I think. They gave us a flyer about it at one point."

"Well, all he's got is our good ol' American e. coli — so that's good."

Wind pressed a newspaper sheet against

the bike rack and sent candy wrappers into a knee-high tornado on the bare concrete plaza outside the library. It was Ellen's third day in a row coming here to work; she'd reserved a faculty carrel in the basement after making sure it had no Internet access and little cell reception.

"When did it start?" she asked.

"He had a fever day before yesterday, I guess, but then it went away . . . and came back big-time last night."

"Is he conscious? Is he in pain?"

"Yes, but sleeping a lot. No, I don't think so." Lacey hesitated. "That nurse he likes has been on shift . . . Rob Base or whatever."

"Rob Beers. Good, I'm glad." Ellen shifted her briefcase strap to the other shoulder. "You can talk about her, you know. About Jane. It's not a verboten subject." *Even if she hasn't called me about this. Or anything.* "Is she all right?"

"Yeah, totally." There was relief in Lacey's voice. "There's no contagion except for direct contact, so she's wearing gloves and a mask. I mean, most of the time. And she's cleaned up their room a little . . ."

"She's staying in Mologne, is that right? In my room?"

"Yes. Look, I'll do whatever you want, Ellen. If you want me to get all up in their business and make sure things are done like you say, I will. You know I can boss the shit out of those kids. Or I can . . . you know, keep it on the down low. And let you know what's going on."

"Be my mole, you mean?" Ellen laughed despite herself. "I don't think that's necessary. I'm sure Dr. Rodwick will get the infection under control, if it's not already. Having Rob on duty will be good for him, and as for Jane . . ." She trailed off. "I'm sure she'll figure it out."

"Right." Lacey sounded as if she wanted to say more.

"How much longer for you? That's wonderful about Eddie's vision." Ellen shook her watch out of her sleeve to check the time.

"Well, we had T.O. orders for week after next but there was a snafu. No surprises there. So it's looking like three weeks now."

"Good, good."

"Yeah, but . . . will I see you before then? Before we get out of here?"

"Probably not." Cloud shadows skittered across the plaza, and Ellen stepped out from under the awning to feel the bright sunlight on top of her head. "I'm very busy with work — in fact I'm at school right now."

"You said your classes were all being

taught by someone else."

"It's not only about *teaching,* Lacey. I have to write too. That's part of my job! In fact I have a tentative deadline for an introduction that . . . Never mind."

"The thing is I think that Jane might —"

"I'm sure Jane is quite happy there's half a country between us. She got her wish. Anyway, I can't simply drop everything and fly back there whenever there's a bump in the road!" Ellen closed her eyes to the sun, dismayed at how high-pitched her voice had become.

"Okay, I get it."

"I'm sorry. I'm a little preoccupied. Could I give you a call back later?"

"Don't worry about it. Good luck on the writing." Before Ellen could think of how to soften her tone, Lacey hung up. Had there been a faint emphasis on that last word? *Good luck on the* writing. So Lacey was mad at her now too. So what?

Edith Wharton wouldn't have given two bits about someone's hurt feelings when there was so much to be done in war-engulfed Paris. Aside from her own prodigious output of letters, editorials, and fiction, Wharton threw herself into war work: raising money, organizing charity efforts, hounding the Red Cross, and badgering friends and acquaintances to do more, give more, be more. During this time the eminent society writer became a single-minded formidable presence on the home front. Ellen had always avoided this time period in Wharton's life (many scholars did, unhappy with the rich writer's energetic prowar stance) but now all she wanted to do was to look right at what had happened to her favorite writer on the home front during war. So without allowing herself to dwell on the sadness in Lacey's questions — or the worry about Michael's fever, or the frustration of Jane, always frustration and Jane — Ellen briskly submerged herself in the library's underground cement layers, flashing the guard her ID and a smile.

Ellen was working again. It had come back to her, slowly at first and then gaining speed, over the course of the last week and a half. She read now, in great swooshing gulps, both new texts and books that were as familiar to her as her own hands. She read in long, steady, intent stretches, pausing only to type a few notes, roll her neck, or pet Maisie. Her desire for words again was as physical as hunger — which made sense, because her appetite had come roaring back too. She ate breakfast, lunch, and dinner. She cooked for herself at home: steel cut oatmeal with dried cherries and brown sugar; buttery risotto with fresh radishes sprinkled in sea salt; one perfect piece of grilled salmon placed on top of a tangle of bitter greens. She went out to dinner with Serena, and with Debbie Masterson, and even (almost) with Paul, who canceled at the last minute. Ellen ate well, she slept well, and she read through Edith Wharton's war fiction period — the novels, stories, and surrounding scholarship — as deeply as she knew how.

That copy of *A Son at the Front* was the first domino. After reading the novel and rereading the well-executed academic introduction, Ellen wondered what it would have been like to encounter this novel at Walter Reed in a popular edition. With an introduction that, yes, situated the text in both Wharton's oeuvre and the political context of the day . . . but went on to explain what this novel could mean to readers today, at home during a war of the twenty-first century? *Well,* she asked herself, *what did it mean to me? Now, after those months in the hospital at Michael's side?* Did Edith Wharton's depiction of the wounded boys of World War I have anything to say to . . . Martha Whitehead, for example, whose boy three rooms down from Mike had lost both hands and most of his torso skin when a grenade blew up in the flatbed back of his truck? She had another son still stationed in Anbar Province. Or to Rosalie, who had run Ward 57's nurses' station since before the first U.S. invasion of Iraq? What could a book like this mean to any of the women who had gathered for spaghetti at Ellen's invitation, burned-out on army incompetence and whooping it up at one another's tales of woe?

What could it mean to Lacey?

Ellen started writing and she held on to both in her mind: years of knowledge about this writer, and the women at Walter Reed. She read and wrote, read and wrote. She kept it simple and personal, for the first time. And through the Wharton-studies grapevine she reached out to a half-dozen editors at literary publishing houses. *Maybe,* they said, when she pitched the idea of reissuing *A Son at the Front* and possibly other little-known Wharton books, with a new introduction "highlighting Wharton's writing about war, now more timely than ever." *Send us a proposal.*

A son at the front. What turned the key for Ellen was the title itself. And the realization that, of course, Wharton, badly married and famously childless, never had a son in the war either. This American-born Parisian writer, with no actual heir or child sent off to the truly unimaginable slaughter of young men (a war in which the total French casualties — over six million — added up to 73 percent of their fighting forces), worked from imagination to tell a story about a parent's pain and fear during deployment. Actually, the stories of dozens of parents who make up Paris during those terrible years — a whole city racked with grief, endless funerals, a flood of wounded men, refugees, looting, blackouts, and food shortages. Wharton keeps her eye on those at home, Ellen wrote, putting aside scenes of fighting (though she made several trips to the front and knew the horrors there) in order to give us scenes like the excruciating one where a man asks a doctor about a medical exemption for his son, knowing the doctor's boy is at the front. Or a divorced couple joined again by the fear of their son's mobilization orders. Or a painter, devoted to art, afraid to sketch his son asleep on the night before he leaves, because he is suddenly made to think of what his boy would look like on his deathbed. How war reaches into the everyday at home and humbles, flattens, changes us.

Ellen wrote, and read, and wrote some more, marveling at all the things Wharton got right.

Later that day, Ellen drove home from the library in early twilight, listening to NPR headlines. *The Senate is expected to take up a nonbinding resolution against the White House's handling of the Iraq War later today. More on Senator Russ Feingold's resolution to censure President Bush. Activists with the group Code Pink disrupted a speech by New York Senator Hillary Clinton calling on the presidential hopeful to oppose the Iraq War. One banner said: "We want a woman for peace, not just a woman." Six people were arrested.*

She let Maisie out into the yard and heated up a plate of yesterday's vegetable curry with rice. She poured a glass of Riesling. Halfway through her dinner and *The New Yorker* she left her plate and called the nurses' station at Ward 57.

No change in Mike's fever, despite the antibiotics. He was now getting fluids and piperacillin to fight the possibility of getting bacteremic. Would she like to leave a message for the on-call resident? No, Ellen said. Thank you. She didn't ask: *And my daughter . . . ?*

The least appealing item on her to-do list read *Jane's room* so she tackled it that evening. Changed the sour and dirty sheets, vacuumed, dusted, and tried to pick up without breaching any privacy boundaries — that was for her own self-interest as much as Jane's. To the sounds of Brahms from a radio station out of Kenosha Ellen finished assembling the abandoned bassinet, and made space for a changing table. *What about some kind of rocking chair?* she wondered, and then had to sit on the bed under posters of howling punk rockers, overcome.

"Sure, a rocking chair!" she said to Maisie. "Where she can sit and crochet a layette!" If the dog was fazed by her exasperated tone, she didn't show it. Ellen lay back on her daughter's bed and stared at the ceiling. She knew as little about what was to come as Jane did.

In bed, after a long hot bath, rereading a favorite Alison Lurie novel, she suddenly laid it down to call the nurses' station. No change. Possible transfer to ICU, but not confirmed.

By 6:00 a.m., she was dressed and drinking tea. Still no change. The team was with him now, evaluating options. Mike had had a bad reaction to one of the antibiotics — the night nurses' notes showed that he had thrown up multiple times in the night — but appeared to be less nauseated now, though still feverish. They were going to try vancomycin next. "Was he in very much pain?" Ellen asked, aghast at the idea of him so sick. Worried for Jane, handling all this. *Hard to say,* was the answer. *In and out of consciousness.*

She took a long walk through the neighborhood with Maisie, umbrellaless in a light misting rain. Neighbors waved from cars on their way to school and work. What should she do? If she called, Jane would probably blow up at her for interfering, trying to take charge, doubting anyone else's abilities. If she didn't call, she'd have no idea how Jane was holding up. And how Mike really was. But the fact that Jane hadn't called *her* said everything.

It was stupid, it was juvenile, but Ellen couldn't figure out how to get past her own hurt feelings and the anger that still sizzled between the two of them. Shame at her own behavior, how she'd run out on all of them, saturated every thought. She was stuck. *He'll be fine,* she told herself. *And so will she. Let them handle it.* Tugging at Maisie's leash, *why are you stopped?,* she was surprised to see that they were back in front of their own walkway at home.

"All I got was a text from her," Wesley said on the message he left midmorning. "Apparently it's day three of the fever, which is, like, not good. They said something about pyelonephritis . . . if it spread to the kidneys. But she doesn't sound like she's freaking out. So . . . I don't know if you guys have talked yet, but, uh, well I don't want get in the middle of anything. Love you talk to you soon okay bye."

In her carrel, a blue metal cubicle about the size and shape of a meat locker, Ellen bent her head over the minuscule text in an article the graduate student department intern had blurrily photocopied for her. She tried to shift the pages so that they caught more light from the fluorescent overhead strip above. After another quarter hour she gave up, rubbed her eyes, and took a drink from her thermos.

Now she felt afraid. Yes. It was too easy to conjure a vivid image of Michael, flushed and sweaty, tossing and turning, the brisk concerned actions of the nurses reaching arms over him to adjust drips, check monitors. Too late, she remembered all the other stories from Heaton, from Mologne — where sudden emergencies sprang up out of nowhere, and recovering soldiers actually died, or nearly did, from banal and asinine medical events, footnotes in some journal later on. A hairpin turn from being okay to not. She'd taken in those stories with appalling complacency, she saw now. *That was them. And this is us.*

Shouldn't Ward 57 have taught her that what you thought was the worst, what you thought you could rest on once you accepted it, was never the end of the line?

Ellen took her phone and purse and went up three levels to fading daylight and cell reception. *Please hold while I get the latest,* the nurse said. It was a long wait. *You should speak directly with Dr. Millhauser. What number can he reach you at?*

She drove straight home, leaving all her work in the carrel. No one called. She swept the kitchen floor in small, careful circles. She made one poached egg, watching it turn in the rolling water, and ate it on top of a thick piece of buttered toast.

It's different, she heard herself think. Her fear, this time. It wasn't the floating existential dread that had suffocated her over the weeks and months Michael was deployed. That had led her to write all those letters. This was — she turned it over in her mind while she sat on the couch by the front window, book in lap — a clear, focused kind of being scared. Strange. The object of fear was the same: that Mike could die. But the approach to it, inside her, was a lightning-flared straight road, not the disorienting weight of a heavy cloud.

Why is that? Because she could understand death in a hospital, death on American ground, more than she could death by sniper or IED or friendly fire in a chaotic country half a world away? Because her mind knew the facts of one, and had to imagine bare horrifying fragments of the other?

"Stop it," Ellen said out loud. *He'll be fine.* Then she went upstairs to her study to make notes about Wharton and imagining war.

At 7:00 p.m., the nurse said no change, still fever. White blood count was higher. She put on a recording of Chopin's Nocturnes and forced herself to listen to 1, 2, 8, and 10 before getting up from the floor of her bedroom. Halfway through brushing her teeth, she tapped Jane's number into her phone before erasing it, one digit at a time. She took a half tablet of Ambien before she could argue herself out of it, and slept from 10:00 to 2:15 a.m. At first the night nurse tried to put her off until the morning and Ellen's voice shook as she insisted on speaking with the on-call resident.

Michael had been moved to SICU an

hour ago. First signs of sepsis were detected and now he was on vasopressors and corticosteroids, and being prepped for emergency surgery to try to remove buildup of pus.

"And my daughter . . . ?" Ellen fought to control herself. "Have you seen her?"

"I'm sorry — who? What's the relation to the patient?"

Ellen apologized and hung up. For one moment she held still, sitting up in bed. *It was happening, then. It wasn't over yet.* The images that kicked her into action, though, were of Jane. What if Michael died while Jane was the only one there with him when it happened? What would that do to her girl? To her pregnant, terrified girl?

The next few hours passed in a series of strobe-lit events as Ellen raced to get there in time. Dressing in the dark, packing one small bag. Ringing the neighbors' bell at 3:00 a.m. with Maisie, her leash, a bag of dog food. Messages for Wesley and her mother's caretakers. Badger cab ride to Dane Regional Airport while she bought a ticket on the phone for the next flight to D.C. Six a.m. wheels up, running past surprised people in Reagan National, telling the taxi driver to *hurry, please hurry,* any way that he could but it was all right because as soon as he glimpsed her face in his rearview, as soon as she'd given the Walter Reed address, he knew. He knew. He blew two red lights and got her there in fourteen minutes.

When the sealed doors to SICU unpeeled Ellen burst in, blood pounding in her forehead and throat. "Whoa," a guard said, and blocked her path. "ID and pass, please."

"But — but I have to —"

"ID and pass, ma'am." Ellen's arms fell to her sides. Her long-term visitor pass was — where? — she hadn't seen it in weeks. All the way over in Mologne, somewhere in her room. Her breath tightened. How would she make it there, and back?

"Mom!" A blue-gowned figure appeared at the end of the hallway, calling for her, waving energetically with both arms high. She pulled her mask down and began to run, dreadlocks bouncing: Jane.

Then she was there, pressing her big hard belly against Ellen, arms around her neck, and she was laughing and crying and talking fast into Ellen's ear. "He's okay, he's okay, they didn't have to operate because it's on its way down! Mom! I've been calling and calling you." Jane pulled away and held up her scratched cell phone. "See? I literally just called you again for, like, the nineteenth time in an hour! Where have you *been*? Wes told me you were coming and I called you and then Mike's fever broke, Mom! It broke, on its own! Dr. Messenberg says he's going to be okay! Aren't you going to say anything?"

Ellen held Jane at arm's length and scanned her everywhere: bags under her bright eyes, pink cheeks, the rows of holes punched in her ears, her strong arms, her heavy round belly under the blue surgical gown stretched tight. "You're all right? Are you feeling all right?"

"Mom, don't cry. Here. Come here." Jane brought Ellen's hand to the top of her stomach and held it there. "Can you feel that?" Ellen closed her eyes in the SICU vestibule and warmed to the feel of her daughter's hand on hers. Together, they waited for the kick.

31

Helicopters buzzed overhead, news choppers getting their aerial views, as the wounded soldiers and their families assembled on a wide expanse of grass in front of Heaton. It took time for everyone to get where they were supposed to be: event organizers jogged around the circle like it was a track, urging people to fill in available seats in front, moving stragglers along, bending to help lift a wheelchair over a particularly stubborn bump in the road. It didn't help that spectators were already tipping their heads back and staring upward, scanning the blue afternoon sky for anything other than its sprinkle of cirrus clouds. The organizers sighed, tried to maneuver around these folks with their mouths open and their binoculars up, the ones blocking long lines of other people, and redirected traffic as the veterans and families kept arriving.

" 'Gospel News Report' calls them . . .

Vibrant vocalists with finger on the pulse of . . ." Announcers on the dais in front of Heaton's steps were thwarted by the windy day and microphone trouble. The crowd could hear only bits of what was being said, not that many were paying attention anyway. "Christian and nondenominational with a creative and powerful . . . Healing of the soul. Please welcome . . . from Bowen, Maryland . . ."

One set of audio speakers fizzed and died, while another roared to life with a squeal of feedback. Soon the rich a cappella strains of "I Need Your Glory" spread throughout the circle; these women in purple robes cared little about what a microphone could do anyway. They could lift songs up to the heavens, let alone across a windy grass pavilion, and they got spectators to clap, to join in on the chorus, to quiet down and rock slightly. Older black women in the audience nodded, murmuring, *that's right, mm-hmm,* while little kids burst out into the grassy circle to dance on a dare, before someone pulled them back behind the cordoned-off barrier.

The soldiers, all whom either were still in Heaton or had been moved to one of the outpatient buildings, were dressed as ordered in formation camo BDUs — or as much as they could manage, given missing arms, pounds lost or gained, misplaced headgear, or pant legs slit off by a medic's scissors in a Baghdad ER and not yet reissued. The more fragile cases — mostly Neuro and spinal — were taken to a special platform area under a many-peaked white tent on the west side of the circle; this was reserved for the full-body wheelchairs and one or two family members each. There they had extra staff, nurses, oxygen tanks, and a quick exit route in case someone needed to be taken back in before the event concluded. Yet except for the most newly arrived or the worst-case situations (infectious, near-death), every soldier at Walter Reed was expected to be present and accounted for.

Kids wore shorts and sneakers; they had shrugged off jackets in the warm sunshine. A number of them wore red-white-and-blue construction-paper hats — at least until they were crumpled or blown across the grass — evidence of an earlier crafts project run by social services. Not many fathers of patients were present. There were a few older vets, locals probably, who had been invited out of respect or nostalgia, who wore pinned-on medals or caps bearing their regiment or memorabilia flags in their lapels.

Women, all ages, made up most of the

crowd. Here at Walter Reed they were known only by association: mother, wife, sister, girlfriend. They wore sunglasses — mirrored, flip kind, drugstore brand, department store brand, dark lenses, colored lenses, attached to a chain around a neck. Murmuring to each other, they stood in groups of three or four, occasionally bursting out in a big wave to someone across the grass, or leaning over to check in with their soldier. They carried no purses, having long ago given those up as unnecessary, here. Instead, they carried canvas tote bags — you were always getting freebie tote bags — stamped with pharmaceutical brands or the names of companies who wanted the charity publicity: FORD TOUGH. LIKE AMERICA'S HEROES. Inside the bags: bottled water, sunscreen wipes, cell phone, and a camera she'd forgotten to find batteries for. Meds he needed in the next hour, Power-Bar because the meds made him nauseated, *Us Weekly* she borrowed from the PT waiting room in case there might exist in this afternoon a slight chance — *yeah, right* — for half an hour of lying down in the peaceful shade of a tree somewhere on the grounds. By herself.

As the gospel singers finished and filed off the dais, Lacey craned her neck to see around the people in front of her. She and Eddie were on the southeast side of the circle, shuffled in with a bunch of others from Building 18 who had walked over together. Figures. Sure, put the blind guy — half blind, she reminded herself with a smile — about as far from the action as possible. "What's he saying?" "When they starting?" No one in their area could hear a damn word from the announcers, and Lacey didn't care anyway. She scanned the crowd, leaning forward until someone elbowed her, annoyed. "Oh, relax," Lacey hissed back. She'd be here, wouldn't she? She knew they were leaving tomorrow, so she'd come to this, right?

Since Ellen had come back a week ago — and thank God Mike made it through that insane infection — she and Lacey had tried without success to get together. Phone calls, texts, and quick hugs were all they had found time for. Lacey knew how overwhelmed Ellen was after what Mike had been through — she'd barely left 57 after he was transferred back there, she and Jane together again spending every waking moment with Mike . . . maybe out of happiness. It was a reunion, Lacey got it, so she stayed out of the way even when they said stick around, they just ordered a pizza. *No, it's okay, you guys do your thing.* She gave Mike a kiss and told him he better get his ass in shape soon or else. *Else you'll come kick it for me, I know, I know,* he joked. So good to see that kid easy and joking. *No way in hell,* Lacey said. *I'm never setting foot in this place again.*

If only her crap phone hadn't died last night! She'd had to call Lolo and Otis using a calling card and the smelly pay phone in the basement of Building 18. But she and Ellen would find time, wouldn't they? It had to be today; bags were packed, and she and Eddie were getting driven to the airport before dawn tomorrow. For coffee or something, just a few minutes together. Where was she?

Eddie shifted side to side; the crowds made him nervous, and he didn't understand why they were here. "Shit, I don't know why either," she said, squeezing his hand. Oh, Ed. "Hey. Hey, Eddie."

He turned his head toward her and it focused, his eye, it focused on her. "Want to grow your mustache back?" Lacey reached up to touch his upper lip. His hand followed hers, feeling for something not there anymore. "Let's do that. When we're back in New York."

"Back home," Eddie agreed, patting his

lip. “Mom?”

“Yes. Mom’s at home. See her tomorrow, okay?”

A purple balloon, set free on purpose or not, wafted up in the air. A ripple of excitement in the crowd — people pointed, faces followed the drift — until most realized it wasn’t related to the event. Soon the purple spot was a soap bubble high in the air, bobbing gently in the direction of the Gait Lab.

On the other side of the circle, wedged between the tent and the announcer’s platform, Ellen kept a hand on Michael’s wheelchair, unhappy that he was jostled by latecomers squeezing their way to the front of the crowd.

“Excuse me!” she exclaimed to one particularly shove-happy couple, startled to notice then that it was the woman in uniform, with a roll bandage taped around her neck. Her husband, in a Dodgers cap, was the one who’d pushed Ellen.

“You’re fine,” he said over his shoulder as they budged in front.

Mike laughed. “Fight, fight, fight,” he whisper-chanted, nudging her.

“Are you sure we can’t go in there?” she said, with a longing look at the spacious area under the tent the aide had suggested they move to.

"No can do, boss. I'ma stick with my boys in coach." A nearby friend from 57 reached down with a fist bump when he overheard this — he was a fellow AK standing on the same C-leg Mike had received. And then there came the usual smack-talk about grunts over officers, only wimps need special attention, those pansies in the shade, etc., etc. — which broadened into the never-ending Marines vs. Army thing, with occasional potshots at the Navy but not the Air Force because why bother. Ellen let it go. It was disappointing enough for Mike to be back in the chair, especially today out in public — even if that was only temporary, until he got his full strength back after the infection. And for his leg to be refitted, based on the weight he'd lost.

"Didn't Lacey say she'd be coming to this?" she asked him, going up on tiptoe to see over people's heads. Ellen was surprised she hadn't called.

"Dunno." Mike shrugged. "Hey — those must be the landing targets." Out on the grass, men in uniform were fastening down black and yellow plastic strips, in the form of an *X*. There were four of them, each in a quadrant of the circle. This did keep the crowd's attention, and now people were taking pictures and speculating about how much longer they'd have to wait.

The announcer: "Headquartered at Fort Knox, the team is garrisoned at . . . Two teams from the finest aerial . . . Utilizing a Fokker C-#1A Troopship specially commissioned for . . ."

"Pretty sweet gig, considering," Mike said. "Except for the circus vibe."

"Don't even think about it," Ellen said, still searching for Lacey.

"Why?" he said. "You could get in on it too, and we'd be a traveling skydive freak show. You could get us a gig at UW! For graduation or something!"

"I'd like you to be busy at graduation," she said. "Graduating."

But Mike was still having fun with the image. "My robo-leg could have its own little parachute." He made a zooming noise, pretending to coast down to one of the *X*'s on the lawn.

His anger and paranoia were gone. Even though Ellen knew it didn't work this way, she couldn't help believing that when Michael's fever broke, those black moods — the ones that held such a tight grip on him for months — did too. Or that the PTSD had withered under the force of this other, deadlier, invasion of his body and brain. "Cooked it, you mean," is how Jane cheerfully put it — right in front of Mike! "Six days of a hundred and four zapped all that being a dick right out of him." When Ellen told her to shush, she'd just laughed. Jane and Mike both had. She even joined in because it was so good to have him back, although she tried not to think of it that way. Jane didn't really know, after all, how bad it had been. Maybe Michael didn't know, either.

Just then four jets pulled parallel contrails across the sky and the crowd let out a huge cheer. The announcer was completely drowned out, even as the planes streaked away from Heaton to bank on the far west side of the horizon. People shaded their eyes, held up phones and cameras even after the jets were gone, positioning their viewfinders up to the blank sky. Goofing-off kids were nudged, told to pay attention. No one knew where to look. One older woman held her hands over her head, an automatic flinch even as she laughed about it. *How they gonna control where they land?*

Ellen had followed the jets' progress west across campus until her gaze caught on the white pillars and gold cupped top of the rose brick old hospital building that dated back to 1909. The first soldiers housed there were the rare surviving injured men of the

Great War. Did Edith Wharton ever travel here? she wondered. Probably not — during that time the writer was in full swing of her war efforts in Paris. Still, Ellen could picture it easily: merciless Edith striding these grounds, issuing orders to any poor underling who crossed her path. Cheering the boys in pain on cots . . . and urging them back to the field to fight for freedom.

How could she? Ellen wondered. There was so much she wanted to understand. The makeshift desk in her room at Mologne — bedside table plus armchair — was neatly set up with books, files, and laptop. Each night after dinner on the ward she worked for about an hour before bed. Michael now shifted in his chair to get more comfortable, lifting his stump briefly, with both hands, an unselfconscious heave.

"Here they come! Here they come!"

"They coming around!"

It wasn't the jets though. Now approaching from the south was a yellow-and-white turboprop that, frankly, was underwhelming after the adrenalined roar of the synced planes. Still, the crowd cheered and shouted, *they're jumping!* Asked one another, *are they jumping?* I can't see. What's that? You see anything? Shoot, better them than me; I don't even like a little turbulence.

The plane seemed to throttle back, to dig into the air above Georgia Avenue. And then it changed shape, grew minuscule black forms on its side that quickly dropped away and became dots in separate space, one, two, three, four of them. The plane moved on, forgotten. The ring of dots hovered, as if in conference. Slowly they drifted toward the crowd on Heaton's lawn.

"I do not believe it. Do not *believe it.*"

"Mom, they gonna fall right on us or what?"

An instant tiny bloom: black and yellow. Then another. Like popcorn in the sky, parachutes burst open and now the crowd could see what was happening: four figures strung to silk curves that cupped air.

"Army's Golden Knights team performs at . . . Most successful sports team in D.O.D. history . . . intensive program of paratrooping skills second to none in . . ."

Tacking on a diagonal, the four parachutes fell toward earth. A couple teenagers pretended to wave them in, air traffic controller style. Now the jumpers were in a vertical chain, a thousand meters from the ground, swinging left and right, left and right, as they circled down.

"Oh!" Gasps as purple streams shot out from one of the jumpers' feet. It was colored gas, set off in puffing funnels from a kind of device strapped to his boots. The smoke faded to violet and obscured the parachutist behind him. Kids made the obligatory fart jokes.

Now they were getting close enough for the crowd to see details: helmets, goggles, and all-black flight suits. Parachutes toggled back and forth, wending their way down. Everyone took a photo, paused to look, took another photo. Cheering rose in intensity as the first jumper entered the area just above the green. ARMY, read the underside of his chute, in black letters against the taxi yellow silk. Feet first, he sunk to the *X* on the farthest side of the grass, the one in front of the tent. People flinched, but he stepped down lightly onto the plastic, running a few meters to avoid the parachute, which collapsed against the ground behind him in bubbled heaps, dragged flat by dozens of cables connected to his harness.

The other jumpers were landing, to wild applause and more incomprehensible announcer's comments, but Lacey couldn't stop looking at the flattened silk on the grass. Ignored, lifeless. The jumper was unclipped from his harness and jogged around the field to accept the cheers, but the puddle of black and yellow lay splayed like a jellyfish washed up on shore. She felt a sharp stab of gladness that the ARMY logo was all crumpled up. *Fuck you. Ed should have gotten that medal.*

"Let's go somewhere else," she heard a woman's voice say, right behind her. "This area is for traitors." Lacey turned to face two women staring at her with undisguised hostility. One was the fiancée of a specialist who'd lost both an arm and a leg, who Lacey had trained up until recently, when a nasty voice mail message cut it off. She opened her mouth but both women wheeled away before she could say a word. Others nearby looked on, curious at the snub. Lacey's face was burning. She put on her sunglasses.

It better be worth it, what she'd done for Shelby. Who had moved on from Lacey and Eddie anyway! To others she could follow, tape-record, write about. *She hasn't even written anything yet,* Lacey felt like calling after those women, two of who knew how many who thought she was a turncoat bitch. *And it's not like I got paid for it!* Everyone knew that, right? Even though the article wouldn't come out until later, or so Shelby said, rumors were flying. On big group e-mails Lacey shouldn't have been cc'ed on, women were writing: *I heard they took a mold sample. Did anyone tell about the elevator, broken three times this week? I need to get my brows done if they're gonna take a picture of me, anyone know a salon?* Lacey couldn't always hold on to why she'd participated — and occasionally would pretend she didn't know anything when a chance conversation in the cafeteria turned to the undercover spy among them — but fuck it, she had and that was that. They were out of here anyway. Still, she edged closer to oblivious Eddie, not jonesing for another encounter.

The purple gas still streaming out of the jumper's boot was making people cough on the side of the circle where he landed. Another musical group — up-tempo Motown, this time — was at the microphone, and the jumpers went to four different directions on the grass. Each seemed to select a person in the crowd to give something to — a small token from the vest he wore.

Ellen and Michael were only a few rows back from the recipient on their side. Ellen leaned to watch as the jumper removed his goggles and carefully took out a folded flag from a side pocket. This he handed gently to an Asian woman in her late seventies, who was flanked by relatives including what must be her grandson, an army soldier on crutches, one pant leg pinned up. Michael's attention had already moved on, but Ellen surprised herself by tearing up at the parachutist's swift salute, his tender smile, and the family's stunned reaction. Only the older woman herself seemed unperturbed, her face round and solemn, as if she thought it were perfectly natural for a goggled man to parachute down from a plane in order to hand her this flag personally. Her grandson's leg was gone in their war. Why shouldn't this be done for her? Among all other things.

To divert all the sudden emotion she felt Ellen pretended she had to look for something in her purse. She checked her phone — nothing. "She hasn't called you?" she said to Michael, dialing Lacey again. Why did it go directly to voice mail? Michael was busy on his own phone, texting Jane, sending her photos of the jumpers. Whatever was between them, they weren't sharing it with Ellen.

Except —

"Mom," Jane had said, tentative and sad. They were getting ready for bed in the Mologne room, a day after Mike had been moved back to Ward 57 from SICU, still shaky from how close he'd come. "He thinks I should give it up. For adoption."

Ellen came slowly out of the bathroom, toothbrush in hand. Jane was cross-legged in the middle of the bed, her big belly nestled in her lap.

"What do you think?" she asked quietly. "Is that what you want?" And then she had to hold still, hold back, while her daughter's eyes filled with sorrow and relief. When she nodded, tears spilled down and Ellen climbed over to hold her.

"But it's going to be so sad," Jane gasped. Ellen was wild with agony, to say whatever could take this pain away from her girl: *Yes, but I'll be there. You're doing the right thing. I will help you in every way I can.* But she spoke no words, only rocked Jane and let her cry as long as she would.

Now, as the parachutes were gathered and the jumpers left the grass for the announcer's dais, Ellen thought about Jane at home, driving herself to meetings at the adoption agency, beginning the process. Ellen had reservations to go back home next week; the doctor had said the baby was head down and all seemed to point to an accurate due date . . . but she and Jane had decided that Ellen would get there at least ten days before, just in case.

"She says hi," Mike said, squinting up at Ellen.

"Hi back. Are you ready to go in?" Long stints in the chair made his back hurt, she knew, and he looked pale.

For a long moment he didn't speak. Then, all in a rush: "It's fine about my leg. About the amputation. I would've said yes, I would've signed off on it or whatever . . ."

Ellen trembled, in the sun. "It didn't seem like there was any choice."

" 'Cause there wasn't. No choice about any of this." Mike screwed up his face in a smile. "But it's fine."

"Thank you," she said, with difficulty. A moment later: "It's not fine."

"No," Mike agreed. They looked out over the dissipating crowd. Where was Lacey?

Waiting for these shuffling ding-dongs to get out of the way so Eddie didn't trip over their slow asses. Thinking about Jim. He knew nothing about what Lolo had said to Lacey about Ed coming back to live with her, or the fact that Lacey had turned those words over in her mind a thousand times, weighing the possibility of actually allowing it to happen, and what that might mean for the shape of her life. Try as she might, she couldn't picture it. All she could see for the future was her and Otis.

"Mom, you know that guy Jim?" The sound of his name last night, through the banged-up receiver of Building 18's common-room phone, had lit her up.

"Mr. Leahy," she corrected.

"Whatever. Well, he —"

"Excuse me. Not 'whatever.' Not to your mom. You hear me?" Aggrieved silence on the other end. "Look, when we get back there is gonna be some work done in the manners department. Just because you got a pass on a lot of sh . . . stuff while you been at Lolo's doesn't mean —"

"Okay, okay! Do you want to hear or what?"

Yes, she did want to hear, about Jim, with pretty much every fiber of her being. So Lacey leaned her head on her hand and traced patterns on her jean leg with the corner of her calling card. She listened to Otis and ignored the other residents who came in looking for phone time and stood around obnoxiously making their presence known. Jim had stopped by Lolo's, O said, and brought three bleachers tickets for the Mariners game at Yankee Stadium next week. Said he wasn't sure if Otis's grandma liked baseball, but that Otis could have a good time there with one of his friends and the friend's dad. Or whoever.

"So I was thinking *we* could go, Mom. 'Cause you'll be home!"

"You serious?" Oh she loved this boy. "I'd love to. But is that a school night?"

Otis ignored this, but his voice dropped in worry. "But, like . . . would Eddie want to come? I mean, even if he can see out of one eye, he might not . . . get it. Anymore. Right?"

Lacey closed her eyes. How should she answer? What Otis was asking could be a dozen different things. And how could she reassure him if she didn't know herself what was going to happen — with them, with Eddie?

"I don't know," she said honestly. "If he'd want to come. But how about this. You and I have a date for sure, and then we'll see about the other ticket later. Is it gonna be a good game? Who do we have pitching? How's my boy Mo doing?" That got Otis to go off on how lame she was, how clueless, how could she not know about Mariano Rivera's *three saves this month already, Mom, what, do they not have the Internet in Washington, D.C.??*

Now, straining to catch sight of Ellen in the flow of passersby, one hand on Ed so he wouldn't get knocked over, Lacey realized she hadn't asked Otis if he'd said anything to Jim about when she'd be home. Tomorrow.

The ring-shaped crowd began to dissolve. Low-angled sunlight slid through treetops and made rainbows on the pavement, bouncing off the light poles' dusky globes. Women tugged on cardigans and hoodies, snapped at children who were fussing. They sighed and hugged one another good-bye, and promised to get together soon. Because they hadn't even scratched the surface today, no way. About the caseworker who forgot her son's first name and then excused herself by saying she had forty files to manage so how was she supposed to keep the details straight; about the dead mouse under the sink still there two days after she made the first call. Her boyfriend who had four sessions of electrotherapy on his wrist before they figured out that was a mistake. Should have been his ankle. The broken dryers, the broken elevator, the loneliness. That bitch in accounting, that bitch in processing, that bitch who gave her kid a D in social science. Did she hear about the suicide in Fisher House? It wasn't suicide — OD. Same difference! How to keep an attitude of gratitude, how to make it to chapel and back before rounds, how to not cry when he does. Do you have Wi-Fi, who's got Wi-Fi, I hear you can get it in Mologne's bar. Oh, you can get a lot in Mologne's bar.

Like a dose of the clap. All right, girl, you hang in there. Love you. I'm praying for him. Text me when you find out. Get some sleep. You too. You too.

Just then one woman spied another across the green circle. Her frantic motions caught her friend's eye and they faced each other opposite the wide lawn, and kept waving, in surprise and delight. *I'm here, I'm here! I see you! There you are.* One held up her phone, the other shrugged, palms up, and shook her head. The exiting crowd flowed around them but the two women stood still, smiling, each with a protective hand on her soldier. One pointed to the midpoint on the paved path — *meet there*? — but they saw it was impossible, blocked, the crowd directed another way. *Meet in the middle?* one gestured, *Can we?* and they considered the circle of grass, where the jumpers' crew was cleaning up and breaking down. No. They cupped their hands over their mouths and tried to call to each other, but words were taken away by the wind. They laughed at themselves, and then fell silent. Time to go. And so they said good-bye in the only way they could, with more waving and a blown kiss. Then the women turned away and edged into the long snaking lines of people filing out from Heaton's plaza. They joined the others, and disappeared.

Epilogue

Madison, Wisconsin
March 2007

Each of them still missed Maisie. At dinner, they felt around under the table for her soft ears, or listened for her paw-clicks trotting downstairs while the coffee machine began to bubble. Ellen had collected her bed, food dishes, and favorite chewy toys and stowed them in a cardboard box in the garage; no one could bear to give or throw these things away. And on this evening occasionally one of them could be found by a window, looking out over the latest crust of snow in the yard, smooth and unbroken by prints, under the yellow porch light.

Her decline had been mercifully fast, too fast for any possibility of Ellen to make arrangements to come back from Walter Reed in time. She had just returned to D.C. after three weeks home with Jane, for the birth of her daughter, and the adoption, and helping her through those hard days afterward. Jane had taken Maisie in to the vet, worried about how she kept falling, and had the tests done, and heard the results. But she couldn't bear to be the one, so it was Wesley who came home from Chicago to do what was needed. He was with Maisie at the end, stroking her head as the injections were administered, driving back to the house alone. That night he and Jane finished a bottle of Macallan someone had given to Ellen years ago, and they called Ellen and Mike in Mologne — Mike having moved there too, rooming with another amputee from 57 — and all four of them cried on speakerphone as they remembered and toasted their good dog's good life.

Now, as Ellen loaded the dishwasher, she wished Wes was here. Originally he'd had plans to come home for the weekend but canceled when the opportunity came up to go skiing with his girlfriend at Steamboat, where her parents kept a condo. She was rather proud of how nonchalantly she'd rolled with the news, on the phone with Wes, but admitted to herself now that she felt disappointed.

"They're not, like, getting *engaged* this weekend." Jane had wandered into the kitchen and hopped up to sit on the island counter. “Are they?”

“What?” She was startled, by both the possibility and Jane’s ability to read her mind. “I haven’t heard anything. Why, did he say something to you?”

“Would you give him your ring to use, if he did? The one from Dad?”

“That one goes to you, actually.” It was in a faded velvet box on her dresser, with her wedding band: a single diamond in a gold setting. “If you want it.”

“Really?” There was so much pleased surprise in Jane’s voice that Ellen glanced at her over her shoulder, both hands still in soapy water. Her daughter had a sunburned nose and cheeks from a snowshoe hike she’d gone on with friends yesterday in the woods near Eagle Heights. Her hair was wound into two coils on top of her head, like emergent horns. With her tangled necklaces, made of string and silver, and the glinting delicate blue stone in her nose, she looked like a mystical woodland faery alighted on Ellen’s kitchen counter. Possessor of great powers for mischief and joy.

“I have an older family ring I had meant to give to Wes, when the time comes. But yes, the diamond one is for you. Would you like to maybe . . . I think I’d like to give it to you now.”

"Now, like — tonight?"

"Why not?" Ellen blinked at the pot she was scrubbing. "Or tomorrow. If it doesn't fit, we'll go downtown and find a place to have it resized." They were so careful with each other now, after the birth, with Jane still living at home — working a few days at the vet. No mention was made of when she would move out, or how or where or what next, but that was all right. It wasn't time yet; they were still held in the space of having survived giving that baby away. They had gone through it together, although of course the main burden was Jane's. But it had drawn them close, in a new way. They were still blindly touching the soft walls of this cocoon, trying to determine what it meant and when the pain would soften too.

The obstetrician had gently asked if Jane would like to give her daughter a name, at least for now. Before she went to her real parents, waiting in a separate area in the hospital. Ellen would never forget Jane's response, the way she held her newborn for those few moments, the expression on her face as she bent close to her. *No,* Jane whispered. Her eyes stayed only on the baby. *No, that's all right.*

"If you want," Ellen said now, to the pot covered in dish soap. So careful.

"Okay, sure."

Then at the same time she began to ask "Is the table cleared?" Jane said "Thanks, Mom." Ellen smiled to herself.

"Could you two bring in anything else that's out there?"

"Mike!" Jane shouted, not moving from the counter. Ellen sighed. "She wants you to clear the table!"

"I can't," they heard him call from the living room, where the TV had been moved from the basement. "No leg, no chores."

"Nice try, stumpy." Jane swung off the counter, her face suddenly alive. "Get off your butt and come help me." Ellen listened to their affection and bickering, the clattering of plates and their coded insults. The things she knew about them and the hints of what she didn't.

After Walter Reed Mike had moved into an assisted living apartment run by the Madison VA. But almost from the start he chafed at the rules and regulations there, and so was now making plans to find a place with a guy he'd met there, a National Reserve BK amputee originally from Indianapolis. In the fog of leaving Walter Reed after most of a year there, Ellen realized she had always assumed Mike would move in with them, at least for some time — she'd never really thought about it. And all the paperwork, all the bureaucracy, involved in detaching them both from Walter Reed had consumed her every free moment for weeks. So she was caught out, embarrassed by her feelings of rejection, when he told her about all the plans he'd made. This was on their first day back, in mid-September. Wes had picked them up from the airport and soon the four of them were on the back patio eating grilled tofu dogs and potato salad.

"But it's no trouble!" Ellen protested. "You can have Wesley's room, and it won't be hard to make any changes to the bathroom up there — We'll all pitch in to get you settled . . ."

Mike looked down at his lap. He'd gained back most of the weight, and his hair was longer, a soft bristle like a black paintbrush.

"I don't mind at all, is what I'm saying," she continued, though the three of them were silent. Had obviously talked it through, between them. "Just until you get on your . . ." *Feet again,* she was able to bite back.

"Mom," Jane said. And her voice was gentle. "It's good this way. He needs his own place."

"But . . ."

"Mom. It's okay."

And in this way, Ellen understood that things had changed. She swallowed her objections and tried to form an enthusiastic smile. An awkward silence settled as Ellen gazed over the brown and brittle grass in the yard; she could feel the three others exchanging looks. *Stay here,* she told herself sternly.

"It's not like I won't be around," Mike mumbled, and bit off half his hot dog. "To hang out, or whatever." And his flash of a smile to her, mouth full and eyes exhausted, did the work it always had.

Mike's C-leg was now leaning against the other side of the couch from where he sat, his stump propped up on a checkerboard-pattern needlepoint pillow Ellen's mother had once made. Jane nudged the prosthetic away from her. "At least *that* sneaker doesn't smell," she said. The two of them were bent over Mike's laptop, laughing at something on Facebook.

Ellen lingered in the doorway, watching them. It was impossible to parse the language of their bodies, utterly comfortable with each other. Jane smacked the back of Mike's head, and then laid hers on his shoulder. He said something that made her wince, then something low and soft, into her ear, that made her smile. This was recent, though, a wary amity. Before, there had been weeks of slammed doors, bitten-off conversations, phones ringing at 2:00 a.m. Ellen stayed focused on Jane, on her recovery. How had they settled things between them, after his injury, after the adoption? It wasn't for her to know, at least now.

"I'm going up to the study," she said. "Jane, you'll lock up?"

"What about the movie?" Mike protested. He held up the DVD case. "You were the one who picked it." *The Mummy III: Rise of the Dragon Emperor.* He ignored Jane's laughter. "She did, she insisted! *I* wanted *Pride and Prejudice.*"

"All right, you two." She dropped a kiss on the tops of both heads. "Keep it down so I can hear myself think."

"Wait, weren't you going to show us something?" Jane said, twisting around to catch her mother's wrist. "Like on the news, that you taped?"

"Oh. No, it's not important. And I have papers to grade."

"You have papers to grade? Mike, she has papers to grade!"

"Papers that need a grading," he mock-

announced. "Many, many papers. On which there shall be grades. Many, many grades."

"Papers to grade, papers to grade," Jane twittered, in a parrot voice.

Ellen rolled her eyes and went upstairs. What was funny about that? She *did* have papers to grade. As always. Even more so, now that she had taken on three courses this spring, continued voluntary penance in the department.

But she wasn't planning to grade, not now. First she went to her desk, where the proofs of her most recent article — "Wharton and War: A Writer on the (Home) Front" — needed correction, and several e-mails about upcoming conferences awaited her response. Ellen cleared this work to the side and opened a file she'd named, simply, "New Book." Here she quickly typed a few thoughts that had occurred during dinner prep, mere notes and sketches that she could flesh out more later, when she wasn't so tired. Because the new edition of *A Son at the Front,* with an introduction by Ellen Silverman, was doing well. Serena had urged her to write the proposal and get a contract first, but Ellen was going to take her time with this book. She had new things to say, and she wanted to build them up slowly, to consider multiple approaches into the material of how reading mattered to women in Wharton's era, during the Great War. Ellen believed she had a different audience now, to be responsible to — and whether that was true or not, it made this work seem vital, and she knew enough not to argue with that.

What she had taped to show Mike and Jane had aired on C-SPAN earlier in the week. One had to fast-forward through many, many minutes of procedural complications, and pockets of dead air, and long-winded speeches received with grim-faced hauteur by the committee members of the House commission. The unmoving grainy long shots were technically similar to footage from a convenience store security camera. It would be impossible to miss Lacey, though. She stood out, not only because of the long, blond, wavy hair, but because of the way her paper trembled as she gripped it and read out her statement in her strong, outer-borough accent.

Ellen had been riveted. Lacey, testifying to Congress! At first she barely listened to what Lacey had to say, those details about her substandard living conditions, shoddy treatment, the different ways Walter Reed failed people once the soldiers became outpatients. She just marveled at the tiny representation of her friend, making known what the army had tried to cover up. Were those reading glasses new? How was Eddie doing? It had been so long since they had talked on the phone, and their e-mails had slowed to a stop.

When the scandal broke, Ellen saw that her own part in the actual newspaper series was small. She recognized things she had said to Shelby, but they were truncated and attributed to "another resident." Lacey's story was a focus, though, as was a photo of her sitting next to Eddie, his face tilted up toward the stained ceiling, a half smile on his lips. Lacey eyed the camera dead-on.

> "What bothers me is that he can't see it," Mrs. Diaz said, referring to Major Diaz's head and eye injuries. She gestured to the mold and the broken bathroom fixtures. "I do the best I can, but Eddie was always the one for cleaning. He'd be up and down this whole hall, bleaching and fixing everyone's rooms, if he could."

There were also several column inches devoted to a mother furious about her son's hopelessly mixed-up medication, and an army staff sergeant who, although injured himself, had taken on the role of social worker, morale booster, janitor, and handyman for his fellow soldiers who couldn't help themselves. The original articles snowballed into further investigations, predictable outrage (both automatic and real), some firings, and now this congressional committee.

"Professor Silverman, when you were there did you know about all this???" a student had e-mailed, sending a link.

"Huh," Jane said, when Ellen showed her the paper. "Can I take your car tomorrow?"

"Brilliant, brave," read the note on the bouquet Serena sent to her office.

But Lacey, Lacey had done it. Suddenly Ellen had a powerful longing to be back there, at the Mologne House bar. Getting teased by Lacey and laughing with her and trying to give her some good advice. She'd thought back then those hours were merely a respite; she'd taken them for granted. *Strange,* Ellen thought, pushing away from her desk. To know now that that friendship was real.

She could phone Lacey, tomorrow. She could tell her how proud she was, watching her testimony, how impressed. *How I miss her.*

Her reading chair, a light wool blanket. Rumbled explosions from the movie downstairs; the memory of Lacey's hoarse laugh. Ellen switched on the lamp, and opened her book.

New York City
March 2007

Apparently this block on Carroll Street was the only one on City Island where it was every-man-for-himself in terms of garbage cans. More likely, Lolo's natural haughtiness and tendency toward daily 311 calls to report minor snow shoveling violations or noise complaints hadn't won her many friends. Whatever it was, no one else's garbage and recycling cans were still out at dinnertime on this evening near the end of winter. Lacey got back out of her car, left the motor running, and hauled the first of Lolo's three heavy cans from the curb around to the side of the house.

"Now she's gonna stand there, get all concerned, what's that noise," Lacey muttered under the window where Lolo was frowning, talking. "It's fine, Mom. Just bringing in the cans." She ignored Lolo's complicated gestures — *What are you doing? I'll do that later.* Not, of course: *Thank you.*

Then she dragged the blue recycle can, cursing when her heel caught on a crust of blackened snow. Wheeling in the last, sticky-handled garbage can, Lacey could feel it starting, the hot throat, the bad feelings. She ducked down out of sight under the windows and wiped at her face furiously. Lacey sat on her heels and pinched her upper arms until they stung, sobbing, while Lolo knocked on the glass above her: *Where are you? What's going on?*

But by now she knew to expect it, each time she came out here to visit Eddie, each time she left him. Jim said it was proof of her caring heart. People from her AA meeting said it was years of built-up toxins finally leaching out of her system and she shouldn't expect it to stop anytime soon. All Lacey knew was she'd be wrung out and mascara-stained, numb, as payback for this weekly afternoon on City Island.

These fits were getting a little easier to take, though, ever since they flew her down last week to Washington for the trial. Okay, Lacey knew it wasn't a trial, but you could have fooled her — with the bench seating and dark wood rails, the podium and hushed seriousness in that giant hearing room where she was called to be a witness in front of not one judge, but half a dozen, all staring down at her from a raised platform with their name plates set out in front. She was so scared she'd had to pee the whole time. They'd said she could read whatever she wanted, her statement, but she'd forced Shelby to help her write and rewrite those two pages, e-mailing it back and forth, until it sounded right and all the mistakes were fixed. In D.C. she got driven everywhere in a Town Car and stayed at the Marriott out by Reagan National, and even though Lacey sort of knew she wouldn't be paying for it she was so nervous about what was and was not included on this trip that she didn't eat dinner that night, didn't order a thing from room service, just watched some cable in the bathrobe before her flight back the next morning at seven.

"I pictured it different," she told Jim then, on the phone, lying sideways across the king bed. "Different how?" he asked. "Tell me." "Well . . . I guess I imagined being back there, at Walter Reed. Saying all this there, somehow, what it was like. But I was nowhere near it. Never going to see it again, probably." "Yeah. What else?" "And nobody was there that I knew. It's stupid, but . . ." She tried to figure it out, while Jim waited for her. *Because he wanted to know her thoughts.* That hit her each and every time. "I guess I thought I'd see people. Like, from the wards. I thought I'd see Ellen." "Was she going to testify too?" "No. I just thought about her, when I was there."

What she didn't say was that at every turn she'd been freaked that someone from Building 18, one of the women who hated her now, was going to pop out and scream at her in front of everyone. She'd seen herself called out on mil-wife blogs ever since the articles came out last month, everything from *who does she think she is?* to *whiny brat doesn't deserve to be called an army wife* to *unpatriotic bitch* to *nice undyed roots, you hot mess.* No, she didn't tell Jim about the late-night reading of these posts, or about how they could still make her burn with shame. In D.C. she half expected a brigade of righteous wives and moms to face her down during her testimony, and the funny thing was she could predict every single thing they'd say to her. She had been one of them.

But if there was one person she wanted to know all about what she'd done — spoken directly to the House of Representatives! — it was Otis, so she texted him photos of everything until they made her put her phone away, the marble halls and brass plaques and a self-portrait of her big face in front of a flag, and she collected a bag full of souvenirs for him: her ID badge, the program schedule, a White House magnet she bought at the airport, two bars of soap from the hotel. Her days of being able to give him extra assignments on top of school stuff were over — he'd like to see her try — but if she could she'd make him research and memorize whatever structure of authority made up the legislative branches leading down to the Subcommittee on National Security. And then explain it to her, since Lacey still wasn't sure how that all worked.

She called him now, from the car, phone wedged between cheek and ear while she idled in Lolo's driveway. In a front window Tego the cat arched his back between the glass and the sheer white curtain. A hand — Eddie's hand — appeared and stroked the old cat, front to back, again and again. All Lacey could see of Eddie was his shadow behind the curtain, but she watched his hand pet the cat, slowly, steadily. She shut her eyes and mentally sent him . . . what? The hope that things would be easier someday, good luck with Lolo's "Texas chili" tonight (she had memories of *that*), and: *I'm sorry.* Always, sorry. Sorry for him and for her and for them.

"C'mon, Otis — pick up, pick up, pick up . . . Hi, honey! Whatcha doing?"

"Nothing."

"So what kind of nothing?" Lacey waved to Lolo, still consternated in the window on the other side of the door. *What's wrong with your car why haven't you left yet?* Then she floored it up Carroll and hung a left on the main avenue. Otis was telling her about the movie they were watching, about a mummy and a dragon and she tried to keep it straight but she was still trying to shake off the remnants of crying so hard, god she wished she could get that together already.

"Uh-huh. What about homework?"

"What about it?"

"I'm not kidding. Did you do that Regents practice test? The one on the computer?"

"Practice test . . ."

"Otis! If I get back and —"

"Relax, relax, I finished it. *And* famous-African-American-person book report. All I have is math journal —"

"Good. You know how much homework I got, right? And you don't see me leaving it until last minute on the weekend, so . . ." Fine, that was obnoxious but true. Almost true. She had no idea how she was going to finish that Kinesiology project by Monday, but somehow it would get done. Last night she stayed up until one to finish chapter review questions for Nervous System and

Pulmonary, so at least those were out of the way.

The divorce had gone through as quickly as she could have hoped. Now the VA checks had started to come in, plus all Eddie's rehab was taken care of. Lacey kept an eye on the money and made sure it all got funneled into the accounts she'd helped Lolo set up. Did those articles help their case? Sure, maybe. All Lacey knew is that she fought for as big a payout as Eddie could get — his rating got up to 85 percent — and then walked away from all of it, even though the lawyer thought she was crazy. Except she'd held back just enough for first semester tuition at Hunter College. She'd allowed herself that much.

Compared to that one preprogram basic-sciences course they made her take, Hunter's physical therapy program was intense. Three years, full-time, all classes held at the Brookdale campus in lower Manhattan. She'd have to do two clinical practicums for the last year, sort of an internship in a health center or hospital, and if she got through *that* there would be the licensing exam. All before she could even earn a dollar. And she was a million years older than the other students, and she'd probably hit menopause by the time she got certified. But Jim said it took as long as it took, and so what, as long as she liked it?

And actually, she loved it. From the first course, Physical Modalities, she could tell she was going to rock this. All that fitness assessing and injury rehab and body typing and exercise program designing that she'd done at Rudy's and for her own clients . . . she totally saw how to make that count now, in the classroom. And who knew, maybe one day she'd be able to work with injured vets like Mike. Really work with them, not just basic core-strength stuff like she'd done on Ward 57. Lacey kept it a complete secret, she didn't even tell Jim, but she had this idea for how you could combine a regimen of PT work with training routines, and how that could really help guys — and women — who were adjusting to limb loss. Maybe she could even design her own method, and write it up online somewhere . . . and get famous, and rich . . . *Oh shut up. First, finish your Kinesiology project.*

Under the City Island bridge there were a few people fishing off the small beach, even in the cold and dark. What the hell kind of catch did they put in those white buckets, and who bought it? Had to bring in some kind of money, because guys were always down there, no matter the weather.

"We're gonna order pizza so he wants to know do you want Anthony's or Famous Famiglia? But not that healthy place with the whole wheat crust, disgusting."

"Actually . . . can you put him on? Love you baby."

"Mom?"

"Yeah?"

"So, uh . . . how's Eddie?"

Lacey breathed out, long and slow. She shifted the phone to her other ear. "About the same, honey. He likes the new shirts you helped me pick for him, because of the zip-ups, no buttons. And Lolo says he's been sleeping good, and the doctor said soon they'll take him off the seizure meds, so . . ." She fell quiet. Why did she always have to put on the good spin? Otis knew how things stood. The divorce, their new apartment, how Jim came over but only on the weekends he didn't have his girls. Maybe someday she'd be able to really talk to O, and tell him what it was like with Eddie both before and after the war, where she went wrong and how she tried to make it right. Maybe someday Otis would tell her what he thought too. But for now, she had to get through these moments where she felt so bad about things she could hardly stand it.

"He said to say hi." Not true. As far as she could tell, Eddie didn't have any memory of Otis. Or if he did, you couldn't tell from the few short sentences he was capable of speaking.

"Okay. Um, so do you want pizza? Wait, here's Jim."

"Hi, baby. You okay? How was it over there?"

"All right. She's got him in front of the TV a lot, as far as I can tell. Or maybe that's the aide. Anyway, they're good for groceries, and the stairs look better." Jim had paid for a guy to tear out Lolo's rickety-wood stairs in the front and back, and put in leveled concrete ones.

"How are you, though."

"Eh. You know." She had to swipe her eyes again, before gunning it onto the Hutch in the split-second gap in the traffic. Jim *did* know. It was still hard to believe this love he had for her, hard to accept it. They were taking it so slow — she had met his beautiful daughters but only in passing, as "a friend." Nobody mentioned getting married, ever, and a lot of times he didn't even stay over, just left after dinner with her and Otis, went back to his place.

But they took every chance they could to

be alone. And together they were as good as Lacey had remembered, had imagined — which was saying something.

One night she was waiting up for him, reading Patient Care case histories half asleep on the couch. But he didn't even come over to kiss her when he came in, just gave a weird wave and hustled off to the bathroom where she heard the shower running. Later in the dark bedroom, after they made love, she asked what was up with that.

Jim rolled on his back, his big arm still under her neck. "Don't be pissed, but . . . I've been going to a few meetings, all right? The ones for family and friends of . . . anyway, I told this lady who was running it about you and how great you were doing —"

"Four months in, that's nothing. It doesn't even get hard until after your first year, is what they say."

"Yeah, well, I don't like that I come home smelling like the bar." He raised his head and stared at her. "My clothes and shit."

"Are you serious? I'm not going to go on a bender 'cause someone spilled Busch Light on your —"

"I'm not joking around on this, all right, Lace? This lady said whatever I could do would help, and there's this Web site, and so I'm going to take a shower after every shift before I touch you or kiss you or whatever. For as long as I want. Okay?"

There was real heat in his voice. "Okay," she said softly. And kissed the side of his face until he brought his head back down on the pillow next to hers.

"Come on home," he said now on the phone. Red headlights flared ahead; there was always a slow-up where the highway crossed with 95. "You can catch the rest of the movie with us." She laughed. "What, it's good. And maybe, you and I can watch a little something different, later on."

"Mm-hmm," she said, smiling at his efforts to cheer her up. She knew the kind of movie he meant. "Actually, I'm going to go to that thing."

"You sure? You up for that?"

"Yeah. Think so."

"So call me after. Drive safe."

"I won't be too late. Make sure he brushes his teeth. And I love you."

She let the sounds of his *love you too* linger, then dropped the phone back in her heavy backpack, full of texts and notebooks. Traffic picked up as she came up on Pelham Manor, tracing the river north until it disappeared under the big intersection at Sandford Boulevard. The moon was out, its cold white sliver winking at the top of her windshield.

Lacey fished out a lipstick and put some on one-handed. No chance to do anything about her hair in a boring ponytail, or this smear of grease on the thigh of her jeans from Lolo's garbage cans. It both mattered and didn't. Of course Martine would look her over, checking out everything about Lacey since the last time, a year and a half ago, and there was no getting around that. But she could handle it.

Martine had reached out, texting her after someone forwarded her the Walter Reed article. At first they both kept it real short, real basic: *How long you guys been back? Since summer. How's Otis doing? Good, how are you guys?*

Lacey hoped for nothing, expected nothing. But last week she got a long e-mail, one that it looked like Martine had written late at night. It said how sorry she was for not calling after Eddie got hit, that she kept wanting to but didn't know how, and maybe it was time they moved on from all that stuff before. She prayed about it. She wished she hadn't burned that bridge. Also, she wrote about how moved she was reading those *New York Times* articles, how upset seeing what they'd been through, and the other families, and how she couldn't believe Lacey went to testify in front of the actual House of Fucking Representatives. And did she hear they were closing it down? Walter Reed. Gonna build a new facility, a better one. Unbelievable, right?

You did the right thing, Martine had typed. *Eddie deserved better by them. So did you.*

Then she invited Lacey over for a girls' night in at her place, nothing fancy, just some of the FRG girls and some wine and apps. She hoped Lacey would come. It had been so long.

Unable to stand it, after a sleepless night Lacey texted Mart the next morning. *You know I'm with Jim now, right?* She couldn't breathe until the response came. *I know. I miss you.*

So now she was taking the exit onto Third Street, scared as shit but full of hope anyway, honking at some clown who thought he could cut her off, dreading the moment she'd ring Mart's bell and have to walk through that door. She'd hold her head up though, because that's what Lacey did, and she'd go in to face Martine and those women and she had no idea what would happen next.

But there was still a little time. Still a few blocks to go. So Lacey turned on the radio, found the right song, and began to sing.

ACKNOWLEDGMENTS

Although this book is fiction, it is based on real events surrounding the housing scandal at Walter Reed that became known in 2007. To learn more, please read the series of articles published in the *Washington Post* by Dana Priest and Anne Hull, whose undercover investigation and reporting (with accompanying photographs by Michel du Cille) won the Pulitzer Prize. I'm grateful to these authors for their insight into the conditions of life at Walter Reed for recovering soldiers and their families, and acknowledge their work as an inspiration for my novel.

Of the many other sources that contributed to my understanding of Walter Reed, the Iraq War, and its home front effects, the following proved especially helpful: *Blood Brothers* by Michael Weisskopf; *Home Fires Burning* by Karen Houppert; *A Soldier's*

Courage by Janis Galatas; *Long Road Home* by Martha Raddatz; *Operation Homecoming* edited by Andrew Carroll; *The War Comes Home* by Aaron Glantz; *Thank You for Your Service* by David Finkel; *Run, Don't Walk* by Adele Levine; *Alive Day Memories* directed by Jon Alpert and Ellen Goosenberg Kent. I also relied on *Edith Wharton* by Hermione Lee and *A Son at the Front* by Edith Wharton, with introduction by Shari Benstock.

This novel would not have been possible without the incomparable Alice Tasman and editor extraordinaire Brenda Copeland. Much appreciation also to Laura Chasen and everyone at St. Martin's Press.

Thanks to the staff and institution of the Pritzker Military Museum and Library, especially librarians Tina Louise Happ, Angela Grunzweig, and Paul Grasmehr.

Several people lent me their time and expertise on matters related to the military and medical treatment. (All remaining errors are my own.) Thanks to Jonathan Popovich, readjustment counselor. A thank-you to Daniela DeFrino, MS, RN, of the University of Illinois at Chicago. In Chicago, a thank-you also to Dr. Paul Defrino, MD, orthopedic surgeon, and to Dr. Ellen Omi, MD, trauma surgeon.

I am very grateful to those who read the manuscript and offered suggestions and support: Liam Callanan, Rebecca Makkai, Gina Frangello, Rachel DeWoskin, Thea Goodman, Zoe Zolbrod, and Dika Lam. And for encouragement along the way, many thanks to Caroline Hand Romita, Jenny Mercein, Lauryn Gouldin, Melissa Tedrowe, Bonnie Gunzenhauser, Valerie Laken, and Dawn Smith.

For time and space and quiet, thanks to the Ragdale Foundation, and the Holy Wisdom Monastery of Madison.

I want to acknowledge the many dear members of my extended family who have or are currently serving in the armed forces, and especially to the women in our family who know well what it is like to be the wife, mother, grandmother, or sibling of a service member at war. Particular thanks to Mary Gray, whose comments on the manuscript — and whose support — were invaluable.

Much love and thanks to my amazing parents and siblings, especially to Lowrey Redmond for taking care of me on research trips to Washington, D.C., and to Jocelyn Gray for sharing her expertise as a therapist for military veterans and their families. Special gratitude goes to my brother Malcolm Gray, who allowed me to learn from his experience as a Marine in Iraq and then to tell my own story. This novel is dedicated to him with love and admiration.

To Courtney, Samantha, and Wendy: all my love.

ABOUT THE AUTHOR

Emily Gray Tedrowe is the author of COMMUTERS: A Novel, which was named a Best New Paperback by Entertainment Weekly. Her short fiction has been published in the Chicago Tribune's Printers Row Journal, Fifty-Two Stories, and Other Voices. She lives in Chicago with her family.

The employees of Thorndike Press hope you have enjoyed this Large Print book. All our Thorndike, Wheeler, and Kennebec Large Print titles are designed for easy reading, and all our books are made to last. Other Thorndike Press Large Print books are available at your library, through selected bookstores, or directly from us.

For information about titles, please call:
(800) 223-1244

or visit our Web site at:
http://gale.cengage.com/thorndike

To share your comments, please write:

Publisher
Thorndike Press
10 Water St., Suite 310
Waterville, ME 04901